ISS

To Lance

ISS

Fiona MacInnes

Mòia MacInnes

Stromness
Books and
Prints

First published in 2013

by Stromness Books and Prints,

1 Graham Place Stromness, Orkney

www.fionamacinnes.co.uk

ISBN 978-0-9927240-0-9

Copyright © Fiona MacInnes 2013

British Library catalogue-in publication-data

A catalogue record for this book is available
from the British Library

Page layout by Iain Ashman

Printed and bound by Bell & Bain Ltd Glasgow

The moral right of the author has been asserted

For Neil

For support of all kinds and some they may not have realized they gave;
Archie Bevan, Elizabeth Bevan, Howie Firth, Peter Urpeth, Anne McLeod,
Judy Moir, Mandy Park, Sheena Frankish, Morag MacInnes, Mhairi MacInnes,
Pam Beasant, Iain, Ashman, George Gunn, John Aberdein, David Walker,
Robert Allan Jamieson, Brian Murray, Liza Murray, Andrew Greig,
Phaemie Matheson, Rose Matheson, Francess Matheson, Maureen Gray, John Gray,
Davy Gray, Colin Sinclair, Seona Dunsmuir, Fiona Menzies, John Zacharski,
Tracie Coffey, Kevin Coffey, Sheena Winter, Tam MacPhail, Marion Sutherland
The Scottish Book Trust, AFSL, The Scottish Arts Council, Hi-Arts

In memory of Billy Wilson who was the first person ever to buy my poetry book.

Contents

Then It Wis

Michael cut the engine on the outboard and let the dinghy drift in towards the Skerry. A petrol feather of peacock blue slipped into the wake of the boat, shimmering in the evening sun. A fine day and a gentle wind blowing offshore.

'The fuckers.'

It was low tide. Brown tangle smeared the black rocks.

'The bastards.'

Michael tipped back his head, the base of his skull connecting with the top of his spine. Above, the Sistine Blue cupola careered away from him. His head felt heavy. He closed his eyes, listening to the slap of salt water against the blue fibre-glass boat hull. *Wooden boats? Far too much maintenance.* Wrapped in canvas in the bottom of the boat was the rifle.

Michael waited.

Then from the town came the noise of the pipe band. The bass drum first. It boomed two beats then was joined on the third by the thrash of the side-drums. With the convergence of the pipes he reached down to unwrap the rifle. The first bullet pierced the skull. Soundlessly the head slapped away from the impact. The crack alerted the others and they floundered with ungainly heavy flopping towards the sea. They were hauled high up on the rocks and Michael had already picked out his sequence of shots. The second shot went in at an angle as the animal was turning. It scored through the blubber and soft tissue like a knife through grease, bruising to rest against a section of vertebrae. The third entered the animal towards the tail flipper, causing it to collapse almost at its destination, the protecting sea, lurching, still alive. All the seals were moving, and the Skerry erupted into a splashing mass of heavy flesh meeting water.

'Wait, yi bastards …

'Wait …'

'Yi fucking maggots.'

Michael let them dive, waiting for the heads to reappear. He lined up the sights of the rifle on the water about twenty metres from the Skerry.

As the heads appeared above the surface, he swung the rifle over. After that he just took potshots but he was pretty sure he got three more in the water. The injured seal was flicking its upper body in ever heavier efforts to move. Michael trained the gun on its head. The boat was only about twenty feet off the rocks. The killing shot landed right above the eye.

'That's fine.' And Michael lowered the gun, keeping his gaze on the still hulk for a moment. Once they had swum out of range there was no point wasting bullets. The bodies would slide off at high water, gently rolling down to the bottom of the sea. It would be a good few days before anything appeared on the shore.

The pipe band was keeping up its medley of Scottish marching tunes. As the parade came through a gap in the houses, the music swelled out towards the sea. Muffled between the cavernous buildings, the volume temporarily subsided, only to swell again further along. All eyes would be on the parade. The police would be marshalling the floats. The pier head would be ten deep in crowds and Michael would take down a carry-out later and mingle with them all.

I canna dae it, mither … the words crackled through his brain and even the shots couldn't dull them. But killing something made him feel easier, it returned some power.

With one pull on the cord the outboard rasped into mechanical life. Pushing in the choke, Michael pulled the tiller in towards him.

He felt better. Setting the boat round the back of the holm and in towards the harbour. Two half hitches on the handrail at the steps up to the old stone pier. Then he folded the canvas back round the rifle, securing the cloth parcel with an old piece of frayed end line from a creel. Entering the black shed from the seaward door he put the rifle up on the rafters, fastening it with a chain and padlock. He would make sure there was no chance of losing his licence.

From the bottom of the close he could see the parade. It was stuck at the hotel because of the traffic coming off the ferry. Through the narrow close he could see the crowd with eyes fixed on one of the fancy-dress entrants. Michael reached into his back pocket for his tobacco tin taking a ready made roll-up from the box and slowly lit up, heaving the sweet smoke into his lungs.

Whit the fuck …?

He felt mild amusement and in that moment superior, spectating on the drunken idiocy of others so ready to make fools of themselves.

Seadhna Rufus. Seadhna fucking Rufus … dancin' aboot in a fuckan' Red Indian get-up. Fuckan' heedcase …

'Pissed as fuck,' he said out loud.

He leaned on the wall and smiled.

'Snotty little bitch she wis.'

Michael walked away from the crowd.

He knew he could lay his hand on the bottle of rum. Still wrapped in brown paper from Harald Jeffrey's shop. Willie Bremner's rum, secreted there like a totem or a threat on the high shelf in the shed. Part of the legacy. Part of the things he knew he must resist or had no right to, like that girl in the parade … Seadhna Rufus. He knew his place and in the shifting sands of belonging there were truly no rules. *Jis' kis yi wur born here disna mak yi wan o' iss …*

'Ah, fuck it. There'll be an end tae it.'

The gala week was reckless and unsettling. It shifted people. Unhinged drinking took hold of the town lurching at the stays that normally held everything together. The community became a restless body loosening the straitjacket. Michael knew that to survive and stay in control he had to keep sober and aloof. But the unsettling stuff had already begun. Seadhna and his mother.

Everybody in the place knew it now – old Agnes McLeay's mind was gone.

Visiting his mother in the Eventide Home, Michael was alarmed at what she might say, what she might ask him to do. More than once she'd asked him *to feenish her off*.

'You could do it, son, pit me oota this useless state …'

'Whit di yi mean, mither?'

'Yi ken fine whit I mean! Pit me ower the Crag.'

Her speaking like that was bad enough, like it was just asking you to go out and get a quarter of pandrops.

His mother, never more lucid, never more serious or rational with this one shred persisting through the dementia. He pretended she was ranting.

'Yi canna spik like that, mither.' His mind in turmoil because she always returned to the same subject in one form or another, accusing him almost. It reeled on and on in his brain, the dilemma, the justifications, getting her to stop that talk.

Yi canna jist feeninsh fowk off, whitever they say tae yi …

Then Michael met that lassie, the postmaster's daughter, Seadhna Rufus, and her one of the clever ones that had been in his class at the school and witnessed every particle of his humiliation. It made him want to flee.

Part One

it wis 1957

Annie hurried Tom out of the house to go for the doctor.

'He'll nivver get his car up here. Yu'll hiv tae get him in the tractor.'

At the top of the hill the snow creamed into troughs and covings, immaculately sculpted between the dykes. Tom tied his scarf round his face and set off hunched. He could see the sky, itself pregnant and heavy with the next fall of snow. The loch was frozen and the perfect flatness of it was like a whole new country, undiscovered. It made you want to walk out onto it and disappear.

Back in the upstairs bedroom of the farmhouse Agnes McLeay pressed her face against the damp plaster to get some coolness. The sweating wall merged into her skin and soon was made warm and she had to turn her cheek again. The fire was too hot. The ripping pain of the contractions was the constant, around which everything else rotated. Grabbing the underside of the mattress and pulling, then becoming consumed with such weakness that everything swam. The smell of Annie's sweat as she leant over her with a dampened cloth, and the piercing glow of the fire that was too orange, a hot wire in her head. Her own voice issuing a moan as if it was no longer part of her.

Then she cranked her body right up into a tight coil. Ratcheted everything up to breaking point and held it for a few seconds. She felt the grating of a boulder in her anus. *So damned hard.* Everything was subsumed into getting rid of this stone lump.

Like shittan a neep.

And it started to go. There was no way back. It might rip her in two but the baby had to move. Any control she might have had was now gone and she wallowed in the great waves that pulsed through her. Unnaturally strong they were, coming from some muscle force unknown with a strength and will of their own. Like being pummelled and pulled, wound up and released.

Annie was darting over to the window to look for the tractor.

'Come on lass, try an' haad back a bit.'

Annie leaned into her sister on the bed and absorbed the possessed groans, the wrung-out sounds that Agnes made.

'Damn thing, get this damned thing oota me.'

Time was different, minutes were hours, and everything was measured between groans and the hideously contorted looks on Agnes's face. Then Annie heard the slow 'putt' of the diesel Fergie as Tom pulled into the yard, quickly followed by the louping of the doctor as he took the stairs two at a time. And she breathed a little easier.

Annie stood back as the doctor took over in the room. He said little, working between Agnes's knees, feeling and measuring with his fingers. His jacket off and his bare arms beneath rolled up sleeves. It seemed unnatural to see a doctor's flesh, his suit trousers stuffed into wellington boots.

'Been going a while?'

'Yes, doctor,' replied Agnes in her special 'doctor' voice. 'She started at five this morning.'

'Okay, the baby's coming, but she's pretty tired.'

Agnes lifted her eyelids dreamily, resigned to submit blindly to whoever took charge.

Within the hour, Michael McLeay was born in the upstairs bedroom of his aunt and uncle's farmhouse, Suster. It was November, and his father Harry, his brother George, his sister Shirley, and a grandmother he would never know, were living in a brown canvas tent, heated by a cast-iron canon-shaped stove that bellowed black smoke over the white landscape. Like a moored steamer draped in tarpaulin. Tinkers.

Agnes slopped back into the bed with the relief of the expulsion.

Annie whispered to the doctor more than a little excitedly, 'That's the caul is it no, doctor? Hid's got the caul?'

He was piercing the amniotic sac that still surrounded most of the baby, feeling for its mouth as you might clear out a lamb's. The doctor ignored her and carried on, slipping the sac away from the mouth, cutting the cord, and swabbing the stump. He held the baby up by its legs. Like a drowsy lamb, the newborn twitched and let out a bleat.

My, hid's like a skinned rabbit … but everything's there, anyhow. Annie made the quick visual check for 'normality'.

'It's a boy, Mrs McLeay,' pronounced the doctor.

Agnes felt a wave of heaviness engulf her. Until that point in the day she had heard only the creaking of the old farmhouse, empty of the noises of young life but full with the sounds of ancient floor joists shifting with Annie's heavy tread and complemented with the delicate fragrance of fungal growth. The sound of the child's snorting breaths seemed strange and loud in that old dead room. The fire sparked violently and sporadically as it ripped through a piece of barnacle-encrusted driftwood that Tom had chopped up. It snapped Agnes back to the realisation that the birth might be over but the work was just beginning.

'Wu'll pit by the caul, doctor ... hid's good luck.' Annie scooped the limp remains of the amniotic sac onto a tea towel as if it was a great treasure. She set it on the dressing table, anticipating the time later on when she would pin it out on a clean piece of lining paper. Annie felt busy and important, and composed herself to wrap the boy in a towel.

The doctor checked his watch.

The baby out, there was still the afterbirth to come. Agnes again gave her body up to spasms and with the final remnant from her womb ejected, the doctor wrapped the bloody placenta in a torn sheet and passed it to Annie. The placenta was of no interest to Annie. It would go into the kitchen stove to be burned.

After it was all done, the doctor took a dram downstairs, Annie shooing the favourite farm cat off a chair for him to sit on.

'Aye, she'll be pretty well tired out. You'll need to give her plenty of time to recover.'

'Hid's a relief hid's all by wi' an' a grand healthy boy too.' Childless Annie beamed with the closeness to it all. 'Don't ken why she had so much bother – he's no that big ... wi' the caul as weel. A sure sign o' good luck, fitivvur.'

The doctor laughed. 'You surely don't believe all that stuff these days, do you?'

Annie smarted. 'Well there's no harm in it. The caul's good luck.'

The doctor conceded, 'I suppose there is no harm in it, though some of these old tales are not so benign ... I was thinking of the fulmar oil the St Kildan women used. The poor things dressed the cord with it. They thought it had protective properties ... Turned out it killed most of them,' and the doctor drained his glass.

His cheeks were flushed with the whisky.

Annie declared, 'If you're born with the hood yu'll never die o' drowning, so they say anyway.'

'I kent a sailor that paid ten guineas for one,' Tom said. There was a silence, then the doctor added, 'But then sailors are a superstitious breed.'

The doctor set off with Tom in the tractor to retrieve his abandoned car. He climbed into the metal box hitched onto the back which that same morning had been used by Tom to pick up a stiff dead ewe from the field.

Upstairs in the house, Agnes was staring at the plaster showing through the faint floral wallpaper where the wall had been rubbed. Awareness was dawning that across the room there was a baby, that she would have to heave herself into its life. She could hear the small grunting noises it made and felt herself resenting its helplessness. Then the irritation changed to a flood of sorrow and she welled with tears at the aloneness of the new child with no one truly but herself in the world.

I made my bed, she was thinking.

Her only act of impulse, just five years before, took her away from the bounds of a simple, damp croft house in the country. Remembering the tart words of her mother, 'Yur bed, yu'll hiv tae lie on it, lassie …'. Pulled in and ensnared by the sweet trickery of handsome eyes. Big black-haired Harry the tinker, as he was then, trailing her away from the islands and off through Caithness.

She burnt hur boats weel an' proper.

Her face and arms were weathered with the tattie-picking, strange against the white sheets in Annie's sterile bed. Agnes lost her place back in her old life, and the only one who still spoke to her was her sister Annie. She knew she was watched and despised, a stranger in her own environment, hardening a place inside herself to deal with it all and shut out the whispering … *a dirty passle o' brats* … Shirley born in Inver, George at Rogart, and now this one, Michael, in Orkney at Annie's.

an' then

Five miles from Annie and Tom's farm and five months from the farmhouse-confinement, another birth was awaited. The year had moved a notch across the bridge of Hogmanay to 1958, and in an upstairs bedroom in the fishing village, Sadie Rufus leaned on the window sill before sitting herself down on the edge of the bed. In the town the people had long given up the superstitions of the country folk. John Rufus was preparing to attend a Town Council meeting. Little Iseabail wanted a sister and had prepared a display of all her dolls in anticipation of the new playmate. She expected an instant friend that would arrive already able to walk and talk.

'Aye, you go, John.'

'Aye,' conspired Sadie's mother, 'yur no use to us here. A man's just a pest aroond a birth.' As if he was a bluebottle that had to be flicked off the sugar.

The house had been taken over by ample-bosomed women with fat arms and brown teeth. John Rufus collected his meeting papers from the hallstand and edged his way out through the front door.

'Yu'll hiv a bairn by the time yi get back.'

He walked down a rugged cobbled hill past the harbour, filled with the varnished hulls of Norwegian whaling ships. The evening was grey and chill, a sullen north wind the reminder of weather to come. Inside the meeting room the town councillors were assembling at their usual seats around the long heavy oak table.

'How's your wife, John? Baby due now, is it?'

The very weight of the table imbued the councillors with solemnity. The joking and greetings were in a different tone from those they would use outside that room. Chairwoman Baillie Harvey's human form took on box-like proportions. She walked unevenly on two corners, her mottled bosom resting like a monstrous toad under the sheen of her blouse. The stiff tweed of her suit-jacket folded over the corners of her shoulders and in the ante-room she transformed herself, donning her chain of office, the cold clunk of democratic responsibility lying dead on her chest.

The room was too small, really, for such grandeur, and the Baillie had to edge her way to the high-backed carved chair-of-office behind the row of lesser red, upholstered ones. She pressed her way against the brocade wallpaper, her mouth drawn down at the corners, her glasses and greying hair framing the heavy folds of her cheeks. She was top of the tree in the town.

The others hushed as the gavel came down and she cleared her throat.

'Meeting of the town council is now convened.'

The eight townsfolk awaited Baillie Harvey's announcement of the agenda. Elizabeth, the voluntary secretary, sat at the Baillie's elbow and the councillors in their accustomed seats around the table – a gift from the consul of Norway. The meeting room overlooked the harbour and many a gaze would drift from the harbour to the painting that hung just above Baillie Harvey's head. The picture illustrated the form of a past dignitary of the town who now brooded vacantly down from a shiny but warped canvas. His features became the study of many hours of contemplation, especially during the lengthier and more tedious agenda items. Of great fascination was the pet seagull he posed with, his hand set gently on the back of the bird.

The secretary leant her sharp features into the minute book, poised to scribe, as the local news reporter, sitting on a mere folding stool by the door, turned to a fresh page in his spiral-bound notebook and licked the point of his pencil.

'We have a lengthy agenda. First, apologies.' Baillie Harvey netted her audience, glancing around them to command their attention, her eyes sombre over the tops of her spectacle frames.

Eventually the meeting wound its way through the repairs to drainage and reached the part that the councillors looked forward to most.

'Item seven on the agenda. Housing allocations. Harbour Terrace. We have applicants to consider for the vacant property at 6 Harbour Terrace.'

John Rufus leant back in his seat, seizing his chance to shoot across the bows of the Baillie. He said, 'I propose without further ado that Mr and Mrs McLeay, whose names are next on the list for a house, be allocated the property at 6 Harbour Terrace.'

There was a moment's silence as the reporter scribbled in shorthand.

Baillie Harvey stiffened and looked at the reporter. 'Mr Walker, would you care to lift your pen?' She eyed John. 'Well, Mr Rufus, I think your proposal may be a little premature as there are other factors to consider in the allocations process.'

John had been waiting for this, of course. There was always jiggery-pokery surrounding the allocations.

'I think we can take this item in public,' he stated, shooting a look at the confused reporter.

With the exclusion of John Rufus, most of the town councillors found the meetings tedious. The housing allocations were always a little more interesting. The merits and demerits of the applicants could be weighed and discussed: Jean Armett, who had an incurable and debilitating muscular disease; James and Rena Flett, whose baby had encephalitis and an outsized head; the Bakers, who were a hard-working and honest family now that Tam had joined AA; and all the while, wafer-thin slivers of gossip were filleted from the selection process.

The town councillors saw their roles as guardians of the status quo and aspired to a town council seat much as they might also wish to be church elders on their passage up the social ladder. It was a type of thin snobbery that irked John Rufus, knowing well the cosiness that could damn and exclude without recourse to reason. He saw through the faint veneers and endeavoured to use his cleverness to manipulate them all around to his point of view.

'I disagree, with respect, Baillie Harvey. I don't believe any of us sitting round this table are in a position to objectively decide on the suitability or otherwise of any of the applicants for the house in a fair manner. The only way we can be truly fair is to take the next name on the list, the applicants who have arrived there by dint of waiting. The next names I see are Mr and Mrs McLeay.'

John Rufus steadily pressed his point, ever so slightly honing the vowels of his speech to remove the chumminess from their common dialect. Even addressing the tinker McLeays as 'Mr and Mrs' was challenging their perceived status within the room. *The Tinkey McLeays?* hovered unsaid between the painted seagull and the brocade wallpaper.

Baillie Harvey pulled her lips together over her tea-stained teeth. The other councillors shifted uncomfortably. She thought it had all been cut and dried earlier. Announcing herself on the telephone by her first name, Ena, in order to cajole through familiarity, Baillie Harvey had already contacted all of the councillors with the exception of John Rufus. She had made sure to outline the credentials of her favoured new tenants for the lease of Harbour Terrace.

'The Patersons are a very nice young couple. He's active in the church and they really would be such an asset to the town. He needs to be nearer to his work.'

'Yes, just started in the bank.'

'Uh huh, the daughter of Angus Williams.'

The qualities of the Patersons had been well outlined in Baillie Harvey's unofficial pre-meeting and she was certain there would be no need for a vote. Looking around the other councillors she failed to catch an eye that would make a counter-proposal.

'Mr Rufus does not seem to have a seconder. Are there any other proposals from the committee?'

No one moved.

'In that case I wish to propose Mr and Mrs Paterson, who have approached me as Mr Paterson needs a house near to his work at the National and Commercial Bank. Perhaps one of you would like to speak to their suitability and we can resolve this without a vote.'

'Oh but I think we should have a vote, Madam Chairman.' John Rufus spoke straight, launching a spanner directly at Baillie Harvey's cosy works, and did not shift his eyes from her direction. The Baillie raised her chin. 'Do we have a seconder for Mr Rufus's proposal?'

A hand was gingerly raised. 'In the interests of democracy, ma'am, I'll second.'

Jamieson the crawling baker, always on the side of the angels, and John Rufus was momentarily grateful for Jamieson's support, whatever the motive …

The secretary and the reporter scribed in unison, heads down.

'Do I have another seconder?'

Three hands motioned and grunts of 'Aye' accompanied them, securing Baillie Harvey's motion.

'Mr Anderson, thank you. Any further proposals before we go to a vote?'

Heads remained still.

'Then you may speak to your proposal, Mr Rufus.'

'On a point of order, Madam, the vote is about whether we take the case of someone who is next on the list for the house or someone who has made a personal representation to yourself for housing and who has only recently joined the list. We should not be discussing personalities at all here.'

The others were reluctant to get involved. They did not want to see themselves quoted in the local paper. Eyes averted to the gully between the edge of the table and area towards the floor.

Tinker trash, that folk don't ken how to look after a decent house. Baillie Harvey was still confident she could win, despite John Rufus and his pedantic communist procedures.

'Very well then, we'll go straight to a vote.'

'A roll call please.'

There was an intake of breath. Now the names of who voted for who would be recorded and maybe even published.

'Elizabeth, will you call the names please? Those for Mr Rufus's proposal, that we should take the next name on the list which is the McLeays.'

'Anderson?'

'Against.'

'Campbell?'

'Against.'

'Rufus?'

'For.'

'Sinclair?' And on it went.

John Rufus won the vote five to four.

'Very well, we'll take that as carried. And I hope you do not have cause to regret your decision in the future.' The Baillie's head twitched back and forth, unsettled by the upset to her preordained plan. She had already told the Patersons she would give them the key after the meeting so they could go in and measure up for curtains.

When the report of the meeting came out in the paper everyone would know how the votes fell. It was unusual that any decision could be pinned on any individual. The political process shambled along nudged by innuendo and gossip, bristling personal hostilities and un-researched prejudices.

But the McLeay children would grow up knowing who, at least, was on whose side.

'It's a girl, John. You have a daughter. And she's got the red hair. The red hair of the Rufuses.'

In the upstairs bedroom a green-painted wicker Moses basket held the baby. All but one of the posse of midwives had left.

'In the end she cam that queek the doctor nearly missed her. He says he'll no be daein' any more home births. It's the hospital noo. Thu'v got oxygen and aall the stuff you wid need … yi ken if it hid tae be needed,' gabbled Rita Ratter informatively. Always at the back of their minds was the horror of a deformed baby. *A vegetable.*

John's wife sat propped up on the bed, red-faced, a Melaware teacup and saucer by her side. Sadie Rufus let her eyes rest on the gilt-edged Bakelite handles of the Ercol bedroom suite. They had bought the whole matching set and it was a huge extravagance, but austerity and the post-war years were a fading memory. She felt the warmth of optimism and contentment.

'Did it all go okay?' her husband asked, still thinking of the meeting in his head.

'Aye it was fine. She slipped out like a puppy.'

'It went to a vote. Aye, I pushed it all the way. They got the house.'

'That's good.'

'But Ena was seethin', though.' John Rufus allowed himself a smidgen of glee at his housing victory. 'You could just see it in her.'

'Will it be "Seadhna" then?'

'Aye, Seadhna. A memory o' the Gaelic.'

Shayna, aye, it's unusual, Gaelic for Jane – they spell it funny.

tinkers though

A housing allocation letter was prepared for the McLeays, offering them the tenancy at Harbour Terrace. Elizabeth the secretary, on her heavy black Imperial typewriter, punched a hole through the thin typing paper with every full stop, then scuttled round to the manse with the completed letter for Baillie Harvey's signature.

Next day, as John Rufus sat behind the post office counter, he saw the portly Baillie as her frame filled the half-door into the office. Their roles had shifted for daytime along with their clothes: John was now the postmaster and Baillie Harvey was Mrs Harvey, or even Ena to her friends in the Church Guild.

'I don't know where we're supposed to send it. Does the post office deliver to tents? I imagine you'll know.'

She pushed the letter under the brass grill of the post office counter.

'Thank you, Mrs Harvey.'

There was a fleeting moment of coolness as the acknowledged opposing perspectives lingered between them. But in the end it was a small place and everyone had to find a way to coexist with everybody. That they both knew.

John left the warmth of the coal-fired Wellstood stove and made his way to the bottom of the lane to take the car, a second-hand black Vauxhall he'd bought from a shopkeeper in the country. Setting his hat on the bonnet, he cranked the engine, and on the third pull it shuddered into deafening life. It seemed like the loudest thing in the world. An uncompromising statement of mechanisation among the streets of footsteps and conversations. Brittle hail-showers were starting, the sky heavy with impending snow. The Paynes Grey colour of winter, so beautiful and foreboding. The hail rattled on the bonnet of the Vauxhall, ricocheting off the windscreen, and soon the road to Skaill was covering in white, the narrow tyres of John's car carving a solitary path into the tarmac.

Not far from the prehistoric village was the McLeays' tent. Brown and sagging with what appeared to be several layers of sailcloth, it sat behind a drystone wall, with smoke emanating from a funnel at the end. Firm hailstones gathered in the folds of brown canvas.

'Aye? Harry? It's John, buey. Are yi there?'

John stood outside the tent. The flap opened.

'Mr Rufus.'

Inside the darkness, the warmth from the stove fused the aromas of breath, sweat and slept-in clothing to a sweetly repelling stench. Two children of indeterminate sex peered from smoke-stained faces, the whites of their eyes the only clean thing about them.

'The letter about your house, Harry,' said John in formal English. He remembered then that Harry couldn't read and he'd signed the application form with a cross. John reverted to dialect. 'Wid yi like me tae read it oot?'

From the back of the tent, a huddled shape in manila blankets and a crocheted cover moved and uttered shrilly, 'Ah'll no kin be movin' there intil a hoose ...'. Sutherland Highlander's brogue. Then something in Gaelic.

'But it's a fine house, Mrs McLeay, and the bairns will be able to go to the school.'

'Never mind her, Mr Rufus. She disnae ken what she's saying. Agnes'll be happy, Sir. She's at her sister's with the bairn. She had a long time of it. Aye, Mr Rufus, the days o' living in tents is weel past, an' the bairns will be able ti go till ae school an' learn ae readin' an' writin'. Thu'll be better 'n me in time, Ah hae nae doot.'.

'I said I'd pit in a word to the baker for yi, Harry. They need bakehoose staff but it's nights, yi ken.'

'Aye, Mr Rufus. Ah'll try that. Ah'll try it. Things is changin' an' Ah'll hiv tae try an' work in a job regular like.' Harry the tinker with the naive enthusiasm of a child in a new world.

Michael McLeay was never inside the tent at Skaill. After a month at the farm he was brought as a baby straight to the new house at Harbour Terrace. There was stuff still in the farmhouse that was so big and heavy that Annie thought it would be grand to get rid of it. All the inherited furniture of Tom's mother felt like a burden to her and she was glad to claim the place for herself. She got Tom to take the tractor and trailer down to the town with the cupboards and bedding as well as a massive wardrobe. The dung-spattered trailer parked on the smart new tarmac like a big clarty animal. The throb of the Fergie engine was terrifying to the children peeking through windows. It was even more frightening than the blasting when the County men had to shift all that pink granite for the founds for the council houses. It was like bombs going off, the same as the wartime when Churchill was a great hero.

Tom had no problem with Harry. He was quite happy to give him work in the tattie-picking. He was a good enough worker. They were just *unco*, them tinks. You just had to be wary. At least that's what folk said, so Tom felt in a strange middle ground with Harry. He knew they were both now related, *but it wisna like hivan a proper relativ, yi ken … a normal relativ …* At least in the country the tinker connections were less obvious.

Annie felt the invisible sneers of the community towards Agnes. She pre-empted disdainful looks and malicious enquiries when she got her chance, rethreading Agnes's story a little here and there to whoever she thought might shift their view a touch, to engender a little sympathy.

'Och, Agnes's just a stupit dreamur. Mithur jist coodna understan' her gaan off wi' Harry McLeay. The first wink that came her waye an' she wis off. Think it wis more that he wis ten years owlder than her that bothered mither, rather than him bein' a tinker. Whatever, mither never lifted her heed when Agnes left the hoos tae git the steemer tae go off wi' him. An' she haaded ontae that bitterness aal her days. Poor mither. Couldna climb doon. Couldna say she made a mistake.' Annie smoothed things over to explain, make it more palatable, build a barrier against outright malice, cajoling Tom to help out and sending him on another trip with the tractor to Harbour Terrace with sheets and food.

'Tak a sack o' tatties an' a pile o' neeps wi' yi, Tom.'

Solid Tom heaved up a hessian sack onto his back, slopping through the mired courtyard from the steading, thinking about better drainage. In the neep shed he filled another sack with a dozen great purple heavy heads, swiping the shaws off with one blow of a rusty knife. Fither's horse harness still hung from the eaves, dusty, with the black leather blinkers hardening into shape.

'She nivver even saa the bairns. It's a shame but there you are. That's thraan-ness fir yi.'

The big plum-red chest of drawers upstairs held sliver upon sliver of starched sheets and bed linen. Annie armed a load of folded linen up out of the drawer, wrapping it in newspaper then tying off the parcel with a firm no-nonsense slip knot. In her head reminding herself – as if she would forget – of the embarrassment that just had to be dealt with.

'I mean they hiv nothing, Tom. Really, they hiv hardly a thing. An' the owld mother's still refusan ti go … an' Agnes, poor daft Agnes, sittin' in among it aal like she his no idea whit's gaan on aboot her. Bairns filthy, peein' everywhar like dogs … Fur the sake o the bairns at least …'

Harry's old mother finally took a stroke and saved everyone another dilemma. No one quite knew how the tinks dealt with burials, but the doctor had certainly been called. He had been seen going up there to the tent. They must have got the old lady into the hospital, but she only lay a couple of days and then died. That didn't stop the stories, though. The tale persisted that her blanket-clad body was still decaying inside the tent on the common land, and after a while the Sandwick children crept around it, firing sticks and stones. Getting bolder and bolder they shouted towards it, fuelling each other with terrifying stories of the old tinker wife who had been left to die.

The stories whirled and grew, ballooning and inflating in cold bedrooms at night with the wind blowing. *The spirit's come back ti haunt the beach an' thur's evil an' ghosts inside the tent and if yi go in yi'll be cursed.* The menace of dares percolated the country school for months as each boy feared he might be the one finally pushed beyond his limits to make entry to the horror tent. But no one achieved the dubious accolade because the entire tent blew away out across the Atlantic in a sou'-easterly gale. The same wind brought rain pouring through the exposed mortar of the farm gables in the country. Floorboards were soaked, and brown earth-stained drips plopped from downstairs beams. On the empty wall where the wardrobe had been in Tom and Annie's, a huge tea-stain of damp appeared, bubbling and blistering into powdery plaster.

The wind whipped nearly all the evidence of the brown tent away. All but the cannon-shaped stove which lay flat on its back, heaved over by the strength of the great canvas sail that flapped and smacked around in the sixty-knot wind before becoming severed from its stove-pipe mast to belly off across the sea in the black night. It finally tailed into the waves and got pulled down into the water.

The owld tinker wife's bones geed blowan aal ower …
They did so, me fither said so.
Her head could be anywhar. Yi might find it oot ploughan or in a ditch.
Fuck, no …?

an thur choochtery Gaelic

In the neatly harled two-up two-down houses of Harbour Terrace, news of the mythical scattered bones of Harry's mother had not yet reached the residents. The town council had built the houses themselves. They bought the field from the Church because there was no real need for such an enormous glebe. The hipped roof of the solitary manse, itself like a great chimney emerging from the heathery field, was now edged with a ragged petticoat of grey cement houses whose eyes steadfastly fixed on the harbour ahead. A row of garages had been built in anticipation of the car-owning masses, but as no one in Harbour Terrace yet owned a car they had been let out to other car drivers in the town. So when Tom's tractor arrived there wasn't a problem with parking. He just drove up to the front door, tractor, trailer and all, and left the engine running as they started to unload the cargo.

Off came a black tin trunk, two horsehair mattresses, the huge wardrobe, an oak table with a central pedestal, an orange box filled with old plates wrapped in newspaper, and the sacks of tatties and neeps.

There was no need for small talk. Harry and Tom could converse about the manoeuvring of the huge lumps of furniture into the narrow passage of the house. There was communion in the shared task. Small social difficulties dissolved through the problem-solving, although they avoided each other's names, embarrassed.

'Aye, I think if we tak her roon' this way, then through the kitchen door, yi'll get the top started up the stair …'

The wardrobe was never made for a council house.

'Maybe we should tak the doors off. Ah'm pretty sure the base unscrews …'

All this time, Harry and Agnes's peat-stained children, Shirley and Geordie, ran around in the muddy backyard. The council didn't go as far as landscaping the gardens, so Geordie dug in the puddles with sticks and Shirley played 'hoosies' with the orange box.

'I'm the mammy in the hoos wi' the babies …'

They were watched from dead-eyed windows.

The name McLeay had been mentioned. *Not a local name.* There was confusion as to how to interpret the union of Harry and Agnes, Agnes Greig at least having the pedigree of local status, but at the same time having chosen to squander it by making such a strange liaison.

Did she hiv no idea at aal hoo difficult it wid mak things fir hersel?

I mean she's made her own bed …

McLeay was a Highland name, for a start.

Heelan' choochters wi' thur heedrum hodrum and choochtery Gaelic.

Whispered disdain. *Uncan folk.* Sniggering that they couldn't speak proper English.

But Harry did get work at the bakers, Jamieson weighing up how the Christian gesture he made equated with the economic reality that he paid Harry two shillings less than the other bakers. Jamieson let him take two cans of Special on tick against his wages and he picked them up in the early morning after his shift. The beer helped him sleep in the daytime. Agnes was trachled with the baby and it fell to Shirley, all of six years old, to get the others dressed and yelled out of the house in the morning.

afore stories

Way back before there were people in the bay, there was always the sound of the sea. But back then even the sea made a different noise as the Atlantic swell spilled from the west into the granite-banked cove and pushed northwards, trapped between the hill on one side and a sleeve of tidal land on the other. Sometimes powered up by southerly wind, a whorl of high pressure in the Atlantic, the sea coursed into the bay like a river in flood, with white-topped waves and shifting veils of grey rain. When there were only the undulations of shoreline to accept the waves they flowed onto the sandy places, spreading out like lace, whispering on the gravel unimpeded by the constructions of men, or slapped the black rocks that one day would become the foundations of sheds, houses and piers.

Untrammelled by hundreds of miles of ocean, the wind hit the western landmass of the islands, slamming into the ragged coast. Over the hill the gusts were blunted by the slope of the land. The street would come to change that sound, creating a funnel that whistled from north to south or buffeted stone vennels from east to west.

On still summer days, when the sun made the flat rocks warm, the cormorants came and stood with their outstretched wings. And the people of the town walked the street, their moods dictating whether their eyes dropped down to their feet or lifted up to the blue between the zigzag roofs.

The town began to form its identity as a place, with an alehouse at Karston and with ships that anchored out of the tide in the lee of the hill. Someone saw an opportunity. It was business. All the wars came from the south: Napoleon, the European kings and emperors and then Hitler made the English Channel dangerous. Shipping favoured the safer northern channels. Merchant ships put into the safe harbour of Stromness to wait for wind or take on water and men to journey to other places. It was a crossroads, a place with a meaning, a place of moving people, of transient people and slow settled people who watched. All with a purpose to that place that soon required a name around which to build its own dialogue. Where some would assume status and rights over others, where there would be tensions and sadness and exclusion. And in the air, where once there was only the sound of terns or fulmars, the residue of unspoken human lives shimmered like a cloud. Local stonemasons used their memory to create the shapes of the buildings. Building-stone quarried from the hill at their backs of solid ochre sandstone. Measurements were spoken and offered from muscular arms as they reached away from their chests. Within the regularity of chisel-cut blocks and geometric precision was the infill of irregular hand-quarried stone. A good mason, they said, only ever lifted a stone once to fit it to the wall. The eye had done all the measuring and trying first. Taut string kept walls plumb-straight and the precious bubble in the spirit level edged the gables up to the chimney heads. A chimney pot for each fireplace in every room. Working in the good weather when there was sunshine and long days of light, the joiners set to sawing up couples for the roof supports using a two-handed saw. Splitting whole timbers that came on the decks of sailing ships from Norway or washed across the Atlantic as bounty from a logging river in Canada. Swaying back and forth in unison, the sweat on their brows, the bare-chested men at the two-handed saw. Each time they took a rest the saw restarted its motion in a slightly different groove, leaving marks on the beams as clues to be discovered by coming generations.

Then, you could build a house in a week on a new croft, everybody in the place helping. All the carts bringing in stone. Flaying the heather off the bank, where the new bigging would go and you could look down over your five acres. But the town houses took longer, with lathe and plaster inside and joiner-made windows. Fields were sold off, houses crammed onto them. Muddy back lanes emerged where cats and children began chasing games. The landowners' names found their way onto the street signs: Peterstoon, Anderson's Quoy, Sinclair Place.

It was fish. Fish in abundance. Big Catholic markets in Europe. The Russian Orthodox Church needed herring. And boats and people clattered into the bay, busy and loud with the first Klondyke of scaly silver.

From Lowestoft to Lerwick went the gutters.

These itinerants were permitted, brown-faced and black-haired, as commerce purchased tolerance. Their salt-soaked hands bandaged and bloody as they dared everybody from their wooden shacks, the witchery of flashing knives and unintelligible talk. Together in sailcloth aprons, not giving a damn, they sang, stamping and working hard and moving fast and moving on, leaving everyone behind wondering. They laughed back at the stony-faced shopkeepers and their nipped wives. Tolerated, they were, needed for the herring. Silver herring, black boats, tarred rope and smoky steamed barrels. Matjes, jam-packed in brine, off to the Continent. Migrants who knew their place in a chaos of moving people, but still the gutters could never belong, even if they wanted to.

The herring paid for everything, and civic aspirations demanded a proper metalled road, and then gas lights, and then the demolition of old houses that were in the way of commerce.

The delivery cart can't get past. Is this a self-respecting modern town or not?

The Lighthouse Board bought land and buildings for a depot. *All choochters* … If the lighthouse tenders came in you could be sure of a right ceilidh. That was allowed. The ships' crews were nomads too. A great diaspora of polished boots and gleaming buttons, stiff peaked hats, schlepping up winding staircases on every kind of lighthouse there was. Horizontal stripes, vertical stripes, all white. Tall and solitary, short and squat, clustered by houses stood the lights. Strong mason-cut stone, even the dykes all good, clear, ninety-degree angles. Polishing layers of heavy glass and setting the meths-soaked burner under the mantel to heat, the keepers. The purple liquid hissing as the blue flame extinguished and the asbestos clamp was set back to sizzle inside the jar. They screwed safe the black tin lid that was just slightly rusted in the damp, then pumped up the pressure on the lamp. The hiss, the glow and the dark coming. Wind speeds, visibility, cloud types. Weather.

The ship relieved, stores out to Suleskerry, a family shift from Oban, changing the keepers on Copinsay, a whole community aboard the black painted metal, and down in the engine room polished brass and green gloss. White gloves on the steward, clay pipes on the deck. Navy-blue knitted jerseys with NLB insignia stretched over well-made chests. An army to light. Then the menacing commissioners whose every whim had to be pleased. Far away in Edinburgh the offices of the Northern Lighthouse Board, 81 George Street, were even more important than the offices of the Church of Scotland.

Up in the Northern Isles, Gaelic was a secret life. A forbidden language, for consenting adults only. If you spoke it you would be accused of snobbery. Of being uppity. Excluding the local folk. Scaring them because they didn't know what you were saying. Wasn't that it? Everybody wanted to know what everybody else was saying, whether it mattered or not. It was their right over the *incomers*, to know what they were saying. Anything that might exclude you was a threat.

you jist had to get on

John Rufus never advertised his Gaelic background. It didn't fit in this place. They soon dropped the language. His mother had nobody to speak it with after her husband died.

'We never spoke Eenglish till we went to skule. And there you *had* to speak it or you would never get on.' She might meet Ella in the Stromness street, Ella Watson that was, which wasn't even her real name. An orphan sent over from Farr in Caithness to an auntie, who gave her a new name that everybody could pronounce. She worked for them, spoke no English and had to learn it fast. Ella might come out with a single sentence in the middle of her conversation with John's mother, describing the kind of bread or the feeling she had when she smelled the snow ... and then they would talk on in English as if it had never happened. A small pit-prop to the great English language, a tiny Celtic nuance.

But Gaelic still sang, half-questioning, half apology, the only clues left in the ghost of its rhythm.

'But you just would *never* get on ...' and old Mrs Rufus shook her head and tisked as if it were an inconvenience. As if that justified everything. The loss of a whole history of thinking and feeling. Nobody acknowledged the dead words. They didn't want to be called 'choochters' and made different.

Incomers.

For John Rufus, it became a thing of the past. A reminder of poverty and the power of the big estates. Once, they could have basked in the skewed grandness of the big house, but now it was a thing to shake off. The bog-sunken shacks of the West Coast with their red, rusting corrugated iron, deep in midgies and the steam of warm peat. Tea-tepid water oozing up through your bare toes. Ragged sheep and barren hills – how could you ever lift your eyes from any of it and see anything other than how it ground you down? Who ever said a hill was beautiful? You walked from stone to stone expecting dead carcases, looking to the distance for a missing ram, excluding all around the ragged edge to the world that was waiting to be redefined as 'majestic' by those who never had to scratch a living from it. A bog beautiful? Slurry of bracken-infested swamp, rashes that sponged up the relentless rain, and a good cow up to her neck fallen between two old peat banks. Getting colder in the hill water of ancient glaciers, and finally dying before you could haul her out ... The drystone dykes, a tithe of sullen carted granite, yard upon yard, in annual payment to the laird. A place to simply weep over the powerlessness of humans, the Highlands.

The mixture of deference and resentment flowed in equal measure through John, a folk memory from the weight of a collective heavy history. The rich who came from the south of England with their assured tones and hunting voices. Different clothes for shooting, picnic baskets and big moustaches. Suits on for dinner, so the chambermaid said.

In Gaelic you could still talk about the aristocracy and laugh at them with all their inbreeding and ignorance. It was a safety valve. And John's mother held onto a strained coexistence of pride and resentment at their contact with the estate. Proud to be the daughter of the head gardener because it put him above the other crofters, and resentful at the predetermined order of estate life where no one could stay. There were no life choices, only enforced moves, gentle or brutal. The order of things was hard and fast and unyielding. Letters from Winnipeg scored in blue crayon, references from the Dominee, a wedding photo from New Zealand. The black hand of the Kirk moved behind everyone.

The Post Office, the Church, the Law, the Lighthouses: these were the routes out of the toil on boggy land that no one else wanted anyway. The passports into more subtle roles of subservience. Hard-working, quiet and used to solitude, minding their manners, the Highland people nursed their resentments in their secret tongue. From one estate to another they went, from the thousand-acre deer-shooting preserve of the rich to another predestined life where the commissioners came round the shore-station houses with their white gloves to run the authority of inspecting fingers over the demure cottage furniture in search of slovenly dust. The keeper's wife already belittled by her place in the economic caste.

So when John tried for the post office it was a shore job, a step up from his father. And he came off the *Fingal* to sit the post office exams.

Back on the estate, still in a corrugated tin house, the old blind Auntie got visits from the Wee Free minister and gradually lost her English. There was nothing there to go back for. John away up in the Northern Isles and Sadie with him, where she felt at once the heavy release from the weight of religion. They would never go back.

The line was surely broken.

it's whit you ken

Shirley had to take Michael to school on the first day. The school was at the top of a long climb up the hill, approached by a heavy drystone wall of pink granite. *Full of uranium, the scientists said ...* But for the Easter intake of new pupils it was not uranium that the towering wall contained, but nests. The nests of starlings ready to burst forth with small, squawking, naked chicks. As the nests were built, the schoolchildren pressed their eyes to the cracks, poked sticks into the crevasses and watched frantic parent birds flit in and out. When the eggs hatched, the journey up the hill was interspersed at sporadic intervals with the shrill bellow of insistent rasping. The school loomed like a castle, frocked by a grubby playground that ran at forty-five degrees downhill to join the rest of the town that tumbled towards the harbour.

Just inside the girls' door, which became unisex for the benefit of the infants, the warmth of the radiator invited, drawing red cold faces into something that might be more pleasant than the outside. The central-heating pipe snaked its low-slung way from the janitor's boiler room through the school. This pipe evolved a strange status of security, a kind of cylindrical comfort blanket, where legs, backs or buttocks, dependent on the contortions of the individual, could be warmed. It was a secure conduit from the girls' door to the Primary One classroom. There, heads brushed beneath the generous brass ball of a doorknob. Centred even higher up on the mid-panel of the door, brass numbers announced the door's title in Times Roman, correlating with the chronological status of its occupants:

'**1**'.

The long corridors of polished sparkling granite delivered everyone into a whole other world.

Shirley yanked Michael by the hand, flattening him against the cold wall in the queue of mothers and infants. Further up the queue, Sadie Rufus stood with Seadhna, who clutched a stiff leather satchel, her hair recently clipped into a severe bob. Across from them all, the legs of the display cabinet towered above the heads of the new pupils. At playtime the big girls from Primary Two and Three would come along and heave the smaller girls up to see the contents of the cabinet. Boys were rarely afforded this privileged view, being famously made of slugs and snails at the very least and usually 'dirty'. As a final statement of the grandeur of school, a tall sash window, with cataracts of mottled glass and the imprint of wartime sandbagging, filtered its cloudy light into the corridor.

From the interior of the Primary One classroom, the form of the teacher, who mysteriously was never seen to enter the room, emerged when the bell rang.

A piercing insistent ring, enduring for longer than was really required, marked the change in two different worlds. Once inside there was a new enclosed world where the register was a hallowed book. The granite floor gave way to pungent-smelling, black-oiled floorboards and a place where ink blots were like a terrible sin. As the names of the four-year-olds were read out, they sat in silence, hands searching for the warmth of oxters, the bare skin of thighs just beginning to stick to the wooden seats. Seadhna barely noticed her mother leaving the room; she was already drawn to the toys set out on the floor. Howling came from the corridor and some heads turned around. The teacher knew of the possibility of contagion. Michael McLeay clung to the door-jamb as his sister tried physically to pull him through the door.

'Aw it's peedie Michael,' said Sadie, lowering herself to his eye level. The hunted eyes refused to connect. 'Will I tak him inside fir you?' she offered to Shirley, who was now grimacing and trying a twist on the wrist as added persuasion.

'No missus, I canna, I sed tae mam I wid tak him right inside and no let go till he was in the door. He'll run off if I don't.'

At that point Mrs Breck appeared with an overly toothy and scary smile, rustling a paper bag of Murray Mints.

'It's okay, Shirley, you run off now.' Turning to Michael, she said, 'Michael would like a sweety, wouldn't he?' Michael's confusion sustained long enough for Mrs Breck to close the door behind him and pop the hastily unwrapped mint into his mouth.

The easel had a column of round holes up each leg where the pegs fitted in, looped by string. Seadhna cottoned on that you were supposed to look at the easel for some reason, but after that you just got to play, once you had said the obvious 'aforapple'.

Seadhna liked the groatie shells that you could pour from a jar. They flowed untrammelled in such a pure way, and were always cool to the touch, unlike the sweaty, unyielding jigsaws that refused to fit. It made her feel calm. The weighing machine didn't interest her, she just liked the feel of the shells dripping through her fingers. She delved repeatedly into the pile, letting them trickle and whisper into a mound. From the top of a tall cupboard, a red tin bus was brought down, and a pram with a solitary doll. The adult agenda only impinged when Mrs Breck snapped a ruler down on her desk and the interval of puzzlement was followed by an announcement.

The janitor was standing, a sentinel by the open door, with a black tooth, his boiler-suit buttons stretching over his gut, awaiting instructions.

'Take him up to the male staff room and clean him up.' Mrs Breck spoke posh Orkney. 'There's spare shorts in the gym cupboard.' Then, sweeping down in one flowing movement, Mrs Breck slapped the thighs of Michael. 'You are a dirty, naughty little boy. Number twos are for the toilet.'

Pulling away the grey elastic waistband of the oversized shorts had confirmed her nasal suspicions. The janitor led Michael through the door, closing it behind him. Once shut into the silent corridor he picked Michael up and strode away towards the no-man's-land of the staffroom. As Michael was heaved up into another perspective he could see the contents of the display cabinet from above. It was scant comfort. The reflex tears were pumping through a moan in his chest and his arm reached to clutch the folds of the blue boiler suit. His blurry view was of the displayed objects from high above. The things the girls got to see. A strange velvety brown burst bullrush from Africa with stuffing spilling out, some pink sea shells and a huge ostrich egg, hard and glossy with a tiny round hole where it had been blown. Michael's eyes lingered on the unbelievable egg as the rich stench of excrement hung in the echoing corridor behind him.

'Och fella, hid's only a peedie mistake. Wu'll get thee sorted.'

an whaur yi ken

'Yur futhur's a communist,' spewed the beetle-browed face topped with a cow's lick and a 'slide'.

It was Edna.

'Allison says she's not playing with you because you're a red,' expressed Sheila in the slightly more refined tones befitting a lawyer's daughter. Seadhna tried to assemble the various statements.

Red. Commy. Leftie. Russkie.

Investigation took a circuitous route. Seadhna wasn't one for direct questions. They gave away too much.

'What's a communist?' she enquired over the liver and bacon one teatime. The reply from Seadhna's father was totally perplexing.

'Well Seadhna, it's someone who wants to share out all the wealth in the world fairly between everybody.' And then, 'Why do you want to know, who's been talking about communists?'

It seemed logical to Seadhna that 'leftie' and 'red' must mean something similar, but with language you couldn't always be sure.

'Tinkey McLeays' was the generic term unanimously and, in the children's view, righteously adopted for all members of the McLeay family. Used openly to the faces of the children only by other children, but adopted by adults beneath their own breathy cloak of malicious privacy. All those who knew they were from 'clean' families felt glad to have escaped the abyss of scorn and kept themselves tight inside their lino-clad, Pledge-polished homes.

Shirley, as the oldest McLeay child, bore the signature title for the whole family, anointed through association with Michael's sorry incontinence incident. 'Shitty Shirley'..

Smell was Shirley's crime, and it was well known that if ever you smelled, you would never live long enough to shake off that particular badge of disgrace. But Seadhna never actually detected Shirley smelling different from anyone else. The edict defining the odour status of the McLeays had never been uttered from a single source but had risen like a cloud slowly enveloping them, and now their status was so firmly ingrained that it was taken as no less than a biblical truth.

Shirley wore thin shapeless skirts, socks and heavy shoes. Old ladies' blouses with thick dull cardigans. The other girls had Clarks sandals and white ankle socks. So she failed the fashion test.

'But then she can't help that, can she, if her parents are poor?' volunteered a plaintive playground voice that had recently been read a Bible story about the widow's mite. The defence was pooh-poohed. Shirley's face was red and blotchy with cold sores round her mouth, and her straight hair was lank, secured in a side parting by one small token of femininity, a cheap plastic hair clip.

Surrounded by taunts and rejection, Shirley remained on the edge of everything. An embodiment of poverty and something nobody wanted to be, despite what it said in the Bible. As long as Shirley was despised, the others were preserved from that fate. Shirley tried to push herself into their world. Sometimes she would just muscle in on others' games. Or be reluctantly called upon to hold the other end of a skipping rope only when need demanded. She would receive unprovoked hits and kicks as the boys ran past her, then make the effort to resolve her injustices through dialogue, running up to the school door, with the first stutterings of a sob, shouting, 'Ah'm tellin.'

Unable to identify a culprit, there was Shirley trapped in the role of victim, with no one to pin her abuse on.

'Tell away, yi big stinky cry-baby.' The perpetrators already knew they wouldn't be caught, that the unspoken ethos was that she deserved to be victimised. The teachers were tired of Shirley hammering on the staffroom door at break-time. In the playground it was sport to taunt her, to see the outsize, ugly girl sob. They ran away laughing. A pattern for future life.

Shirley pulled Michael away from the other children as if he was her safety blanket.

'Come on, wur gaan.'

'Yur futher's in wi ' the stinky McLeays.'

Seadhna felt alarm. They were making it up because they had run out of people to pick on.

'That'll mak *you* stinky as weel.'

'Stinky, stinky, stinky. Shitty Shirley and Shitty Seadhna!'

'He is no ...'

Seadhna was sure that there could be no basis in their assumption, but again it was possible to find yourself swept up into terrifying situations wholly by accident. There were all kinds of things that could happen without you knowing or realising. It was unravelling which mattered and which didn't that was the difficulty. The playground squabbles and the serious issues of the world were all on the same level.

Edna was a font of knowledge on grown-up life. She watched wrestling on ITV on Saturday afternoons with the curtains shut to keep out the light and told Seadhna about Churchill's funeral. She told her about what a sad day it was since he had saved the world from the Nazis and how she had watched the whole thing with her granny, and the coffin was on a gun carriage and everything. The only thing Seadhna watched with her granny was Calum Kennedy on the Hogmanay show and it was all in Gaelic, but she got to stay up until midnight. And then somebody said that the wrestling was all faked. So maybe Churchill's funeral was too. Edna's mother was wearing dark glasses that day and she said it was because her mother *wis alerjirc* to the light. George McLeay, *that tink*, said it was because Edna's father hammered the living daylights out of her, it was nothing to do with the light.

fir knowledge is power

John Rufus was in a frenzy over the secrecy of the Nuclear Industry.

'They want it for bombs, of course they do …'

'Atomic power goes hand in hand with nuclear weapons.'

Seadhna's father stood out in the autumn air with a circle of gaberdined listeners, pointing his finger at the sky as if to challenge God. He wanted a Labour government to be elected that year of '64, one that would end the race for nuclear power. Back in '58, the year of Seadhna's birth, the secret decision to site the reactor at Dounreay in Caithness had all been signed and sealed without the people on its doorstep knowing a thing.

'Nuclear weapons are an abomination in society. We must not stand by and be led into a future of more evil weapons. Remember the horror of Hiroshima? The most callous war crime ever? And why do they want to site the reactor in Caithness?' He narrowed his eyes to question his public. 'Yes, you've got it, because it's remote, there are no people … or very few! Yes, friends, we are an expendable population. To Whitehall, we fishermen, farmers, bakers …'. As he spoke, he confirmed the faces he knew in the audience. 'We don't matter. If we're blown to kingdom come, will anybody really care? We must ban these weapons. We must end the nuclear arms race. No to the Dounreay Reactor!' As he ended there was polite handclapping.

It was in the cupboard under the stairs that all the 'Ban the Bomb' placards were. There was talk of marches and scientists. Aldermaston was a faraway and dangerous place. But it was the banners that attracted Seadhna. Each one had the CND symbol deftly painted in black on a white background, with 'Ban the Bomb' beneath. An upside-down 'Y' in a circle. Her father's assured hand. For a long time Seadhna couldn't figure out the word 'Bomb'. It was the silent 'b,' and eventually she wrote it on a piece of paper and asked Iseabail.

'What does that word say?'

And Iseabail big-sisterly explained it. 'It's bomb, band the bomb.' She sang the three words as if they were part of a nursery rhyme, rising in pitch with 'bomb'.

'What's band the bom?'

'It's bombs that can blow you all up, and banning them.'

Iseabail's ignorance of the wider meaning was cloaked in the confidence of a little superior knowledge. The placards themselves, under the stairs, seemed empowered with some awful menace. The black and white and the strange words. The'blow you all up' that was somehow associated with them. Blow up what? A house? *No, a whole town. Lots of towns. Blow up the world …*

How can it be that you can make a thing that blows up the whole world?

The world's too big to be blown up.

Seadhna didn't go in around the banners while they were there, even though the room under the stairs was the best place for hiding. All the coats hung there, the scratchy long woollen ones with their silky linings, the exotic feel and smell of the fur coat that you could pretend you were a bear in. Hats, jerkins, old coats for outside, and the scary upright hoover with the black bag that might burst into roaring life at any time. A small, secret world of its own with the door shut and a tiny window low enough for Seadhna to reach and open herself. She did not like the contaminating presence of the banners in there. Their sticks jutted angularly, whereas the cupboard world was soft and enclosing and safe.

New

clear

power.

The reactor. Just across the water. The guvver mint. The bom.

One day they were gone.

She and her sister had been in the car, an old, black, leather-smelling Vauxhall, which crawled behind the protesters as backup. They had bottles of lemonade and sandwiches, but it was just another interminable car journey that might bring you to some strange place. The long boring hours were spent tracing wrinkles in the leather, finding the bits where the burst stuffing of the upholstery could be pulled out, and watching for the indicator stick to flick up between the front and rear passenger seat. A piece of magical engineering.

'God will send you to hell if you're a commy. And he'll strike you down with a bolt of lightning if you swear. God could just destroy the whole world if he wanted. Just like that.' Edna had learnt how to snap her fingers, but Seadhna's index and middle fingers slid limply off her thumb.

It was inside the stair cupboard that she tested her theory. God and Nuclear Power in a strange marriage. By Edna's yardstick, 'Hell's Bells and Buckets of Blood' should definitely merit a swearing bolt of some kind, but none had materialised when her father said the words. *Could it be*, thought Seadhna, *that there was a range of bad words that applied differently to different people? Were bolts only for certain words like the 'f' word? Or maybe only children got struck down. Was it only if you said the words outside where God could hear you?*

There was nothing for it, she would have to take the risk of being struck down and try the theory out. To minimise stress and disruption to the rest of the house, she thought the under-stair cupboard would be the best place. If she was rent asunder, her bits would at least be contained within a small area. She didn't tell anyone about her experiment. God had never been a topic until her arrival in the infant's class at school when they all had to shut their eyes and say the Lord's Prayer in a drone. Hands clasped and elbows on the oak desktops and eyes tight shut. The harder your eyes were shut, the harder you prayed. She had no idea what it was all about, but she copied everybody so she wasn't caught out.

'Forgiveusourtrespassersandthosewhotrespassagainstus.'

Among the coats, and looking furtively to the side, she said it. 'Hell's Bells and Buckets of Blood.'

And waited.

Nothing.

She waited again, in case the bolt took a minute or two to get fired up.

Still nothing.

She tried it a bit louder. '***Hells Bells and Buckets of Blood*.**'

After a while, untimed but at a suitable interval, it appeared as if there was going to be no bolt.

But then, she thought, *maybe it was the wrong bad word or phrase.*

With all the sophistication of a scientific study, she narrowed down the variables. So she tried 'Bloody'.

Then 'Hell'.

Then 'Bloody hell'. Then even whispered 'Fuck.'

She went out of the stair cupboard with a feeling of elation. The world had shifted. One thing was clear. There was no God. There was no bolt from God, and all the things Edna had claimed as certainties would never be quite as sure as before. She knew something that Edna didn't. It gave her a feeling of power and elation, and outside on the washing green she jumped and danced, shouting 'Hells Bells and Bucket of Blood,' over and over again. She taunted God to come and strike her down, staring up at the sky to invite his biggest bolt.

What's an atheist?

an' ignorance costs

'Michael?' The teacher's voice raised in pitch as she spoke to draw out the latter vowels in Michael's name. She was from the country, a First World War spinster.

'Bring your sum book out to the desk.'

Her voice was not unkind. But she could still narrow her eyes and whip a cutting look to Sandy Baker, ready at the slightest loosening of control, to rock in his seat and paste a big glakish grin onto his face.

Now in Primary Five, aged ten, a familiar pattern had emerged for Michael. The class of thirty pupils had self-sorted into groupings closely resembling cliques of who was cleverer than who, who had white socks and Clark's sandals and who possessed Dinky cars. The rankings were more finely tuned than any school test or sociologist's data.

Michael walked the oiled corridor between the desks to what was his regular position at an appended lower desk to the teacher, Miss Manson. There he and outsized Sandy Baker, who at ten had the build of a fourteen-year-old – still, however, with his fat thighs raw beneath grey shorts – would sit, haltingly producing 'reading' from their vocal cords. The chasm between each word was a defining silence marked by the rest of the class. Sandy and Michael's heads bowed, their fingers willing the words out of the page as if pressure alone would do it. Even the 'bottom group', in new-fangled jargon called 'the yellows', had already finished the reading that was a whole book ahead of Sandy and Michael. They could look forward to filling in their nature diaries, with the satisfying prospect of using the coloured pencils that had arrived from Reeves. The pencils, still sitting in a cardboard box, proclaimed all their newness on Miss Manson's desk. Sandy and Michael, as the 'poor readers', were issued the name of 'white group' as if the dilution of colour denoted their proficiency.

'Sit down at the desk, Michael.'

She always sang his name as if she enjoyed its sound.

Taking a clean piece of squared paper from the centrefold of a new jotter, Miss Manson wondered how far back in the logic of multiplication she would have to travel to pick up the place where Michael had gone adrift.

'Do you remember, Michael, when we talked about sets?'

Michael nodded, mostly because he liked to sit beside her at her desk. He could smell the strange fragrance of her cardie and see the tiny pearly earrings clipped onto the soft lobes of her ears. Her hair was twisted into a kind of hat brim round her head. You couldn't see the join, but it sat like a long sausage from her brow to the nape of her neck.

'Here is a bag of six oranges,' and she drew six circles onto the paper, then enclosed them in another looser shape. Michael was mesmerised by the big strong numbers she drew on the paper.

When she first said 'sets' he had started thinking about wireless sets, and he had to push that image of sets out of his mind in favour of the sets you got on the blackboard. The wireless image kept pressing in. He could see it sitting beside the fireplace in the living room. Polished brown wood with brown glass and the gold letters of indecipherable places written on it. *Luxemburg, Tirana, Helsinki. Budapest.*

'Don't you go touching the wireless set,' his mother said.

Miss Manson was reading Michael's face, registering the blankness on it.

'All right Michael, let's go over and look at the milk crate.'

Michael approached the milk crate as his mind simultaneously drifted back to the wireless set in Harbour Terrace. His head was back in the bedroom with his brother Geordie ranting at him the night before. The bass of the speaker boomed through the ceiling to the bedroom where Geordie, he and Jake slept. Another *peedie wan* was imminent too. Shirley had announced it to them, confirming that the new baby already had a name although it wasn't there yet. It seemed certain to be a boy, also called Malcolm or, 'Malky for short after Mam's brother that died in the Russian convoys or summeen,' she informed.

The wireless set seemed like a booming person in the house. Kept switched off while Harry was sleeping, but put on in the evenings when he went out to the bakehouse. Michael shut his ears to Geordie needling at him from his bed. Jake and he shared a mattress on the floor.

'Ah'm gonna fuckan' batter Norrie Inkster the morn. He's a fuckan' cunt. He's no gettan awaye wi' fuckan' shuvvan me aboot.'

Geordie couldn't walk away. 'Fuckan'… Fff…, it's no him that sez who can pit thur cars on the track … Ah'm gonna fuckan' get him the morn.'

Geordie only ever saw one route to sorting his injustices, and spoke on and on to himself with Michael as the tacit but affirming audience.

'Who sez he wiz the boss o' the track?' Geordie rehearsed his monologue to the room, Michael and the sleeping Jake, recounting the slights, massaging them into proper full-bodied wrongs, and firming up his rights and finally resolving his determination to sort the matter.

'You lisnan' tae me, Mick?'

As Miss Manson smiled and talked about sets, Geordie's earlier rant forced its way into Michael's head. He couldn't switch off Geordie, who was really mad, really upset, and Michael was the sounding board that concurred that Geordie's campaign was pure and just. He tried to switch on to the music coming from downstairs, with Jake farting pleasurably under the covers. *Aw, fucking stink.* It was a great muddle of talking and sounds.

'Well Ah'm gonna get the little cunt and see him greet all ower his cunty face.' Geordie's hate spiralled, until there was nowhere left for it to go and he just had to lie there rigid, staring at the ceiling, the blood coursing through him, his teeth clenched and brow creased in the dark, steeled with the prospect of tomorrow.

'Did you understand that?' Miss Manson waited for a reply.

The collecting of the milk crate was a coveted classroom job. It had to be picked up from a red handcart at the back door of the school where it was delivered along with a churn for the kitchens. The milk crate duty had to be strictly on a rota to ensure absolute fairness. When Miss Manson led Michael to the crate, heads surreptitiously glanced towards it, sitting on its familiar perch beside the radiator, lest some unlegislated favour was bestowed upon Michael.

'What are you looking at Edna Alexander?' snapped Miss Manson, which of course was code for *The rest of you get back to your work and do not dare snigger*, emphasised by the visual cue of a particularly hard stare.

Seadhna, too, let others catch the teacher's stare, although equally interested in who was getting the coveted classroom jobs. The foil tops of the small glass bottles, a third of a gill, were still wet with raindrops, and the cream had settled enticingly in the top inch.

When he saw the milk, Michael became thirsty for it.

'Now, Michael, first of all. Count all the bottles in the crate …'

Michael counted with his finger hovering over the lid of each bottle, inhaling the numbers on his breath as he reached the final total.

'… twenty-two, twenty-three, twenty-four …'

'So how many bottles all together then, Michael?'

Never sure whether it might be a trick question, he replied faintly, 'Twenty-four, Miss.'

'Well done, now can you count how many are just in one *row*?' Miss Manson traced the row with her finger up and down as she spoke.

If there was to be a trick then this was surely going to be it, but in that second Michael felt safe with Miss Manson, that she wasn't trying to catch him out and that what she said, she meant.

With his finger he followed the path of the previously traced row.

'Six, Miss,' and he allowed his eyes to reach up to her face, almost in trust.

'Good, Michael. Now all these rows are the same, aren't they? Will we just check? I'll count one then you can count one.'

They counted.

'Yes, Miss, they're all the same.'

'How many rows of six are there, then?'

Michael was safe in an untouchable bubble with Miss Manson. He was oblivious to the current of incredulity radiating round the room, sparking from the 'red' reading group to the 'triangles' maths group, and back to the 'yellows' and the various combinations which made up all the other groups of which Michael was not a part.

Did you see what the teacher was getting Michael McLeay to do? What an ijut! We did all that in Primary Three. He is just so stupit. Di yi ken this?

They're not ganna let him into the BBs because he's that stupit ... An' smelly. Yeah. Tinks.

'Michael, when you are big you will need to learn a trade. You are excellent with your hands. Your weaving is perfect.' Miss Manson always tried to find something good to say.

Why is she no merreed? Me fither sed there wis no men left efter the waar. It could be that. She wis engaged, tho. More likely nobody wanted hir kis she hid that big mole on her face. Whit, Old Manny Manson engaged? No likely. Yuch.

And they giggled. The little girls knowing full well that being left on the shelf was a dire state to endure. To be unwanted, not getting a man, was something they needed to avoid at all costs.

Spinsters. *Yeuch.*

Miss Manson held up Michael's Dryad handicraft tea mat for all to see.

'Do you see how neatly Michael has woven his mat? Every tiny stitch is exactly the same size.'

The class looked on in dutiful awe.

'Well done, Michael. I think that deserves a clap.'

'It's boring colours, though,' whispered Edna, stuffing the cut-outs from the back page of the *Judy* into her desk. Seadhna tacitly agreed with her, as it was better to stay on Edna's side than not.

Geordie's battle to right the wrongs of the car-track did not turn out as he had planned. The churning injustice had all started the week previously around a mud hump in the school playground which miraculously became transformed into a coveted car-track when surrounded by the eager circle of boys clutching their toy cars. It was strictly the preserve of boys, where Dinky models were brought and hurled over cliffs then 'broom-broomed' round the track again for another high-speed take-off. The pecking order and queue at the coveted track was rigidly enforced by the boys with the best cars. Norrie Inkster had two racers with numbers on the doors, and he took the lion's share of track usage. A couple of other boys shuffled, waiting, running their cars up and down their forearms in anticipation of their 'shot'. Even Sandy Baker had a tractor which wasn't exactly meant for the track, according to Norrie, but he was still permitted a shot. Norrie drew the line, though, at Bert Johnston passing his shot on to Geordie.

'Nope, the shot's fur you, no Geordie.'

Access was strictly tied to ownership.

Geordie hung back behind the clump of boys and watched Norrie's endless goes on the mud ramp. He had been willing to wait, nursing the feeling of anticipation that the use of Bert's lorry provided, and still thought that Norrie would relent with a little pressure from the others.

'Come on Bert. It's no his track. It's no like he owns it.'

'But Ah'm in charge. Fur *I* have the top cars.'

'How come yur in charge? Yi are no.'

'It's everybody's track.'

'No it's no.'

'It's jist for wans that owns their own cars.'

The boys didn't hear the bell and the dispute rattled on unresolved until the janitor came over to chase the huddle into their lines.

Geordie smarted and the humiliation burned through him. In the shifting rules he couldn't win.

On the day he came to right the wrong, he only had fists and insults. At dinner-time Geordie's resolve failed him. The car-track was returned to a mere mud and gravel hump. The direction of the boys' interest had shifted. Instead of the car-track, they had opted for football and Geordie was thrown. He pulled Michael along for support like a mascot.

'Hey, come wi' me a minute Mickey.'

The demand that he right the wrong was hammering into his head. But his anger was rendered impotent, robbing him of any kind of release. The abandoned track had no magical lure. The cars were ranged on the edge of the sloping tar macadam football pitch, 'looked after' by Sandy, the non-playing minder who was temporarily bequeathed a small favour. Grinning and leering over at Geordie and Michael, even Sandy was in with the others. His allegiances shifted like water in a bottle.

Geordie sat by the track, moving his taut cheeks around his jaw, the resolve ebbing, the unfairness rekindling, the injustice having to be born, simmering. He turned to Michael and booted him in the back, propelling him suddenly forward, sprawling his bare knees onto the gravel.

'Hey, what you do that for?' Michael attempted rather more strongly than he intended. 'Piss off, Geordie.'

'What you say? Don't fucking tell me to piss of or I'll fucking hammer you.' The blood was coursing and Geordie needed a punchbag, so he stamped with his heel at the mud hump, but it was too solid to respond to his kicks.

whit yi learn

Back home, Shirley unrolled a second-hand *Bunty* comic that had arrived from somewhere unknown with the *Beano* and the *Dandy*. The woven mat fell out of Michael's bag at the back door and lay there until Shirley picked it up and set it on the sink.

'We never got mats, it wis purses,' she pouted.

Agnes propped it up against the window.

'Michael made it at the school,' she told Harry when he came in with a paper bag of six spongy, soft rolls in the morning. 'Hiv yi yur wages fur the rent?'

Harry said nothing for a moment, then, 'It's readin' an' writin' yi shid be learnin' at they school, no that poncy girl's stuff,' and he thudded heavily up the stairs to sleep in the bed still warm from Agnes and Shirley. Soon he was snoring fitfully in his semmet and trousers, the diluted daylight playing on his eyelids.

The knock at the Rufus's back door was unusual. It was where the black-faced coal men came in to offload their sacks. Dusty hessian sacks heaved off their stretched backs clad in ripped old suit-jackets. Only people you didn't know knocked. Pulling the kitchen door shut against the wind that blew in through the house, Sadie spoke to someone in the back lobby.

'Jist hold on a minute I'll get him.' And in another tone, 'John, it's Harry McLeay.'

The tall heavy man in a big black overcoat passed through the kitchen, led by John Rufus. He seemed exceptionally large. Harry McLeay averted his eyes, as if it was an intrusion to survey the private interior of someone else's home. He made no sign that he saw Seadhna clinging onto the handle of the kitchen door as she swung it back to compress herself between the sink cupboard at the limit of the door's arc. From there she could fix her eyes unseen on the face of Harry McLeay. Greying white hairs curled from under a tightly pulled cloth cap, well drawn down over the dome of his skull against the wind. Black stubble stippled the entirety of his face except for the soft tops of his red cheekbones where unshaven tufts emerged. A black man with a jute sack and a brown paper parcel under his arm.

Michael McLeay's father. The stinky boy that shat in the class.

John Rufus shut the door to the sitting room behind them.

'Siddoon min, siddoon.' He repeated himself in an effort to make Harry feel at ease.

'It's aall right, meester Rufus, A'll no keep yee long.'

'Whit can I do fur yi, buey? Whit can I dae, min?' John Rufus swung in and out of dialect.

'Ah brocht ee a hare meester Rufus fir Ah wis oot shootin' an' Ah got five like an' Ah only shoots fir ee pot like. Ah cannae use this een. An' yiv aye spoken up fir is like.'

John was breaking in with protestations.

'Ach buey, there's no need fir that …'

'Bit I wees windarin sir if yee might like tae buy a lamp. See I heev this auld lamp, and she's sure aal bress an' burns right gid. Ah wis jees wonderin if ee might like tae buy it fer Meeses Rufus fer an ornament ur sumthin ... a lot o fowks like iss aal lamps noo.'

In the pause that ensued while John tried to find a way to recognise the request for money dignified as a sale, Harry unwrapped the lamp from its parcel.

'Bit iff ee hiv nae use fir it like ...?'

'No, Harry min. It's not that. Ah'm no needan' tae *buy* the lamp ... But Ah'll gie yi some money an'... yi kin think o' it is a loan if yi like ... but Ah'm no needan' it back ... the money, yi ken.'

Harry insisted on leaving the lamp.

'No, Ah'll no be takkan' charity, meester Rufus. Ah'll sell ee ay lamp.'

'Hold a minute, buey ...' and John went to the kitchen to get money.

'Hiv yi a fiver in yur purse, Sadie?' He only used her name when it was serious.

'Aye, I wis going to pay the butcher, but there should be a five there. Gie him this for the bairns.' She passed a bolt of comics like a relay baton into his hand.

Harry took the five pound note, folded it up and put it inside the lining of his cap.

'Good night ti ee Mrs Rufus. Thank ee Mr Rufus.'

And Harry McLeay was shut out into the black night with hail skiting into the cracks between the flagstones.

In the morning the lamp was standing on the kitchen sideboard and the hare was hanging from its hobbled hind legs in the back kitchen, dripping blood from its mouth onto the stone floor.

'Why was that man here last night?' The question went unanswered. Talk of money was a taboo. The exchange of money was an embarrassment. But now the smart of the 'Tinky Mcleays' was a conspiracy of betrayal in which Seadhna's parents were implicated. The world of adults was a complex and shifting place.

my word

They were playing down in front of the garages with a ball. It was sometimes rounders, but that day more likely three and in, because the boys liked that better. It wasn't the ideal pitch because of the slope, but the garages were good for goals and you got a good bounce on the new tarmac. The goals presented a defined area, visual and auditory, which minimised disputes. There could be little argument about 'oot' or 'in'. It was either on the concrete or the wood. It was between the garages and the freshly harled gable of the new council houses that Seadhna learnt a wholly different word she really liked. It was one she'd never heard at home, and she loved it.

'Cunt.' The word had a perfect deep hollow sound to it, a satisfying mixture of consonants and vowel. It was like a grunt measured by two edges. George McLeay was using it happily and the context made sense. It was a form of friendly endearment surely, gentle teasing maybe.

'Pass us the baal here, ya cunt.'

And the ball was thwacked over to Geordie. Geordie belted it in past Edna and it boomed on the garage door.

'Wan tae me, wan tae me,' chanted Geordie.'

They put Edna in goal because she was girly and useless, and the boys just liked to score goals.

'Well done, ya cunt,' congratulated Bert.

A new word.

Michael watched, pressed against the harled wall.

Seadhna didn't have to ask the meaning, it was surely a new word for good things and exclamation.

'Yur a peedie cunt, Michael.'

'Yur jis' a greedy cunt, Sandy.'

'Yur ma's a fat cunt, Bert.'

Seadhna used the term with all the fascination of something novel. Everything was *cunt* this and *cunt* that.

'That's a cunt of a goal, buey.'.

She passed the term on to her sister Iseabail with authority, and they both assimilated the new word with ease. It was Edna's mother, however, who put a stop to it all.

'You said a bad word,' said Edna, suddenly teachery in tone, happy to report crime and grass on offenders. The pursed-up face always carried a threatening fleck and, in addition, Edna's ample covering of flab was ably used to complement her raft of intimidation techniques.

'I tell't me mum, you said a bad word, and she said you're to stop using that word right away or she'll tell YUR MUTHUR.'

Rising in crescendo to the peak of her opening statement, Edna stood proud in her coup de grâce, arms folded and righteous.

'What word?'

'*That* word. The one that starts with kih.' And she spelled it out. 'Kih, uh, in, tih.'

Seadhna felt immediate wrong welling up and leapt into a defence.

'Well YUR BRUTHUR was saying it first …'

Family loyalty could switch situations in a flash and Edna snapped quickly to the defence of her pack. However much her brother teased her and sent her running in to her mother wailing, a challenge to him meant a challenge to her.

'Are you accusing me brother noo?'

Edna was practised for fights. She heard the preliminaries often. The pre-fight verbal sparrings and the rise in intensity. The constant undertone of indignity and quick accusations. Eyes steadying and the whipping of looks … Then on to denials and defences, culminating in the thuds at night when she was in her bed.

Seadhna backed off quickly. She was out of her league.

'Well I didna ken it was a bad word.'

Comfortable she was winning, Edna drove home to savour the kill. Ignorance of the law, even in the jungle of the playground was no defence.

'Well it's a *really* bad word. One of the baddest words there are. It's that Tinks that's been learning Stevie it. And YUR MUTHUR will belt you if you say it.' The finger was raised advancing now.

Maybe, Seadhna thought, Edna knew things about what her mother would do that even she herself did not. To date, Seadhna's mum hadn't 'belted' them, although 'beltings' were in common parlance. *I'll tak the slipper tae yi if yi don't stop that howlan'.* The prospect that there were forms of punishment possible from her own mother that Seadhna herself had not yet encountered was truly chilling. It transformed the word 'cunt' from something that was part of a new liberation down at the garages with the big kids to a Trojan horse of terror. She never spoke the word again, and even when she was grown up and said fuck and prick and bastard, something would always stop her saying cunt. It was a word too far.

She quietly told Iseabail not to say it as well, hissing it from between clenched teeth. If leaked, the source would get back to her.

Stevie and the others carried on saying it, to the stroppy protestations of Edna, but Seadhna took no part in this, dropping her head an inch and pulling her lips firmly closed, all the while keeping her gaze fixed on Edna and Stevie to see what they did. The power of a single word was indeed something mystical.

'Did yi see the darkie?' Edna whispered, 'Sandy Baker sez there's wan at the minister's.'

'Whit diya mean, a darkie?'

'Ken, a wog, a nigger? A black boy. Thur diffrint fae us yi ken, kis thur made black.'

no jist bricks an' mortar

Stromness was made from work and stories. The colours of a working fishing town were the blackness of the tar sheds and luggy boxes, the brown livery of the lighthouse ships, the green paint that came buckshee with the free coal from the NLB. Yellow was only used on the thin lines round the hulls of the boats in a superstitious colour code, which told of the fortunes or tragedies of the boat's family. Red to ward off bad spirits in symbolic flames of fire all the way round the hull against witches. Blue for a death in the boat's family. Before chemical paints retouched the world in sugary hues, a simple choice of limited colours covered everything from the flatties to front doors, rabbit hutches to sheds. Limited colour pared down the world and made it simple. But those simple days had slipped away. There was new thing called progress. *Yi canna halt it min ...*

By the Fifties, a Ford tractor engine could power a boat just as well as a vehicle. Second-hand engines were stripped from old tractors and heaved into the hulls of the traditional yoles. The steam-stretched timbers were cut into and modified. Wheelhouses were dropped onto the clinker-built hulls and new rows of planking were added as well. You could go to sea and be protected from the weather. Get a gas stove in and brew up a kettle. The harmony of the old lines getting lost, the handful of untouched old sailing yawls left high on the beach by old men too tired to embrace engines. *Changes the whole balance o' the boat. Ah'll no be butherin'.*

The boatyard that once launched schooners developed a design for motorised fishing vessels and got into negotiations with the Highland Board to get the prototype accepted for grant assistance. In the Sixties it was time, they said, in the interests of the fishing industry to modernise the fleet. Steam-bent straps of larch were boxed over to house plotters and radar. News of the Highland Board percolated through to the fishermen and they talked, standing up on the piers, about the costs of new boats. The figures were astronomical, the loans impossible.

Far too big a cost. That's jis' crazy, that kinda money!

But yi'll pay it back bit by bit ower the years.

No way am I gettin in hawk tae the bank. Ah'm nivver owed nothin' in me life …

Weel, Ah'm thinkan' tae go fir a new een …

Drawings of the new MFV were being shown around. Two were ordered already for Wick. Building a brand-new boat, now that was something. Watching the planks getting hammered onto the staves. Copper nails, seeing everything was good, smelling the cut wood and rubbing your cheek on its smoothness. Knee-deep in shavings, all around the deafening rasp of the electric saw.

Getting a grant for a bigger boat. *What is this grant? Surely you hiv tae pay it back sometime?* Putting heads together to identify a guarantor. The bank wouldn't lend without one. *All that risk.* There was money on offer for expansion, chances to take and brand-new spanking boats to bring home and feel proud of. There was the buzz of building something. Launchings, painting a girl's name on the bow, *Our Rose*, then the fishing numbers underneath. A photo in the paper.

A lot of forms were involved with the Highland Board, and it was still a time when men dealt in unwritten agreements, eye contact or a clap on the back. Handshakes were not a thing in that community. Too formal, too distant and not for their class.

On a night of rain a knock might come at the Rufuses' big front door and the figure of a man would manifest itself. This unfamiliar territory initiated the hesitancy of unsure roles.

'Is yur fither in? I was wondering if … eh … Mr Rufus could help me fill in me form. It's aboot a boat.'

The visitor stood at the door, giving the eleven-year-old Seadhna too much information, and she, unfamiliar with the etiquette of door-answering and this unsettling feeling that a grown man needed help with a form, hesitated like a domestic servant. 'Just wait.'

When John Rufus saw the man waiting on the doorstep for permission to enter he rushed over. 'Come in, buey, come on in. Whit kin I do fir yi Andrew? Don't stand oot there!'

He talked in their accent, calling the man by his first name to cover over the uncomfortable rucks in the encounter. Their difference.

There were nights like that, of Force 9 southerly winds that drove right up the harbour where there was no shelter, and boats broke moorings and smashed up below the houses while children slept. Precious engines then had to be hauled to safety. Things had to be salvaged. Everything was at risk. Everything could be lost in one night of weather.

In the Rufuses' kitchen the radio whined. It swelled and veered on and off its Home Service station. The beeps heralded up to the six o'clock news that suddenly amplified in sound long enough to hear the headlines. *The prime minister, Mr Heath, has won the second reading of the European Communities Bill …*

Sadie was breeing a pot of tatties over the sink, the steam rising up to condense on the glass window. Setting them down on the stove to air, she cut a lump of butter in, and took down the wooden masher from its hook.

Mr Heath secured the vote in the House today. By just eight votes, swooned the RP announcer. *That means that Britain's entry into the Common Market is now secure.* There were no fishing boats on the Thames. Nothing down there was built for seventy-knot winds. Sadie rattled the pot of mashed tatties. She would just have to keep everything hot until John finished speaking to Andrew.

Apparently Mr Heath played the piano, there had been something about it in *Women's Weekly*, Sadie remembered, but no one had ever seen a grand piano till the piano-smashing contest in Shopping Week when an ancient Broadwood was lain to smithereens like a three-legged dinosaur.

Behind the sitting-room door, the mysteries of the Highland Board form were unravelled and solved, and the Andrew, Jack or Bobby, whichever of them it was, left the house with loud hearty relieved exchanges, moving from the sitting room to the steps outside accompanied by talk. The shuffling men who had climbed the hill to John Rufus's big house would leave reassured in the knowledge that you could ask John for help and not feel embarrassed. He was still *wan o' iss*.

John had done well, and, to some, it put him above them. He had a post office salary and had bought a terraced villa, and that inevitably meant he had moved out of their world forever. Cleverness shifted you. Old Ella Watson had stung him when she said, 'Imagine that, John? You a wee heelan boy buyin' a big hoos like that! But yur doin' weel noo. Yi'll be above iss aall. Yi'll be gentry noo.'

by noo yi should ken

The domestic science teacher made Shirley tie her hair back, and then took her into the back room off the big kitchen with its washboards and back-to-back deep porcelain sinks. *Shanks England.*

'Personal hygiene, Shirley.'

Michael's sister sat unfamiliarly close to Mrs Wilkinson, each on a faded green arm-chair. The sofa doubled as a bed when required for the 'sick bay'. Shirley waited with her hands in her lap, looking out through her eyes in unsure anticipation.

'Now when a girl reaches your age, Shirley, and you are fifteen, aren't you, there are things that you need to do. Ehm … To keep your body clean, and so that you look nice and smell nice and fresh.' The teacher was trying a new tone, which was mellower that the one she normally used in front of the class.

'You'll have to take her aside.'

It had been discussed in the ladies' staffroom.

'I mean it's really getting quite whiffy.'

'Obviously nobody's told her about *menstruation*.' The dreadfully un-public word.

'Well when you grow up, your body starts to sweat much more, and you start growing hairs in place like here.' And the teacher demonstrated a vague hand gesture somewhere towards her oxters and then her knees. 'And here.'

The high-ceilinged room resounded like a bell tower of disconnection, as if all the air and space surrounding Shirley and the teacher was made of iron filings.

'Now all that hair traps dirt and sweat and it's very important to wash these areas thoroughly.' The teacher pronounced 'thoroughly' as if it was the key word in a magic spell that required every vowel and consonant to have maximum value. THORRROLEEEE.

'Now the other thing that happens to girls of your age is a thing called "menstrOOation". It means you are growing up. And it's when blood comes out of you … down there, and it tells you that your body is ready to become a woman and make babies.'

Shirley sat in frozen alarm.

'Has that happened to you yet? Have you had any blood?'

Shirley allowed her head to nip in and out of a very quick nod.

'Right then. That means that every month you will have these drops of blood and I'm just going to show you something that you can use to mop it up.'

The teacher stood up and opened the door of the wardrobe that somehow was part of the sick-bay paraphernalia and pulled out at bulky bag of Dr Whites.

'These are sanitary towels.' And she pulled one out from the layers in the bag and swung it in front of Shirley. The cotton netting and loops were altogether fascinating and alarming, like a strange toy hammock. But the teacher went on to explain.

'You get a little belt that you wear around your middle and these loops fasten on to it.'

She rummaged again in the wardrobe and came out with a fleshy strap-like thing with hooks and clips.

'This is it. Now … I believe you can get things nowadays that the girls are using that don't have straps and loops, but just stick onto your knickers.'

The teacher was ploughing onwards, with Shirley betraying no sign of having any knowledge of sanitary pads or the mysteries of the *privates*.

'When this is soiled …'

Such a strange vocabulary, this was leading the teacher into. *Soiled must be the same as dirty, or bloody. Feuch.*

Mrs Wilkinson with the sanitary pad lying over her knee.

'You can't put it down the toilet because it blocks the drains, so you have to put it in the incinerator. Now there's one in the girl's toilets.'

Incinerator?

'Is that okay now, Shirley, do you understand everything?'

There was another sudden nod.

And in a lowered tone, 'If you need pads and you don't have any, there's a store in here, and you can come in and help yourself. Okay?'

Another nod.

The bell went, announcing playtime, or break as they said in the big school, because by then everyone was too grown up to play.

'Just a minute Shirley, before you go.'

She was standing up.

'Now boys can smell the smell of you when you're … *ON*, you know when the blood's coming, and it makes them want to, well it makes them, well ladies give out a kind of an animal smell that boys can't resist.'

The seconds were whizzing and expanding. Shirley was wide-eyed with the terror of this peculiarly unexpected world that was being described by Mrs Wilkinson.

'And boys, when they smell that smell, want to come after you and touch you and kiss you and things …'

Mrs Wilkinson's monologue had become so unhinged that she was becoming slightly reckless in what she was saying.

'What I'm saying, Shirley, is that boys will want to touch you because they can smell you're a woman and they'll want to poke their thingummy into you, you know, their penis, and you mustn't let them touch you, especially down *there*.'

And with the coy hooking of her forefinger several times toward the area of her skirt, Mrs Wilkinson was finished.

'Okay, Shirley. Off you go.'

As the Victorian panels of the door were pulled behind her and Shirley left, Mrs Wilkinson let out an audible sigh, pressing the demonstration sanitary towel back into its packet and returning it to its mildewed wardrobe. She strode across the playground, mission accomplished, heading for the staffroom and the restorative properties of a good cup of tea.

Such elucidation was denied the boys, the assumption being that it was pointless, as they were controlled by unstoppable biological urges. After that, Shirley spent a lot of time in the domestic science room, hand-washing net cloths and floor cloths. Rinsing things out the way Mrs Wilkinson showed them, pinkies together.

'That way you get much more strength into your arms, and you can ring out even more water.'

And it was true, they felt the weight of a cloth wrung out using the thumbs-together technique and another using the pinkies-together technique. There was no doubt which one wrung out more water.

'That's very neat, Shirley.'

She was folding cloths lengthways to lap over the pulley, the red stripes like a row of flags, each one perfectly aligned. The summer leaving date was approaching and the domestic science room was getting more sunlight through its high mottled windows.

'And what are you going to do once it's the leavings?'

'I think I would like to work in a hotel, Miss.'

'And do you know one that you would like to go to?'

'Well I'd like wan in the sooth, Miss.'

'You come in at dinner-time and I'll help you write a letter to some. There's a very good one I know of in Wick. And the good thing about hotel work is you get your lodgings too.'

That summer she found out what Mrs Wilkinson meant about men smelling women as she wrote her sweaty biro letters of application to hotels up and down the A9 and waited for replies. Walking by the pier, the Norskies clicked their tongues and tried to say, 'Good morning' in their foreign accents. The whaler men had no prejudice, and they didn't speak enough English for anything to matter. One called Lars walked along behind her, then fell into her step, and by the time the whaler disappeared, after three days' sheltering, Shirley was able to show off the engagement ring that Lars had given her. This betrothal, however, was met with derision and envied scorn by her sniping peers. *That's no a ring, that's jist paste. He probably dishes them oot tae ivrybidy.*

Shirley was not going to be allowed to share any second-hand happiness. No one was going to pretend or even go along with it to humour her. They had all solidified into rock-hard roles. Shirley had to stay within her allotted parameters and there were no Hans Christian Andersen swans in her script. That could only threaten everyone else's parts.

When the whaler put in again after a couple of weeks, Lars and the Norskies again marched up the street from their boats wearing their red Norwegian jumpers with braid trim and metal clips.

'Did you see Shaarley? I vas lookeeng for her?'

'No, Shurley's geen awaye. Och, she geed awaye tae Wick. Shiz cleanan it Mackays.'

'Sank you. You weel tell her I vas asking for her?'

'Oh yes.'

They knew they wouldn't see her again and the message would never have to be passed on from Lars. Shirley had one chance of rewriting the role she had been allocated by others, and leaving for Wick gave her that chance. In her absence Geordie became king pin.

The McLeay's house was simple rather than dirty. Agnes could not be accused of being unclean. Perhaps the children wore their clothes longer than others, and the stains were sponged out to spare a wash, encrusted mud was scraped off and rubbed between fists to powder. Agnes wanted to avoid any more babies, so after Jake was born she managed to keep Harry off her. It was a subtle thing that worked away just beneath her conscious thought. The exhaustion of the births produced a cumulative slowness in her. She never quite drew herself out of the swirling tiredness that engulfed her. Her self, such as it was, functioned just under the burden of wailing and dirty washing, rent money and squabbles that were the constants of her life. More children meant slipping further under and maybe losing her grip completely. The shift-work helped keep Harry too tired to notice she was evading him and the cans of Special finished the job. Once he was upstairs asleep, she left the house to walk the long cobbled street to the bank-house.

The National Commercial Bank was where Mrs Paterson employed her to wash the breakfast dishes, put on the washing in the twin-tub, make the beds, hoover with the Electrolux and clean the toilet. It was a parallel world. The quiet of the bank house when it was empty. The lives of other people. The smell of their suspended activity. She could sit for five minutes on a kitchen chair and almost remove herself from her own life.

Geordie moved into Shirley's space, filling it with the heavy frame that mirrored his father's. Imbibing injustices from all quarters and harbouring them, then letting go of them where it was easy.

'Will yi get in some coal tae me, George?'

'Fuck off, get it yursel.'

Agnes heaved the coal scuttle without challenging him, while Harry slept on. Michael watched silently, trying to work out his place in the shifting current of power. Just a little too late he moved to take the handle of the scuttle as his mother set it heavily on the grate.

casting a net

John Rufus let the door shut just a little too violently behind him. The wind took it and the shuddering vibration wakened Seadhna from a hot and fitful daytime sleep. He was on his way to the laird's house and she was off school with an illness. Some time before, she had presented her tongue to the doctor and said 'Ah,' and a small brown bottle of red liquid penicillin stood on the table.

The fishermen needed land for a net store, so John Rufus was asked to talk to the laird. They came to him because he read books and knew about forms and the rights of things.

'Politeness costs nothing,' he said, 'and can win you many things.'

So he rang for an appointment first.

He felt conspicuous on the long walk up the tree-lined drive to the house, trees being so unusual on the islands, thinking all the time of how he would put the case to the laird. It didn't do to demand.

Whispered through the tenanted farms, the folk called him a parasitic inbred old bastard, who would be shot first when the revolution came. Angry at all the land he owned, with them squashed into the seaward strip to the east, not daring to ask for a roof repair in case he might think they were troublemakers. And it was true, way back they had had to get the laird's permission to build their houses, even if they already rented the land. Nothing moved without the say-so of the laird, the type of crop, the kind of boat, the denomination of Kirk … John agreed with them when they spat in indignation and looked out from the corners of their eyes, but then went on to say he would talk to him, he knew how these folk worked. It would be better to make the laird feel that he was being philanthropic. They liked the thought they might be well remembered, the aristocracy. Like the Duke of Sutherland and his 'grateful tenants'.

But most of them had never heard of the Duke and Duchess of Sutherland and the statue high above Golspie. The islands were a world away from the cantankerous crofters of the north coast and the correlating brutality of the Sutherland Estate.

On Orkney, the island laird couldn't command a property equal to the vast estates of the highland lairds, but still owned big swards of Arctic tundra on the cliffs. He owned the jagged wind-carved hill and the expanse of land that moved through the seasons from green to purple to brown and included all the tenanted farms and crofts. Mister MacKenzie came every summer to Scotland from Africa where they kept black people in sheds to run their big farms. That's what folk believed, anyway. But the laird's money didn't come from his farm. Somehow he had struck lucky on a patch of land that contained the type of lime perfect for high-quality cement and so that was where his fortune came from. They called it a fortune, because his wealth was in the realms of royalty. Almost divine. A fortune in dusty brown bags of cement, that spilled and leaked, leaving a powdery trail, or got soaked and solidified rock hard before you got weather to dig in new corner posts. Perhaps he saw the Orkney place advertised in a London paper. Maybe a pal in a men's club told him. Perhaps his accountant advised him to get rid of some money and put it into land. Whatever the reason, the cement-rich laird bought the estate, and got with it a big hunting lodge. There were no deer, of course, mostly hares and rabbits, but they bred pheasants for shooting, and he would come north after the twelfth to pepper the hapless flyers with lead shot.

John slamming the door woke Seadhna from her sleep. The library book Iseabail had brought her slid to the floor, opening at the page showing mud huts. Seadhna had heard her father talk about the laird and his estate in Rhodesia. Little was excluded from the ears of the children in the Rufus house, but it was still too great a leap of possibility to place the figure of the laird anywhere in the context of the black-and-white photo of the mud huts.

Everyone mused at the comings and goings of the laird, and to Seadhna it seemed a strange thing when someone so posh and rich, with his wooden-framed shooting-brake car, was involved with a thing as lowly and mundane as cement. You imagined that the alchemy of wealth was more like spinning straw into gold than bags of cement into heather. His big house stood empty all year until August, when Breck, the farmer who looked after it, opened it up to put fires on in the rooms he used. He didn't use them all at once. Some rooms got opened up if there was a guest party coming. *How do you 'open up' a room*, she wondered, *just open the door and let the air in maybe*? It made it sound like it was strangely sealed all the rest of the time. Unbreathed, still, yellow air. *Mister McKenzie*, Breck called him. But there was nothing Scottish about him. Breck revved up the shiny car in the garage and from then on the laird's unusually tall figure could be spotted with a spaniel. He had no wife. The folk looked at him from afar, feeling small motions of excitement when Breck dropped some information about what the laird had been saying or doing. It brought them all close to the strange greatness of him. His big posh English voice like Prince Philip. The worlds of cement and Rhodesia that could only be imagined. Tom's uncle had been in the Boer War and brought back a native's spear. Now it was in the museum.

For Seadhna, it was the only time she saw her father deferential. Outside the ironmongers, when the tweed-clad laird had raised his hand in a greeting to John as they passed. He didn't acknowledge her, of course, but her father had said, 'Good morning, *Sir*.' Something he would never say other than in jest to any other being. But it was the Highland memory, the Rufuses, from crofters to white collar in two generations. Being deferential was in the blood, or at least it was a well-honed inherited act.

Up at the big house, the laird answered the door himself – he didn't have any servants. Still fixed on his mission, John let the laird usher him into the mosaic-tiled vestibule. It was at once dark with heavy wood. Inside, he offered John a dram and he took one just to be courteous. His eyes looked around the interior of the house, absorbing the inner sanctum of wealth and silence. The slightly musty elegance of the place. The library, floor to ceiling in books. Books on the islands, Scottish books, rare maps. Arts and Crafts wallpaper. Stained glass. The Lethaby features. Big smooth carved stone mantels. The laird began to talk about his hobby of trying to find a chemical fertiliser from seaweed. Breck had hauled a whole lot of tangles up to the back of the lodge from the shore in his tractor, and the laird had them spread out in the kitchen. Some were being chopped into tiny bits, some were being put through a mincer, others were being dried on the pulley above the great Aga. Jars of brown liquid stood around labelled like chutneys at the produce show.

John Rufus nodded and expressed his interest, talking about iodine, and the medicinal cures that could come from bladderwrack. He'd set by a whole afternoon for the visit so there was plenty time to talk. The laird babbled away like an ordinary man. Eccentric, you could see why he had no wife. Not the marrying kind, he was completely obsessed with his chemical projects, labelling, noting, testing, cataloguing. He was in a side-world that existed just outside the realities of everybody else.

The laird never even said much about the land for the net shed, just wondered whether it was above or below the road because there was to be an electricity substation built too, the North of Scotland Hydro Electric Board had written. There had to be permissions and way-leaves and suchlike …

Seadhna spent the languid afternoon, while the deal over the net shed was politely firmed up, dragging her fingernails over the loose cellophane cover of the mud-hut book. It made an irritating yet pleasing rasping sound and by the time her father returned home the cover was all scored.

'He has no idea of our lives,' John told Sadie, adding, 'I thought he'd probably be out o' kilter wi' the rest o' the gentry set as well. An odd ball but harmless,' he concluded.

'Aye, maybe, but he's got Breck running about like a lackey. Gets him filled up with drink and sometimes he never gets home. When the laird's there, Bella never sees Breck. He has some kinda hold over him.'

An aversion tae weemin?

John eschewed any form of gossip. 'Och, that's just talk.'

John's negotiations were successful and the fishermen got the land for the net shed. The laird agreed to sell outright rather than lease, which meant they had the security to go ahead and apply to the Highland Board for a grant for a building. The London lawyers were to sort it all out.

By the time the deal was struck, the polythene cover of the Africa library book was barely hanging together and it still had to go back all scratched and scored to the library.

The County set by then all knew that John Rufus was a 'red'. The brigadiers and retired colonels, who met at the Pisky kirk or the Conservative and Unionist Party meetings, chuckled patronisingly.

'A straight enough chappy, as far as one can know, but a bit of a 'red'. You can never tell with these Highlanders – they're a bit different.'

In their decaying Victorian follies, hoarding their cut-glass accents and tatty superiority, they would give a wry smile to ward away the fear, placing themselves momentarily in the same context as the Romanovs.

'Do you remember, darling, we passed him in the car on that ridiculous anti- … what was it? That march. I mean nuclear power, it's going to be the new thing … clean. It's progress, you just can't stand in the way of it, and I know for a fact old Thurso fought damned hard to get that plant there. Bloody hell, what is there in Caithness, for God's sake? Nothing but acres of bog, and if people want jobs, they've just got to make compromises.'

In time, John got the by-name 'Kremlin', because the Kremlin was in Russia where all the communists were.

when it wis simple

The year 1970 brought the *Partridge Family* and David Cassidy to Seadhna and a temporary realignment of Michael's place in the rigid pecking order that his contemporaries assigned him. Swelling their ranks in the secondary school were the children from the country schools who at twelve were bussed away from the coal fires of their safe single-teacher classrooms to join the town kids. The farm boys spoke thickly and hung around brooding, in home-knitted jumpers. Edna and Seadhna felt superior again because they had tan tights, knee-high boots, tank-tops and bought the *Jackie* every Thursday. The secondary school was only a shift from one end of the building to the other, but there was an indoor toilet block.

Michael, like all the boys, wistfully coveted ownership of a Wrangler jacket and matching jeans and felt the shame of his cheap clothes. Seadhna made herself a crocheted waistcoat and scanned the ad page of *Melody Maker* for mail-order LPs. The jeweller's was the only place in the town you could buy records and even then they only stocked fake *Top of the Pops* cover compilations.

The journey through their secondary years was marked by an increasing chasm between the terminally slow, and those destined for exams. For Seadhna, report cards were a comfortable affirmation of safety among the exam elite, while for Michael, the comment boxes filled with repeated 'poors' in a variety of different forms of script and coloured biro. Woodwork got a 'good', with a comment from Mr Sinclair, the technical teacher, that Michael could make an excellent joiner one day.

Along with all the others who couldn't do English and maths, Michael found himself in a designation entitled 'L' for leavers, a holding area for all those waiting to get out of school as soon as possible. The other third years were channelling towards exams, feeling the edgy awe of 'O' levels and Highers. There was new jargon to talk in, *prelims*, *practicals*, *assignments*, things to make you sound big and clever and different and way above the 'leavers' class. In reality, the schism had occurred well before. Seadhna, Edna, Norrie and all the clever ones had long ago discerned that they were part of another world.

The teachers who still had to contain the leavers until their official release date had to think up tasks to keep them out of bother. A posse was sent to pull up all the weeds in the school garden, using the time out of the eyeshot of the reluctant supervising teacher to pass around a Number 6. The 'L' class was a diversion for Bert Johnston and Willie Bremner, a source of entertainment as they used their animal smartness to spin their gullible classmates into ruses and pranks that sent the teachers into neurotic rages. Sandy Baker was persuaded to take the wedge out from under the massive cast-iron grass roller that careered down the sloping tattie beds and right through the school greenhouse.

There was an inquiry.

'William Bremner, I know fine that you're at the back of all this.'

Willie could sit out any inquisition, stony-faced, and cool as a practised poker player. Like a cat playing mice, teachers and fellow pupils were his pawns. He controlled everything.

'I saw Mickey behind the shed. Maybe you should ask him.'

Willie knew the teacher had reached a stalemate and was looking for a way out of the confrontation. He flung a red herring, and the teacher went off sniffing the wrong trail. The headmaster had tried to persuade Willie Bremner to stay and do exams, but he had just laughed and said he could make more money at the fishing in a couple of months than Mr Sinclair got in a year. Bert Johnston knew he was going to the farm and just waited for his release date so that he could drive the tractor every day and hot-rod his souped-up mini round the field till he could get a legal licence to drive. He already knew all about Aberdeen Anguses, Massey Fergusons and acreages, *five furra ploos* and barley subsidies. You didn't learn any of that stuff at school.

George McLeay was a message boy at the butchers, where he sawed up bones in the back shop and threatened anyone who looked at him the wrong way.

There was no career plan as such for Michael. Mr Sinclair struggled to find a positive way to say that although Michael found the academic curriculum was not for him, he could work a saw well, was very practical and that he was an honest quiet lad. All things that still counted for something, but you could not pass an exam in them.

Mr Sinclair said there might be some labouring jobs on the new ferry pier.

There was a lot of building going on for the new ro-ro …

Seadhna had eight 'O' levels and a violin exam to pass, and Edna had blossomed into a mini-skirted wonder with an ample bosom and a curvaceous backside that gave all the boys uncontrollable and immediate hard-ons. She was developing all the extra-curricular skills for a world where beauty meant a lot more than brains by practising smoking her mother's Embassy king-size and trying out Dubonnet and lemonade.

The leavers and the exam-destined all had one last time thrust together in a show of social harmony. Before any of the 'L' class could leave they had to attend the Christmas Dance.

There was no way out of it. Michael had to go too.

'I can't afford a ticket,' he told Mr Sinclair, but Mr Sinclair had given him one anyway for free. It meant he had to dress up in a shirt and trousers. Geordie was needling him, telling him he looked like a real dick.

'You'll have to get that bumfluff off your face. No birds'll snog you wi' all them plooks.'

Michael reddened in an uncontrollable flush. He had tried using his father's razor and sliced through the myriad of raised volcanic eruptions on his face. The pus and blood had mixed and the wispy hairs of his first beard growth matted together. His face was carnage. The combed-down black hair was like an alien liquorice topping. He wanted out the house without anyone seeing him and hoped he could keep his jacket on and his hood up without being noticed.

'Hey Mickey. Ah'm cumin tae the dance. Get us in through the lavvys.' It was Geordie.

Michael grunted. 'Fuck, Geordie. What you wantan tae go tae the school dance for? You said it was a lot of pish.'

'I'm gonna smack that poncy fucking Norrie Inkster.'

'Yur no gettan' me inta trouble.'

'Why no? Yur leavan anyway. Why should you be buthered?'

'Yi should jis' forget it.'

'Fuck off, you. Trying to tell me what ta do, ya peedie poof?'

Willie Bremner took a bottle of rum into the gents, while upstairs on the badminton courts the stiff rows of girls and boys kept themselves awkwardly separate under the full glare of the strip lights, only to be gyrated into forced contact through a Paul Jones or a Strip the Willow. Michael didn't dare cross the bear pit of the floor to ask any one to dance, and was dumb with stoic embarrassment when Mr Sinclair's wife made him hobble through a St Bernard's in a ladies' choice. He managed to hide himself at the end of the trestle serving neep and clapshot until Willie Bremner shouted him over. 'Hi Mickey, yur brother's wantan yi doon below.'

Geordie and the other previous year's leavers were hanging around, being shouted away from the fire escape by the teachers. Willie Bremner was keeping his options open between the inside and the outside of the hall, passing his whisky bottle to Geordie, who was smoking No. 6 behind the gates. Outside, the wheeze of the accordion music echoed all the way down the street.

Michael appeared at the toilet window.

'Get us in, Mickey. Go roon' the fire escape and sneak us in.'

He mumbled something akin to 'Aye'.

Michael knew he could say 'Aye' and then disappear and pretend to have done Geordie's bidding. There was no way they could get Geordie in unseen. And Michael didn't want Geordie inside, anyway. Mr Sinclair was earnestly operating the Dansette attached to loudspeakers. It would be wrong.

Edna and Seadhna were clacking up the stairs in platform heels. Seadhna wore a purple rayon dress she had spent three weeks making and a matching velvet choker. Nobody had anything like it. The school dance was an opportunity for display. Edna had just reapplied her lipstick and taken a quick swig from a quarter bottle of vodka in her bag. She offered some to Seadhna but she declined, beginning to get a little alarmed at Edna's wantonness.

'Won't you be glad when the dross like Tinkey Micky leave and it's just the clever ones?'

Edna said it just a bit too loud so that Michael had to pretend not to hear.

Seadhna rattled her shoes on the stair as if to scrub out the insult, returning to her function of escort and confidante to Edna's romantic entanglements with Norrie and the difficulty she was having deciding over him or Bert Johnston. Bert's saving attraction was that although he was leaving (so formally in the stupid bracket) he could already drive, albeit illegally, and really just pretended to be stupid. With the last dance producing a sweaty clutching session lurching from heel to heel round the floor, the unclaimed dancers, either relieved or smarting with rejection, made their way to the coats. Seadhna, not wanting to be prized into the unspoken groping duties of the last dance, went to collect Edna's coat as she flopped round Norrie's neck, her head lolling ever so oddly on his shoulder.

In the crisp December night of stars and constellations, the Plough and Orion, and all the same black and sparkle as the Neolithic peoples had seen, the sweaty bodies spilled out into the cold. Seadhna waited inside the door for Edna to finish snogging Norrie, feeling the draught chill her bones. She had nothing on over her dress. It would have spoiled the effect.

Edna went into the toilet while Norrie went outside, Willie Bremner calling him round to a waiting Geordie.

Whisky invincible, Geordie got hold of Norrie just outside the back wall. There he grabbed the arm of his brown cord velvet jacket. 'Hi you. Yeah you. Arsehole.'

Geordie clumsily lunged for Norrie, and Norrie, trying to dart out of his reach, tripped as Geordie clung to the corduroy sleeve. The mass-produced foreign stitching burst under the oxters as the two grappled between the gravel and the sodden winter grass verge. Norrie wasn't a fighter.

'You fucking cunt, you.'

There was no form to the fight. It rolled and heaved and staggered itself on and off the harled wall.

'Go Geordie.'

Willie Bremner threw the whisky bottle into the school garden.

Seadhna came out. 'What's happening?'

Michael appeared and hung around in the shadow.

The emerging crowd was mesmerised by the fight that took place deftly round the corner away from view of the main door.

'I better get Edna,' said Seadhna to nobody.

Norrie's pastel shirt was covered in mud. Geordie flailed his arms full at the kicking form of Norrie. They pushed faces away, heaving and panting, Norrie breaking free, with the tails of his jacket slipping through Geordie's fingers and finally making a staggering escape. With the sound of Mr Sinclair's voice the crowd melted. Norrie was running the long way round the hall and back to the other door.

'The fucking bastard. Fucking tinker cunt. Psst, Seadhna, tell Edna tae meet me outside the café.'

Seadhna nodded.

Willie Bremner stood watching. Sandy Baker was grinning.

Edna appeared, tottering in her hot-pants and platform boots, Maybelline eyes fluttering, and dabbing her lipstick where Norrie had smeared it kissing her. She emerged after everything was over.

Norrie was the top catch. Captain of the football team, and Edna was good enough at typing to keep herself out of the bear pit of the thick. She was working herself up to the position of Shopping Week Queen in the coming summer. You could go no higher in the schoolgirl popularity stakes.

The also-rans of the dance floor emerged, the unchosen beetling off as inconspicuously as possible into the night. Michael, unable to get away unspotted, was left to take the filial flack for Geordie.

'Yur brother's a bastard an' … an' yur sistur's a fuckin' whore. Shuz doon on a Norskie trawler way her knickers roon hur ankles. Shiz the biggest ride in Wick.' That was all the redress Norrie could muster.

Geordie had disappeared.

'Fuck off, ya poof.'

And then it was 1973.

ti earn a pay

'Ah'll learn him tae use ay gun,' said Harry. 'If ee kin shoot fer ay pot ee'll nivver be hungry.'

On the links the rabbits sprung up everywhere. The town council had been trying to create a golf course, 'for locals and visitors alike,' they chimed in civic generosity.

Aye, the only eighteen-thousand-hole course in the whole of Scotland!

Everyone laughed heartily at their own home-grown humour.

They were trying all the methods they could to get rid of the rabbit population, netting the holes and sending a terrier down, getting ferrets in, filling up the holes and gassing them, but there were just so many. The eighteen-thousand-hole golf course seemed more of a reality than a joke. The golf club decided to offer a bounty.

'A sixpence a tail. Ee best waye really is till go oot it night wee a lamp. But wu'lll jees hae a go in the daylight till ee git ay hang o't.'

At dawn, Harry lay in the undulations behind the dunes, whispering. 'See aat een?'

The air rifle was lined up on a fat rabbit about ten yards away.

'Ee hiv till aim good at ay heed.'

Harry was steadying the rifle on the crook of his arm. The pellet fizzed out of the barrel like a lemonade bottle and hit the rabbit with a thud, tossing it into the air. It spun and landed about a yard away, its back legs galloping.

'Like aat.'

Harry stood up and walked to the kill, picking the animal up by the hind legs.

'Iss een's deed, but yi jis' need till mak sure.' And he clutched the rabbit by the shoulders and smacked its head against a stone in one deft movement. The head lolled and the eyes stared cold and Harry slung the dead rabbit into a sack.

'Now it's your turn. We'll walk this waye a wee bitty.'

Michael lined up the airgun. It felt too long and awkward in his hands. He had to stretch to get his finger on the trigger.

'Hiv ee got ay barrel on ay heed?'

Michael pursed his mouth.

'If eer sure ee hiv it, jes squeez ay trigger gentle like. Keep ee rest ay yi still like.'

Michael squeezed. The gun ricocheted against his chest, thumping a shirt button into his sternum.

'Ee got him.'

The rabbit was trying to run, dragging one hind leg and squealing.

'Ee'll need till feenish him off. Hae anither go at ay heed.'

Michael took another aim at the slow-moving rabbit's head.

'Jis' aim a bitty in front of ees heed.'

Michael squeezed the trigger. This time the pellet hit the stomach. The rabbit flicked onto its back, contorting and convulsing, pedalling its one good back leg into the grass.

'Dam't, ee'll hiv till feenish it off yursell. Go ee an' get im by the scruff o' the neck, Same waye is ee pick up ay kitten an' jis' gee the head a good smack on a stone.'

Michael went to pick up the wriggling animal. The pulse of its kicking made it hard to hang onto. It was heavier than he had anticipated.

He was looking around for a stone.

'This een?' And he looked up at his father.

'Aye, try it. Try it.'

Attempting to get the head to smack onto the stone was impossible. The convulsing body conspired to render his tries at a clean kill feeble. He was hitting the head on the stone, but without enough force. The animal was stunned but still making reflex running movements.

'Tak anither stone and gie im a good big thump on the back o' the heed. Near ay bottom. Aat's whur ee main nurvs is.'

Michael took the stone from his father and kneeling on the ground with the rabbit pinned to the grass by the neck brought the stone onto the skull with such force that he heard and felt the collapse of the skull.

'Aat's it. Aat's it. Ee've done it. Ee've ernt yursel a sixpence.'

The blood was running from the skull over the fur, and he felt its warmth on his hand. He looked over to his father but he was already searching for the next rabbit.

money an' sense

In the Outer Isles, 'hippies' were throwing themselves in the path of seal-shooters, but the cull barely made the local paper. It was big news in the cities. The isles folk looked on at the strange protesters with their peculiar clothes, pink hair and earnest arguments. Everywhere they went they were a conspicuous entity. *Earrings on the men…!* Long hair. Patchwork skirts. A TV crew came. There was something on BBC Scotland about it all, and Jimmy Prentice got three hundred pounds for one day's hire to take them all out in his boat. *Better than a whole week at the creels.* All of it was way off Seadhna's radar, too. She was fixed on being a city girl, getting to a place where your voice mattered, changing the world through the alchemy of art. *I mean, didn't Picasso change the world? What about* Guernica?

Everyone, it seemed, needed a cause to follow. John Rufus was reading scientific tomes on nuclear power and penning handwritten letters to the paper. He even had one accepted by *The Scotsman*, bringing it through to the kitchen to show Sadie. All in their different perspectives, earnest, naive and powerless in varying measures – all, that was, except perhaps the seal protesters.

it the sels

'There disna need to be any waste.'

'Yi kin use ivry pert o' the animal.'

'It's the twentieth century, for Christ's sake. Nobody needs to kill animals in such a barbaric way to survive.'

'They're fill o' oil. Hid's the best thing tae stop yur car rustan.'

'No one needs to depend on seal oil and seal meat. It's a hangover from an antique culture.'

'And what's so different about carving up the sea-bed to get black oil?'

All of a sudden the seal cull was a hot potato. Politicians shuffled uncomfortably, thinking they might be linked to an outmoded culture with barbaric practices; votes would be lost in the big population areas. The Sea Shepherd had money and publicity. Bearded environmentalists were being interviewed on the news. They had to be taken seriously. No one, however, showed pictures of slaughtered sheep, which the islanders said looked pretty much like a blood-covered seal pup. Sheep lacked the cuddly, human-baby facial proportions that set off welling triggers of emotion in the city-bound population. The upshot was that no UK company would take on the cull, so the Norwegians were doing it. They still needed to hire extra men.

The ro-ro caused redundancies in the bake-house. It was supposed to be 'last in, first out', but Jamieson decided to keep on the Robb lad. It was the Masons. His father was the Grand Master, so Harry had to find something else. The new Co-op sold Mother's Pride from new long shelves illuminated by strip lights, transported straight from a bakery in Inverness on a lorry.

'Can you shoot well?'

'Aye, mister.'

It was one hundred pounds a week and a hundred pound bonus if you stayed until the end of the cull. That was serious money.

'Have you got your own gun licence?'

Harry and Michael each packed a kitbag with boots and jerseys and headed on the bus to Kirkwall.

The Norwegian boss, Knutsen, said there was a caravan they could stay in at the village, as the company had hired it for the season, so it was free accommodation, just paying your own board.

'Can you handle a boat? We need people who can get in and out to the Skerries.'

'Aye, I can dae that.'

whaur's that then?

Her last year, and there were things she thought about now that she could no longer share with Edna. They had schismed apart too, into yet finer delineations of clever. Seadhna's dialogue was with herself inside her own head.

Christ, it's like a prison sentence. She sat every day in the art room, painting and repainting the reflection in a purple chemist's bottle. The new owners of the old Victorian chemist's did up the old shop and ripped out the curved oak counter. Everything was cheap, honey-coloured softwood and tacky display cabinets. All the old bottles got chucked out except two that Mr Henderson, the art teacher, saved for the art room.

The chemist's bottle had a mesmeric quality; the heavily blown glass was like looking into another world. *Maybe if I can paint all that, all the reflections, all the images going back and back into infinity I'll unlock some key or something …*

That's what that time was, waiting. Waiting for a key like Alice in Wonderland. A release into another world. She was in a world of Van Eyck, immobile like the stunned woman in *The Betrothal*, not sure, and everything waiting to burst. She kept painting that bottle.

Super-realism is the key. Andy Warhol. Neatness.

Anal retention.

I mean anything with texture, any viscerality, is just messy.

I can't stand it. I've got to get out of here. Everybody knows who you are. They know what you're doing. It's so narrow. It's strangling me.

Seadhna had to plan an escape route.

You're trapped in a script that they all write … What they don't know they make up.

Transcending time, dissolving hours. The heavy leg-slowing syrup of minutes spent waiting for the endurance of school to be over. She was held in a straitjacket of age with prescriptive hurdles set out ahead. No escape visible and no protest worth pursuing. All she could do was dissect the length of the sentence and measure out the mental endurance required to go through it. Every limb ached from battering on the unyielding obstacles that blocked her way.

Seadhna got her head down in search of a way out of the place. She needed a legitimate passport because she was too unsure just to up and off. *That's all the exams mean to me. I'll get my head down. Get it done. Because I am predestined …*

There were no choices.

And the supreme sacrifice that she saw was necessary was to lock herself away from the sun with her revision, hoping it would never have to be endured again. Cleverness would get her out.

The day she went into the headmaster's office for her careers interview, she was angry that her life seemed mapped out by others. *I have been assigned. Assigned to university. The stupid man. The pantomime dame that he is. I hate them. I hate how they think they know me … How they think I'll just do what they expect. Why should I please him?*

Through the sunny afternoons, she slogged inside and wrote out reams on 'The Hundred Years' War', Lord Richelieu, German adjective endings, the plays of Arthur Miller … Outside the sun was bright and the sea a flat Prussian Blue, the hills were fresh with new growth, and the greens held the effervescence of new grass. It was building towards the sunniest summer in twenty years.

Der Die Das, die die der den. She incanted the bold inscriptions from the German grammar text.

Up in the North Isles, as they did every year, they were shooting seals. Issuing licences, counting out quotas. Skinning and tanning, stretching skins through the good weather, getting them out to dry in the sun, taking sharp Sheffield steel scissors and cutting out the patterns from the pelts. Sewing hats and waistcoats, making moccasins with blanket stitch round the uppers, and sticking glass eyes onto quizzical seal faces. Posing the miniature stuffed seals artistically on stones, then gluing them down. *A present from Orkney.* For the tourists.

Boom … boom boom crack.

All ready for the summer visitors.

Michael behind a rifle.

aal the time

Seadhna was trying to find out what the place meant, what she meant to it, too many worlds colliding. The loosening gyre. Art was magical and different – there was something unmeasured and dangerous. Midsummer brought her into the fantastic world beyond the purple glass.

The town was buzzing with the news that the new folk, *English of course*, who had moved up and bought the chippy were 'kinky'. *Well, the wife*, went the lascivious story, had appeared in *Fiesta* in the 'Readers' Wives' page. Then there was Lewis Gerrard. He came in like a pirate on a schooner, swaggering through the street with his posse of hippy followers on a kind of arty hippy trip.

'This is exciting. I'm gonna go with the flow …'

All the copies of *Fiesta* sold out in a single day as the identity of the chippy owner's wife was affirmed.

Lewis was leading his followers on an art trail, tracing the path of the builders of the ancient monuments from the Mediterranean to the Northern

Isles.

What's Fiesta*? Do you mean men actually take photos of their wives naked to send to magazines?*

Seadhna checked the 'Cathy and Claire' page for hints about sex and what it was like.

Intercourse?

Surely it doesn't happen on purpose? Oh my God.

There must be people here that buy those magazines. Maybe the butcher? Everyone was suspect.

Mr Henderson invited Lewis to give a talk at the school, and the final-year pupils had to display their exam work. You could tell Mr Henderson was in awe. Like this was real grown-up art. He sat there mesmerised, with Lewis dancing around holding a sheep's skull he'd plucked from the still-life shelf.

'What do you think art is? Well! If only we had the answer to that …'. Pointing like a magician he said, 'Our mission is to be artists. Artists … do you know? … are the most important beings in society,' and he fixed his eyes on Seadhna.

I think I'll be that – I want to be important …

Seadhna watched him move around the room enjoying the captive audience. Smiling. Brown skinned. Curly hair, almost like David Essex, telling them all how privileged they were … how lucky … 'to live in a place like this, in this landscape, this ancient landscape with the imprint of the ancient peoples all around.'

He stood in front of her, blowing through the eye-sockets of the sheep's skull.

Seadhna let his words drift over her. Her mantra ran, *I want out … I just want to get to a night club … out of here … somewhere big and exciting.*

'Art is not about passing exams, it's … it's about the beauty in a flower, the moment of death …'

Seadhna tried to follow what he said, but got lost. It was a million miles away from the Higher art syllabus and the powdered poster paint that you spooned out of tins. *Maybe I'm stupid … I'll just have to look like I know what he's talking about … I don't want to look thick …*

Lewis had them all in the palm of his hand. Balancing the sheep's skull on the tips of his fingers like a Fabergé egg, he gesticulated. 'Is this art? Is art of the concrete, or is it in the mind?'

He sounded wildly exotic and Other, with his Cork Street accent that knew all about real things and real art. 'We must get inside the psyche of our ancestors. We must travel in their footsteps. Follow their trail. I … *we* are following a trail from the Mediterranean to the Northern Isles. Artists are the most important people in the world.'

His eyes flashed and twinkled, and he swept round, enjoying his role. 'But they *are!* Artists built the Pyramids and the burial tombs here in your island!' And he offered the skull to Seadhna, but she sat unmoving and so he placed it on the table in front of her.

Then he was talking with Mr Henderson and laughing, and Seadhna felt ignored.

So if it's not about passing exams, why have I been bothering?

Exams were what everything was about. The world was defined by Higher pass results. It was the way out. The passport.

And it was as if someone had just disproved a long-held theory, collapsed an entire religion, shot through a political ideology.

Next there was a trip out to the standing stones. Mr Henderson drove the minibus. Edna was supposed to go, but she never showed up and so Seadhna was on her own with all the strange artists, who did not belong to the world of exams. And Lewis Gerrard.

He danced at the head of his well-heeled American entourage of art seekers. They had all paid handsomely to get the 'experience', mediated through Lewis, and they followed him like puppies. They hung on his every word. He knew how to play them – like a trickster or a shaman.

It had been too sunny all week and fog rolled in from the east to compensate. You could barely see three feet ahead, let alone the stone circle. Spilling out of the bus the artists ran towards the ghostly stones, trying to feel the power of the 'lines', making efforts to commune with alien forces. They were hopping and flitting around, whooping and exclaiming. A woman in a kaftan splayed her arms across a stone in an embrace. Seadhna was a fish out of water.

Maybe I will have to be like them if I want to be an artist. There must be some special thing you have to tap into … I think I am too ordinary … Too rational, maybe. Like I don't think could ever be hypnotised.

The Americans all disappeared to follow the 'glimmer of the sun through the mist', Mr Henderson with them.

He never asked her name, walking up behind her to fall into her step. He stopped her to run his hand over the surface of a stone. 'Look,' – he knew she was watching without turning round – 'think of the hands that have touched this stone, of the rituals, the sacrifices.'

She watched politely.

'Come here.'

And he placed her in front of the stone and looked at her.

'Stand there …,' and she moved as if what he said you did, what he said you believed.

'You could be a druid princess. Do you think perhaps this is where an ancient princess stood?' He looked at her.

What am I supposed to do?

She moved at his bidding, wide-eyed with the moment, knowing something was going to happen, scared of what it might be, yet wanting it to take her to a new place she had not been.

I can't seem a fool …

And he stood square on in front of her, while she was backed onto the stone and she quickened with his closeness … too close … way beyond the legitimate space … as he laid his hand on her head in a fake ritual manner.

'Your crown, princess.'

He played. Drawing out the moments, savouring her awe and innocence. Trailing his hand over her cheek. Knowing she was dumbstruck.

Maybe this is all normal … maybe this is what you do …

She was rigid, and she could smell the tobacco on his clothes.

Things were lurching in her head and she felt that wash of drunkenness. The melting of butter inside her body. Lewis let his body press against hers. She, pinned there against the stone.

What do I do with my arms … I don't really know him!

He talked aloud. 'Should I kiss you, sweet island princess … or should I not?'

And Seadhna felt he was weighing her up, whether she was worthy of his kiss, and she did not want to fail the test.

I want to go there … I want to tumble over that cliff.

hid's time

There was another nude picture in *Men Only*.

God I can't wait to get out of here.

Of the chippy man's wife.

Nothing on at all. I mean? Disgusting … She did have a wig on, but it's her, fir sure – the name and address were printed this time!

Seadhna had had enough of small places. After Lewis she felt that some strange new presence had entered her head and her life would never be the same again.

Can people see that? It must be so obvious … I am not the same person. It must be written all over me … like you can't hide this kind of change …

Walking with her father on the cliff she was sure he must know but he carried on as if everything was the same.

'Nothing between us and America,' he said, as they walked over the wiry grass, the Primula Scotica under their feet. 'See that ocean out there. Well, if you just keep going you'll reach Newfoundland – America. That's it! There's nothing between us and America.' He said it with pride, as if there was no other place that could boast such a thing.

'Nothing between us and America!'

Seadhna strained to try and catch a glimpse of America far away. The arc of the horizon became blurred and spotted as she stared and stared, knowing really that it was impossible to see.

'It's way over the horizon, far *far* away.'

Yes, and they both looked out over the sea in their own silent communion, before turning back to the car, parked beside the redundant red-brick wartime buildings, the wooden lookout collapsing on top of itself, and John Rufus, ever the didactic, carried on. 'America only came into the war at the very end, after all the sacrifices had already been made. It was Russia that suffered the most. Without Russia we'd never have won.'

Seadhna listened politely, her mind in faraway places. His voice tailed off, and the subject was left behind. War, like America, was incomprehensible. It was long ago and distant, just as America was far away.

Seadhna could still feel the rawness on her lips, the smarting rasp of coarse stubble on her cheek. The quickness deep in her groin when she thought of it. It seemed to scream over the top of everything.

And she started to think, *Nothing between me and Edinburgh.*

Lewis's ship set sail for Leith, but there was a terrible summer gale and the entourage were all seasick and had to put into Wick instead for shelter. Then a bus took the discovery travellers back to Edinburgh, truncating the final creative leg to jolting up and down the Berriedale Braes and the incidental views from the hairpin bends.

Seadhna was left to wish her life away in her last summer on the islands. Trying to get away, despite what Lewis had said about retracing her ancestors into an ever-diminishing vortex. It was life that Seadhna wanted to be part of, life in a city, not life on an island surrounded by water, or even in an academic institution marooned by its dreaming spires.

The acceptance letter she waited for finally came. The passport out was secure. There was no going back, and all it needed now was for October to come around, and the coiled spring continuing to tension inside her. In her head she had already left the place, so nothing mattered. She had used it up. She sat languid in Mac Peters' split-screen classic Humber at four in the morning, watching the sun rise up in the north east. Mac was the forty-year-old stay-at-home bachelor that every small place has, who cruises the annual crop of young girls while he still has some good looks, a car and a pay packet. Once it would have been the most coveted and daring thing you could possibly do. Even Edna had never gone with Mac Peters. With a joint in his hand, he passed it back to her, his arm creeping round to pull her towards him on the leather front seat. All night, drinking Southern Comforts and lemonade in a Kirkwall bar, 'Hotel California' on the jukebox. It was the most exotic you could ever get.

Part Two

two sides

There was no sign of the protesters to start with. In fact, up north on the remote island of Selsay, the cull went on much as it had done every year. The 'factory', a tarred shed at the end of Dena's washing green, made hats and jackets. The visitors bought them. It was no big deal. 'Hand Made Orkney Seal Skin, Island Craft of Selsay' is what they got embroidered on the labels from a supplier in the south, the women unfurling the silken labels from a card spool, and nursing the soft smooth embroidery thread against their nimble fingers. They boxed up parcels of clothing and ornaments for the Kirkwall shops. Business was expanding since a craft shop in Edinburgh had requested miniature sealskin brooches and wanted a dozen hats on trial.

For Harry McLeay, shooting outside was good work. After years of working nightshifts and fighting off the daylight, it was liberating to get up with the sun and follow it through the day with the other men. He enjoyed the good crack there was with the shooters, being part of the common end. You crept up slow, using your eye, feeling your muscles. He felt proud and confident at his skill. Harry was one of them. After a day at the cull the shooters all got pie and chips up in the hotel and a dram or two after that. Elbows on the bar, side-on talking, slipping a palm into the back pouch to take out the note you knew was there. Then the bar till ringing and counting back the change – 'Have one yirsel, Peter' – and directing the barman to let the pennies clatter into the big glass bottle for Action for the Crippled Child.

The Anti-Fur Trade protesters brought a VW Combo. They drew up to the Scrabster terminal, piling out of it to look out over the horizon at the distant islands. The broken swings in the tatty play-park and a westerly swell coursing past Stevenson's lighthouse. Those autumn days had all the cold angularity of tired metal. Rust in the weather. The protesters stowed six of their party hidden in the back of their VW under blankets and saved a good whack on the ferry fare. When they reached the other side of the Firth, the Stromness folk were shocked at their audacity, watching the strange group emerge cramped from the vehicle a few hundred yards down the road. The party emerged as if they thought they would go unseen. Pink hair, bleached hair, long plaits, frilly dresses, big boots, heavy coats, long striped scarves, bangles, earrings *on the males as well* … To the islanders, they seemed like a circus act. A confetti of people … *complete weirdos …*

The islanders were angry at the attempt to outwit the burly purser. *That kind of thing jist dis not happen here*, and silently they were indignant. As a result of the campaigners' initial ruse, the next leg to the seal protest was thwarted. The purser on the Selsay ferry was well warned by the locals, and when he examined the patchwork hump in the van, the stowaways were swiftly ejected. Out they tumbled unceremoniously from the camper on to the pier, where they masked their embarrassment by laughing loudly. Then there ensued a huddle while they gathered up a whip-round. Eventually enough money was scratched together for the fares, the protesters muttering and scowling. Out came roll-up cigarettes from Drum pouches and Old Holburn tins. Then the clattering laughter tumbling from their group welded them apart from the islanders.

It was a case of *them and us.* That was sure … *hid'll no just be tobacco in them cigarettes Ah'll bet …*

The terror of *drugs* struck a note of panic. *Soothmoothers, hippies and cannabis.*

On Selsay, the shooters were up before dawn and away from the pier in a hired seine net fishing boat. The dinghy and outboard was towed behind to ferry the men into the shallow water within range of the seals. The object was to shoot the seals on land, before they could get to the water. The pelts were all to be used, so the shooters wanted to get the seals in the head, not on the body. Once the animals got wary of the humans they would be away off diving out to sea and the men would have to wait for them to haul up again on the tidal rocks. The pups just lay on the ebb, abandoned. Killing them was easy and quick, but it was heavy work dragging a hundred adult carcasses over slippery rock and into a dinghy.

'No we don't club them, the bullet's best,' Knutsen the Norsky laughed. 'See if they come round, not dead, in the dinghy and then try and bite you … Look!'

He showed them the puckered white scars on his arm. 'They get pretty mad.' Knutsen was the go-between with the hired men and the Norwegian company. No British outfit would touch the cull these days on account of all the publicity.

One pelt was worth a week as a farm servant. The locals chuckled. *Wi' the sels, buey, yi dinna need tae dose them, buy in replacements, herd them, feed them or pit in the ram. An' year after year back they come, more and more. Jist dandy!*

It was good business, and others saw that too.

But ivribody's wantin' thur cut … Nothing stayed a bonanza for long … *The landowners is wantin' such an such fir ivry pelt noo …*

In the south, sealing was getting a bad name; Sidney the boat skipper had been there.

'Last year we geed tae the Farnes,' he recounted in the bar, 'and yi coodna move fir newspaper men, an' yi ken *they* nivver pit a good slant on things.'

'Some o' them hippies cam' off the steamer the day,' said Peter as he set down the pints. The men muttered that there was a lot of stuff on the radio about the seals, their elbows mechanically shifting the dark liquid up and down to their mouths. They mulled over their position in what seemed like a distant squabble.

'Weel wur only here ti dae a job,' announced a moustachioed mouth now bordered with a delicate frothy edging from its owner's draught McEwan's Export.

'Ah'm no getting involved in politics. Politics is notheen' ti dae wi' me,' stated his neighbour, wiping his own wet top lip.

'Hid'll be best no tae get involved', was the consensual statement that finished the brief discussion, the speaker yet to lift his untouched glass, savouring the minute before the nut-brown liquid streamed cool over his tongue and down his gullet to settle in his gut. The smell of chips wafted from the hotel kitchen.

The protesters parked their VW by the football pitch and set up a camp, watched by the Selsay folk.

'Weel I don't see as we kin stop them. They hiv a right tae camp.'

The campers had an old bell tent, and a kind of awning that extended from the camper van.

'If it wis me I widna hae let them on the island at aal,' was the shop conversation.

Some of the campers went off collecting driftwood to make a fire.

'Don't see how yi kin dae that …' and the groceries were rung up on the till.

The protesters' presence on the island was cemented and the area around the football pitch took on a whole new aura. It became theirs, and though people never realised it, or felt a desire to walk on or possess that part of land, they now felt that it was a place they could not easily go. Around their fire, sitting on fish-boxes dragged up from the shore, Justin, Brian, Hetty, Louisa, JoJo, Sassy, Steph, and Pete the grown-up, waited for things to unfold.

Two of the 'hippy' girls came into the pub and sipped half pints of lager and lime. They were unaware of Dena's silently steady watch as she kept her eye on the grandbairns in the front room. Usually nobody came in during the day. In fact, if anyone local came in, they just served themselves and left the money. That wasn't something you could do with strangers, of course. The girls paid separately for their drinks, Dena handing them their change from the till. Nobody knew what the protesters were going to do.

them and us

At the soft flicker of time between night and day, just before the sun came up and kitchen lights went on, you could almost imagine the Stone Age people seeing that same landscape. On days when the sun kept a lower arc in the sky, the splash of a rose-filled dawn crept along the horizon, casting long shadows that showed just a glimpse of the toil of the past, the undulating secrets of other lives still locked up under the land.

The October nights were cold, so the protesters slept fully clothed in their sleeping bags. They awoke with aches, still chilled in the morning, their bones stiff and their clothes damp, staggering half asleep along the shingle to make their early morning protest. One morning the camper van was parked across the entry to the pier. The protesters were lined up in front of it. As the men approached the pier in ones and twos they saw the obstruction and hung back, whispering, 'Hid seems like wur path is blocked.'

The protesters began a chant, the timbre of their accents alien. 'No Seal Cull, No Seal Cull, No …'. The entire sound and sight of the protest was foreign. The shooters stood perplexed. Sidney the skipper was nowhere to be seen and the men did not want to enter a confrontation.

Suddenly there came the rev of an outboard from a mooring off the beach. One pull and Sidney was underway. He had seen the obstruction and rowed out for another dinghy. As he swept in towards the huddled shooters at the top of the pier he shouted, 'Pick you up at Sinclair's Noust. Hid's high water. Ah'll get in there no buther.' Sidney curved round in an arc towards his boat, *Andrina*, and was soon aboard with the dinghy tailing behind. The big engine rattled into life followed by its unhurried, steady purr. A Gardiner 6LX, you couldn't beat it. Sidney was away from the pier, throwing off the stern rope and heading back into the wheelhouse with the protesters still chanting.

The shooters made their way along the cliff path to the boat noust where, as he had said, the *Andrina* was able to nose in, and they each stepped onto the bow.

'Weel done, buey. Yi outwitted them this time.' The men clattered into the wheel house, jocular at their first triumph. After it was over the protesters dissolved away from the pier.

The girls shouted on. Then the noise from the engine smothered the protest, Sassy and Louisa heading down to the end of the jetty to continue the chant. The young girls were fired up and angry, Sassy almost weeping, JoJo muttering about getting back for some coffee. 'This ungodly hour ... I'm wrecked.'

On the *Andrina* there was back-clapping and laughing. The tension from the pier melted. Standing on the deck of the boat, they looked towards the land where the protesters' chant had changed to a medley of disorganised insults.

'Murderers, MURDERERS, butchers, blood-money MERCENARIES.'

Back at their campfire, the protesters tried to second-guess their adversaries.

'I can't understand how they can do it.' Hetty was wistful.

The isles were not a place where the *Guardian* newspaper penetrated much.

'They're in it for the money. I mean they've got no shame, no conscience about the cruelty they're inflicting.' Brian was scathing.

JoJo was disdainful, 'Most of them are just ignorant hicks.'

'Yeah.' Louisa just agreed.

'They managed to outwit us this time ... but we just have to be smarter.' Justin wanted a strategy. Collective experiences from Scout camps, the morality of the Famous Five shaped the plan of action.

'Bridget Bardot's with us,' Hetty announced.

'Pete's managed to get the World Service on the radio.'

'Can you get Radio 4?'

'They're going to send up a camera crew.'

'Oh that's brilliant. More publicity.'

Pete stirred the brown rice, which always took an interminable time to boil, and listened to the youngsters without comment.

'They are probably just misguided, being taken advantage of by the machinery of big business. Capitalist interests. The fur companies.' Steph began a political analysis.

'Don't be stupid Steph ... its greed, pure and simple.'

'They're getting some fantastic price for every pelt.'

'Well they should find other work.'

'It's barbaric.'

'Can you make out what they say?'

'Is it another language or what?'

'Do you know what? We need to get a boat.'.

Later they made their way to the post office to enquire. Justin bought a couple of postcards and some stamps, then asked, 'I was wondering if you knew where we could hire a boat? Is there anyone on the islands that does hires?'

'Oh I couldn't say.' Mrs Park felt propelled into the role of go-between and worried slightly about the potential for collaboration, so she passed the information relating to Justin's request straight to Dena when she came in for her mother's pension.

'I don't think anybody will gie' them a boat here. I mean hid's aal very weel and folk can protest. But hid's a good living fur a lot of the men ... and for the island.'

'You could try Pip Baxter,' was the devious advice given when the request was made at the shop. Justin thanked them and got directions, still unaware that anonymity was unknown in the isles. 'Down at the far end of the island,' nodded Mrs Park. 'The only house that still has a windmill.'

As the shop door shut behind Justin, Mrs Park switched tone and attitude to Coll, burrowing in a box to find a pair of hinges. 'It's no like the skins are wasted. Aal the stuff that you can mak, hats and waistcoats.'

Pip Baxter had a glass pyramid of empty Teacher's bottles under the sink in his kitchen. He couldn't afford the big bottles, so bought a quarter each time from the mobile shop. He would take ten pounds from anyone for booze. And Pip's boat was no threat. It was dried out and gizzened from sitting in the sun all summer. He was long past bothering to scrape and paint it.

Justin handed him the ten pound note, glimpsing inside the chaos of Pip's house, the opened tins sitting on the table, Pip's unshaven face and solid spittle at the corners of his mouth, all the while smelling the stench of cats.

'We've got a boat!' Brian was jubilant, returning with Justin. 'I gave the guy a tenner. Dead cheap. We can get right out to the Skerries now and actually get properly involved … and we need people who are willing to actually put their bodies between the gunmen and the seals.'

Justin agreed. 'Direct action. We'll stop them that way.'

mutual need

The seal carcasses were the weight of a dead human. Michael stuck the hook well in behind the skull, dragging the body with the rope over his shoulder. He heaved it into the dinghy and it flopped onto the floorboards. They could take three at a time, the weight putting the boat well down in the water.

Brian and Justin in Pip Baxter's dinghy had made it out to the Skerry. Their thin figures were tightly skinned in black denim. Sidney had seen them from the wheelhouse and watched. Brian managed to get out of the dinghy and run up the slip carrying something.

The men were far along on the beach, heaving carcasses into piles, too far away to see what was going on back at the slip. The shooting was finished for the day, and they were collecting up the bodies. A pile of carcasses had amassed on the pier, waiting to be loaded on at high water. It was easiest to just slide them onto the boat on a chute.

Brian took his penknife to the lid of the paint tin and emptied all of it on to the pile of dead seals on the pier. The paint slid over the bodies, trickling down onto the lichen-covered flagstones to congeal into a sickly jam pudding of custard and blood. Sidney stuck his head out of the wheelhouse window.

'Hey, what yi think yur doin', yi bloody idiots?'

He emerged from the wheelhouse, but Brian had already leaped down onto the dinghy, rocking it violently as he landed, and the paint tin clattered over the side of the boat into the sea. They got the outboard going and Pip's boat was away and off back towards the land. The shooters looked up towards the commotion. Harry was nearest, Michael working at a distance from him and the others round the corner of the Point. The light was starting to go and they could feel there would be an early darkness. Once the clocks changed it would be like a shutter going down at five.

'Vandalism. Jis' pure vandalism.' Sidney was righteous.

The men shook their heads.

'Now that's just a total waste.' Malcolm counted the loss in the value of the carcasses. 'The skins are completely ruined.'

'Fuckin' ijits' and Jimmack moved their collective anger on a notch.

'Why on earth?' Harry wanted a reason.

'Fuckan' hippies,' said Jimmack, 'fuckan' hippy … bastards,' tarring them well with the brush he felt they deserved.

The yellow paint was running down the slip into the sea.

'Hid's gloss as weel,' which in Lennie's view was the worst of the crime.

On the way home in the boat there was a murmuring of dissatisfaction, as if some unwritten rule had been broken.

'Beyond a joke.'

'In Pip Baxter's dinghy.'

'Weel, I widna go across a paddling pool in that.'

They summoned up as many negatives as they could to pour onto the experience they had just witnessed, and to distance themselves from the protesters.

Just two hundred metres from the safety of the bay, Sidney saw the same dinghy.

'Shuz gey low in the watter.'

'Reckon thu'll hiv tae bail pretty queek tae get in afore hid sinks,' said another. The wheelhouse was crowded, and the men had just worked up their annoyance into a comunal disdain towards the protesters.

'This his tae be reported.'

'Wu'll hiv tae get Knutsen ontae it.'

'Jesus, hid'll sink.' Malcolm saw that the dinghy was in danger.

The protesters had no bailer. They were scooping water out with their hands.

'Christ, yu'll hiv tae go an' get them, Sidney.' Malcolm could see it was sinking.

'Aye aye,' he said slowly. Sidney had already swung round the wheel.

'Let them bloody sink,' muttered Jimmack.

'Get a rope on them, Michael.'

Michael was coiling a rope ready to throw. When they came near, he yelled out, 'Oi, catch the rope!' One of the boys in the dinghy looked up as the *Andrina* sidled slowly in to the stricken dinghy, Sidney knocking the engine into reverse. 'Tie it roon' the seat.' Brian was holding the rope in his hand.

'Mak the rope fast,' insisted Sidney, getting more impatient. 'Come *on*, mak the bloody rope fast. Tie it tight roon' a cleat.' The boy followed the instructions and did as he was told.

'Now you better get aboard … quick.'

'No. I think we'll stay on our boat. If you can lend us a bucket we'll bail out the water.'

'Don't be bloody stupid. Get on board. Wu'll tow the boat in.'

The shooters took over. They were making to tie the dinghy to the side of the *Andrina*. This was stuff they knew about. There was no need for words.

Harry offered his hand out to the two in the dinghy, the water lapping around their calves, but they were already climbing aboard without making eye contact.

The journey back to the pier was silent, the protesters opting to lean on the stern as far away as possible from the mound of seal carcasses. The hunters huddled round the door to the wheelhouse.

The men unhitched the outboard and heaved it onto the deck of the *'Andrina'.*

'Lucky this didn't get knackered.'

They went on to pass the heavy outboard up and onto the pier, in what to them were easy lifts, their arms full of muscle.

'Best thing yi kin dae is git it runnnin' again. If thurs any salt watter in it, hid'll be fucked.' Malcolm's good nature was not subsumed for long by the previous incident's anger.

'Is there a mechanic on the island?' Brian enquired.

'Aye, wur all mechanics,' replied Sidney without smiling.

Pip's boat was tied up to a mooring just off the pier.

'Let it sit for a few days an' hid'll tighten up,' Sidney offered.

The rest of the shooters headed over to examine the desecrated skins, leaving behind Brian and Justin with Sidney. Finally, once they were alone, the two lads muttered their thanks to Sydney.

'But we'll have no more o' these silly stunts wi' the paint, I hope.' Sidney gave them a cool look. 'You need tae ken whit your doin' on the sea. Hid's no a playgrund.'

The protesters said nothing. By this time their friends, who had been watching the action from the shore, were arriving. 'God, what happened, Justin?'

'Are you two okay?' simpered Louisa with her doe-eyes.

They ignored Sidney, spiriting Brian and Justin away into their huddle.

a good skin

The paint-covered carcasses were abandoned on the pier to rot. The three on the bottom were less contaminated, although the gloss was smeared and had solidified into sticky patches. Harry shoved at them with his foot, shaking his head. The rest of the men wandered off up the hill to the hotel and he and Michael were left.

'Ah'll learn ee hoo tae skin em anywaye. Shame tae waste a good skin.'

Harry pulled over the heavy bodies, looking for the best ones, then took his knife and slit a carcass from the anus to the throat over the belly. 'Disnae tak long till ee hair starts tae part fae i skin.' Harry tugged. 'This een's still a'right, an' 'ers no bullet holes in ay back.' He cut a collar round the neck above the eyes. 'We dinnae need 'iss bit.' Michael watched. Gripping the skin, his fingers sinking into the blubber, Harry tickled the knife along the taut white flesh that bound outer and inner. 'Hid's a pile easier tae start whaur 'ers plenty o' fat.' Two inches of skin flapped. Harry, deft with the knife, was wiping it on his trousers. 'An' work each side even like …'

Michael observed, conscious that they were also watched from the shore. The girl with the blonde hair, who had been shouting and weeping, cut looks into them from the road.

'Yu've tae get through ay blubber, an' keep it off ay pelt. It stains ee fur, see.' There was a good two inches of blubber beneath the skin. Harry rolled the blubber over as the knife scored towards the back. Then the pelt was released. 'There.' He lifted it up and flapped it like a sheet. 'Wu'll stretch em oot an' pit thum in Malcolm's shed. He'll no mind and wu'll clean off ay paint marks.'

He handed Michael the knife, the blade curved and thin with repeated sharpening. 'Tak that een, hid's no bad ither.'

Michael rolled over the mottled carcass of a blotched black-and-white seal, now with the ludicrous yellow additions. He could feel the girl's eyes burning into him. He knew she was standing near the telephone box.

Harry tipped the white body of the skinned seal over the edge of the pier with his foot. There was a great splash. 'Ers likely nothin' wrong wi' the blubber, but ae company'll no tak it noo.' The heavy carcass disappeared into the water, revolving and sinking fast. 'A feed fir ae crabs or ae black-backs, fituver gets ayre first.'

Harry and Michael skinned three seals and left the rest. 'This lot'll start tae stink soon.'

They rolled the flopping skins up and carried them under their arms and headed up the pier. The girl at the phone box moved off, turning her head back to follow them with her eyes. Michael heard her Doc Martens crunch over the brittle tang and shells as she headed back to the camp.

Malcolm bobbed out of his but and ben as he saw them approaching, offering a brew, but Harry declined, showing him the skins. 'We need tae get these sorted, buey, and thocht yi might let iss use yur place.'

Malcolm was glad to be asked, and began looking for more ways to help.

'No problem lads, jist help yursells tae whit yi need.'

Inside the shed Michael knocked up some stretchers from driftwood and four-inch nails. He pinned out the skins as instructed by his father. Malcolm had all the stuff there, in among the engine parts and the bits and pieces he was fiddling with. 'Aye beuys, yur right enough no tae waste them. Jist plain stupeet that kinda vandalism.'

Michael mixed up yellow diesel and bicarbonate of soda together in a pot until it made a heavy paste, following Harry's instructions. 'Like wi' a sheep skin, get as much o' the fat off as yi can …'. When they were well scraped down he painted on the mixture. Harry exchanged curing techniques with Malcolm. 'That'll git ae cure goin'. We used tae do it 'iss waye wi' they deerskins. Harder tae shoot em though, there wis ay more holes in ae bodies.'

There was so much fat on his hands he couldn't grip. They stank of fish.

'Wu'll get ae bottle o' turps an' git that paint off.'

In the pink-tiled bathroom of Malcolm's cottage, Michael and Harry washed down their greasy hands. Michael felt like an invading bear in a dolls' house. The pink crocheted poodle constructed from a lemonade bottle fixing him with googly eyes from atop the cistern. They had a dram with Malcolm in the kitchen, not heading back until late.

actions and words

Next morning they awoke to see that their caravan had been daubed with paint.

'MURDERERS'.

The word was splashed in dripping red gloss across the entire side of the caravan. Large confidently executed letters, which only became smaller as the calligrapher ran out of caravan to complete the word. The 'R' was squashed and the 'S' turned the corner towards the Calor gas cylinder that piped the cooker.

'Wis that ayre when we got back last night?' Harry asked.

'Don't ken.' Michael was pretty sure who had done it, though he said nothing.

The paint was dry except in the thicker parts where the brush had been overloaded. Harry smeared a finger across the top of the 'M'.

On their way to the pier the shooters collected to observe the graffitti, standing silent and irked. Shuffling on to the pier, they tried to lessen it. 'Och that'll soon come off.'

'Bit a turps and a rag'll shift it.' Lennie was upbeat.

'Hid'll be that stupeet soothmoothers again,' Jimmack scowled. 'Some o' them should ken better ... thur owld enough.'

But Harry was uncomfortable. 'Ah'll hiv tae apologise tae Malcolm. Fir that damage tae his property's ma fault. Swear Ah nivver heerd a thing in ae night.'

Michael shook his head. 'Me neither, I nivver heard a thing.'

They were all quiet getting on to the boat. Things were scaling up, but Sidney sailed on regardless out to the Holm.

'Wu'll hiv tae see whit the company's line is on aal this. This is gittan beyond a joke.'

hearts and minds

The first of a series of TV crews arrived. To start with, they filmed Sidney's boat heading out to the cull, then hired him to take them out to the Skerry. They paid cash from a wad of notes that must have been near a thousand.

'Ah'm no shy o' thur money,' said Sidney, justifying the duality of commercial realities, 'but Ah'll no tak them when Ah'm contracted ti the company. Thu'll hiv tae find anither boat ti dae that.'

There was a flurry of excitement as the TV crew booked into the hotel, spending big lots of cash in the bar. The shooters were all up in the bar too, trying to put their case to the reporter, getting a chance to tell their stories of the sea and the place. Michael avoided the hotel. Instead of joining the flurry in the bar, he went up to Malcolm's shed to examine the skins. The curing process fascinated him: how the paste was drying out the flesh and blubber and leaving a soft smooth white texture. He tugged at the fur; the hair was holding. *That's good. Jist wan hole where a bullet hit the shoulder.* He placed his finger through it, feeling the hard edge of the punctured dried skin, the toughness of it, the gentle rasp of the hair. He smoothed the hairs of the skin against his palm. You could hardly see where the paint had been. The white spirit had eased it off. It was only superficial. He pressed his top lip against the smooth pelt, and rolled over the dried skin. It was stiff like thick paper. Malcolm came in and stood watching. 'Hid's a job tae git the skins saft. The Eskimau weemin chows them an' the Shelties send them tae the tanneries in salted barrels. Drying them on stretchers is hard work, running to get them aall in if the rain comes on. Come inside an Ah'll show yi summeen.'

Malcolm took him into the house and right through to the good room. 'Here yi are, luk.' He handed Michael some offcuts to show him how the skins should be when they dried. 'I started wi' the heedmaister. He hid a rabbit club in the skule. Wi shot rabbits an' skinned them an' cured them, an' made gloves an' stuff fae them.'

He showed him the skins hanging over the backs of chairs.

'Whit's this wan?' Michael smoothed his hand over the sleek fur, more like a cat's.

'That wis an otter. Hid wis tame. He lived in a basket in the hoose. He cam up injured off the shore and we nursed its back leg, and then it jis' stayed. I skinned him when he died, but he lived tae thirteen … Lily named him. She called him Smokey. He was a smokey kinda colour, yi see.'

The pair of them quietly acknowledged a space in the empty living room, Lily absent with her illness in the hospice. Michael collected up the offcuts, Malcolm offering him a paper bag to put them in. 'You could mak someen' oot o' them. Gie ye a feel for hoo the skins work.'

Michael left to go but as he turned out of Malcolm's yard he ran straight into the protester girls. There were two of them, Hetty and Steph. Straight away their combined body language commanded. Although Hetty was small, her entire stature was superior to his;

'Hey. Are you one of the hunters?' Steph was skinny and pushed herself in front of Hetty, standing her ground before Michael. He tried to negotiate past them.

'No, stop. I asked you a question. Are you one of the hunters?' She had a shaky boldness. 'You are, aren't you? One of the seal killers.'

'Mibbe, what if I am?'

'Do you realise what you're doing?' Steph fixed him with cold, angry eyes.

Michael knew he could not pass, and that he would have to hear out the assault.

'These are innocent animals you're killing. Helpless innocent flesh and blood. How can you do it? You're a human being.'

Michael looked at her dumbfounded. She had a smooth thin almond face. Curly black hair and a scarf tied around her head. Her bloodless lip was shaking.

'It's nothin ti dae wi' me. Ah'm jis' daein me wark …'

The other girl laughed, and looked towards her friend. 'Pff! That's no excuse! How can you do it? Maim them and leave them to die?'

'We don't leave them tae die … we don't waste …'. She cut in on him, spearing him again with her eyes, and short clipped angry words.

'What about all the pups. Motherless pups? Babies squealing …'

'I have tae go.' Michael felt embarrassed. He didn't talk to girls. It simply didn't happen.

'You're a murderer, an animal murderer. You think about it … think about it.' She paused. 'We'll get you stopped. We'll win this. You are history.'

The words jumbled in his head. He could feel he was flushing red all over. The embarrassment was more from the encounter with the girls than their accusations. He headed up the single-track road to the paint-daubed caravan. The girls watched him.

'God, what a moron,' Steph declared to Hetty, who then shouted 'MORON!' after him. 'I mean he can only be about our age. He's like something from the Stone Age.'

Michael kept his head down and let himself into the caravan. He saw them as they gesticulated after him before turning back down the hill. Hetty threw her arm round Steph and they skipped off as if they had won a bitchy playground encounter.

There was a week of bad weather and it was too rough to work the small boat, so the men were all stuck ashore with nothing to do. Harry was at the hotel, enjoying the company and the crack. He was appreciated as a story-filled character. They liked his tales and his humour and listened when he talked, then bought him more whisky, fuelling him until he got well past it and staggering drunk.

Michael was careful to avoid the anti-fur girls, keeping to simple, necessary routes around the island. That week he took it in his head to go up to the island shop and, after a long list of other things, he asked the shop-girl for thread and needles.

'Whit kind o' thread? Mending or embroidery or what?' She rattled out the question like an interrogation, her eyes flicking him up and down like a guard. Michael was unprepared for choices. He didn't enter conversations willingly. 'Eh don't ken rightly.'

The girl brought out a selection from where he could choose.

'Yur wan o' the hunters, ur yi no?' The girl persisted in her one-sided questioning, boring her eyes into his clamped face. 'Hiv yi bin gettan buther fae the protesters?'

Michael was practised in answering with conversation stoppers. 'No really.'

The fattish girl continued as she placed reels of thread on the counter top for him to survey. 'Thur's a dance in the hall. Ur yi aal gan up?'

Michael hurried to make his decision over the threads and needles. 'This wans 'ill do.' There were some needles like the ones they'd done the weaving with long ago at school.

'Dance's a week on Friday,' she added curtly as she handed him change from the till.

Back in the caravan, Michael cut round the ragged edges of the skin remnants with his knife, running the cut to follow the direction of the hairs. Nothing would be wasted. He patched together the offcuts, pulling the edges of skin tight and oversewing the seam. He folded over the joined skin, pleased at how little the stitching showed. *That's good*. He soon made a pouch with a flap. It needed a button, something to fix it down securely with.

Up in the hotel with the other men, Harry was telling stories of his days on the salmon rivers in Sutherland. There was no mention of tinkers, because it was a place that embraced new people through curiosity and common aims. Harry and Michael were accepted. They were completely on a par with everyone else. People enjoyed their newness. They were hunters and they were equals, without baggage or an inescapable role that had been assigned to them by others. Harry revelled in the bonhomie, being with the local folk against the newspapers and the *hippies*, knowing that the incoming protesters had different agendas that could never gel with the local folk. Being in the right camp, on the right side.

Meanwhile, Justin had been telling his camp of someone he knew called Felix who had bought a farm on the neighbouring island – 'an absolutely snip. Dirt cheap. Property's at give away prices up here. We should think about it. Club together and buy somewhere. Have a collective. Run it on a communal basis. We could be self-sufficient.'

Justin said he'd get the money from his father, quickly adding that it would, of course, be as a loan. He had already seen an eighty-acre farm for sale in the local newspaper with a two-storey house – 'in need of renovation with a collection of outbuildings …', the advert read.

'It's perfect, just look at what you could do with that,' and off he went across the sound to Dingasay to look at the place. When he came back he could talk of nothing else. 'We can all move across, Felix says we can use his place till we get our own and we can still continue our action from across there. Felix says it's all fine with him … the more the merrier kinda thing.' He looked around to see who was with him. Brian shook his head.

'I think it's important we stay here. This is where the cull is taking place. We need to be a physical presence here.'

'Brian's got a point,' said Steph.

Lines were dividing along the parameters of sexual attraction lightly dusted with political necessity. Pete who had the camper van kept silent. No one was thinking about the small print at that stage.

splits

Felix's commune on Dingasay had already got the bush telegraph in Selsay alerted. The local folk ferreted around, peering at the commune from a distance, commenting on the frailness of the girls, *fir yi could hardly call them weemin …*

Wispy girls arrived, trailing blankets and babies. Pregnant, with unkempt hair, they gave birth in their shack and washed nappies in cold water from a well. The doctor was apoplectic because they all insisted on home births, then needed the ambulance plane at the last minute when things went wrong. Kids ran around barefoot, then needed tetanus injections, and everybody was dirty with smoke from the fire blowing back. They always had a job getting the fire to draw and the east wind was hopeless. The boys huffed around the dead embers, desperately trying to reignite both their distant hunter-gatherer status and the flames from the damp driftwood. Unspoken tensions hovered around the ability or failure to make the fire go.

Felix's land was unfenced and the goats ran around eating other folk's daffodils. Despite this, he evangelised to Justin how he was setting up a new society, away from the towns, which would be an untainted Utopia. The old local folk looked on perplexed, their long accepted mores challenged, muttering. *In the commune nobody's merrit tae anybody. Hid disnae seem tae metter tae them … aal the bairns hae diffrint fithers, an they seem ti pass the women aroon' like a hareem! Them delicate lassies, that skinny yi'd think they'd fall apart.*

So Justin decided he would move with Hetty and JoJo, and still hoped to encourage the others to do the same. Pete indicated that he intended to stay put at the football pitch, Steph remaining too, feeling that it was a diversion to move the agenda onto setting up a Utopia.

At the end of the week they went, Justin and Brian still committed to joining the others in sorties to the Skerries in their boat. Felix had loaned an inflatable rib and now they felt like daring raiders with an important mission to fulfil, running amok among the seals, blowing whistles and shouting abuse. They were angry, venting all their own frustrations into their cause.

Out on the Skerry during these confrontations, the shooters ignored them. The protesters were an annoyance. *Yi jist hae tae watch yi dinna shoot wan o the eejits.* The company said just to get on with the work. Knutsen instructed them not to respond to any taunts.

'It's bloody hard sometimes, boys.' Malcolm spoke the common thought of all.

'Aye, but if yi start shouting and causing agro, they'll get you for breach o' the peace. You have to just keep yur heed doon and dae the work yur gettan' paid for.' Sidney kept his commercial head. They all nodded and strode out onto the Skerry, dodging the protesters who ran among them, hurling stones at the rocks to scare off the seals, and popping up in the sights of the rifles.

'Wan o' them'll get shot, and then whose tae blame? Ah'm no ganna be responsible for that.' Lennie's patience was wearing.

The protesters, annoyed at the lack of response from the gunners, tried to hike the insults and harassment up a notch. They imported a strain of callousness that came from some repressed place inside themselves and catapulted them all into a new world of uninhibited menace and insult. The well-brought-up lads felt wildly liberated at being able to hurl insults that were alien to their manner and palate. Conspiratorial smiles that the women and girls would never see were saved for a male environment, one that sanctioned a more brutal code.

'Who's your wife fucking while you're out here? Eh? Eh? Who's she shagging?'

Brian's eyes glinted as he honed the insults towards his dehumanised quarry. There was no one in the playground to tell any of them to temper their language. It was a new kind of freedom because no one had to think before they spoke. A free for all of total liberation in a war with no rules.

Among the shooters, there was more tension to release ashore. They eased off in the hotel, now a no-go zone for the protesters. There was a new ugliness that made everyone uncomfortable. In the caravan, Michael cut the bottom button from a shirt and fixed it onto the sealskin purse. Positioning the flap over the button, he carefully cut a hole in the skin, then oversewed the gap for extra measure. He could hear voices outside the caravan and stuffed the purse into his back pocket.

'Yu'll no believe iss, buey, bit ers talk boot em calling off ay cull.' Harry had a good drink in him. He came in heavily through the small caravan door. Malcolm poked his head in, then carried on round to the cottage. The acceptance and ease that whisky brought was an irresistible combination. 'Ee shid come up ay hotel wi' me. Er's gid crack up er. Er's a dance later on.'

'Come on, Michael, hae a dram wi' ae boys.'

the wounded

Everyone was congregating for the dance in the hotel. Because the hall was dry you had to get a good fill beforehand and the hotel was packed. Almost instantly, a line of whisky glasses were ranged in front of him and Michael found himself laughing out loud, talking to the men as if there was no difference, in age or place or learning. He downed the whisky as every glass got easier. Whisky, the magic potion. Soon everyone was moving like one body from the hotel to the hall. Michael found himself in a world where he floated.

The girl from the shop pulled him onto the dance floor. It seemed easy. All the tightness disappeared. His face relaxed and smiled, the lights of the hall whirling. It was all dream-like. He let the girl lead him outside, where there were more half-bottles passed from hand to hand. Although the Kirk said no alcohol inside, outside the car boots opened up, full with portable bars. He could smell the slightly bitter smell of the girl's sweat. Lesley, it was.

Everything flowed. They were at the back of the hall among the uncut nettles, the music muffled through the wooden walls. His hands were working all over her as if it was something he'd always done. Kissing her, pushing his face into hers, running his hands over her bare back, down over her buttocks, grasping them deeply. His hands rough, her skin clammy with acne. Pressed against the back wall of the hall she heaved up her frilled nylon skirt, pulling at Michael's trousers. She took hold of him and pushed him inside her. He felt the warm of her, swallowed her smell and her skin and her hair, pushing up through her, she on tiptoes for him. The pulsing ramrod that led him on. And then it was over in a great rush, the explosion that went off inside him, and she was pulling down her skirt, and he struggling with the fastener of his jeans.

The next thing, he was staggering hand in hand with Lesley, red-faced and saliva-smeared, back into the hall. She clung to him as the carousel of the dance continued.

In what was sudden for some, but took a long time to penetrate for others, the merry-go-round went into slow motion. It was breaking up, and an urgency from another dimension started to infiltrate the secure bonhomie of the dance hall.

A yell went up. There was shouting, then the words became clear.

'There's a fire!'

'A fire!'

'Whar?'

'Doon at the caravan. At Harry's.'

'There's a fire.'

'A fire?'

The caravan was ablaze. The crowd spilled out to see the fire from the back door of the hall. The men jumped into cars and headed down the single-track road to the shore where the inferno was well alight. A horrible bonfire against the black sky. The caravan went up like a paper lantern with everything inside. The ammunition from the rifle cracked like fireworks. The Calor gas bottle exploded, sending a jet of flame into the night. It was a spectacular blaze if you were watching as entertainment. But a disaster if you were calculating the cost. All the cash that Michael and Harry had been paid for the job was in a cloth bag behind the stash of bean tins in the cupboard. Deep inside the inferno the tinned beans bubbled and hissed long after the cash became cinders.

There was nothing anyone could do. Everything was gone, the heat of the blaze even scorching the gable of Malcolm's cottage. The men hurled buckets of water at the shed to stop it going up too. Harry was so drunk he couldn't comprehend what had happened until the next day. Sidney dragged him back to his house to stay the night, with Harry still protesting. Michael woke up on the sofa at Malcolm's.

There were no police on the island so no one would ever know what truly caused the fire. In the morning they made their way to survey the burnt-out remains, each scratching for clues.

'There's a right smell o' petrol.'

'Ah'm sure I heard an engine.'

'Never thought anything o' it till efter, but I definitely heard a boat.'

In the whispering justice of the islanders, the protesters got the blame, but there was never any proof, not even after the Kirkwall police came to investigate. Picking among the sodden contents of the caravan, they looked for evidence to support their suspicions. They deliberated over the congealed plastic of the turps container.

'Na buey, we bought that wursels …'. Harry wouldn't be seduced into false blame.

'Cooda been ae gas jis' geen up itsel … a faulty bottle. Cooda left summeen on …'

But some wanted it to be the protesters. They wanted a terrible act to hate them for.

'When they said that tae Malcolm aboot his wife, I mean, hid wis jis' no right, when she wis lyin' in the hospital …'

'Ken we wur no meant tae retaliate but that went a bit far. Lily no weel an' all.'

But there were no rules of engagement, there were no lines that could not be crossed. The protesters were blind with their right. A cause sanctioned anything. The hunters' irritation was hardening. The biggest hurt to the islanders came from receiving misplaced slurs that were no part of their way of life that came imported from another place, a whole different culture. The city protesters couldn't know that when they randomly hurled the insults they calculated in an offhand and safely anonymous way to irritate the men, they might by chance land home with a force they could never realise.

Malcolm ignored the abuse and taunts out on the Skerry, closed his ears as the lads yelled and the words echoed deep into his brain: 'Who's she shaggin'? Come on, whose yur wife fucking while you're out here?' Out on the Skerry the words burned through him as he set his eyes silently on the rocks ahead, judging the range of his rifle, Lily yellow against white hospital sheets cocooned in fawning hope. He pulled the trigger and felt good at getting a clean shot, a simple death, knowing the protesters' taunts could never hurt him. The twenty-year-old boys grinned at each other between insults.

The acrid belongings were hurled from the caravan, blackened and wet, into a heap for the lorry to pick up and dump in the quarry. All that Harry and Michael had left were the clothes they wore at the dance. The two men were taken in by each household in turn and set up with spare jerseys, boots and food. Everyone wanted to do something to help them, to show the goodness they were capable of, the more to amplify the badness of the arson attack. There was nothing they could do about all the lost cash. Nobody worked with banks, but they had a whip-round, the hunters piling a handful of notes into Harry's hand, 'tae keep the pair o' yi till yi git yur bonus at least.'

Harry worked out the season, but the fire killed the feel of the place. He drank his wages in the bar, and owed his bonus by the time he left.

the spoils

When Harry got back to Agnes after the season at the seals, he had barely five pounds and the roll of skins which had escaped the fire in Malcolm's shed.

'Ah well,' was Agnes's response, unfurling a skin to lay it over a chair-back, where it remained stiffly, the grain rubbing the wrong way as Harry's head slumped against it. She had two cleaning jobs, one at the bank and the other for the new young doctor. She polished the brass door plaques as if her life depended on it until an untouchable world of syrup shone back at her from another dimension. With the pages of the *Scotsman* and a bottle of vinegar she worked the paper balls hard into the corners of the glass door as if dirt was a conspiracy to catch her out.

'Ah'll head sooth an' see if Ah can get ony work on ay estates, or maybe ae docks,' said Harry, softly addled with drink.

Michael stayed in the North Isles. He had unwittingly been claimed as new blood.

'When the sealing's by wi', yi can come wi' iss tae the seine net,' offered Lennie. The other men too were going back to the fishing. Michael thought about giving the sealskin purse to the girl in the shop, but in the end he didn't. It stayed in the pocket of his jeans, the ones he'd been wearing at the dance and which were now all he had of his original clothing, bar the Icelandic-style jumpers that were all the rage among the knitters.

'Yu'll no be gaa'n anywhar. Wul hiv tae git merrit noo.' Lesley wanted an engagement ring from the catalogue. 'An' then iverythin'll be right.'

winners and losers

In the year of the Sex Pistols, the Selsay jukebox was stacked with Charley Pride and Crystal Gayle. The protesters got the cull stopped and it was indeed 'history'. Louisa and Steph went back to their university courses, others disappeared back to the big cities, Pete decided to go to Afghanistan and import ethnic crafts to sell, and Justin, Hetty and JoJo stayed on the commune.

The islanders smarted. Somehow, collectively and unwittingly, their lives had been shamed and they felt tainted with something unclean. Things they had always thought of as fine, without question, were now unsure. Michael, still on the island and staying in Malcolm's house, battened down with the rest of them for a long dark winter, Lesley herding him about like a sheep, snapping behind him like a dog.

Embra

'I'll tak the bus doon,' said Seadhna. Eileen, she thought, had the potential to be a new pal.

'Say that again! Whit did yi say?' Eileen, in her skin-tight jeans, looked askance.

'I'll tak … I'll *take* the bus … doon,' repeated Seadhna, trying to acknowledge the joke and mask her discomfort at being ridiculed.

Eileen laughed. 'That's just so funny. The way you speak. I've never heard anything like that before. Say it again …'. Eileen had been to Majorca on holiday with her parents and spoke Joppa.

It was Seadhna's first term at the art school walking everywhere because she didn't know how the buses worked and feeling a door key in her pocket for the first time. At home you needed nothing in your pockets, not even money.

It was Friday afternoon in the old red Lauriston Place building and the students were dismally sticking fragments of broken stained glass onto a window pane with Plasticine. It seemed to them that they were studiously ignored by the tutors and the superior older students. The Head of Department, they had been pompously assured in the induction lecture, was world famous, so by osmosis perhaps his greatness would feed into them. That appeared to be the unspoken ethos of the place.

Seadhna never realised she had an accent until then. At home, the island accent could sound oafish and she eschewed it just a little. After Miss Fraser's class in the primary school they all learnt that you shouldn't say 'ken'. Miss Fraser had been unequivocal: dialect was *not* to be used inside the school. The thick ones forgot, and carried on saying, 'I dunna ken', only to be repeatedly corrected.

'We don't say "ken" in school, we speak properly, don't we? What do we say? What do we say, Seadhna?' Miss Fraser's eyes drilled.

' "I don't know" is the proper way, Miss.' Her correct response cemented her apart from the linguistically impoverished others.

Seadhna's mother pooh-poohed the country accent, dispelling it as common. She had relatives in Nairn and explained the virtues of the Nairn tongue. 'The people of Nairn are the best spoken' – as if there had been an official edict. Nairn had the best weather too, apparently.

There were only certain things you could say in the treacle-type island voice. You would certainly never read the news in it or make a speech in Parliament. Seadhna could speak it, but that voice was strictly limited by place. She tempered it when she spoke to her mother. She noticed that her father used it along with his west coast twang when he spoke to the fishermen and the country people. You could tell the kind of person he was talking to on the phone by the intonation he used. But when he was arguing a point, he too diluted it. You would never dare talk like that in school. *Why was it always about how you spoke and not what you said?* Since those times long ago with Miss Fraser, she thought she had it worked out, and could flip subtly from playground to home to school-speak. She was an adept chameleon of intonation and inflection, whether it be sing-song or assertion. She could adapt her speech to her audience and knew the prosody and rhythms that mattered to different ears. She could feel assimilated or distanced as the situation required.

Eileen's outburst unnerved her. She hadn't come all this way down south to the city to be laughed at. A country girl in the city. One of Edna O'Brien's hapless Galway Noras. *I'm not going to be caught out twice. I'm not a 'girl with green eyes'.* She carefully bound up and stored away the narrow blade of anger she felt for Eileen.

However, it was still the case that in Edinburgh, people thought her accent quaint. They exclaimed and pulled around an audience to make her speak, so that others could marvel at the linguistic oddity. They weren't interested in what she had to say, and that's what ended her island voice. How she spoke, Seadhna decided, would have to be sorted as a matter of urgency.

In a month she was talking Muirhouse. 'Ah'm gonnae go waye the bus. See yis there.'

'Chum us ti th' stop, then.' It cemented her with the people she wanted to belong with. The choice was between that or the plummy tones of someone called Melissa who hadn't done exams and went to the Steiner school. When Melissa spoke out in a tutorial it was with a boomy authority. She always sounded clever, astute and, without question, *right*.

'And what does *yor* father do for a living?' Melissa, with her sleek black hair coiled into two ram's horns against her head, and her powerful features, smoked a cigarette in the drawing break with the ample gestures of a Gatsby. She had no idea that the question might come as an embarrassment to some. Thrown together in their first-year drawing class, Melissa already had demonstrated scary dexterity over the rest with a rotring pen, arranging her materials confidently on top of her desk on the first day.

'I'm going to become a *theata* designer,' she proclaimed, and no one doubted it. Apartheid of accent.

Then there was Cammy. 'See when thon stuck-up cow came oot wi' that! Ah jis' thocht, that's me. Thu've got me. Thu'r oota ma league. So Ah just got it right oot right awa'. So Ah sez "Ma da's a loo attendant. Aye, ken a lavvy cleaner." Ah'm nay pussyfootin' aboot coverin onythin' up. Ah'm prood o' ma da. An' aw' they posh dames ur goin roon' sayin' "Mummy works for Oxfam, Daddy's in Dubai, Daddy's this an' Daddy's that. Daddy's in business …". An' I thocht, well maybe, yeah, I can get a handle on that, but oh noh, it's noh just a wee corner shop Daddy's got or onything, but hey, it's Scottish and fucking Newcastle Breweries! An' then it's "I went to a finishing school in Switzerland. After Steiner's." An' Ah'm thinking, what the fuck's Steiners? Ah never heard o' Steiners. Ah didna ken it wis a school. Ah thocht it wis a kinda posh pianna. Ah thocht Ah kent sumeen about posh folk, but then Ah felt like Ah wis in a kinda different posh league. Thur faces! Tryin tae be aw' polite when Ah sez Ma da's a bog attendant, he cleans other folks shit affa loos. An' yi ken what they said? They posh yah dames? They went in their posh fucking Steiner speak "Wow, Cammy, that's so fascinating. I've never met anyone whose father was a toilet cleaner before." An' Ah thocht, this is fucking unreal.'

chameleons

Seadhna needed a way to be heard that was as far away from Melissa as she could get. That was one of the choices to be made.

'Ah jis' fuckin' hate thon arty farty patter,' Cammy snarled, and soon cut off his Marc Bolan locks. He appeared from Brian Drumm's trainee night with a Mohican. That was when Seadhna knew where her vocal identity belonged. In the big, crumbling college club down in the West Port, the dank walls of the old church boomed with The Clash. Cammy leapt about behind a Formica coffee bar, whirling singles onto a deck. The air was thick with smoke. A black cavern of a fire-risk, the students blinked, their eyes shocked into the bare electric light beyond the swing doors to huddle up the stairs to the ladies' toilets. Cracked flaking lino, broken toilets, heavy eyeliner and plum blusher on cheekbones, and the dismal sanitary dispenser.

Finishing-school Melissa did her eyes up like Cleopatra, but punk was way too noisy for Eileen, who retreated mouse-like to her steady boyfriend in Portobello.

Everyone sagged together on the big sponge cushions with lager and limes and Embassy Regals.

The art school was about music and bands really. Art was just a reason for a bunch of misfits to land up together. It was the world on the other side of the glass and Seadhna walked home to Marchmont with the whine of loudspeakers in her ears, all the way over the cold Meadows. Cammy, still buzzing, headed off to yet more parties and all-nighters, getting into college on autopilot after a night on speed.

The swill of working-class boys and girls at the art school were consumed with trying to negotiate the alien planet of higher education. They were all frantic for something to cling onto. It was a world of shifting sands, so they sought each other out in thinly disguised desperation. None of them had factored in the class issue.

The learning establishments was where it really drove home. Edinburgh University swelled with the 'yahs' as they called them, who came up from Cheltenham and Gloucester and from strange-sounding public schools. *Is Gigglesworth a place somewhere? Yeah, it's got summan tae dae wi' Russel Harty,*

Ah think.

St Andrews was the first choice of the Oxbridge rejects. *Pff! Yi might as well be in England as in St Andrews.* Next came Fine Art at Edinburgh University. It was a more acceptable pursuit for those who wouldn't need to work too hard for their living. The art school was for pretty girls fresh from European finishing schools, the heiress to a whisky dynasty, maybe, or the doe-eyed daughter of a Tory peer. The peculiar collection cast their eyes around the top floor of the newly opened Hunter building with its gun-slot windows, and positioned their portfolios against the uniform grey table tops.

For the 'yahs', the working-class kids were colourful diversions, eccentric collisions with tatty disorganised lives.

'Oh Shuggie, you are so funny! Come and tell us all about the time you worked in the bottle factory.' On cue, a Hughie or a Boab would relate an oft-told mythical story, well embellished in the many retellings, about the missing workman who fell into the glass-works, or the canners who pissed in the peas in the cannery. The storytellers felt again the temporary age-old tingle of flattery, embarrassment or attention from the days of servants and masters in the big houses. *Fuckan' bastards. Fuckin' arseholes ...*

There was nothing that got you places like the full confidence of a posh English voice, and nothing that kindled centuries of resentment and inferiority like a working-class brogue. For Seadhna it was a matter of allegiance. She was from neither world, really. The posh kids held soirées in the Colony houses in Stockbridge, with Tanqueray gin and tonics, or Pimms for the summer time.

'Wur huvin a partay!' shreiked Cammy. 'Ah'll dae invites on the college photocopier' and so he copied a photo of Lenin and the Kremlin from a library book, cut round the images and collaged them onto a master, recopying until he had an A4 sheet. Letraset and felt-tip in black and red.

Come to a White Russian Party!!
!!Vodka kitsch and revolutionary style!!
BYOB
!**Водка китч Водка китч!**

A hundred invites were distributed round the college and the trendier university students, the ones who liked to circulate on the fringe of the art school. The ingredients of a party were simple. A place, music, drink and plenty of the right crowd ... an excuse for imagination, the brief magical transformation of anxiety into style anaesthetised by booze.

Vodka kitsch was anything from Anna Karenina to Rudolf Nureyev. And revolutionary style, *well yeah*, everybody looks good in black and red. *Eat your heart out, Mayakovsky!*

The plum taffeta dress came from the Lifeboat shop. It must have been at least a size eighteen, with swirly embroidered beadwork on the hips and neckline. The feel of the cloth was rubbery with quality. It only had to appear Russian in essence, in this catalyst for imagination not accuracy – the beads would provide a hint of Fabergé or Romanoff.

Cammy got yet another dead man's suit with pleats at the waistline, and full Oxford bags tapering down to turn-ups. He was loving it, becoming a Potemkin extra one day with the option of Fred Astaire another.

'Whit aboot this?'

And he pulled an astrakhan hat from a brown paper carrier and said he was going to shave his head.

He showed her what to do with the dress. 'Jis' cut a seam up the back 'n pit a big fishtail pleat in ... then yi kin cut the top off 'n mak a bolero jacket.'

Organisation was precision planning, clearing the big living room in the tatty top-floor flat. Georgian decrepitude. *Now is that an architectural style?* High above the rumbling spin dryers in the ground floor launderette, the bared and splitting floorboards sloped towards the Tollcross clock. Subsiding foundations with masonry features crumbling onto pedestrians below. A dust-filled, once coloured, once expensive, Indian rug was rolled into a collapsing sausage, then heaved with a couple of staggers behind the sideboard pushed up against the windows.

'Wu'll yi never ken, dinae want onyboday fallin oot tha winda pished.' Cammy had done all this before. He was an events pro. The junkshop ornaments were rammed into cupboards, everything breakable cleared from view. All superfluous furniture was removed. It wasn't going to be a sit-down affair – by one in the morning the place would be jammed, full to the gunnels with stylish drunkenness in degrees of posing, lounging, dancing, flirting and *bagging off*. The anticipation became tangible.

Dan, the slightly nerdy architect with a drum kit and enough money to buy a good hi-fi was leant on to allow use of his precious Garrard deck and Wharfdale speakers. He was already twitching unassertively about the gear getting wrecked. Cammy was reassuring him.

'Ah'll be on the deck aw' night. Wu'll pull the sofa up against it like a barricade. Ah promise it'll be fine.' He grinned a big, winning grin with his newly *baldy heed* and winked at Dan. 'Ah promise.'

The sofa was dragged, the remains of its missing caster hooking the floorboards and digging a big skittery scratch towards its final resting place. Its significant weight was finally positioned in such a way that Dan was at least superficially persuaded that all possible had been done to mitigate drunken crashing and lurching. The speakers themselves were wedged into matching alcoves on either side of the marble fireplace, the cables run along the top of the almost intact cornice.

The preparation and the dressing was a delicious ritual. The tools were collected and laid out ready. Unladdered tights new from John Lewis's with seams up the back, black satin stilettos worn by long dead feet, eye pencil, mascara, eyeshadows and lipstick. The final look had already gelled in her imagination and she knew exactly how it would go. It would take a steady hand, some time and concentration in front of the mirror. The taffeta skirt slid on like a dream. She was loving the way the skirt tightened over her bum and swung in and out. Wiping a window in the steamed-up mirror, she backcombed her hair into a roll at the front like a ginger Hedy Lamarr, *not Russian, oh shit*, fixed it secure with kirbys and a skoosh of Elnett. Then got the deep-port-red lipstick out and savoured the joy of defining her lips, first with a darker pencil, then filling in the cupid's bow, taking the opportunity to pout and wonder for a second about the other lives that she might still have. Next, the black eye pencil, running it along the inside lip of her lower lid – it stung just a little. Watery black, smokey grey and a touch of pink smudged together to feel a bit on the tarty side of revolution but *shit, who cares?* She felt good, gave herself a sidelong glance, stepping into the (Cancer shop) satin stilettos, loving the reinforced heel and toe of the quality tights, bending round to straighten up the seam over her calves. The mirror confirmed the transformation, and that was it.

In the kitchen a stack of unmatched plates and thrift-shop glasses sat beside the pasta salad, the French loaves cocooned in tin foil with garlic butter, the Oddbins booze laid out on the dresser, and the three large Smirnoff bottles. They had a kitty to buy the food and booze, but proper Stolichnaya was too dear. The White Russian cocktails had to be tested – vodka, cream, Camp coffee and ice cream. *Ah yes, perfection and a kick too. Whoo!* She dabbed her lipstick.

The furniture-less, carpet-less living room seemed big and echoey. A wooden lemonade crate held the amassed singles collection, pooled from the tenants of the flat.

Music suddenly blasted from the sound system. The intro riff wailed and echoed, then the words. 'Ziggy played guitar'.

Cammy grinned, his body fitting into live sculptured shapes before leaping over the sofa and thumping onto the floor. The vibrations stuttered the needle over the vinyl. 'Fuck! Hope Dan niver heard that.'

The two of them danced and swung themselves around the entire empty room, feeling the liberation from the engulfing music, the connection of that moment and the joy of what the night might bring, intoxicated already with anticipation, giving themselves up to the helter-skelter.

Time got lost; after a few drinks, Seadhna hit the place where you live only in the moment, where there is no other place, no outside world, nothing to drag you away. The front door banged open with the stream of partygoers, invited and crashing. Eventually it was wedged open, the flat crammed all the way down the hall to the living room and into the kitchen. It was a good party. You could hardly move. Sweaty and packed and loud. One of the essential skills of life.

Boom! *Like a bomb going off inside.* Hit. *A hit, I see what you mean.* Whoosh. Warm big open loose immersion in pleasure. *Yeah.* Liquid gold, warm, running through her body. *Ahhhh.* The power went from her legs and she collapsed back onto the sofa. *Whoa. God that is brilliant.* Cammy took the bottle from her and screwed back the cap.

She never knew her body could feel such an intensity of pleasure. The prospect of it was invigorating and yet tempered by the electrocuting thump that had thrown her back off her feet. The power of it was fearsome.

By three in the morning the initial cocktail ingredients had degenerated into a slop concoction of milk, any alcohol still left and maybe a straw taken from an unwashed glass with a cigarette stubbed out in it. Nobody cared. The music mood had subdued and the floor was strewn with people lying or sitting smoking droopily. The willowy, anorexic girl who went from catatonic to incapably drunk in one single stage lay foetus-like in her black, oversized jumper in front of the empty fireplace while others stepped over her. She always felt cold. *D'ya think she'll be okay? Yeah, she'll be fine. She always does that at parties* ... was the assurance.

The sofa had been dragged round again and was fully occupied by one prone body and six sitters perched on the remaining space and arms. Dan had long since crashed out in his bed, oblivious to the new vulnerability of the hi-fi. Eventually the last stragglers fell asleep where they were, or staggered towards the door and out into the early morning. No conscious life remained, only the mechanical rhythm of the stylus wavering back and fore with an amplified hiss and click on the last LP on the record player.

Seadhna managed to get her stilettos off and crashed fully clothed across someone's empty bed, a calf-to-thigh ladder in the new John Lewis tights.

The kitchen sat silently curating its apocalyptic transformation, awaiting the first body to emerge searching for a dirty glass, the cold water tap and a seat to collapse back onto and wait for the world to stop spinning.

That was the art school and its transparent divisions. The comprehensive-school achievers out of their depth. Drinking cheap wine from unmatched thrift-shop glasses and trawling second-hand shops to revive Gene Pitney and Ska. Between Mono Dansettes and speaker stacks of crippling decibels they recalibrated poverty into kitsch collectables with plastic jewellery. They pierced more and more holes, curving up the cartilage to the top of their ears, and dangled anything from safety pins to fishing floats from them. Brushwork skills were displayed in eyeshadows flashing like kingfisher's wings or the unexpected beauty of a glinting starling. The girls mimicked Eva Peron one day and Marilyn Monroe the next, always just off-kilter and slightly on edge. The boys found baseball jackets from Fifties movies, braces and flat-top haircuts. Rife with the smell of mothballs, painted jeans, ripped T-shirts, hair coloured with food dye and stiffened to exotic spikes with PVA. Snakebites and singles in dark caverns with the see-saw riff of the Sex Pistols' 'God Save the Queen', Blondie's 'Denis Denis' and Devo's 'Are We Not Men??' All the time living out of each other's pockets while the rich kids played at it, secured by the insurance of their preordained connections.

Life was an everlasting fancy-dress party punctuated by appearances in the college canteen, waiting in line for a hot buttered Breadwinner roll, a coffee and a smoke. Then there came Mondays at Tiffany's rock nights, Tuesday mornings stumbling late into the dark and soporific art history lecture, with the projector well through its box of slides, where it was impossible to keep eyes from drooping into sleep.

You did, however, need to be awake for the life studio.

the anatomy of life

In the studio, the long single-bar electric heaters glowed around the model. The rainy sky over Edinburgh Castle cast big tonal contrasts on the buttocks and scarred stomach of Francesca, the model. The smell of warming oil paint rose from the spattered floor, and the silence of concentration gave the studio a feel of religious meditation. Then came the rasp of a match on a matchbox as a cigarette was lit, the flame shaken out and the dead Bluebell match fired to the floor.

Seadhna loved the discipline of the life class. Securing a large white sheet to her board and hoisting it up onto the easel. Walking around the pose to find the best composition. Narrowing her focus to enjoy the way the spine pulled a long furrow of skin between the flab of Francesca's shoulders and waist. Francesca was her favourite model. She anticipated the joy of drawing Francesca, laying out her materials like surgical instruments slowly and methodically on a spare chair. The preparatory rituals. *The scapula.*

The big brown breasts. Francesca had wrinkled skin in folds and a vertical Caesarean scar on her stomach. One night Seadhna had stood at the same bus stop as Francesca, who had spoken to she unprompted. In broken English she prattled away.

'All ma babes. Dat way. Sezarreen.' She spoke openly to Seadhna and said she recognised her from the class. Francesca had no embarrassment about sitting naked all day. Seadhna was thinking she could never ever do such a thing. Francesca was on her way home to Pilton, aeons away from the art school.

The questions that pushed forward into Seadhna's head she could not ask. They would reveal something about her that Francesca had already gone well beyond. *Do the folk that get off the bus with you know you come and pose nude at the art school? Do you keep it a secret? Would they be shocked?* Even as she thought those questions, she realised how ridiculous they were. As if she read her mind, Francesca volunteered, 'Eez good monay. Eef I cleanin', no near as good monay.'

Italian. *How did you end up in Edinburgh?* The legacy of Leonardo's Madonnas. None of the questions needed an answer. They were questions that probed what Seadhna was asking about herself.

At the bus stop everyone was anonymous; Francesca could have been a secretary or a shop worker or anyone heading out of town after work.

'For God's sake, Seadhna, you are such a prude,' Cammy laughed at her when she tried to discuss it all later. The farmer boys at home would have tittered and staggered around clutching their red tins, leery-eyed. *Luk at the fuckan' TITS, buey!*

illumination

The type of light dictated charcoal. There was far too much heavy contrast to endlessly hatch with a pencil. Seadhna's fingers moved through the black marks, softening thighs and bringing some shadow in under the breasts. She stopped to carve a point into a fresh putty rubber with her Stanley knife, then lifted some light onto the spine.

The time was swallowed in concentration, each student locked in their own singular world between model, paper and marks. So deep was the communion that the model's break came as an annoyance. Seadhna tried to work on the hands clutching the seat of the stool, feeling the stretch of the tendons at the wrist and the helpless lolling of the splaying belly.

There was a collective sigh as the taut wires of tension released. In the breaks, the students wandered round each other's work. Those confident students didn't bother to survey the other easels baring their varied abilities to all. Some efforts were lumpen and crude. The lack of sensitivity could never be softened. They simply couldn't see it. Seadhna noted it. Some drawings were highly technical, with guidelines, dots and marks of symmetry. Others flowed with undulating line and apparent ease.

Groups of students huddled in twos and threes. A nervous boy remained isolated, protected behind a huge board, visibly shaking. Drink or neurosis, it was hard to tell.

Embassy Regals or Number 6s in packs of ten were opened up and offered round and crumpled cellophane fell to the floor. The smoking ritual unleashed a plethora of differing styles. The thumb and forefinger of the worky boy who had done a decorator's apprenticeship, whose drawings were tight and controlled. The girls bowed over shrinking ribcages, pulling thrift-shop cardies around, trying to get too skinny. A girl in impossibly high stilettos perched precariously and almost rooted to the spot except for tiny Chinese steps; Lizzie smoked without shifting her gaze; Cammy was getting more camp as the term went on, inhaling the nicotine hard as if his life depended on it, and eyes flashing about, anticipating an attack from someone or somewhere.

In the break, Seadhna slipped out onto the sculpture court. Within the towering silence of the columned vault, its plaster casts of Greek heroes and heroines shoved unceremoniously into corners, she traversed the open wooden floor. In moments like these she loved the grandeur of the college, the big paintings looming down from the walls. Her favourite was the Kitaj, but she hardly dared to hope that one day she might be able to corral and balance all the dexterity of colour, image and composition brought together in that work. She knew she was at the start of a long apprenticeship and there was still the memory of Lewis, an insistence daring her.

a muse

One Saturday she took a bus down to the New Town in search of Lewis's new Scottish Gallery, a branch of the Cork Street one. It was one of those days when Edinburgh was a perfect grey, and whirling round the Mound and down the hill on the top deck of a number 23 was joy, seeing Fife across the Forth. She craned at the window to decipher the house numbers, irritated that they got lost with a series of antique shops, and let the bus go further than she needed to before she got up to ping the bell. Swinging down the stairs holding the silver rail, she felt just like someone who was used to buses and the way they slewed your body in all directions. She leapt off and walked back up past the clock at Canonmills. On the opposite side of the street she went along Henderson Row and past the gallery before doubling back. She stood at an angle looking in, but could see no one. Big abstract works hung on the walls. It was clean and empty, and she curved the card he had given her in her palm. In her head she rehearsed what she would say. *Ah, hello, you told me to call in when I got to Edinburgh?*

The versions changed as she reshuffled the words, the subtle meaning shifting, the degree of distance or friendliness. It would have to be done.

Pushing the huge, heavy glass door, she immediately felt untidy. She was obviously not a buyer. Inside the gallery the silence was oppressive. It did not look like the kind of place where you browsed. A door opened and a woman emerged, ignoring her. There were voices in the back area and she strained to hear if one of them was Lewis's, then looked around for a few minutes, eyes glued to the paintings so that she would not have to glance away. She feigned her absorption, trying to think what to do, then realised that no one would ask her. It was not like a shop. She would have to make the advance. So she turned to approach the woman at her uncluttered desk.

'Excuse me, I was wondering if Lewis Gerard was here, ehm, he asked me to call in.'

The woman looked up with all of her assured and classy make-up intact. She was no shop girl. Sophisticated and moneyed, she wore the kind of clothes that were dull but expensive. A pearl necklace. 'Who is it that I should say is calling?'

'It's Seadhna … ehm … Rufus. I met Lewis in the summer in Orkney.' Saying the word Orkney seemed to give her away. It put a sudden bump of island naivety into her delivery.

'Awknay, did you say?'

'Yes, Orrkney.'

'Oh yes, Lew was up there in the summer. Wait a moment.'

Seadhna felt uncomfortable having to declare herself. It put her in an inferior position. The woman disappeared, then reappeared.

'He'll be with you in a moment.'

It was an interminable time. Seadhna felt she should leave. It was stupid going there. But by then she was trapped, and it would look even more stupid if she left. However, Lewis emerged, a ready grin on his face, used with smooth talking, winning people.

'Ah, if it's not the little Orkney Lass. You made it after all to the big city..

He said 'lass' as if it was a word he would not normally use and it confirmed right then that this it was all wrong and would now just have to be an ordeal she had to get through.

'My muse of the Standing Stones. I thought a lot about you, you know, after we left. How are you, Shona?'

He got her name wrong. All Seadhna could muster were wan smiles and 'Oh's.

'I'm at the Art School now.'

'Come, my little Orkney beauty.'

He took her out on to Dundas Street for coffee and they sat in a claustrophobic small café. He ordered real coffee. Her taste buds had not yet acclimatised to black ground coffee, but she forced herself.

'So how is the big ivory tower on Lauriston Place? Still making you draw plaster casts?' He blew smoke from his cigarette and leant back, examining her. Seadhna made the mistake of trying to answer his questions seriously.

'No, we don't have to do the casts anymore.'

'Bet you still have life drawing, though?'

The coil of smoke from his fingers dangling over the adjacent seat was going right up her nose. Seadhna loved the life drawing. 'Yes, we get two days of life drawing.' She was about to expand on her fascination with anatomy.

'God, so old-fashioned, so passé. I mean, life drawing?' He grimaced. 'It's like performing an ancient ritual. It has nothing to do with creating meaning. Don't you think, Seadhna?'

He eyed her slowly. 'Perhaps you're not there yet. Here,' and he reached into the top pocket of his jacket and handed her a private view card, 'come and see this show. It's opening on Friday. Beautiful work. I'd be interested to hear what you thought.'

She left the muddy grains in the bottom of the cup, glad to sidle out of the café without knocking things over, Lewis chatting with the café owner as if he knew him, Seadhna feeling she should pay for her own but then deciding not to go there. She was just glad to get out and away from the encounter, feeling stupid and embarrassed, striding manically up the hill and not stopping until she had to wait at the green man to cross at Princes Street. Lewis had unsettled her and hooked her curiosity at the same time. There was another art world away from the college that was nothing to do with still lifes and life drawing. *I need to know about it, find out about it*, she thought, *because I am going to be a real artist …* But there was no way she was going to Lewis's opening on her own.

'Will yi come wi' me?' asked Seadhna, knowing Cammy was someone she could ask.

'Is it free wine? Aye, Ah'll chum yi fir a bit. Ah'm no hingan' aboot wi' aw they posers tho.'

So Cammy on his best behaviour went with her, whispering, 'Arty farty shite or whit?' as they entered through the door. Lewis watched who was coming and going out of the corner of his eye, simultaneously hurrying away to court a buyer. He was seriously busy … it was money.

'You must excuse me … but hold on, I'll introduce you to someone …'

He cast about the packed room, where the noise level had escalated with wine glasses clinking and the chiming of rich confident laughter.

'Help yourself to wine.'

'Dinnae mind if Ah dae,' and Cammy set off after the waiter.

Seadhna made an attempt to look at the work between the press of bodies. There were no prices on anything, but it was selling.

'I just love that,' a woman swooned loudly on the arm of a portly man.

'Ah there he is,' and Lewis found Henry, glass in hand, smoking. He flashed a conspiratorial look to everyone and no one. 'Henry, you must meet Shona – the island muse ... You don't mind if I call you that do you?'

'No ... no ... it's Seadhna, actually, Shay-na.'

'Of course. Unusual ... Norse or something. You're all Norwegian's up there really, aren't you?'

'Well ... it's actually ... ' she started, but Lewis wasn't listening.

'Meet Henry ... Henry Sinclair. He'll tell you about his famous namesake, the *Prince*' and Lewis seamlessly offloaded Seadhna onto Henry while Cammy twitched around the blank but meticulously layered canvasses, saying nothing but bursting to get out.

'So, a famous link?'

Seadhna presented almost genuine interest, feeling momentarily sorry for Henry as Lewis's satin-clad back disappeared into the private view crowd and they were left marooned together.

'Yes, he always does that.' Henry drew on an un-tipped cigarette. 'No relation. Prince Henry Sinclair. Discovered the native Americans. Do you know of him?'

'Well, no, I don't, you must tell me.' But he didn't. She was drinking her wine too fast.

'Lewis said you were at the college?'

'Yes.'

'What do you make of it?'

'I like it.' She was trying to gauge the answer she was supposed to give. 'So far ... anyway.'

'I think it's a fucking shit heap,' he said quietly and poshly.

'Well ...eh, I'm finding drawing fascinating.'

'But it's so stuck in the past. It's like there's been nothing since the Colourists.'

'Oh.' She wasn't sure what it all meant, but tried to wing it, hanging in. Henry had a kind of aloof fascination.

'I'm doing the university course,' he informed her. Henry talked in the tones of Fettes or Merchiston, always calculating and measuring before he spoke. As the crowd dwindled, the wine fuelled a feeling of recklessness in Seadhna.

'Shall we head off somewhere else?' asked Henry.

She was ready to follow. Cammy was hunting around, swigging back the last of his wine. They all headed up Dundas Street together to a nondescript pub where Seadhna tottered and swayed, eventually comfortably leaning against Henry's oversized wool coat. Cammy vanished into the night after some time hovering behind Henry trying to communicate gooseberry signs across to Seadhna. She waved him off blearily, knowing she was helplessly intrigued by Henry's otherness.

'Watch yursel hen, ken what they public school boys are like,' he whispered, not too quietly.

When the pub closed, they both made their way up the interminable hill, Henry lurching out at taxis. None were stopping. The comforting orange lights were all switched off. Finally they stood on the High Street, looking in all directions for a cab. The city felt dark and empty as if they were the only two people left in it. In the silence there was the sound of glass smashing. Somewhere the plate glass of a shop window shattered over the display contents and an alarm began to ring.

It was the Highland shop where tartan-clad piper dolls toppled like dominoes onto each other as the soft red Stewart travelling rugs were sprinkled with turquoise shards. The pyramid of round shortbread tins clattered to the floor and rolled to a stop while a mouthless model with a sealskin hat rocked and fell against the locked jewellery cabinet. '*End the seal slaughter*' was penned in felt tip on the breeze block that hit the floor.

The alarm bell was still ringing when Seadhna slipped her arm under Henry's coat and round his waist. 'Looks like a break-in.'

'God, who would want to steal all that tartan tat?' He pulled her into a lane off the High Street to kiss her, with the moon traversing the cavernous medieval closes and the plague ghosts deep below, walled into buried streets.

no going back

When the year turned the corner and spring came, the low Selsay landscape emerged into a cold, brittle March. The bleached green land was scummy and muddied by the feet of sheep. Sucked dry and wrung out, wetted and soaked again like an overused floor cloth. The land, scorched bare by wind, was depleted and drained. The faces of the island people were tired and pasty, starved of sun and cheered only by the blur of beer and whisky that buoyed them through the dark days of the end of the year. Everyone colluded in the comfortable aura of bonhomie, staving off the days when they would have to grind back into work, get up before dawn in the cold, and clamp out the soporific intimacies of a warm bed.

Michael was swept along too. Armed around like a docile puppy by Lesley. Brought to the family home, he was sitting at the Formica table in the too-bright kitchen, the collie dog chained at the back door. Before they entered the house, Lesley slowed on the mass concrete path and whispered, 'Wu'll no say anythin' aboot … yi ken whit … this,' and she patted her stomach in code. It had not sunk in yet. Michael still thought it could all be a mistake. But nothing was sore or difficult. If this was how things were, it could be worse.

'Wur engaged,' announced Lesley. Simple, round, pleased Angus, her blacksmith father, took out the bottle of whisky and poured a dram for them all. Her mother, Alice, went up to the cupboard, nipped in the middle by the ties of her wrap-around apron, to take down the remains of the black bun, then opened up the door of the stove to break up the clinkers. She busied herself with dishcloths and shovels and the setting of things in their place. Lesley stood with her fleshy face, awaiting a reaction.

'Weel, that's certainly news,' said Alice.

There was not much of a choice of suitors on the island. Associations had to be pragmatic and quickly formed. The new nurse was assigned within seconds of her arrival. The pecking order of lesser bachelors retreated then to turn elsewhere.

The whisky helped Michael speak, nodding to agree with Lesley as if they had such a bond that everything had already been discussed and sorted. 'The boats ur gan back tae the seine net noo, and Lennie sez he'll tak me on.' A whole new career was opening up for Michael.

'An' that's a fine job' encouraged Angus.

They were all building a picture of future domestic bliss, somewhere between *Woman's Weekly* and the Flash adverts.

'And then wu'll build a hoose. Everybody's building new noo. Yi kin get a kit.'

'Aye, hid's far cheaper than tryan ti dae up an owld place,' Angus agreed.

They all smiled. Lesley was full of ideas for this and that. Weddings, houses, holidays. There was a whole agenda of life in her head that Michael, it seemed, had unlocked.

casting loose

It was all fitting; Lennie needed somebody to wind in the ropes. The McDuff-built wooden boat creaked against the pier. 'Needs recaulked,' he grunted.

'Aye.'

'An' shuz needan' a paint. Wu'll beach her at neap tides and do the bottom. But wu'll wait till the big tides. Michael, buey! You go up tae the store an' get yursel' a set o' oil skins. Jis' mark it doon tae the boat's tab.'

So Michael came back to the *Northern Dawn* with pristine yellow oilskins stiffly folded over his arm.

'Hing them on the wheelhoos door,' and Lennie smiled.

The crew jumped from the ladder onto the deck, swinging off the metal rungs a few feet from the bottom. Willuck passed down a box full of bread rolls, tins of Spam and soup.

'Hope there's more than a' that tinned shite,' glowered Max.

'Aye aye, Bob's pittan doon bacon and sausages,' Lennie assured them.

'Thank fuck fir that.'

Willuck, Lennie and Max were passing out cigarettes. 'Whar's Jimmack.'

'Still pissed, likely.'

'He better fuckin' hurry up. Wu'r no waitan' on him.'

'A fuckan' liability.'

'Aye, Michael. Catch this stuff, will yi.' Willuck threw a tyre onto the deck and started firing down wooden fish boxes onto it. They bounced off at all angles, slithering down to Michael's feet. The pile of boxes sitting on the pier gradually diminished as the heap on the deck grew. 'Stow them doon below.'

Michael scrambled down into the hold as the boxes lurched and stuttered towards him. Max was pitching them down from above. 'That's it!' he yelled up into the square hole of blue, at the same time dodging to avoid any more raining boxes, 'Watch me heed, min!'

Michael's eyes were growing accustomed to the darkness of the hold and he could make out the firm staves of the boat. He stacked the boxes beneath the square of sky, hearing the voices of the invisible men. Then came the stutter of the engine starting up, changing to a purr as she settled into neutral.

'Shiz cold a' right.' Lennie had a grease smear on his face from the engine room.

'Here's the next load. Watch yur heed!' yelled Max, and the square of blue was obliterated by the next load of boxes bearing down.

'Pack them as high as you can.'

Michael threw them up on top of each other. *Return to Lochinver. No unauthorised use.* By the time they had loaded on two hundred empty boxes the hold was full.

'Any more?' he shouted. But there was no reply, the voices had moved off. The main engine clanked and clattered, the whole boat throbbing with vibrations and permeated by the smell of diesel. Michael pressed through the hold to the metal ladder, pulling himself up on deck again.

'Get that for'ard rope,' Bob was handing the fresh meat in a cardboard box over the rails to Willuck.

'Stick that in the ice.' Willuck passed the box to Michael.

'What ice?'

'The ice in the fish hold.'

'Whar's that?'

'Bloody hell, lad, di yi ken anythin' aboot boats? Come wi' me so yi'll ken fir next time.' The path to the fish hold was blocked by boxes. 'Sorry mate, yi'll hiv tae shift this lot. There's special bits whar yi pit the boxes. See? An yi hiv tae pit this wedges in 'atween. Then thu'll no shift at sea. Yi better rearrange aal this afore we git unner waye.' Michael began restacking the boxes.

'Yi'll git the ice in there,' and Willuck pointed to a battened-off section.

'That's whar wi' keep the fresh stuff. No fridge on this cruiser but plenty o' ice.' By the time Michael had rearranged all the boxes down below there was no one above deck, and the pier was an indistinct mark in a long grey-green mound. A plate of wrinkled grey stretched away on all sides. They were heading west.

Through the tight door to the galley, the crew sat around a cramped table, the gas stove at their backs. Willuck warmed himself against the exhaust pipe. 'Get yirsel a brew, Michael.'

The blackened kettle sat penned onto the gas ring by metal guards. Swinging from hooks were two remaining tin mugs. Tea, milk and sugar were all mixed together in the black kettle. Michael poured. 'Ah'll hiv a fill up' came from Max.

'Aye, me too,' said Jimmack

'An' me,' added Willuck. The tin mugs were pushed to the rimmed edge of the galley table.'

'It's an intravenous tea-drip that Jimmack needs, eh?'

'Don't tak the fuckin' piss, Willuck,' and Jimmack recoiled into his crippling drouth, emptying a crushed cigarette from the battered pack in his back pocket onto the table before straightening it out and lighting up.

Above in the wheelhouse, Lennie sat on a high stool, his foot playing with the wheel. He had the wireless tuned into Radio Scotland's discussion programme, whining loudly against the intermittent crackle from the VHF. It was a capsule from another existence, the furniture of the plotter, the radar, the sonar, the switches for the deck lights, the windows that slid down into their casing with a thud and from which Lennie yelled his instructions to the crew. Rolled up and jammed behind the plotter were the grubby and fingered charts. Each chart well worn and marked with a pencilled cross here, a halting line there, some shading or a hatched area in red. Those charts mapped the sea for Lennie, the places he had been before, where he had discovered the bottom was sandy, or muddy, where the edge of a rock shelf was or the water depth suddenly plummeted. The marks described places where there were fasteners or rocks to tear a net on and the unknown lore of the fishermen who knew where every wreck was, a sub from the wartime, the missing evidence of a disappeared trawler. *The sea cannae haad its secrets for ever.*

The geography of the seabed was another dimension for those who were unfamiliar. Michael listened as he heard the names of rocks shouted over the radio, dropped into conversations about overcooked bacon and big hauls as they waited in the galley. The silent spaces in the mess room conversation were filled by the insistence of the most enthusiastic talker, the one who didn't get bored with his own voice, who could always find a cheery anecdote, and ignored the indifference of the group.

'Whit? You lot aal deed? Got nothan' ti say?'

'Shut up fir a minute, Willuck. Yur fucking doin' me heed in.'

'Aye, when I wis speakan tae Eric off the Harvest, he said last trip they pulled up a whole human *torso* in the net. No heed on it, though. Maks yi shudder tae think thur's a skull rollan' about doon there.' Willuck enjoyed the word torso. You didn't get many occasions in which you could use such a word.

'Fuckan' shut it, Willuck.'

'Aye, but that's the trawl, they get all the shite off the bottom.'

'Mibbe, but they get Monks an' a".'

'No a patch on the seine.'

'Monks is two hunner' pound a box.' And whispering, 'See if there's no a better price in the haddock, Ah'm gan off on a Peterheed boat.' Jimmack was never happy.

'Yi think the Scotch'll tak yi? Thur right clannish. It's all fisher families. They keep tae thur own.'

'Wu'll see.'

'Half o' them's drunk a' the time an' half o' them cannae git the nets shot fir prayin".'

'Cannae be buthered wi' that God lot. No sailin' on Sundays.'

'Aye the choochters.'

'That lot's doomed.'

Lennie headed for the Stormy shoal. He had a plan. They would fish till they got a good two hundred boxes. There was always the chance you might get two hundred in the first shot, but it would probably be that he'd have a go at Stormy, move round to the next bay, then the next and be within easy time of landing the haul at Scrabster. There would be better prices in Peterhead, but then it was a longer sail. He would just see. He kept his plan in his head.

'What are we doin' then, Lennie?' Willuck asked.

'Och wu'll hiv a go at Stormy and see whit's doin, and then jis' see.' He wouldn't give more than that. It was the skipper's privilege to hold the plan, not tell anyone what was happening, feel good when it worked and feel the annoyance when it didn't.

'He should 'a stayed for anithir haul at The Patches. We got a heap o fish there last time 'stead o' gan fur more smaa shite at the Middan.'

Everyone else always knew best what should have been done. Lennie heard the grunting and the low rumblings and always ignored them. There was no discussion with the skipper. The debate remained in the galley.

'Ach, Lennie kens whit he's doin. If anybody kin find fish he kin.' Max kept the balance.

'Kin he find a price, though?'

'Weel, thur's no point haulin' in at the top o the day. The best two are always first thing and last thing.'

time and tide

Lennie was pretty sure he'd get fish at Stormy. There had been nobody out for days, and the fish would have collected. Whether he spoke aloud to himself or to Michael, Michael stowed away his words. *They just work like a herd a sheep. Yi'v got tae unnerstan' thur behaviour. How they work. Then yi jis' hiv tae be cleverer.* He slowed down the engine, and the whole atmosphere on the boat changed into a different key. The sonar was showing grainy images like mountain ranges on the screen. To the untrained eye it was meaningless, but Lennie could tell exactly what the marks meant. His eyes narrowed, the hum of the engine like a sinister sound accompaniment. He sipped his coffee. Whispering to himself, 'Aye, there's a mark,' and only when he was sure he shouted out the window, 'Aye boys, Ah've got a mark. Wu'll try it here.' At that, the boat wheeled round to begin its encirclement of the fish. Willuck took over Michael's instruction.

'Watch this, they work jist like a flock. Whit wu'll dae is kinna herd them intae wur net wi' thi ropes. Yu'll see hoo it works when wi dae it.'

The first thing to go out was the dahn with a flag on it and two buoys. The two coils of rope stood shaped like small cooling towers in the for'ard section of the boat. Michael was assigned to watch the rope paying out and make sure it went out smoothly.

'Whitivver yi dae, keep yir feet away fae that rope. Thurs no stoppin' it wance its runnan' oot. If it sticks or tangles up we need tae stop the boat, so shout up tae Lennie.'

Michael watched coil after coil whip off the thick column. Jimmack was muttering. 'He should git rope reels. Wid be a lot easier. Too bloody mean, though.'

Willuck pointed to a level in the coils about a foot off the deck. 'Thurs two mile o' rope there. You shout when there's aboot that much left.'

Michael found himself a position below the wheelhouse window where he could monitor the rope winding off. The boat settled into a quiet chug, setting off in a straight line to a point somewhere in the distance that only Lennie was aware of. The other men departed into the galley for more tea and Penguin biscuits. The Twixes had already all been eaten, and the Penguins were second choice. Out front the rope was steadily feeding off the coil and slipping into the sea and under the water. The flag on the dahn was getting ever more distant, waving like an abandoned toy soldier from a parade.

Far away now, the islands appeared like a grey smear, barely a mark above the horizon. It seemed impossible from the world of the boat with the chug of the engine and the purpose of trip, its narrow focus and magnified individuals, to imagine the life and activity ashore. It was as if it had disappeared and had become utterly meaningless. Out at the fishing all that mattered was the sea, the boat, the flick of the rope, the gentle line it made in the water and the ocean covering everything over again. To Michael it was mesmerising.

'That's it. That's it!' Michael shouted. 'Lennie, that's the rope oot.' He ran to the opened wheelhouse window.

'Aye, buey. Fine that.'

The connection of the men was through commands and statements. The engine clunked down a rev and Michael felt the boat slowing.

'Get that owld weemin' oot the galley!' yelled Lennie. But the men had already heard the change in engine pitch and were emerging through the door.

With practised assurance Willuck stepped forward to clip the rope onto the net.

'The wing goes oot first,' he announced. 'Should all go oot even as long as hid's been stowed right.'

The wing of the net followed the rope into the water, then the bag.

'Right?'

'Okay.'

'The bag clear?'

The net was heaved over the side, buoys clattering together, a giant's fistful of plastic orange baubles which then separated out like beads in the water.

'Gotta keep the bag clear o' the mouth.'

'Stick her ower the starboard side.'

With the first rope and then the net out, the first two sides of the herding triangle were formed, and then the second tower of rope completed the third side of the trap.

'That's hoo it works. Simple. Yi lay oot yur rope, then yur net, then yur ithur rope an' its all sittan' on the bottom wi' the fish inside and then yi jis' pull yur ropes in. Aal that dust an' mud that the ropes kicks up maks the fish swim intae the clear bits.'

Willuck was warming to the role of teacher. Nobody ever asked him about how it all worked, and explaining how it operated gave him a new importance. He left Michael to monitor the second rope tower. Max and Jimmack were just bored with it all and repaired back to the galley to get smoke time.

'Och, yiv got tae help the laddie oot. He's no idea aboot hoo this all works,' Willuck protested.

The rope flicked its momentary hoops away into a line making towards the original dahn buoy. And sure enough, they were down at the last three coils by the time the dahn appeared up close.

'Wu'll pick up the dahn and get both ropes onto the winch. Then yi hiv tae mak sure they both come in even. Yi canae let wan git tighter than the ither, that means wan side o' the net's higher than th' ither an then the fish kin get oot.'

Lennie poked his head out the window, checking the ropes. Jimmack was leaning over the side with a boathook to pick up the dahn. With one dextrous move he had the buoy up on deck unhooked and the tail wound round the winch. He conserved his energy only for the parts of the job where he was needed, and for those parts he knew exactly what was required and what he had to do.

The other rope was already fixed, and now the net waited, flowing behind the boat like a great bride's train under the sea, filled – they hoped – with fish. Lennie kept enough power in the engine to keep the boat still, the winches pulling and the ropes moving steadily in. Under the sea, the triangle softened into a pear shape and then to parallel lines, all the time the fish swimming in together, closer and closer, trying to escape the sawing menace of the ropes. As the trap narrowed and the fish slowed, the net advanced over and under them, with the ropes finally closing tight together.

On deck the miles of rope had to be recoiled, and reformed into their towers. As it spewed back off the winches it was fed into the mechanical coiler that spun around to make perfect circles. In pairs they lifted the rope from the coiler and replaced them back on the deck, ready for the next shot. The deck was gradually replenished with rope, accompanied by the noise of the winch grinding, the coiler squeaking, and the interest of a few expectant seagulls, waiting for what was coming next.

Max was at the stern watching for the bag, and he could see the buoys. 'Fuck, that's the buoys coming up. Thurs no much there.' Sure enough, by the time the ropes were hooked onto the hauler they were all muttering. The net came up thin and light, the haul like a single mandarin orange in a large string shopping bag. There was maybe half a dozen boxes.

'Ach well, it's only the first shot.' But it set the tone. Like any roll of the dice, it was the double sixes that were anticipated before the throw, which now offered only the indifferent three and one. The cod-end lacer from the bottom of the bag was undone, and the haul slithered onto the deck.

'Och, there's a few good haddocks there.' Willuck trying to keep upbeat, Jimmack silent, Max setting to sort the fish that were there. Three boxes of haddocks, some coley and a few flats. Jimmack was gutting and chucking them into baskets.

'Hose them doon, Michael.' Max lit a cigarette, throwing the fish into their allotted baskets with a perfect aim each time. Jimmack stowed the net ready and silently disappeared to the galley, clutching his mug of coffee with fish scales encrusting the palms of his hands.

'Ach, yi jist hiv tae pick away.' Willuck filled the mess-room silence. 'Wu'll git more in the next haul.'

The gambler's optimism, and the pessimist's gloom. Each balanced the trip. Willuck was full of the big hauls they'd had, when they'd gone into Peterhead so low in the water that the boat was like a great bellied whale and they were the talk of the market. 'Yi shoulda seen it, buey! God, that wis a haul an' a half. Eh Jimmack? Mind that wan?' Jimmack glanced over. The big hauls were drops among the tedious pickings and the many small ones.

But Michael did see one. It took a good while, but it explained Willuck's optimism. It was like a pools win, and five weeks into the fishing.

The days began to stretch; the fishing week had set a pattern of sorts. Loading up stores on the Saturday, sitting in the hotel with pregnant Lesley on the Saturday evening, away on Sunday night, fishing until Thursday, landing Fridays and home for Friday nights. It hadn't taken long for the whole process to become routine. Michael accepted his role as the 'boy'. The 'yop' who had to stay outside and watch the ropes while the others sat drinking tea. He didn't mind the separation. He fixed a roll-up and leaned on the wheelhouse below the front windows, balancing himself in the centre of the boat. He could judge exactly the time it took for the rope to pay out, moving round to shout up to Lennie. He did his job right. If he saw a kink developing he banged on the window, waiting to hear the boat slow to a stop while he sorted the ropes.

'Okay noo, Lennie,' and Lennie revved the engine up again. The simple communication and common purpose of the untrammelled rope sealed Michael's worth.

That day, they were waiting at the stern.

'Fuck, buey, there's a heap o scorries.' Willuck had his eyes on the place where the net was due to appear. 'Thur no there fir notheen.' He knew what he was looking for and that was the secret of most things, *aye knowing what to look for*. 'Buey, I think this is ganna be a big een.'

Gannets plummeted into the sea. There was a chatter of frenzied excitement among the birds. 'Yi only hear that soond when thurs a pile o' fish.' The birds' excitement was infectious. Willuck prattled on. Max straightened himself up like an alert rabbit. Willuck had a new commentary to impart to Michael and volunteered the answers before there were any questions. 'See that bubbly kinna way in that water. That's a big een, no doot. The haddocks float up, yi see. Wance the net starts pullin' them up they float up, and they let go o' all the air.'

There was a fizz in the sea like the air from a thousand lemonade bottles.

'No buoys. See thur weel pulled doon in the wattar,' and the bag emerged like a huge balloon of fish. It rose up above the water, six or eight feet, propelled by the force speeding it up to the surface. Then the bag settled down again and began to spread out on the surface of the sea. There it was, a huge moving mass, the net, live with fish. The men got to their places in a flash, everyone knowing the urgency of getting the haul aboard before it started to sink again. Before the quality was damaged, the scales rubbed off. They got the ropes into the block and the machinery whined. The hauler groaned under the strain of the weight, heaving on the first lift.

'Thurs seven or eight lifts there, Ah'm damn sure.' Max was infected.

The net bulged at the stern, canting the whole boat so that the bow rode up, threatening to pull her end-under with the weight. Fish-heads and tails pressed through the mesh. Even Jimmack was moving fast. Max and Willuck were smiling, the big win like a release. Counting the boxes, mentally they were all working out the price and estimating their share. Imagining the cash in the settling up.

'Noo yur seean' sumeen, Michael,' Willuck beamed, his prophesy at last come true.

The bag opened and fish cascaded onto the deck from a height. They were up to their knees in haddock, flapping and jumping, bodies bending, eyes fixed, cold and moist. The boat was a seething mass of slithering fish, filling the sides right up to the gunnels.

'Buey, yi want a photograph o' that!' Willuck shouted, elated.

Lennie came down out of the wheel-house, beaming. 'Shovel them intae the pond, queek,' and the fish were heaved into the fish pond, ready for shovelling into boxes.

'An' wu'll get the next lift aboard.'

The operation went like clockwork. Section by section the net was emptied onto the deck. Filled boxes were stacking up, lift after lift, seven and a half in all, and the full net gradually emptied.

'Wu'll head right in tae Peterhead an' land for the morn's market. Thur's a pile o guttan' there, boys.' Lennie headed back to the wheelhouse, while below the gutting began. From above, the bickering gulls in their hundreds swooped down almost right onto the blades of the knives. Great feathered squabbles erupted around the grey guts hurled over the side. Black-backs dived on the herring gulls. Seaborne battles wheeled off into the sky as screeching crowds descended on one bird forced to drop its pickings to fall into the beak of another. There were more angry pursuits and the bird that could fly the farthest was the only one that kept the prize. Another fist-load of offal flew into the air, the flock diverted, the boldest birds sitting on the deck, catching the guts in the air before they hit the water.

'Bloody scorries,' said Jimmack.

'Thur souls o' deed fishermen, yi ken.' Max slung a haddock to one of the birds sitting on the rail and it swallowed the fish whole, too heavy then to fly. That was as far as any of them ventured into the romantic lore of the fisherman's life.

Michael was slow at the gutting so they put him to the fish-washer. The cleaned, gutted and sorted fish were swung down from above through the hatch in boxes, Smalls, Mediums, Bigs, and there they were put on ice.

'Wan shovel in the bottom o' the box, then the fish an' then the ice,' Max showed him. Newly dead, they shone and glinted. The big ones head to toe, the length of the box, alarmed gaping mouths, shocked expressions all sequinned with sparkling ice. The entrapment had been quick, the killing smart. They were in pristine condition for the market.

'The trawl ruins them. Thur aal squashed and battered. A' the scales rubbed off ...'.

Willuck was an advocate for the old ways. But the drive was to the trawl. Bigger boats and more horsepower and higher value catches.

The hold was filled and the catch safely stowed like a wet treasure.

Everybody aboard was infected with the optimism. Lennie stuck on the boat's autopilot and made an announcement: 'If thur's a good enough boat share wu'll get a telly fur the mess,' and even Jimmack smiled.

landing

They made Peterhead at two in the morning, deck lights on, and the glow of orange sodium from the streets their first view of the Blue Toon. Lennie woke everybody up.

'That's us, boys.'

There was already a queue of boats waiting to land. Slipping into the quayside behind the other black, splintered hulls, scored with rust and rasped from barnacle-sharp stone piers. Big tractor-tyre fenders rubbed and squeaked along the quay, ropes were made fast and work lights blazed out among the shouting.

While the town slept, the night-time harbour was a casino of activity. A man's world of accents and banter and scowling and spitting. Earnest discussions among skippers took place with pointing and laughing, back-slapping and then the landing. Swinging up the heavy, dripping boxes two at a time from the hold, then slithering them over the wet pier into the big open doors onto the market floor. The screaming bright market, ice glinting, fish-tainted water skimming everywhere.

Michael felt the pull on his arms and the weight in his back as he stretched his whole body to slide the boxes in, working his palm into the comfortable curved slot on the end of the box and heaving up the heavy load into position. Eight stone in each, filled to more like ten stone.

'Here, stick a couple o' them on all wur boxes.' Michael was handed the green labels like long raffle tickets that said 'NORTHERN DAWN K366'. As the boxes were loaded, the thin paper identifying the boat's catch soaked onto the ice, ready for the auction.

Third boat in. Third to land. Far enough up the queue that there might still be a good price. Lennie stood with his arms folded across his chest and a grin on his face. Casting a quick eye over the rest of the competition on the market floor, he felt confident, anticipating the pay-off. He was waiting to watch the buyers. Eyeing up the next haul coming in.

Trash, he was saying to himself with a snigger, *Thu'v been at the east side.* The small haddocks, the inferior fish. 'Shit catchers,' he snorted, 'they jis' pile everything into the market for the withdrawl price. No quality. That's whar it's all gaan wrong.'

The two boats ahead of them were no competition either. The *Northern Dawn* had the best fish, no doubt. The boys had already set off to shift the boat up beyond the swing bridge, take on new boxes and ice and then head up to the office to pick up their advance money. There was fifty pounds each waiting in cash in brown self-seal envelopes. The unloaded boats moved out and over to park in front of the Union Bar. Opening its doors at six in the morning for shift workers. The blue and red reminder of the butcher's apron displayed its tired themed colours in the sign above the blanked windows. The crew tramped into the bar, ripping apart their envelopes and shouting out orders. Sinking down pints in seconds, the boat's crew were hot, sweaty and stinking of fish, sinews and muscles taut from the days away.

In the market, Lennie was wandering up and down. The auctioneer came in with his white wellingtons and a clipboard. They were ready to start. The timing of landings or where the best port was to go were all part of the intricate variables of the fishing. Catching the fish was just the first part. Land on the wrong day or in the wrong place and you'd get no price. The Farquars went out on a Friday and fished all weekend so that they could land into the first market on a Monday. That's when the best price was. Too many fish in Peterhead might mean waiting for a second sale. Then it was better to opt for a different port where there were fewer boats. The farther down the line, geographically, you could land, the better the prices, because it was less distance for the fish to be trucked, but then you lost another day steaming back up north. There were no constants. Lennie knew it all. There was luck, intelligence, guessing where the boats were fishing, what they were thinking, outwitting the others, and second-guessing the markets. Listening to the number of boxes landed. The radio helped: *6,000 boxes were landed at Peterhead today. One thousand, five hundred and fifty landed in Fraserburgh this morning …* So did the prices. Megrim, coley, whitefish, monkfish …

'Awfy low on Friday.'

'Aye, the processors hiv whit they need by then.'

Scrabster prices were lowest, being the port furthest north on the mainland. At Clash and Lochinver you had no choice but to take what you were offered. Sometimes a couple of the skippers might take the huff in Scrabster and refuse to land into the market, hire a lorry and consign the whole catch to Aberdeen in search of a fair deal. Off the catch would go, loaded onto artics, the melting ice spilling from the rusty back doors as the cargo lurched down the road to Inverness. In its wake the lorry kicking up spray, blinding the following drivers for miles until a straight in the road let them pass. The skippers just hoping that the gamble would pay off or at least that the grasping buyers might get a shock.

Ah'm no givan' that catch awaye fir nothin'. They can fuckan' lump it and bring thur prices up. Robban' bastards.

the payoff

The auctioneer and his clutch of buyers were moving down the line of stacked boxes in the centre of the market. They eventually paused at Lennie's haul.

'Seine-caught haddock. Twenty-five boxes. Large. We'll start at eighty.' Lennie listened to the price rise, watching the nods and tight mouths of the buyers. It was out of his hands now. Everything was at the mercy of the market price, the vagaries of the amount of fish they needed to process in Hull. The proximity of the Catholic Friday, the number of football supporters a Glasgow chippy anticipated for the Old Firm game … Lennie was willing the price higher, the buyers fixed on how little they could get away with paying. The 'bigs' and the 'mediums' sold well. There was plenty demand, and even the 'smalls' got a good price.

'Fish fingers.'

Lennie was content, the boat's share would be a good big one, and the boys would get a good cut. They could breathe easy – 'At least Ah've no the bank on me back' – and Lennie idly watched the auctioneer progress to the next boat's haul. As he had thought, he saw the price stutter.

'Two pounds?'

'Two pound fifty.'

That'll be withdrawn. He watched as the auctioneer consulted his clipboard. The price refused to make its way up to the minimum value.

'Withdrawn.'

There were no buyers. Too much good stuff in the market. Worth nothing.

'Fuckan' waste,' Lennie whispered to himself as he watched the blue dye slosh over the ninety or so boxes.

'It's jis' shit bit even so, thur's a world starvan' oot there.'

Unfit for human consumption. The withdrawn fish went away for fishmeal or bait. There was more than enough withdrawn fish going for bait already and the skipper who had landed the withdrawn haul had already left for home. Every box in the next haul was withdrawn also; this time the contents were heaved out to the edge of the pier and dumped in the harbour, a deathly film of upturned fish-stomachs swirling among the spilt diesel.

'He's only fishan' fir the withdrawal price anyway. It's no right. Hid's jis' no right.'

'Aye,' agreed Max, who'd slipped out of the pub to catch the prices.

'Whit's the point? Fishan' aal that crap jis' fir an EEC guaranteed minimum, kennan yi can land any old crap an still get the minimum price?'

'Its' no right.'

'Aye mebbe, but hid's the system.'

Lennie's stomach knotted with the frustration. He looked at the tally. They would be heading back home with fifteen thousand pounds.

'Ah'll better send the lad up tae Dixon's fir that telly. The boys shud be happy this time anyway.'

He worked out the boat's expenses, diesel, harbour dues, ice, stores. Then there was half to the boat and half to the crew. With the cash rolled up in his back pocket he headed to the Union Bar to settle up. Pushing through the ochre double doors, one side still with its original engraved glass and the other long ago substituted by a frosted pane, he was met with thick cigarette smoke and the clatter of a packed pub, filled with loud talk and laughing.

The crew were already buying nips to accompany the pints. Each lot of fifty pound notes circling round the bar and into the publican's till to sit. It was seven thirty in the morning. They'd be well on by ten o'clock.

'Wu'll head off at eleven, boys. Michael, you can tak a taxi up tae Dixon's when it opens and get us a telly.' There was shouting then, and cheering, with Jimmack getting enough of a fix to see him through the trip home. Lennie sat down on a burst leather seat in the corner of the bar and began the 'office' work, peeling off the twentys into piles. The crew waited like well-trained dogs to reach out their hands and receive the settlement. Each with the nonchalance of a card sharp, they secreted the wad into a top pocket or a back pocket, or rolled up the loose notes into a comfortable bolt for a front pocket. Wherever they stashed the pay they could feel its reassuring presence as it nudged against their own flesh.

Everyone was Lennie's best friend.

home trip

Dixon's, like suddenly being transported into the sci-fi world of the *Starship Enterprise*, was filled with flickering screens, and permeated with the smell of warming plastic and electricity. A dozen TVs displayed the BBC test-card. The shelves were filled with instant cameras and stereo record players, and huge speakers stood on the floor along with stacking hi-fi systems. Max had jumped in the taxi too, like an excited boy, to be part of the buying adventure. As he and Michael shambled towards the humming TV display, the suited assistant was at their side instantly. Everything about them yelled 'fisherman', which in turn meant money, big spending, cash and commission.

'Can I help you gentlemen?'

There was nothing that couldn't be bought and taken home on the boat. Everything from the conveyer belt of *The Generation Game* and more. Washing machines, spin dryers, cookers, the latest in hi-fi and even a piano from Bruce Millar's in Aberdeen.

'Aye, wur lukkan' fir a telly,' said Michael with unusual command.

'It's fir the boat, like,' added in Max.

'It'll be a portable then you'll be after.' The assistant, like a human of a slightly different species from the fishermen, was gliding towards the end of the

TV section, Spock-like. 'Be colour, is it?'

Michael stopped in front of a black-and-white Sony TV encased in white plastic.

'Oh aye, colour,' Max was saying.

'That'll be a bit dearer then.'

The colour TVs were resplendent, luxurious, fantastic panoplies of movement, detail and clarity. It seemed that they embodied the kind of magic that could truly transform your life. Like entering the fantasy world of ice-lolly wrappers. Even the news readers and the colours of the weather maps were intoxicating. Max weighed up the pros and cons of the different makes. Michael was dumbfounded by the sheer volume of stuff in the shop. The prices came to hundreds of pounds, even thousands. He felt in his pocket the notes that could buy him anything he wanted and his eyes were drawn to the stereo systems. *Bush, Garrard, Wharfdale.* Max had settled on a colour TV.

'Eh, Michael. This een'll dae. Whidya think?'

Lennie had left no budget limit. The instructions were just to go and get one.

'Yeah, that looks good.'

The assistant went off to get one boxed up in the stockroom.

'What aboot aerials an' that?'

'Oh aye. Wu'll better get wan.'

The aerial and booster were set on top of the box.

'Anything else, gentlemen?'

He'd seen Michael lingering over the hi-fis.

'No. No the day,' added Michael, feeling the intoxication of a gambler who might just lose all his cash at a stroke. They carted out the boxes to the taxi waiting in the street with the engine running.

'Anywhere else, boys?'

'No, driver. Jis' tak iss back tae the harbour.'

'Hold on,' said Michael.

Lesley had ordered a wedding dress from a catalogue. 'Ah'm supposed tae get a suit.'

'A suit then? Aye aye! Come on up tae Burton's and wu'll get yi kitted oot.

'Tak us roon' tae Burton's first, driver,' Max instructed. So the taxi made a U-turn on the cobbles and headed up the street to stop outside the men's outfitters.

'This man needs a suit.'

'Wedding or funeral?' asked the driver.

'Is there a differ?' and they all laughed.

The Burton's salesman saw the money coming, not the fish-soaked working clothes, and studiously feted them with 'Sir' this and 'Sir' that. Michael didn't want to try anything on.

'This'll be fine.' He clutched a coat hanger from the first rail he saw.

'But you'll have to try the suit, Sir, for length and fit.'

Eventually he was persuaded, the shiny lining sliding over his arm, then fastening the glossy black buttons with his calloused fingers.

In the mirror he cursorily viewed his face with his matted black hair, and his neck protruding from the top of a tightly buttoned waistcoat as if he were a well-stuffed if grubby puppet.

'Come on oot, buey, and let iss view yi in yir glad rags.' Max waited by the polished counter, the assistant straightening coat hangers in feigned activity.

'No, this een ill do. Hid's fine,' he mumbled from the dressing room. At least, he was thinking, he would never have to be in the shop again, so no one could report on his embarrassment. Only Max, and that would just have to be endured. Removing the suit, he folded it over the chair.

In this Men's Outfitters' dressing room Michael felt truly naked, his white legs covered in dark hairs, thickening up to his crotch. Then his white underpants grubby from days on the boat. No one changed clothes at sea. Everyone worked, ate, slept, hauled and gutted in the same gear. Their clothing became like a skin and it felt strange to peel it off to expose the under layer. Michael hurried to pull on his working jeans, which had become comfortingly soft and shaped to the muscles in his legs. The Old Holburn tin clanked, hitting the floor as it fell from his pocket. It too had worn an outline in his back pouch, delineating the place it always sat. When Michael pulled back the grey, shimmering curtain the assistant was waiting to confer on the fitting.

'Are you absolutely sure, Sir, that this is the suit you would like? We have a line over here that come with a matching shirt and tie.'

But Michael was already shaking his head. 'This wan's fine.' The ordeal of having to remove his protective layer, and make decisions over something as strange and alien as a suit was overwhelming.

'No. Ah'll tak this een.' He just wanted to be out of the shop, hurrying the assistant to let him pay as fast as possible. 'Hoo much?'

'Twenty-five pounds.'

'Christ! Helluva price fir a suit,' Max muttered.

Michael was peeling the twenty-pound notes off his wad of cash. The assistant noted that there must be near a thousand in his hand.

'Thank you, Sir, is there anything else, Sir, tie? A special occasion, is it?'

But Michael didn't reply, only shook his head, waiting for the fifteen pounds change as the sleek carrier bag with plastic handles crossed the counter towards him.

'Come on, let's go.' They departed in the taxi, which took them along the harbour front, right to the side of the boat, then slamming the door Max pushed a five pound note into the driver's hand.

'Keep the change, pal.' The TV and the suit were loaded onto the deck. Max was good with electrics, so he set to climbing up the mast to fix the aerial, running a wire down into the mess.

'Right, that should do it,' he yelled from above, clinging onto the mast with one hand. Soon, with a bit of tweaking and fiddling, a grainy picture of *Playschool* was beamed onto the TV wedged up between two shelves in the mess. The crew applauded.

'Yess. TV!'

Jimmack went straight to his bunk, and after the morning's booze they were all soon asleep, slumped in the mess, the reception having gone from the new TV by the time they sailed into the Moray Firth.

this man and this woman

Lesley planned the wedding. The relatives from Kirkwall got sent invitations with silver writing on them. 'Whit aboot yur femlie?' Michael shuffled half-a-dozen white cards and envelopes in his hands, unsure what to do. 'Och, jis' you give me the list then an Ah'll write them.' Lesley whisked them back from him.

Michael had no idea of his brothers' addresses, nor his sister's. In the end they enclosed their invitations in the same envelope as his mother's, with a handwritten note from Lesley asking that they be forwarded. 'Yi hiv tae invite yur femlie.'

The rest was easy. The whole island would come. There was no hierarchy of friends. It was a small enough place that feuds could be masked, only to ferment slowly beneath the surface, and everyone knew their behaviour had to be civil, at the very least, in public. The boat's crew were invited, of course, and Lennie.

Lesley, the pregnancy, the marriage and his life was a machine that had taken off, with Michael somehow strapped onto it. He went to the hotel out of the road where he could pick up with Jimmack or Lennie or whoever was there. It was like another home and the crew felt like his real family. The swirly carpet of green and red, the bar stools and the coal-effect electric fire. Getting sat down there with his feet comfortably on the foot rest and only stepping down to go to the fag machine or for a piss, he stayed there till last orders.

Willuck was to be best man, although he was forty-five, with the duty of patrolling Michael through the various nuptial duties. He faffed around Michael like an old hen but took his duties seriously, propelling Michael through his vodka-fuelled stag night and then into the grey dawn of his wedding day. From then on, the events unfolded like a blotchy hallucination of disjointed, strobe-filled actions.

'Christ, buey, yi'll hiv tae hiv a shave. Yi kinna go gettan' merrit lik that.' Willuck propped him up and sloshed cold water on his face, then steered him on a course to the church. There Michael appeared in body, at least, as half of the catalyst for the grunting incantations spoken over him and Lesley by the minister.

Everyone looked on in their party frocks, the men with cheeks scoured pink by razors and smarting with cheap after-shave, the women with forced lacquered curls. To follow there was more vodka and whisky and then the reception in the hall. Malcolm made a halting speech. Trestle tables were grandly laid out with white linen. Paper chains decked the walls. 'Good luck' was cut from crêpe paper and plastered across the stage with 'Michael and Lesley' scribed in twirly writing inside a heart. The design theme was dictated by the length of a roll of paper and the garish colours available in the shop.

Harry was there with Agnes, well drunk before the celebration started, and stood bleary at the new bar-hatch which had been negotiated with the kirk for 'community events'. Agnes, knowing no one, stood unsure of her role, or her place, in a borrowed suit from her sister. The others had RSVPed to decline. Fleetingly, the receipt of a wedding invitation provoked a slight thrill at the exotic nature of wedding etiquette.

Oh no, the mither jis' canna wear the same colour as the bride ... Agnes suddenly worried that she would do something terribly wrong.

RSVP means Répondez s'il vous plaît.

What is that anyway? Is it French?

So Lesley and Michael were duly married.

cut adrift

Agnes, Harry and the married couple all boarded the next steamer out of Selsay the following day, the happy couple about to start their journey for a honeymoon at Mackay's hotel in Wick. Lesley was in her 'going away' clothes but Michael remained in the rumpled suit. He had spent the first nuptial night, in a double room specially booked in the hotel, lying comatose atop the nylon counterpane.

'So ee got a bun in ee oven,' went Harry. 'Weel Ah nivver thocht ee hid it in ee. There ee go.' Michael said nothing, still reeling and vibrating with the accumulated booze, his eyelids half shut, dustbin lids crashing together in his head.

They were following the script of some strange soap opera that no one was terribly sure of. Lesley was the only one who had a definite plan. They were to stay the night before the boat to Scrabster in the morning. Agnes put new sheets on the bed.

'Wu'll hiv tae let them hae the double. Well yi ken hid's a daughter-in-law wi' hiv noo.' Harry grunted and went out to the pub.

Lesley escorted Michael upstairs early. 'Weel, thur's a boat tae catch in the morning.'

Agnes sat up waiting for Harry, making a bed on the sofa, but Harry collapsed onto the armchair when he landed up out of the pub and was still noisily asleep there the next morning.

'That's them off, Harry.' Agnes moved his arm. 'Thu'r awaye in a meenit.' But he still didn't wake.

Michael and Lesley were up early, the single suitcase symbolising their union sitting on the kitchen floor.

'Och, he's soond asleep.'

'Wu'll hiv tae go. Wu'v wur tickets tae buy yet.'

'Hold on a minute.' Agnes reached into a tea tin above the fireplace, taking out a crisp ten pound note.

'Tak that, Michael son, towards yur holiday.'

Lesley fidgeted, zipping up her coat over her generous stomach. Michael took the money. *I cannae offend her.* Agnes had no idea of the money he spent, the Klondyke there was in Aberdeen and Peterhead. How ten pounds was nothing over the bar in a night's drinking. *Oh fuck …*

'Noo you head off an' git yur tickets an I'll come doon the pier and give yi a proper good bye. Mind Ah'm comin noo.' Agnes cleared the dishes away.

'That's them gone, Harry.'

But Harry didn't stir. She left a mug of tea beside him and headed out. On her way she passed the doctor's wife. 'Ah'll jist be along, Ah'm seein' Michael an' Lesley awaye on the boat …'

It was almost as if she had some status. An event had occurred in her life. A married son. A community achievement. 'Yes, gan tae Weeck on thur honeymoon,' she told the woman in the baker's with unusual candour. But when Agnes got to the pier the new couple were nowhere to be seen. Michael had already gone up the gangplank and got talking with the purser, who was Willuck's brother.

The suitcase was stowed in the luggage rack. Lesley had decided she should get her head down and had gone in search of a long seat to stretch out on. 'An' don't you get stuck in the bar,' she threatened her new husband.

'Whar hiv they geen? They said they wid say good bye.' Agnes strained to look. *Whar hiv they geen?* Agnes had her apron on under her coat, waving to the boat as the ropes were thrown off, standing for those few seconds when any normal sense of the world was cut adrift and no one was sure whether it was the boat moving or the pier moving. She carried on gazing up as the bow receded into the harbour, ready to make its reversed turn and line up past the navigation buoys. *Maybe thur on the starboard side?*

a real artist

Henry Sinclair had the kind of name that suggested a northern connection. He intrigued Seadhna because of his stature. He had bad skin, but that became secondary and almost attractive too. He stood well, tall and aloof, holding his head high although his physique was slight. His nostrils flared with all the appearance of confidence and breeding. There was a Nordic blondness to his hair, but there the similarity stopped. Henry didn't do the kind of things that ordinary people did, like go to a barber's; he cut his hair himself. The mane at the nape of his neck grew long and as he walked he tossed the locks off his face, looking straight ahead over high cheekbones. His eyes were a shrill sea-blue.

He appeared to be everything she was not. After that first evening at Lewis's, she saw him as a key that would unlock all the mysteries that puzzled her. The mysteries of the city, of books, other cultures and art. She was ready to head off the end of the big dipper into Henry's world, cocooned by whisky, and in the Edinburgh cold they became a couple.

Without alcohol Henry was crippled with shyness. He could barely talk to her. Sitting across from her at the stripped-pine kitchen table in the Bruntsfield flat his parents had bought, he sipped black coffee from a Japanese bowl. He never ate in the mornings. It was as if to be witnessed doing something so mundane diluted his aura. He pulled his flared Levi jeans onto his bare skin, and his white shirt over his naked, hairless chest. It was as if the warming undergarments of ordinary people lessened him. He did not subscribe to the merry-go-round fashions of the other students, only occasionally donning a 1940s vintage flying jacket. It was as if he disdained such frippery, having already emerged with all the attributes of a fully fledged serious artist.

He likened her to Nora Joyce when he was drunk enough to talk to her, imagining her to be imbued with a similar type of earthy country-ness.

'My brown-arsed fuck-bird,' he called her, using Joycean borrowed words. Seadhna allowed his fantasy because that small country difference gave her a kind of rarity among the others.

From their perspectives of sexual segregation and fee-paying enclosures, the 'yah' boys and girls struggled to relate to the opposite sex of their own kind. They laughed, talked loudly, swaggering in groups, and smoked king-size cigarettes. But like the lords and ladies of the big houses, they went looking for tenderness and comfort among the common kids. And so it was with Seadhna and Henry, drawn by their polarisation, their complete ignorance of each other's worlds, and the unreal fantasies they could weave around each other. In the mornings they walked through the college gates together then separated off to their different studios.

In Henry's final-year studio, Seadhna negotiated the makeshift booths, looking for his space by the sink in the corner, a coveted spot. His stack of tall monolithic, canvasses stood raked against the wall but he was nowhere to be seen. Seadhna looked around at the carefully arranged brushes. She noted the absence of personal clues. No cuttings of inspirational photos or mishmash of messy clutter. Three library books sat on the table. Pollock, Jasper Johns, Rothko. She knew she was prying. Henry had been priming a canvas. Searching for the ultimate neutral, looking for earth brown, the colour of all colours, the unification of opposites.

He had been mixing Cerulean Blue and Cadmium Orange together into a soup of gravy-like mud. The huge canvas he was about to work on was smooth as silk and no texture survived from the weave beneath. He had applied layer after layer of creamy gesso in order to eradicate the past, transforming the structure into something self-standing with an obscured and hidden history.

'Ah ha, what brings you here?'

Seadhna jumped. 'Model's break – thought I'd come and see what you were doing.'

She suddenly felt awkward in his space.

'What I'm doing,' he drawled, 'is I'm making marks.'

She could not quite tell if he was irritated.

'Fascinating, isn't it?'

She always had to work hard to guess the right answers for Henry. Something in him made her feel that her responses were tallied up and scored in his head in columns of correct or incorrect.

'Tell me about it. I want to know.'

But Henry was not one for explanations. He practised and layered his enigmatic persona, casually allowing the cover of a Beckett play to show from inside his coat pocket. In classes he stood silent in front of the model, aware that his drawing was superior to everyone else's. Always a 4B pencil on silky Leonardo paper. It took him over an hour to form the contour from the heel to the base of the backbone, but the quality of line was exquisite. It already suggested the rest of the pose, the distribution of muscle and weight, the softness of fat or proximity of bone, and there was an alchemy present that showed many more things than those that could merely be seen. He rarely finished a drawing, snorting disdainfully that he had to turn out a quota to keep the college happy.

Seadhna was mesmerised. His secrecy worked, his inaccessibility tantalised her. The challenge to understand the convolutions of his thinking intrigued her. The literal painting of Standing Stones that stood on her easel suddenly seemed crass and simple, even with its flash of Kitaj orange. It dawned on her that there was a whole world of unwritten rules that bent and broke, then reformed, and she was unsure whether she had any right to venture into the maze of that world. But that was the world Lewis and Henry were part of, and like Alice she had to see what there was beyond the locked door.

Seadhna took to buying the glossy Leonardo paper too, hoping some of Henry's magic might rub off. Charcoal seemed inferior, the material of peasants, Van Gogh and Degas. But slow deliberate pencil work wasn't her forte either. She spent too long, overworked her drawings. They became flat and lifeless.

In their nightly rendezvous in the pubs of Rose Street, Seadhna and Henry met with Lewis after he closed up his gallery for the evening. In the Abbotsford she listened wide-eared as Henry and he talked. They whirled names into the discussions. Palladio, Sufi, Ellman, Balthus … They were in tune with all that they talked about. Swilling whisky, she kept her ignorance well wrapped up in her silence. Like someone in a foreign country trying hard to grasp a new language, she kept her senses super-alert, waiting to connect a word, a reference or a phrase. She felt included when Henry tapped his Gauloises packet on the bar table and shook out two cigarettes. Lighting hers for her and then returning his gaze to Lewis.

When they talked about James Joyce, she went away and read *Ulysses*. Then everything shifted, and they were talking about Palladian villas. She was always behind, and felt she could never keep up, never feel on an equal footing. The things she had learnt and had valued were never rated by Lewis and Henry. They had never heard of *Sunset Song*, so by that token it was immediately devalued. The only Scottish writer they acknowledged was MacDiarmid, so in Rose Street they tumbled from pub to pub, tripping over his tatty mysoginist ghost among the flashing one-armed bandits. Still Seadhna thought that if she listened and learned quickly enough, eventually she would understand it all. Lewis poured whisky into Henry, who loosened and became puppy-like, smiling, with the pock-marked tension easing from the corners of his mouth. His eyes opened wider to swim towards Lewis's.

'My apprentice,' guffawed Lewis, waxing over the quality of whiskies. 'Let's try a Lagavulin.'

Seadhna became edgy with the excess of drink, as night after night the five o'clock sessions stretched until closing time with nothing but cheese and onion crisps for food. But she never dared suggest they should leave early. She knew it was a waiting game and that it would only end when Lewis stepped off Hanover Street into a taxi and the emphasis shifted. The time when Lewis's spell on Henry would break and he would turn his attention to her. Lewis always headed off to a flat somewhere in the north of the city to a woman he never brought out with him. Then Henry turned drunkenly to Seadhna, like a lost sister. Using second-hand words from the lives of other artists and writers, Henry spoke in contrived tongues. He never said that he loved her. Those were the words of mortals.

On a cold Princes Street after all the pubs had shut, Seadhna eased her hand under his heavy coat and inside the waist of his jeans to feel the warmth of his buttocks. Henry lurched unsteadily into her, his eyelids drooping. Into the night they went, the long walk up over the Mound shocked her into sobriety,

Henry walking trance-like. He never wore underpants.

something to say

Inside the college the time arrived to make decisions. Decisions about the kind of artist you might be. Whether it was all about the mind or the concrete, as Lewis had asked back in the school art room. Money or ideas. Artifice or truth. Mere sleight of hand or full-blown intellectual deceit. In Edinburgh, the art world was like a huge supermarket. You had to browse though it and find a brand to adopt or else blindfolded just stick a pin in a higgledy-piggledy lucky dip of styles, eras and movements, then just go for it. Do it and be it. There appeared to be no genuine requirement for connection; you could invent a history and make up a justification. All along she had wanted away from the tight, closed parochial world of the islands where everything was cemented into the permanence of stone and now it seemed to her that what was the *real* world was within reach.

Seadhna worked hard to pare out all the things that pulled her back to her old world.

Still the imagery of the place invaded her being and she had to purge it from herself. The standing stones, the pudding-bowl hills and the patchwork harvest fields would not leave her psyche. The greens and the ochres, the toytown unreal blues. They were like illustrations in children's stories. Too literal, too realist, too obvious and too simple. *Too much colour.* It was so clear to her now that art was about complexities; the kind of art that said important things could not be easily understood. Cleverness and intellect were all about making things mysterious and difficult, with hidden clues and obscure references. Figurative painting had no intellect and nowhere to go. Lewis and Henry were right. It all ended with Duchamp and that was fifty years ago at least …

Down in the college basement where the priming room was, Seadhna took the canvas that displayed the Stones. She laid her painting on the long trestle table in the paint-spattered workshop where the technician repaired the careless mortise and tenon joints of the students. She charged her brush with the milky white primer, plunging it into the tin. It creamed onto the painting, obliterating her old art, and liberated her into Lewis and Henry's world. Inside she felt a glow of pride at how pleased they would be. *Now that's interesting*, they would say. The paint buried her past and her old figurative imagery.

She went to Greyfriars Market and bought a pack of henna. Black henna, mixing the green paste up in a bowl and plastering it onto her long red Pre-Raphaelite locks. She piled the cowpat of hair up on top of her head and secured it inside a polythene bag, insulated by a torn towel, and the strange mixture steamed quietly and fragrantly. After a good two hours, when the cake had all but dried on her scalp, she washed away the gritty mud pie into the bath. Gallons of black swilled down the plughole like the blood of an alien, getting weaker and fainter until it was almost all gone. Seadhna eyed her new self in the mirror and felt a twinge of excitement. She mused on dark red lipstick and something to bring out the hollows in her cheeks. Next, away went the long velvet skirt that she had sewed herself and instead she grabbed anything that was strange out of the PDSA shop. All the while she was deliberating what kind of artist she should turn herself into. *Kathe Kollwitz? No, too expressionist …*

She bought beeswax from a furniture shop, and white candles, and took them into her studio to crush together and melt in an old black pot. The pure white canvas stood tempting her, propped against the wall. She could smell the honey, the thick gold tallow from the pot of melting wax. *I'm going to be Eva Hesse … tragic and interesting with long black hair …*

There was no right or wrong, no design no plan. It was easy, too easy almost. She dribbled the wax from the hot pot onto the pristine canvas and let it run where it wanted. It skewed down the centre then dribbled to the side, solidifying before it reached the corner of the stretcher. She repeated the process, letting the wax find its own way, letting it stutter and drip then run fast on the incline or slowly as it cooled. She stood back and looked at it, then wondered about red. *Would that be too corny, too clichéd? Too much like blood?*

In front of the mirror she took a black eye pencil and drew round the outline of her lips, then filled the shape in with dark red. Sucking in her cheeks she created hollows with the plum lipstick. She studied her profile and felt the decisiveness of it, the newness, the eradication of the old Seadhna. Melissa had asked her to go to a meeting. She thought she'd give it a go. Melissa had great style despite the headmistressy voice.

Meanwhile, Cammy strapped himself into bondage gear, sewing his bone-thin legs into trousers, and headed off to hear the Sex Pistols in Glasgow. 'Ah'm fucked waye this arty-farty shite. Ah dinnae want tae be a famous fuckin' artist. Ah'm chaingin' tae fashion.'

At the end of second year, Seadhna opted for Fine Art. After all – she believed she had something to *say* and in her head she had already made the break complete. A cheese and wine party was held for students to meet their new lecturers.

'So it's the northern islands you come from Seadhna … and what do you think about the seal cull? It all seems very bloody, these defenceless little animals getting bludgeoned to death by barbarous islanders.' Her new lecturer invited her agreement. The seal cull was never an issue of talk at home. There were some English folk who wrote letters to the paper and there had been a handful of protesters. But the consensus view from home was that people ate sheep, killed rabbits, and shot rats on the shore, and seals were no different. She hadn't realised that the seals were such big news down in the city. At home it was one of the things that had always been. Anyone with serious political concerns was more worried about nuclear power, like her father who had been collecting signatures for the petition against Dounreay Expansion and in all his letters to her had never even mentioned the seals.

'Well, I haven't thought that much about it, to be honest,' Seadhna replied, as the lecturer slowly looked her up and down.

'Really! I thought that coming from up there you'd be totally up in arms about the whole thing. I mean. All that cruelty.'

At that point, Seadhna recalled a night she had spent sitting in a bar watching the TV with the sound off. Waiting for Henry, she knew it would be a long sit, going through the indignation and then the anger of him not turning up. Feeling embarrassed, then getting another drink and after another wait buying a packet of ten Regal to smoke. Time passing interminably slowly as she tried to appear engrossed in deciphering the plot of *Coronation Street* from the visuals only. Then came the Scottish News and there on the screen were the Islands. She'd recognise that landscape anywhere. It was as particular and personal as a signature. A serious, bearded face gesticulated and pointed throughout the interview. The camera panned over a black Skerry, showing seals swimming. There was a reporter and a suited man, and then some shots of what looked like a burned-out caravan. It was another world, a million lifetimes away, so she made no attempt to ask the barman to turn the sound up.

'Yes, all a bit primitive.'

The indolent drawing lecturer continued toying with her innocence, knowing how green these non-city girls were. Seadhna, always suspicious that she was being led into a trap, searched for a redeeming counter. 'I've been more concerned with issues of nuclear power, really.' It was untrue. It was just something to say to fill the void.

drifting

By the time of Michael and Lesley's shotgun honeymoon in Wick, Shirley McLeay had already moved on from Mackay's to a head housekeeper's job at the Station Hotel in Inverness. Later she took a job at the Lochinver Hotel for a season, but Inver was too remote, full of toffs on the one hand and drunk fishermen on the other. By that time she had long ago determined to keep well away from the hotel bars, so as she headed to her bed after shutting up the dining room she sniffed disapprovingly at the raucous noise coming from the drunkards.

The *Northern Dawn* had landed at Inver, and the crew were well settled into the bar. Unaware, brother and sister shadowed each other, never connecting in the same place. None of the crew could remember leaving the bar or getting back to the boat, although Lennie must have been sober. Michael and the rest of the men lurched away oblivious from the whooping Inver gentry to stagger and fall onto the deck of the *Northern Dawn*. Jimmack nearly broke a leg as he landed astride the hold, buckling and bending, his rum-soft limbs anaesthetised to pain.

The boat must have left the harbour around one in the morning. They all fell asleep fully clothed in their bunks with the grinding of the engine and no rhythm to the motion of the sea. Michael woke and felt the ache in his head and the insistence in his bladder about the same time. Still drunk, and trying to evade the inevitable whisky seizure, that metal vice tightening like a torture implement round his skull, he hauled himself up the vertical ladder on deck for a piss.

The sea was grey out to the west, with a pre-dawn shuttering just picking out land masses and planets on the horizon. They had all celebrated, drinking until well after closing time to recoup on the lost days locked away together at sea. It was Michael's nineteenth birthday, standing on the deck, urine trickling over the side of the boat, and back north in Selsay there was Lesley waiting, sullen, with a list of failings to berate him with. The bairn and she were the things that shackled him and had started pulling him under.

Married life took place in the small powder-blue spare bedroom of her parents' house where Lesley quietly seethed at him. Michael had no responses. The intricacies and shifting rules of the liaison he found himself in, he did not pretend to understand. All Michael could do was quietly let himself out through the glass front door of the dank, ill-fitting extension while she was busy out the back, and escape away in the car to the hotel.

They could not row openly in her parents' house, so dissatisfaction was conveyed in whispers and sullen looks. By the time she heard the car engine it would be too late and he would be on his way, deliberately not looking back.

The hotel and the whisky with the boys helped numb him through the days at home, and when Sunday came round again they'd be away to sea. She was always needling at him. 'Kin yi no git a shore job? Thur wantan' a driver fir the shop van.' Lesley intercepted him at the back of the house out of earshot of her parents. 'Whit d'yi think yur playin' it? Yur no gan doon that hotel again.'

She would say her piece. Michael would make no commitment either way and then slip off regardless. Lesley tried to control his movements, demanding all the money from the trip, thinking that would keep him home behind the stifling net windows. Lennie, however, could always be relied upon to give him a loan against the next wage packet, so Lesley was unable to starve him of money for the pub.

'For Christ's sake …' he would begin, then run out of words, not really knowing what it was he would say, or what it was that was all so wrong about everything. Lesley couldn't let go of an argument. She had a whole archive of grievances stored up which could be dipped into and whipped into life for any misdemeanour of Michael's that required added substance.

Then came a day when Michael shocked himself. His head was splitting and Lesley was nipping at every part of his being. The anger fired itself up inside him and he found himself with his hands up around her neck, her eyes staring out at him with animal terror. It was seconds only, but he felt the danger of his strength, how he could smash her, how little power she really had. He silently withstood her tirade, and then inside his head he started to smile cruelly at the picture of her, thinking she was just like an angry crab, its eyes on stalks filled with twitching red anger. The tolerance inside him was cracking and something else was building. Something he knew was ugly

The jagged harling of the toilet extension gouged Lesley's skull, as her head thumped on the wall. He let her go, still feeling the possessed surge of rage that was in him. 'Jis' leave it, wull ya,' and he strode off cursing. After that, the ability to feel such undiluted cruelty towards her ended it. He knew his hate could only build.

Lesley rattled into the house, shocked and fearful. She sat on the bed in the stinging silence, listening to see if her mother had heard anything. She could hear all her movements in the kitchen, the heavy steps on the sagging floor in the old part of the house. Then she went into the bathroom to dab the blood from her bleeding head with damp toilet paper.

It's no use, this being merrit. The thoughts formed at the back of Michael's skull. *It's no fair on her. She disna deserve it. Shu'll be fine wi' the bairn. She his it tae keep her occupied ...* The baby, born while Michael was at sea and already distanced from him by the time he got home, was always spirited away like something Michael might break or dirty. Lesley absorbed herself in the child, building up a new fortress that excluded him.

On one of the trips home, when they put into Wick to pick up a net from Duncan's, Michael just stayed behind. He didn't rejoin the home leg. 'Ah'm ganna hiv a try on a trawler fir a spell.' And Lennie nodded. 'Okay, buey. Weel, hid's up tae yirsel. Wu'll be happy tae tak yi back though, if yi decide yi want back at the seine. Though hid's aboot finished, if yi ask me.'

Michael watched the *Northern Dawn* sail from the Harbour Café and rolled a cigarette. He savoured the moment, enjoying the smooth gentle simplicity of the cigarette paper against his upper lip, nursing it along and playing it over the sensitive skin. Then he used just enough saliva to moisten the gummed edge and not make an ugly tube, nipping off the strands of Old Holborn. There came then a mental severance, and he sighed.

The trawlers, however, were full; everyone was asking for a berth. He'd have to wait his turn. Michael couldn't go back to Selsay and Lesley now. Awkward messages intercut with demands for money, or for him to return right away, or never dare show his face, were conveyed via Willuck. There was nothing for it but return to his mother's.

legitimate greed

After the cull, Harry went AWOL. He got addled with the drink. Seeing visions and pin-balling away from his old softer self. He did a spell at the docks in Aberdeen, waiting in the Crown between ships. Slapping the backs of cattle on and off the North boats one day, then grain flowing from the grab into the hold another. Fertiliser bags swinging high above the dockers' heads in a job it was easy to do drunk. Harry boozing with the mate of a coaster in the bar, then seeing Sidney from Selsay somewhere through the blur and waking up out over the North Sea, with nothing for it but to do the trip and see what happened next. Next thing was Harry getting the DTs in Rotterdam and lying sweating in his bunk, unable to go ashore, no passport and too ill. That was him, propelled away by alien forces. The lives he'd had before, getting more and more distant, less easy to retrieve.

There wasn't ever a parting, there just elapsed such a length of time that eventually it seemed as if Agnes had always been on her own. The family were fragmenting and Harry couldn't write. Postcards were too flippant anyway. Geordie never left Harbour Terrace and still worked in the butchers. Malky, the youngest, had joined the TA and got into the regular army, and Jake was labouring up in Shetland, fourteen-hour days and seven-day weeks with no time off, amassing a temporary fortune in the oil.

So Michael returned home to sleep in the lino-covered bedroom that he'd shared with Jake and Geordie as a boy. Each morning the contact with the cold floor came as a reminder of all the days past when he got up in that house. His bare feet on the lino, the coldness of the metal studs of his jeans against his skin as he pulled them on. In the dark, there were the same sounds as there always were of his mother raking out the fireplace down stairs, the padding noises of her in the kitchen and the pulley, heavy with washing, above the deep Belfast sink, squeaking through blocks at the ceiling.

Then, out of the blue, Shirley returned with Douglas. They arrived together on the new ro-ro, driving off in a yellow Austin Maxi and went straight to the hotel.

'Company car,' said Douglas.

They all sat round the table, too large for the small kitchen at Harbour Terrace.

'I do near two thousand miles a week,' informed Douglas, whom she introduced as her fiancée and a rep for Tennent's, the brewery that was buying up pubs all over Scotland to remodel into their unified corporate image.

Shirley and Douglas had the idea Agnes should buy her council house. The 'right to buy' was all the rage. Shirley had thought it out and decided to sit her mother down in the modest front room with the coloured glass budgies on the fireplace, and explain why it would be so good. She knew it was only a case of leading her mother through it all. She just needed her to sign the forms, then Shirley would pay the mortgage payments through a standing order. They had to set up a bank account for her, of course. Douglas was the one who was good at figures and had assured them it was all a dead cert. He twitched and fiddled, looking round all the time for opportunities, seeing potential here, there and everywhere and things that were 'just ripe for development'.

'You cannae miss oot. It's pure stupit no tae buy. An' wi' a' that discount yir muthir will hiv! Hoo lang's she bin a tenant?' Nearly twenty years added up to a considerable discount. 'I mean the house is already worth five times that! And they're gonna go up. The second-home market's very buoyant. And there's the possibility you could rent, you know.'

'Michael, you an' Geordie'll need to get yourself on the council list. You can stay on but you'll have to pay a rent. After all, it's us that's taking out the risk.' Shirley flashed around, sorting out the details.

'It'll be for the best, mam. Doug and I will buy it, but your name will be on everything. Then you just have to will it to us. You won't have any rent to pay after that.' Agnes was taken to make a will in which she would pass the house to Shirley.... She had never been upstairs in the solicitor's office with its heavy, brown leather chairs and shelves rammed with files and papers. In slow script she signed her name, 'Agnes Jean Bixter McLeay', then looked up to Shirley for approval.

With the house duly purchased, Agnes no longer walked the weekly route to the council rent office with her money in notes in an envelope. She had become one of the property-owning masses. *Aye ... yi'd be a fool no tae buy ...* And others said *Weel Ah'm no buyin' even if I could! Whit's the young folk ganna do when thu'rs no hooses fur them?*

bucking the trend

Douglas worried about missing out on deals; he bought up two lots of BT shares, waited to double his money, then suggested that he and Shirley get married to maximise their tax allowance. Ordinary folk were unsure. *Whit is all this shares? I thought we already all owned the phone company?*

'If yi don't move wi' the times yi git left behind,' confirmed Douglas.

Shirley was managing a hotel near Nairn. 'I'm thinking of moving to one of the big chains – like Trust House Forte, or something like that. I've got the experience now.' She talked about putting in double-glazing at Harbour Terrace – 'I mean you want to upgrade a bit.' The council were implementing a programme of removal of the old porcelain sinks to replace them with stainless steel, but once Shirley had bought the house, theirs was omitted from the 'planned maintenance and improvement scheme'. She looked disdainfully at the surrounding council houses as if they polluted her space. Shirley was itching to rip out the old sash-and-case windows and get Everest in to make a statement about the purchase. It would mark the house out. Everyone would know then that it had been bought, when the plastic double-glazing went in. Meanwhile, the remaining council house front doors were to be repainted and a contractor went round systematically scraping each to expose the bare plywood underneath. When the job was finished, Agnes McLeay's door stuck out even more among the lupine blue of its freshened neighbours. But Shirley was away by then and unable to feel the affront.

On her trip back, few people recognised Shirley McLeay. She had a whole different persona, appearing with bleached blonde hair, painted pearl fingernails, and always wearing skirts, tights and high-heeled shoes. She spoke completely differently, too, and there was no trace that she had ever been part of the place. She and Douglas stayed in the hotel, not at her old home, and she deliberately avoided searching for faces from the past.

'I don't like to talk about it,' she said to the housemaid, who did recognise her from school. 'Those were the bad old days.' It was almost impossible to fit the face of this Shirley into the one who was shunned and taunted and had disappeared from the conscience of the town as soon as it was possible.

'I started at Mackay's in Wick. Worked up. Spent time in Inverness. I never wanted to come back, but you know, I have to make sure me mither's aal right.' Just one tiny slip into her former accent.

Shirley banished her rejection and had no intention of going anywhere near that place. There was no talking about old times, and only once she was gone did people then make remarks. *That was Shirley McLeay. D'you mind her? How dirty they were? I mean they had not a thing … Shitty Shirley*, someone nudged, colluding in prepubescent security. *Well, she's certainly transformed herself. Mind you, she's never been back. The first time in as many years. I suppose her mither's getting on.*

Somewhere they wanted Shirley's story to follow the predicted route. To show that their rejection of her had been justified. That they had been right. Bucking the trend made the community uncomfortable with itself. *That was a pure gold watch she had on. Mind you, I think he has money. The fella she came up with.*

After the house-buying deal was concluded, Douglas and Shirley left. There was a brewer's conference that Douglas had to get to, so Shirley left her bank account details with Michael, including strict instructions to be followed.

fish out of water

When Seadhna left the islands it became difficult going back. Things didn't fit the same. She had to switch back into another language, for a start. The attitudes she adopted from the big city jarred in the tight little street of her home town. The clothes she wore in Edinburgh, won from getting up early for jumble sales and relentless monitoring of the incoming stock of second-hand shops, caused stares that she had to brazen out. At first she revelled in the attention of the shocked looks. She swaggered over the ancient cobbles, that once steadied the horses, in her stiletto heels with a 1940s dress belted with a Sam Browne, Paisley-patterned socks and a tight, tailored jacket. She had become used to lipstick and felt undressed without it. At first she didn't realise how much it screamed among the soft ochre stonework of the herring-fishing houses, how much it shouted, *I've left you all and I am not part of you any more.* The bent and rounded backs that turned away from her into the baker's shop were thinking, *Ah yes, there's Seadhna, been in the big city and thinks she kens it aall.*

Seadhna was so concerned with herself that she did not see how things were changing in the street that was too narrow for traffic. Its quaintness was now a major selling point for estate agents' brochures. Eager 'good-lifers' and second-home owners all wanted a *period fisherman's house with original features intact* where they could sit and imagine they were living some kind of mirrored simple life that never existed. Despite the promotional blurb, Artex exploded with a vengeance in the Seventies and covered up most of the plaster cornices, but on the outside you would never know …

Coming back with her new plumage wasn't enough, and after a while she had to bring back a capture from this other world, to show off. So Henry Sinclair was the exotic catch she took home to exhibit.

Henry and Seadhna, removed from their common environment, slept stiffly on the train from Edinburgh to Inverness, waking up in their clothes, sweaty and overheated, only to spill onto a cold platform at four in the morning and blunder onto the Thurso locomotive. The train creaked out of Inverness and towards a chilly dawn. It swallowed the Sutherland landscape as the sun rose weakly, gathering the Caithness bogs as it rattled to Georgemas junction and on to Thurso.

Once on the ferry, Seadhna took Henry onto the deck of the *St Ola* to see the Old Man of Hoy. The wind plastered his long hair against his head, somehow weakening him. They sat together in the lounge, she leaning into his coat and watching the TV swim in and out of signal while he slept. The new boat was taller that the old one and so the slope of the gangway down to the pier was much steeper than before. For Seadhna it was a more precarious descent than she was used to, her feet slithering on the metal rungs, just then catching sight of her father, diminished in the distant waiting crowd.

natives

When Seadhna and Henry arrived off the boat, John Rufus met them in his car with a small show of ceremony, even though their house was walking distance from the pier. Seadhna noticed there was a new colour TV in the living room. She stood there uncomfortably with Henry, like a visitor in her own home. Malts were only opened for very special occasions and usually for old men. Her father offered them a drink after the long journey. It wasn't the done thing to specify – normally you just accepted what was offered by the host.

'I'll have a malt,' announced Henry, as if he was addressing a barman. Seadhna winced as Henry talked on, unaware of the condescending tones he had and was unable to modify or disguise. He attempted to employ the narrow social skills he had gleaned from his sterile home, which passed suitably in company as 'good manners'. In himself he was perfectly sure that his repertoire of talk fitted with the drinking banter of Highland and Island 'chiels', of whom he perceived Seadhna's father to be one.

'I do have a Glenmorangie, would you like some of that?' offered John Rufus, showing no discomfort, but stretching to take a bottle from the back of the cupboard.

'Yes indeed, a fine whisky …' Henry felt some common ground. 'I'm rather fond of the Islay malts myself … Laphroaig is excellent. How do you rate them, Mr Rufus, the Islays?'

In the isles they didn't go in for rating malts. Malts were for export. Any allegiances in the bars were between the optics dispensing Bells or Grouse. The brand name of blends was what the hardened whisky drinkers asked for. In any case the malts were too expensive.

With every word uttered, Henry clanged like a discordant bell. Seadhna knotted. None of it fitted. She wished her father would bend himself a little to accommodate him, as she did, gently manipulating all the time. But in the Rufus home, Henry was doomed from the start and would never be able to understand why. Sadie was more forgiving, fascinated by watching her daughter orbit this ill-fitting boy.

The claustrophobia of them all in the family home was tangible. Henry could only relate obliquely through his time as a hooker on the rugby pitch and what he mistakenly perceived was 'drinking man's' talk. Against her father, Henry appeared like a sorry, jumped-up lad, toffed up to speak posh, and full of misplaced arrogance. Still Seadhna was loyal and defended him. She was seeking the hidden core, of what made him seem so rare and exotic and her so common and dull.

The Isles, she had told him as she had tried to persuade him to come with her instead of going to London with Lewis, were green like Ireland, and she attempted to seduce him to become enchanted with the place she had rejected. It was the only thing that made her special in the city, this tenuous and confused link she had started to work up, just ever so slightly, that she was indeed a country girl. She wanted Henry to be fascinated by the ancient romance of the Isles with all of their archaeological sites, dramatic cliffs, standing stones and the runic inscriptions. They seduced others, the visitors, the folk from south, all those things she took for granted and had rejected so soundly. She thought the Celtic links would mesmerise Henry too, bring them closer to James Joyce, but Henry always shifted the goalposts just out of Seadhna's reach.

She could tell that her rejected islands didn't really impact on him. Taking him to the cliffs and to watch puffins, he was passive when she had somehow expected awe. She could tell he wasn't touched with any wonder. It was superficial politeness that he displayed. He was fixated on Galway, and the Martello tower near Dublin. Still trying, she took him to one of the outer isles and they camped in a bothy. He let the stubble grow on his face and the acne subsided.

'You should grow a beard,' she teased, but he was uncomfortable, out of his skin, in a different place.

'God no, must get a proper shave and get rid of this,' and he rubbed his chin impatiently.

Their last night before heading back to Edinburgh was the Saturday night of Shopping Week. Seadhna felt trapped in the middle of colliding worlds, by the small town and its attitudes. By the lack of intellectual arty-ness which she now realised was her essential link to Henry and the world of 'real' art. The new craft shops with their tourist tat and tight watercolours embarrassed her. She said little about the Grand Finale of the gala week and its 'fancy dress and tableaux' parade, just announced it as a bacchanalian summer festivity with no real historical links, merely an excuse for lots of hard drinking and awful competitions. 'You'll see, it's like Brueghel come alive,' and she used the art reference to both link and repel at once, avoiding Henry's eyes.

She parcelled the forthcoming event negatively to distance Henry, and suggested they get to the pub early as it would be chock-a-block later. 'Well, people more or less drink all week, and on the Saturday it's the culmination of all that.' Seadhna wanted to be out of the house as much as possible until this ordeal was over.

Henry sensed John Rufus's coldness towards him. When one of them entered a room, the other exited. Seadhna tried to fabricate a bond. 'You could talk about books, my father's really well read … all self-taught, but he can speak about anything.' Henry at least knew that it was hopeless.

'He doesn't like me,' he hissed.

'He's not the kind of person to "not like" somebody,' she hissed back.

'Well maybe it's me and you he doesn't like.'

They got down to the Central Hotel in the late afternoon, everything packed up for the next day's journey. Outside, on a makeshift stage, the talent show was in progress and Seadhna ducked through the assembled chins jutting upwards, appreciating the strains of 'Danny Boy' and 'Cheatin' Heart'. She hoped now that people she knew would not see her. Henry embarrassed her in the place and the place embarrassed her with Henry.

In the back bar of the hotel they got a seat at an already beer-soaked table, the ashtray awash and filled with carefully knotted crisp packets. The bar was heaving. The bodies of the town's working folk pressed and lurched together in one sweaty mass. Heads swivelled as glazed eyes tried to encompass the complement of the room. The jukebox could barely be heard above the rumble of talk and laughter.

To Seadhna it was safe and there was no risk of the embarrassing exposure Henry invited. His awkwardness would be well diluted in the pub. The blaring incongruity of them as a 'couple' could be lost among it all.

Maybe it will all still be okay in Edinburgh.

small ponds

Seadhna forgot how stifling it was in a small community, why she left in the first place. The islands cast everything into hard immovable shapes. Seadhna's escape was into the art world, or what she thought was the art world. Back home everyone assumed a right to you, your business, what you thought, who you were. They made a story for you to fit. You had no control. There were no consents given, everyone was part of the cavalcade with or without giving their permission.

John Rufus's daughter. That's all she had ever been. *John's daughter.*

Soon drunken generosity was flowing in the bar and strangers came up and leaned over them and talked for a while as instant friendships were made. Drinks were bought, stools dragged across, and the tables expanded and mushroomed into an undefined great social melee.

'What's yur name?'

'A whisky, Henry?'

'Aye, Seadhna, Ken yur fither.'

'Pleased tae meet ya.'

Drinks were shouted over the heads of the crowd standing at the bar.

'Yi want a chaser, min?'

'Half and a half.'

'Wan fir yirsel.'

Seadhna eased through the crowd with the whisky numbing her. It felt good with all these folk. She felt happy as everything was connecting. Henry was fitting, and everyone was accepting everybody. There were no edges. Sideways, she pressed her way towards the toilet. There would probably be a queue, she thought. The single ladies' toilet beside the telephone box was indeed queued out. Drinkers sat on the stairs holding pints. A girl crushed an empty cigarette packet in her palm and tossed it to the floor. Heavy eyelids sank over distant eyes, and mouths laughed and arms embraced.

Seadhna found her place at the end of the toilet queue and folded her arms across her chest, trying to calculate the ability of her bladder-control in relation to the length of the queue.

'Ur yi home fur yur holidays, then?' A middle-aged woman was asking her.

'Yes, just for the week.'

'Bet yur glad tae be back. I couldna live in that city mesel.'

'Oh I don't mind it.' Seadhna was wondering who on earth the woman was. She was smoking a Number 6.

'D'yi ken me?' Seadhna knew her face but not the name. 'Weel, I ken you,' the woman continued without waiting for an answer, 'and I ken yur John Rufus's daughter. He wis right good tae me, yur fither.'

'Aye, everybody kens me father.' Seadhna was polite, but almost allowed a little resentment to show through.

Undaunted, the woman continued. 'We wur gittan' thrown oota wur hoose, see. Me husband wis a docker.' She took a deep suck on her Number 6. Seadhna could see the end of the cigarette burn down. That was serious nicotine inhalation. 'A tied hoos fur the stevedores. Hid geed wi' the job. Ah'll no say a bad word, bit that no-good MacIntosh, when me husband died he wis only thirty-eight and I jist hid me two bairns, he hid a brain tumour, me man that wis. Becis the hoos geed wi' his job, MacIntosh comes roon' efter the funeral tae tell me I'd hiv tae shift. Fir it wis a tied hoos. Kin yi imagine that, Seadhna?'

'No that must've been awful for you' – a pat response.

'This is the only night o' the whole year I come oot. I nivver drink any ither time an' this is me only night oot in the year. Anyhoo, me sister Maggie says go on up and see John Rufus, he'll sort it oot tae yi. He's a socialist.'

Seadhna was nodding and inching further up the queue, anticipating that the story would have to find its conclusion before her turn came in the toilet.

'Yur fither went right tae MacIntosh hissel'. He told me nobody can pit you oot yur hoos. You jist stay right put, Ah'll sort it. An' he geed right tae MacIntosh and tell't him whit fir. An' I got ti stay in me hoos right up till they got me a cooncil hoos.'

Seadhna never knew quite how to respond to the stories of her father. He was either known as a beacon of equality or a 'bloody commie'. She never knew which response she was going to meet when the stories started, so learned not to show immediate emotion lest there came a twist that changed the end comment. It could be 'Fuckin' bastard' or 'A good man, yur fither, Seadhna.'

The communist postmaster John Rufus, husband of Sadie, father of Iseabail and Seadhna. But on that night she wanted to forget him and punish him for the unworkable thing that was she and Henry.

When the parade went by they were deep in the pub and saw none of it. The drinkers stayed hemmed at the bar. *God I should have recognised her, it was Rena Ratter*, thought Seadhna and Rena Ratter went whooping out to the door, ready to drop what was left of her shop wages in the collecting cans and follow the magical fancy dress procession to the market green..

The crowd outside were childlike in their anticipation, waiting for the spectacle.

When Henry and Seadhna came out of the pub it was dark. The doors were closing early for the street dance and Seadhna needed the toilet. 'You'll have to look after me, Henry,' she said, gripping onto his hand, with the rest of her body swaying. She was usually the one looking after Henry in his drunken states. 'I've got to pee.'

There were thick crowds of people everywhere in remnants of fancy-dress costumes.

'I would so like to watch you pee,' he swooned. In what remained of her sober brain Seadhna remarked to herself that he must have picked that quote up from Henry Miller. *It would fit; Henry Miller's pretty dirty.* Then through the thickness of her drunken state she thought, *You fucking idiot, can you not make up your own dirty words?* And some thread finally separated.

The two of them staggered down a close to an unlit doorway and Seadhna undid her jeans, lurching as she heaved them down over her bent knees.

Squatting over the flagstones she released a jet of urine. 'Hold me up,' she slurred to Henry as she tried to pull up her jeans. Awkwardly he yanked on an arm to pull her up and they leant into the doorway. Henry had a half bottle bought from the bar before it closed and he took it from his back pocket. Seadhna put the bottle to her mouth and the liquid dribbled over her face. Straight away Seadhna's world was dark, spinning and swaying.

'Gonna be sick.' Henry pulled the hair out of her face as she vomited on the pavement. 'Home, gotta get home.' Her legs would not work, they slid from her hips, bending and collapsing. Henry held onto her hand, with her arm round his neck.

'Look, try and walk, can you?' He was a touch impatient. It seemed miles to the house. Seadhna shut her eyes and rested her head against Henry's coat. Eventually he got her back to the front door. The lights were on but the house was silent; Seadhna's parents had long ago gone to bed. He heaved her up the stairs into her childhood bedroom. The half bottle fell out of his pocket onto the floor as he tried to swing her onto the bed. By now she was limp, with flecks of vomit on her trouser-legs, and he left her fully clothed on top of the candlewick cover.

After all the noise died down, Sadie, who had lain awake throughout, crossed the landing to Seadhna's room and silently tiptoed in. She set the whisky bottle on the bedside table. It was the first thing Seadhna saw when she awoke dry-mouthed in the morning – the sickening gold liquid.

worthless catch

They left on the morning ferry. John Rufus again drove them down to the pier. Silently shaking Henry's hand, he wished them a safe journey. Seadhna couldn't wait to make the separation, which occurred at the point when you mounted the gangway and made your connection with the boat and left the land. All she had to do was get herself onto the boat and the ordeal would pass. It would ease with the train journey south to Inverness, as events would slowly dilute, and she would be able to sleep and gradually sober up.

Waiting to sail, Henry took out his camera; Seadhna, by his side, gazed morosely at her home town from the elevated vantage point of the deck. A trawler had come in during the night and the crew were mending a net stretched the entire length of the New Pier.

'I know that boy,' said Seadhna.

'Which one?'

'Him there at the far end. His name's Michael McLeay.'

Seadhna found herself explaining everything to Henry, as if she was analysing a piece of literature. 'He's a peasant. Well I mean, one of Zola's characters. You know, the lumpen. You could never have an intellectual conversation with someone like him. He's part of the old life of the place.'

Going below to be sick, Seadhna felt she had lost any grip on what anyone or anything really meant anymore. It had been so easy to say that about Michael, way down below them, oblivious, working the net needle and twine on the pier. She had betrayed him, betrayed them all.

lost places

In the past, touring was not something the ordinary folk did. You visited relations. The rich travelled, keeping their distance from the poor, cocooned in their distinct, hermetic world. The Gaels visited the people they had been forced to leave behind, before the places. Those with little or no choice but to move far away to find work and a better life came home on a once-in-a-lifetime trip from Australia or London, unaware that they'd lost their accents.

All of that was changing though, and up in the Isles some could see the potential for making money out of visitors. Travellers became a commodity rather than a social interest, and they turned into tourists. There was a new ro-ro, and the capacity of the bigger boat meant that far more visitors and their cars could flow onto the island. The tourism group were excited. It seemed like money for nothing. *We must get numbers up,* went the mantra chanted by all the good burghers wanting to see progress and the islands compete.

Tourism's the future. Aye it is ... But you'll always need yur agriculture ... and yur fishing. Weel ... Ah'm no so sure...

The old boat to the mainland of Scotland loaded cars singly, tyres padded and clamped, then swung up over the heads of the watching islanders. Men shouted and guided, and the motley collection of pre-1970s models were stowed on the deck after a thorough public display of the state of the chassis. You reached the galley down steep stairs after stepping through bulkheads where the mixed aromas of diesel, bacon and vomit percolated together to accompany the long crossing to and from Scrabster. Latecomers running along the pier simply threw their cases over the rail and vaulted onto the deck.

When the new boat came there was a big launching party and a plaque to mark the occasion. Cars streamed out of the stern door, dispersing and disappearing into the hinterland of the island. No longer could passengers be unwittingly and individually vetted as they came down the gangway, disorientated and dizzy from a tossing on the Firth, with the locals already a step ahead, identifying as they emerged their relatives and long-lost friends. To be unmet was a rarity. You were truly a stranger then.

The councillors discussed the new tourist bonanza. How you had to increase numbers. That it was the future. Baillie Harvey and Jamieson with their subcommittee were the main movers. John Rufus protested that it was the indigenous industries they should be looking out for – fishing, farming and boat building. They should get more control of the prices, the markets. There was stuff happening in Europe, he said, that was nothing to do with keeping small communities going. 'The EEC is just a Tory club,' he snorted.

Baillie Harvey sniffed. 'You would want us all in the Dark Ages, Mr Rufus, still in gutter's aprons. It's progress. You can't stop progress.'

'Progress? Have everybody running round in poorly paid seasonal jobs with no security? Could it come that your tourism group will have us all dressed up as gutters and fishermen, performing the jobs we used to do for real like actors in a circus?'

The Baillie ignored his taunt.

The marketing subgroup spent countless meetings honing and trimming the copy for the brochure, selecting photographs and embellishing descriptions. They compiled a list of Bed and Breakfasts, collating atmospheric pictures of the Standing Stones. They decided to go for niche marketing for outdoor holidays. *Niche*, they liked that word and the way it already sounded foreign, as if they were already connected with faraway exotic places where no one could understand the language. It began to feel as if their ordinary working place was one of these exotic places too.

The net of photographic paper was cast and there was nothing then but the waiting. When the visitors started to come the shopkeepers eyed the takings in their shop tills, helping to count out change, picking coins from outstretched foreign palms.

talking big

All the creel boats were getting short of crew.

It's the oil. The folk spoke of it as if it was an evil magic absorbing everyone and everything. *They can get three hunner' pound a week steady money labouring on the site so thur no interested in the fishing.* There were jobs and big wages at the construction site.

Sandy Baker, with cement-encrusted steel-toe-capped boots, was making big money and getting a big ego to match, driving a giant earth-mover at the oil camp.

'Days o' the big fishing money's gone,' he declared.

Geordie McLeay hosed down blood in the butchers for one pound twenty an hour. He tickled the water out the shop back door and over the road into the street drain and was always being told he was lucky to have the job and how many other boys had been down asking. Rob Anderson the butcher kept him well in his place, and there would be no question of asking for an increase. It just wasn't done. If you were disgruntled you could go elsewhere.

Rob's porky eyes leered at the ladies coming in with their shopping bags clutched tight. He counted out their change with bloody fingers, returning when the shop was empty to the pile of sausages he was making in the back. Geordie scuffed through the sawdust in his blood-smeared white apron and fed most of a whole cow into the mincer.

'Once the steaks and the good cuts are gone there's wan hell o' a pile of mince,' commented Geordie on butchering. He could tell you all about mince and sausages, and although the quartermaster at the construction site was buying a ton of mince from Rob, he still didn't put Geordie's pay up.

Skippers were desperate. They were forced to look outside the families and the traditional local networks for crew. Willie Bremner was still creeling and had everything invested in his boat and gear. 'Ah'm no bred tae work a shovel nine tae five,' he declared and looking around decided to make Geordie an offer.

'You'll get a crew share,' Willie Bremner said, 'We split the money, a share to the boat, then among the crew. There's good days and bad days, and you'll just have to lump that like we all do. And we settle up at the end of the week.' So with Willie's offer, Geordie was out of the butcher's, though he'd never been in a boat before.

'That your brother back fae the trawl, is it? He looking for work too?' And Willie took on Michael as well.

Heading out of the harbour, water sloshed across the deck as they steamed out west. Going through the tide as they brewed up tea on the gas cooker, the motion slammed the wheelhouse door shut until they were clear of the ebb. Under the cliffs they hauled up the creels. *Six baskets of crabs, a basket of lobsters.* Creels full of crab. The big brown partans wrestling and slow-fighting like sumo warriors. The wee velvets nipping at the fingers so that their hands were full of cuts from the spikes and rough shells, the salt water making them swee. In their heads they worked out the money, resetting the creels way close into the land on the rocky parts where the lobsters lived.

After a day's hauling they came home into the harbour with the work lights on, heaving a last skittering velvet off the deck at a gull, old carpets over the baskets to keep the birds off and everything stowed. The wake from the boat cutting between the navigation buoys like a proud announcement.

The hotel stood at the top of the pier, a honey-trap of company, warmth and beer, and Geordie, like the partans lured into the creels, could not go past the door with his pay. The wad of cash from the week's settlement made him feel he could buy the world. He could step into the bar and stand beside whoever was there at the counter and buy them a rum. There were instant friends and camaraderie and someone would buy him one back. Acceptance. The buying of rounds was a ritual they could all follow until everyone there melded into a bubble that was the world of the bar and forgot entirely that there was another world outside.

Sandy Baker, full of boasts and money, talking big from the oil camp, was courting Edna, the very same girl who had been Norrie Inkster's. She had a job in the camp office but her good looks were on the slide. *The drink, weel her mither pat whisky in her bottle when she wis a bairn.*

'Whit way does an ugly cunt like you get a bird like that?'

Sandy hesitated for a moment, judging whether Geordie was insulting him. 'Fuck off, ya bastard. Whisky?' replied Sandy.

Michael took the cue to leave the bar. Geordie soon got ensconced with Sandy.

'Shuz got wan on the way,' – and that was as far as talk of Edna went.

'Pit that shite off,' demanded Geordie, and the TV was switched to snooker which played with the commentary turned down and the juke box turned up. Louder and louder until everyone lost count of the rounds and it was closing time.

'Gimme a kiss, Marie.'

'Away home ti yur bed, Geordie.' Geordie began to leave only when the bar had finally shut, with Sandy away in a taxi and the building emptied of the last stragglers. The barmaid headed him to the door firmly, her sweeping brush in her hand, and Geordie finally lurched towards Harbour Terrace.

Michael heard him come into the house, crashing into the front door, the sound of brittle glass shuddering in a cheap frame. 'Get up, yi owld bitch. Come on, yi owld cow. Get oot yur fuckin' bed. Ah'm fuckin' hungry!' he shouted.

Michael heard his mother rise from her room and tramp downstairs barefoot to the kitchen. 'Had yur tongue, George. Ah'm comin'.'

'Get a fuckin' move on, mithur. Ah'm hungry. Ah'm been oot aal day.'

There was the hiss of Tennent's tins being opened as Geordie set his carry-out by his chair, falling asleep there till morning. The plate of sausages and beans his mother brought sat beside him as he slept. When he woke in the morning he ate it cold, washing it all down with another tin of beer.

By the time they were at sea again it was too cold and wet to talk, and by the time the booze wore off, Geordie was getting irritable and itching for the pub again.

'Don't treat ma like that,' said Michael when they had finished stowing baskets on the pier and before Geordie made for the pub.

'Like whit? Whit you spikkan' aboot, prick?'

'The way yi do. Shoutin' at her an' that.' The brothers didn't look at each other, Michael nursing his gaze back and forth over the cracks in the stone pier.

'I can dae whit I like, shuz me fuckan' mither.'

Michael smarted. He couldn't find a way to pull Geordie into line. Almost inaudible, he said, 'If you ever touch her I will fuckin' kill yi.'

Geordie laughed in his face. 'Ho! I'd like tae see that! Jis' try it, yi fuckan' mammy's boy.'

finding your feet

Once back in Edinburgh, Seadhna found some common ground with Melissa and moved past the barrier of her plummy voice. Abortion. Melissa had a flat-top haircut now and looked like a boy, and had taken up the reins of the feminist cause. It wasn't Henry's stuff, politics. He told her he was more of an aesthete.

What's an aesthete? God knows. Seadhna was finding it all a bit tedious. The repetitive nights with Lewis in the same pubs, the same drunkenness – getting boring. Anyway it was a women's thing. Very few of the boys got involved, although Cammy did, but then he was gay and didn't have any machismo image to keep up.

They made banners, got old sheets from the Red Cross shop and stretched them out on the floor of the art school. *Stop the Corrie Bill. Free Abortion on Demand.* Painting on the slogans, the indelicate brush stuttered over the folds in the sheets. Gardener's canes, stapled through the brushed cotton, rolled up and ready to be unfurled on the day. Melissa confessed to Seadhna in the canteen. 'I had one when I was fifteen, big hush hush, my mother just marched me down to the doctors and got it sorted. God, it's just a lump of cells. A blob of jelly, it's not a *person.*'

'So did you have a boyfriend then?' asked Seadhna.

'No,' laughed Melissa loudly, throwing back her head, 'my fucking forty-year-old cello teacher seduced me.'

The run-up campaign included Melissa getting up to make an impassioned speech to an ignoring captive audience in the college canteen as they tried to have a coffee break. A conceptual art installation of empty gin bottles and knitting needles placed on all the tables was constructed to highlight the dangers of illegal abortion techniques. The lecturers chuckled indulgently.

The earnest protesters were all up early that Saturday and ready down in King's Stables road, waiting for the bus-loads to come in from Glasgow and Dundee. Henry was still asleep in bed as Seadhna left his flat. They wound themselves up into an indignant mood. Laughing one minute and looking surly the next. Passing round cigarettes and then feeling the cold. Somebody went up to get sausage rolls from Martin's.

The Anti-Corrie protesters prepared to shout, to be angry and voice the injustice. Melissa had a megaphone. Seadhna, like all the girls, had gone on the pill 'in case'. It was part of the kit of student life. Now her head was brimming with the arguments of the abortion debate. Viability and weeks, the number of illegal abortions, the queue of women from Southern Ireland, and she threw herself into the demonstration with the confidence that there would be no one who would recognise her as they slowly chanted along Princes Street and up the Mound. *Melissa's right, it is just a blob of mucus. There's no way I'd have a baby now ...*

losing your head

Everyone was deciding who it was they thought they wanted to be. Inside the art studios some of the students were doing Picassos, some were being 'the Colourists', others were trying to be Andy Warhol. There was a boy who wore a beret. Everyone was searching, all worried in case they were caught out and exposed as not really having a clue. The race to find a style became frantic. The centuries of art history and the limitless choice. The overwhelming diversity of the whirling merry-go-round of voices demanding to be heard. All those tiny people with their ideas, frantic to be noticed, and among it all Seadhna's voice was diminishing to the faintness of a feeble reed, wondering what else you could do with dribbled wax to be interesting and noticed.

I just want to learn how to draw, she thought, as if it was still the core of something in the ungainly whirl. She over-worked, over-drew and over-hatched her life drawings, aping Henry's style, losing confidence in her own. *Too messy, too sketchy*, she chastised herself. *It can't be as good if you just do it in five minutes. They don't count*, and she flicked on some white highlight in chalk.

The Protestant work ethic wore through. Nothing was allowed to be easy or enjoyable. While the gyro of art school became top-heavy, skewing out of control, Seadhna clung to her tense life-drawing ritual of pencil sharpening. Henry continued getting drunk every night and she continued propelling him to his bed. Exhausted, she made him her cause. She became his minder and got him up with black coffee and Gauloises in time to get into the college by break time in the morning.

'Whit the fuck you playing at, Seadhna?' But she wasn't listening to Cammy.

'Art is the most important thing, even if it means facilitating Henry. He is, after all, a genius. Lewis says …' and then 'I don't think I know enough to be an artist …'

Cammy rolled his eyes and went off to be in a band with a bunch of punks.

With a postgraduate show under his belt, Henry intended being the next Mark Rothko, but in brown with a manifesto of 'opposites'. He switched to tiny canvasses, obsessing over layers of brown, painting and repainting, scratching out, dribbling and slopping paint on then displaying a meagre four pieces in a huge empty space and that too was part of his statement.

The place Seadhna escaped to that seemed so alluring, so glossy, so liberating, this city place of ideas and colliding philosophies with its enormous intellectual horizons, began to stretch and stretch until there seemed no edges and everything started to tip out of control. She clutched at Henry, terrified of losing her link into this unintelligible world. It seemed impossible in the maze of it all that there was any place for her.

Her final-year tutor surveyed her white canvasses with their dribbles, as Seadhna sat embarrassed, attempting an explanation. 'Gravity pulls the wax in the direction it wants to go.'

'I see.'

'It's about being pulled by all sorts of forces, not being in charge of things.'

'Yes.'

Her drawings were splayed out on the floor. 'But I still think drawing is important.' She feebly looked up at the kindly monosyllabic man, wishing he might pat her on the head and say it was all okay.

'Surely you only achieve quality with work and time and pain?' she asked. Seadhna sat high and dry among her motley display of pained minimal canvasses, with the realisation dawning on her that it was all at an end, and the flicker of confidence that she'd briefly felt making her first-year painting of Standing Stones had been extinguished. After that, there was nothing honest about anything, only the desperation to survive. The final survival test was the opening night of the diploma shows.

Her mother Sadie came all the way south on her own by train. It was a long way to travel. John Rufus couldn't get away because there was a meeting he had to attend about post office closures and it clashed. It felt thoroughly alien to Seadhna to have her mother there in this other world of the art school that she had inhabited alone for so long. Cammy arrived at the opening resplendent in a full dinner suit he'd got out of the Lifeboat shop, with greased-down black hair. His diminutive parents stood close by him, full of belief and trust.

'This is ma ma an' da. Jeanie an' Pat,' and Cammy introduced them.

The huge sculpture court milled with students and perplexed parents.

'This is Seadhna. Shiz a painter.' They greeted each other, unsure whether you shook hands or not.

The Marilyn Monroe girl, rigid on five-inch stilettos, minced around with her enormously fat father who resembled a Corleone. Like a robot she smoked and drank her wine, constrained by her tight dress and her shoes. Seadhna was already detached and floating off through everything. Not there. Swimming and drowning. Sadie smiled at Cammy, whose father leant over and whispered something in his ear.

'Aye, da,' Cammy nodded encouragingly, 'yir allowed tae smoke in here,' and he opened up a packet to offer them round.

'Naw, hiv wan o' mines,' said Cammy, taking a silver cigarette case from his pocket and flicking it open. Seadhna declined. She didn't want to smoke in front of her mother. But Cammy had already offered her one, which gave the game away. Seadhna was gone; there was no point pretending anything anymore. She was absent from everything around her, as blank and directionless as the bleached minimal canvasses that she silently led her mother to see, tucked away in an inaccessible studio upstairs in the college.

'Oh yes, dear.' Then Sadie paused over the taught pencil drawing of a thin man in a jock strap.

Back downstairs, Seadhna got Melissa to take her mother over to the pub so she could smoke without guilt. Sadie stood there among the bizarrely clad art students, displaced and clutching the handbag she took to the Stromness shops. Melissa was good with other people's parents. She was like the assured host at a diplomat's party.

Henry swanned around. Lewis thought he knew someone who would buy one of his works and sailed off looking for the potential buyer. He didn't refer to them as paintings any more; they were 'works'.

Cammy sat Seadhna down beneath a rubber-clad tailor's dummy with pink expletives screen-printed all over it. 'Look, come on, hen. Yi ken it's a' alot o' shite.'

'I'll need to get a job ....' The outside world was pushing in. 'You know, Cammy, I think I understand how Catholics feel. I'm like that. It's like when you're born into a religion and it gradually leaves you. The whole art thing has left me ....' She was talking past Cammy into the distance, '...diluted and evaporated. I don't believe in it any more. I think it was always just a fiction. It's like I'm a Catholic, yes that's exactly it, a lapsed Catholic. Lost the faith. I've lost the faith in my religion.'

Henry, whom she was now too tired to try and grip onto, talked about the Royal College and maybe doing a masters, then Lewis getting him a show at the Cork Street gallery. Scotland was *just too parochial* ... In their quiet, sustained tussle Lewis won out and she was ready to admit defeat, battle weary. Seadhna sat white and sallow, sucking on a steady supply of cigarettes in the echoing studio in the aftermath of the opening, with Cammy twitching around her.

'Fir fuck's sake, hen. Ah'm the fuckin' pape, nae you. It's me that's the lapsed fuckin' Catholic an Ah'm a fuckin' poof tae boot.' And Cammy armed her over to the Tap o' Lauriston, the garish art school pub.

emancipation

It started off well enough, until they heard she had been an art student. Jovial anybody's-grandad-that-you-could-feel-sorry-for Bobby asked her to paint a portrait of his dead Scottie dog. The sole remaining blurry photo was entrusted to her to copy and the dog portrait became an enormous impossible burden, albeit her first and possibly only commission. Seadhna's new job was in the regular drinking hole of the railway workers, aptly named The Footplate, secreted up a lane at the back of Marks & Spencer's, where no normal person would ever know of its existence. Seadhna was interviewed in an upstairs room by an overly bloated and pink owner resembling a cross between a shaved pig and a pimp. She did not feel inclined to unbutton her coat for the duration of the interview, but she did have a skirt on. The owner was picking the girl who would most encourage the railway workers to stay longer and drink more. But naive Seadhna thought she had struck lucky at last and that some buried skill had been recognised when the manager offered her the job.

On the dot of eleven the early shift arrived to heave themselves onto barstools in their railway jackets. Nurses and students were fair game because, as everyone who read the *Sunday Sport* knew, they were into kinky sex, uniforms and nude modelling. Nessie was the head barmaid. The ugly and brash one, there to act as surrogate wife and nanny to the hard-drinking railway workers. 'Aw, son,' she crooned, turning to the Bell's optic with two glasses in one hand, 'never mind, jis' you fill up yir gless an' Ah'm sure that lassie'll see sense. That's awfy. Awa 'n left a' the weans? Och.'

The domestic ups and downs of the early shift. The skills Seadhna had to learn were a lot more complex than what glass you poured a nip into. It was hard work thinking up the one-liner replies. She learnt fast, but it didn't come to her second nature as it did to Nessie. Nessie was from that world. Seadhna was learning a new part.

'Tired, are yi?' leered the railway men in a barrage. 'Been up a' night? Yi'll hiv tae tell that boyfriend ti leave yi alane. Tel him if he cannae keep it up, Ah'll gee him a hon.' They winked and laughed and the innuendo kept flowing like an unstoppable river, with Seadhna's retorts batted back with what became a more threadbare and sprung racket, weakly plugged by a feeble dam of winks and pretend laughter. You could not, of course, ever say *Fuck off back to your sad life, prick.*

The banter got to her. Seadhna truly was an object of titillation. There in the bar to be looked at and fantasised over. To provide buttocks wobbling just under the tight seams of her skirt and legs that stretched up to a fud of mysterious wonder, covered perhaps by knickers and lace or whatever thumb and finger-squishing possibility there might be in that dark place. She could see it in the men's eyes, the drool that kept everything bestial just under the surface. There was a hair's breadth between the danger of eye-contact and the unleashing of something uncontrollable. In their eyes the possibility was there, that under her jumper their hot hands might wander, pushing beneath her bra and over her breasts. It was what she saw written in their faces as plainly as if they spoke the words. That was her key part in the lurid little stage under the optics, to be gang-raped by looks and words.

The pig-faced owner came in every few hours, to press past her on his way to the till. His official mission was to straighten out the crumpled fivers and roll them into a tube to feed into the mouth of a drawstring money bag. He used the opportunity in the tight space behind the bar to tease his cock against her. The unwritten rule was strictly on the side of 'look but don't touch'. But the play of the railwaymen's eyes unnerved her more and more. They were all over her.

'Ur yi wearin' a bra, Seadhna?'

They used her name like they owned her. 'What aboot tryin' it oot wi' nane, like they wimmins libbers eh? Eh hen?'

'Aw, Ah kin smell a cunt. Naw naw, nae you, Seadhna, Jimmy's jis' walked in.'

'Ha ha. Ha ha.' Big guffaws. It was all so funny, obviously.

Nessie was her protector. 'Hi,' she scolded, 'yir embarrasin' the lassie. Pay no heed ti them, Seadhna. That's far enough, Shug. Cut it oot.'

When Nessie went to change the barrels it was worse. It was as if the schoolteacher was out of the room. Seadhna girded herself up but dreaded the twenty-minute lunch break. She wore baggier clothes. Stopped the skirts.

'Whit yi done wi' yir tits, Seadhna? Cannae see them.'

But in the end even Nessie betrayed her. She took Seadhna into the office. 'Look, hen, Ah ken the lads kin be a bit rough bit they dinnae mean it, ken.' She paused. 'The boss his asked me tae spik tae yi.' As Nessie leaned over conspiratorially, Seadhna could see the dark gums between her yellowing teeth, the lipstick edges of her mouth. 'Yir lettin' yirsel go. Could yi no wear a skirt mare often, smarten yirsel up a bit? Dae sommin' wi' yir hair? Yi ken?' Nessie was pleading for her to accept the trick they all had to play. Say it was fine. Pretend it didn't wear you down. Humour them.

'Okay,' she said, playing along. Humouring her instead. 'Will I put my hair up or something?' Pretending.

Nessie smiled. 'Aye, hen, Aye, summin' like that. The boys like tae see a bit o' shape, yi ken.' Seadhna, pretending she was ignorant and that the penny was only now dropping, said, 'Yes, I've got some skirts that would do,' and in that moment Seadhna made her decision.

She nipped into the bar when Nessie was off shift to slip the photo of the Scottie dog into the Bobby's personal beer tankard. Jimmy hardly lifted his head. 'See Bobby gets that will you?' And she never went back, not even for the wages due. She did feel bad about the Scottie dog. The old guy had just been widowed as well, but that day she had to be hard. *If you're in with the crows you'll get shot with them.* Economy of equality.

Seadhna bought an *Evening News* from the first paper-seller she saw. She felt a rush from the release she had just awarded herself, of doing something bad but right. There was nowhere to take any grievance, and she knew there was no point in complaining. She was too tired to fight any more battles. It was just the way the world was.

After scanning the jobs column she phoned up a place called Marco's. It was Marco of Marco's who spoke to her in his slightly refined Edinburgh voice, and so there was another interview. She wore her black waitress skirt made out of taffeta. No one could see that the zip was burst, because she wore a patterned blouse on top which came down over the waistline. She had a good pair of court shoes and a flowing, full-skirted coat that she bought out of Wallis the summer she left school. It looked more normal than her usual art school clothes.

If first impressions counted she looked good, flowing into the bar with her hair washed and brushed and floating about her shoulders. It wouldn't have mattered that her tights had already been on for two days because she hadn't got to the laundrette and that the toes were encrusted with sweat. She had to get another job.

'Yes, I've got experience,' she said, which was technically true, hoping Marco wouldn't check up on her three weeks in The Footplate.

Marco's was different in that everything was a degree more subtle. She sat in one of the snug seats to be interviewed, Marco keeping his eye on the door and checking who was coming in. The Mafia instincts were all there with Marco.

'Well, I will train you *my* way of running bar. In here we don't use optics. Everything's poured from measures. The old-fashioned way.'

Marco too was an art collector of sorts. There were paintings of stags on the walls.

Seadhna had embarked on the slow-motion helter-skelter, inching downwards. A force of heavy, leaden momentum relentlessly crushing her through level after level in a grim skyscraper of downward life. It hit her like a breeze-block in the stomach, the realisation that her art school degree was worthless. Shut up in that hermetically sealed world for four years, gradually discovering that fame was unlikely and that it was always about money and connections. Then the sober reality taking root, that her aspirations would have to be calibrated. First, down towards a library job maybe, *or something in a gallery? That would be okay* ... Then even that thin rung of possibility fell away.

There was the Iron Lady in London with her perfectly coiffured hair of spun metal and her cruel 'Spitting Image' impassivity. She stooped to bestow her bequest of acceptable unemployment on the already tumbling youth. They were sacrificed as the necessary price, and all had to ditch their modest hopes to scramble for low-paid work in a world where society was banished. *Thatcher, the bitch.*

Seadhna got the job at Marco's out of twenty-three applicants. Marco told her himself after she was successful, and she was grateful and relieved.

Like the Footplate Seadhna found that bar work was an act and she could walk onto the stage of Marco's pub theatre and perform. It became second nature. She didn't need to think. Her stock of chatty replies tumbled out. You would never have known it wasn't the real Seadhna. There were customers she liked and those that she wondered at like the advocate who boasted he'd sent Jimmy Boyle to prison. Then there were those simpler humans who just annoyed her, the ferret-like shop manager from the Bridges who insisted that *she*, not Marco, should serve him, who called her 'dear' and waited like an expectant master for her to trot to where he stood at the bar, where he would underscore his familiarity by asking for 'my usual, Seadhna.' When she returned with his drink and the transaction was complete he went on to ingratiate her with a tip of twenty pence. Her role dictated that she should gratefully accept the coin he had waiting in his palm and proceed to place it in the tip glass.

The customers' attitude of right over her clamped her further down the slide. Offence was not something she could feel, it was almost too arrogant an emotion, and had no place now. In the domino game of thin power, she needed someone in the equation to despise. Outwardly she could pretend, but inside she could be free to hate, and from the bottom of the pile gain a tainted sense of self.

Seadhna could see the shop manager's cheap overcoat come in through the pub door, ahead of his grey smoker's face, and she would turn her head away before he could register her actions. She would move to the opposite end of the bar, busying herself with her back to the customers. Deliberately she ignored him just a little longer, and moved cheerily to serve someone else, still pretending she hadn't noticed him. In those seconds she enjoyed a brief whiff of power. Then Marco hailed him and her private spell was broken. '*Mister* Duffy!'

Marco would notice that she hadn't served him. 'Over here, Seadhna!'

'She's coming,' clipped Mr Duffy, as if Seadhna was his pet dog. 'I'll just … be … patient,' and he rolled his eyes toward Marco, as if waiting on a dippy wife in the shops. He tapped the correct money in coins up and down on the bar. Everything about him annoyed her, *the withered old bastard …*

Seadhna went home, fell asleep on the Bri-nylon sofa in the new shared flat. Six of them, in various types of low-paid work and non-legit jobs, cheating the broo. All sharing the Housing Association's only multi-occupancy property and driving the neighbours to distraction with their parties. It was unfurnished, with bare boards, and huge art school student paintings on the walls. Through her disturbed evenings dozing on the sofa, with the buses flashing past the Georgian windows, filtered the perpetual sound of the Channel 4 test card playing on a black-and-white TV. Inside Seadhna's head there was constant action to this soundtrack. An unstoppable crazed movie in which pint glasses were constantly filled up, gin tumblers emptied into the sink and slices of lemon jammed in the plughole. Round and round went the movie, with no end or rolling credits, as two fists again forced glasses down onto the brushes of the glass wash in robotic unison, then slid them onto the stainless steel draining board under the bar to dry. Trapped in a bar of Kafka's making, her brain filled with the impossible arithmetic of enormous orders that she mentally added up in her head. *Two large gins, a whisky and ice, three pints of eighty shilling, oh and two bags of pork scratchings, Paul whatareyouhaving, vodka and lime, lime or is it tonic? Okay tonic no ice, hold on there's more, one Tia Maria 'nd coke …*

Marco didn't sell crisps because he didn't like the bags cluttering up the tables. All the slops from the hand-poured measures went into a stainless steel slop tray and from there were funnelled into a Christmas bottle. He made a punch from it and resold it all to the punters at a pound a glass. That's how you knew it was Christmas.

Then someone shot John Lennon and it really felt as if the world was coming to an end. Sudden collapses were not in Seadhna's genetic make-up. Managed disintegration was more the way of things. She realised, as if a fog was lifting, that she was going to have to stop working in Marco's.

Seadhna still had debts to pay off. While she worked at Marco's she never went out and all her pay went into the bank, slowly paying off the days of whisky and ostentatious meals with Henry and Lewis. They had both receded from her life, although Henry still came up and spoke to her, oblivious to the fact that his presence reignited all the burning hurt and failure she felt. She had never loved him, only loved the habit of him, the difference, the challenge to wrench him from Lewis and the proximity to the rarefied mysterious art world that he seemed to provide. He told her he was going to Vienna with someone who had been invited to do some lectures. He would be building connections, talking to galleries and eventually getting a show. Then there was Lewis, of course, already looking for new protégés. She had saved Henry from himself, and drowned silently in the process.

in the end

The only news she got of home was when she phoned from the call box at the bottom of the street, systematically feeding in the pile of ten pences from the metal shelf into the slot. There was always a queue of impatient others waiting to use the kiosk, banging on the glass to hurry the callers up as they spoke. It always felt that everyone in the queue heard everyone else's conversations, so there was perpetual urgency to finish, say what had to be said before the beeps.

The news of her grandmother's illness and death came with no space in between. The illness came through a phone call and the information that she had died came as a PS on the back of the ready-sealed envelope which contained the prior news of her pneumonia. The old folk's friend, they called it. Seadhna learned of everything backwards, which was a little strange, but even so she didn't feel great sadness, as she had never known her paternal grandmother particularly well. She had never been a woman of warmth and communication, but that too was a mystery unsolved. The closest she had ever come to her was one New Year, sitting in a 1960's living-room setting, trying to figure out what the canned laughter on the TV was responding to. They were watching the Gaelic programme at Hogmanay, her grandmother giggling privately at the kilty jokes.

'It's not very good Gaelic,' she had said in a confessional, using the soft voice of someone still negotiating sense among the foreign words on their palate. 'It's Tinkers Gaelic,' and then she added wistfully, 'but you know you had to have Eenglish to get on. You couldn't get on weethout Eenglish. It was better for the young ones not to have the Gaelic.'

The death gave Seadhna a role to fulfil and a sense of duty to perform. *Have I got black shoes?* And she remembered there was a pair of sensible fake-leather black lacing shoes in the bottom of her wardrobe. It was to be a cremation and all the uncles would be there. She asked Marco for time off and he gave her paid leave, 'Of course, of course, take as much time as you need.' *Great for families, the Italians,* she found herself thinking.

Even when she got on the train to Inverness, she didn't really know why. Perhaps it was so that she could be part of an event and be something other than a barmaid, someone with connections elsewhere. She hoped she might see the body, but when she got to the crematorium the coffin was well screwed down. It could have been anybody inside. Seadhna had never seen a corpse and secretly ached to see what dead flesh looked like, how it would make her feel. That was one of the few remaining unknowns of the human body. The protocol of funerals, however, was alien to her. The mystery of the Gaelic grandmother was her language. And now both were truly dead. No one had thought it important to pass on. Even a nursery rhyme. And Seadhna, too, felt the dreadful inevitability of being present to witness the extinction of a language as the thread broke between her grandmother, her father and herself. The first household in generations of time since the language was first uttered, that did not run and play to the background prosody of Gaelic.

'Don't you remember anything? Anything your mother said to you?' Seadhna tried to will the language back from the broken threads, asking her father.

'Och, only stupid things. *Duine bheul*. I remember that.'

'What does it mean?'

'Shut up, shut your mouth.'

Her father, with atheistic vigour, belted out all the verses of 'The Lord Is My Shepherd' as the tinny electric organ bleated through the notes. The funeral was a cartoon of consolidated misalignments, the soulless cremation parlour, the Seventies decor of velvet and cheap polished wood and the weariness of precision-cut polished granite.

They left the crematorium as the next service began to queue in the foyer, with no breath of the hidden narratives stretching and aching to break out of hearts.

The drunk uncle with his own stash of Special Brew was in the funeral garden having a smoke. Then there was the uncomfortable after-funeral gathering, with Aunty Bet ushering Seadhna into the kitchen with the women to proffer sandwiches and tea. She wanted to drink with the men. There was no resolution of anything.

Seadhna felt a pull to get back north. The metal plates of the city were clamping around her and boxing her in. The rainy wetness reflected puddles of failure and there seemed no respite from the spasms of want, rejection and injustice that met her like billboard adverts round every corner. She felt the tiredness of an overused hoarding plastered with last year's concert gigs, and the hopelessness of an abandoned back green filled with sodden mattresses and broken washing machines.

'We're not together any more.' She had told her mother that she and Henry were living together as if it was some big modern gesture. But they didn't refer to Henry in their correspondence.

'Oh well dear, these things usually turn out for the best.' It wasn't quite *I told you so.*

She didn't tell Marco she was cracking up. All she said was that she wanted to spend some time back home. That she wanted a break from the city. Marco nodded. He thanked her for being such a reliable employee. It was true. She had never cheated him. She had never skived, always turned up, even done extra hours on the Saturdays when all his publican pals came round to watch the rugby internationals in the bar. She never even gave Henry a free drink in the days when he came in to pick her up. She liked Marco because in the end he treated her fairly.

Seadhna was able to leave without a stain and Marco even said that she could return for a job any time she wanted – if, that was, she came back to Edinburgh. Seadhna's polite face thanked him and agreed to work on until he found a replacement for her. It was an interminable week and she was dreading the goodbyes.

'I don't want any big fuss about me leaving.' Any change to the expected parameters of the role would throw her, she knew that. Collections of money and farewell presents were not in the script she had memorised. The man from the Bridges was on his annual leave so she did not have his egregious questions to fend off. On her last day, Marco handed her an envelope with cash.

'We had a whip-round. Thought you could get what you wanted with this.'

She felt at that moment she could have hugged Marco, but that was not part of the script either so she just said 'Thank you' and meant it. On the bus she opened the envelope to discover one crisp fifty-pound note, and transferred it straight away to the notes section of her purse.

As if in a dream, she packed her belongings into boxes and shoved them to the back of a cupboard in the big flat to store. It was as if she might never see any of it again. All the objects, their fleeting memories and the astonishment that she had collected so much stuff in her time in the city. She remarked on it all silently from a cotton-wool space within her head. The polka dot cups seemed a pathetic icon of must-have kitsch from the fancy-dress life she had been enmeshed in, but she wrapped them carefully all the same.

the dreams

Seadhna held her brittle self together like thin, fractured glass. She conserved her energy, knowing she would collapse, drained, at the finish. As if even speaking might suck away what precious being she had left, she conserved that too, avoiding all but essential communication. Robotic, she got the train to Aberdeen, checking off the markers in the journey that brought her nearer its end. In the spaces between essential communications with other humans she shut herself down. The ticket collector did not need to know the weary story behind her. Her bag, always too heavy, wore into her shoulder as she dragged her way round the grey-granite corners of Aberdeen Harbour. Her head was low and she fastened her eyes on the erratic cobbles. Among the no-man's-land of the quays she recognised at last the livery of the P&O ships, the safe, ochre funnel of the twelve-passenger cargo boat, *St Rognvald*, that would take her overnight to Stromness.

On board there was a strange lack of crew, so unlike a passenger ferry, but eventually a steward appeared and gave her a key and the number of her cabin. Before leaving he asked what she wanted for breakfast.

'Scrambled eggs,' she replied in a moment of optimism. Seadhna went to her cabin, unaware of where else you might go on a ship that mostly transported cattle. The old-world wood-veneered cabin had stiff white sheets, proper blankets, cloche lampshades and brass, and she felt abandoned in an old-movie time warp. She could hear no sound of any other passengers. The *Rognvald* sailed at seven so there was nothing much else to do but get her head down.

She wormed herself between the tight sheets. Unused to sleeping clothed, she thought it best, in case she had to get up suddenly in the night, to keep her knickers and T-shirt on. Eventually she made out the sound of the ship's engine grumbling into motion and knew they must be away, wending through the long river exit from Aberdeen Harbour and out into the North Sea.

She tried to force sleep and disengage from the feeling she was all alone on a deserted ship, but felt crazily alert. The night on board was long and there was such a storm that she barely slept. She kept waking, then would fall into half-sleep. She truly thought that something had befallen the boat, that everyone had left it and they had forgotten she was aboard. Apart from the bass hum of the engine and the crashing and lurching, there was no clue to the presence of any other humans. She lay staring in her bunk, then got up and opened the cabin door to peer into the deserted corridor. If the ship was sinking, someone would come for her, surely? She never wore a watch so had no idea what the time was. It seemed that far too many hours had passed. The cattle boat had no stabilisers so she was slung like a bag of potatoes from the top to the bottom of her bunk. She clung to the sides to stop herself rolling off. It was such a waste of the pristine, starched white sheets that invited a clean, peaceful sleep but instead gave no rest at all.

But she must have slept because suddenly there was a knock on her door and a voice said that breakfast was being served in the galley. It shook her abruptly into a confused awareness, trying to piece together bits of her rolling dreams swirling around in a doomed ship. Heaving on her jeans, she went up to the tiny galley room. She was the only passenger there.

'Was that no a bit coorse last night?' she found herself saying.

'Coorse? Na, na that wis nothing.'

She was unsure what to believe. The whole world was shifting on its axis. The scrambled eggs, toast and silver teapot were set before her on a white tablecloth and the steward ferreted away back through the door. She could hear the noise of the crew laughing in the mess room.

Coming down the gangway her head still swam with the motion of the ship. It was the first time she felt nauseous. She was sure it *had* been a bad night.

The steward was winding her up. She wobbled as she tried to walk, her balance shot with the sea journey.

Her father was there to meet her. She looked at him, small at the bottom of the gangway, and noted how white his hair was. In a second it made him seem vulnerable but he sprang up the steep gangplank to take her bag from her, then pressed her into an affectionate yet clumsy hug.

'Was it a rough crossing, Dad?'

'Well it must have been about a Force 8. Did you feel it?' He put his arm round her and she felt as if she would collapse right there. 'Come on, lassie, let's get yi home.'

For the first fortnight she slept. Mute, she moved around the house, drying dishes in duet with her mother, then her father. They watched her and signed to each other silently so that she would not see them.

'I just don't want to have to speak to any people,' she said quietly. In the shortening days, Seadhna waited until the darkness overtook the afternoon before going out of the house, and even then kept to narrow closes between the old houses, keeping her head low when she was forced out into the open street. She thought that everyone saw her shame, her embarrassment, her nothingness.

'Ah Seadhna, you're home now,' folk said to her, as if it was the inevitable end to those who tried to leave. She did not disavow them of their assumptions; she smiled faintly, her eyes disconnected from her inner brain, feeling as far away as it was possible to be, from the town and the people around her.

She went through the winter in a trance while her parents went about their normal lives, letting her mesh in and around them and waiting for a sign that the pall might lift. In time, Seadhna felt the age-old insistence of work and sanity. The Calvinist pull of the simple equation.

'I suppose I'll have to think about a job. I'll have to do something.'

'There's no hurry.' They smiled wanly. There was little talk.

'I could do that,' she thought, as she read the 'Vacancies' section in the local paper. 'I really could do that … I could do that so well.'

'They're building a new Art Centre.' *For putting art in.* 'And you've got your degree,' her mother tried to encourage. The weight and hope that they had as her parents, that there might be a future for her, and their shy, understated pride shimmered around her. 'It's the oil money. They're gifting the building, and getting grants and it will be a great thing for the tourists.' Sadie stopped herself before she began to sound too eager.

Seadhna thought *Yes, I could do that*, and picked up the phone in an optimistic minute and phoned the council administrator for an application form. They asked her to spell her name and she repeated it. 'It's Gaelic,' she replied.

'What's that?' said a bright chirpy non-local voice, 'S-E-A and then what?'

She felt her heart sink, plodding through the foreign spelling of her name, her optimism gone by the end of the call.

'Iseabail's coming up for the weekend,' tried Sadie again. 'Why don't the two of you go out? You could look up some of your old pals.'

Yes, Iseabail, big sister who had got it right, thought Seadhna in a flash of bitterness, *about it being all about bombs and them blowing you all up.* Early on, Iseabail fixed her logical eyes on a straight furrow, then unswerving forged her way into medicine. How could her parents not be truly proud of Iseabail? Seadhna smiled weakly back. Behind her eyes a smattering of envy.

'Are you okay?' asked Iseabail.

Faintly amused, Seadhna remarked to herself how easily fooled people were. Mostly they were content with a smile, or merely your reassurance that you were indeed 'okay'. It's what they wanted to hear, and because *they* wanted you to be okay they were willing to believe you without question.

Right then, for Seadhna, her whole self was schisming in two, and the cavern between her public face and her inner cascading soul was opening up ever wider. She could smile and say she was 'okay' and no one knew how loudly empty metal trash cans and fragile china were crashing and tumbling inside her. It was the easiest lie in the world. She looked across to her mother's eyes, knowing her mother could never appreciate the gulf that now existed between that Seadhna from before and her old pals. The old place that was there before she left was out of reach, too, and had become somewhere else.

'Come on we'll go to the Reel and Strathspey concert. It's in the town hall on Tuesday night.'

Seadhna did not have the will to resist. So Iseabail duly took Seadhna to the concert, following the earnest whispered instructions of her mother: 'You've got to get her out among people.' Iseabail escorted her silent sister down the familiar road to the hall and they queued outside, waiting for the great double doors to open.

'Remember queuing here for jumble sales?' tried Iseabail, attempting to conjure up a shared memory of buying jumble presents for their mother, which after a suitable time on display got secreted under the sink in the old wash-house. Seadhna smiled back but in her head could only remember the ugliness, her mind transported back to the age of seven. The jumble sale queue with the boys and girls in her class, Edna, Sandy and the rest, and the time they were all in a frenzy over the 'darky'. There had been a black boy whose name she could not even remember. He stood there with the other kids, mesmerised and puzzled as the leering, self-righteous face of Sandy Baker sang unchallenged.

'Way down south where the darkies shovel coal
A darkie shoved his shovel up a nuther darkie's HOLE'.

The doctor's family had wanted to adopt the black boy. Sandy's rhyme transfixed Seadhna with horror way back then. It resounded and yelled among the pack of kids who had never seen a black face. It forced itself out still. The guilty pain of being among the crows. *If yi fly wi' the craws y'ill get shot wi' them* …

'They called fir thi doctur,
Bit the doctur coodna come'.

Sandy glanced about looking for his audience. No one told him to be quiet and his sing-song burned through the years as the adults at the front of the queue remained oblivious. The seven-year-old Seadhna ached for someone who would stop it.

'So he died of constipation
WITH A SHOVEL UP HIS BUM.'

The performing seven-year-old Sandy looked around at once for audience approval, sure that he sang on behalf of everyone, but on this occasion he was disappointed and diverted onto something else. He shouted loudly to another kid who might elevate his status by being belittled in front of the others.

ISS

'Geez a Spangle, Bert, yi fat bastard.'

The black boy decided himself that he preferred Barnardo's in Glasgow to staying with the doctor. He was more used to the city, they said, and it was true that some Glasgow children had never seen a cow. It seemed unbelievable at the time.

Seadhna felt the tears from all those years welling up. She so wanted someone to stop it, and felt the shame of being there and not being brave enough.

waving

The twenty-third of March was the spring equinox, bringing a full moon and big tides. Willie Bremner knew there was bad weather coming. The shipping forecast had indicated low pressure out in the Atlantic so there was an urgency to get the creels picked up and taken in. There would be no time to set them further out in deep water. At five in the morning Willie hammered on Michael and Geordie's door.

'Wu'll need tae be away at slack water and let the tide tae tak us along the face,' Willie yelled, striding off along the dark street to get the boat's engine going. Geordie was surly with a hangover, and Michael got him out of bed as usual, the two of them following Willie to the pier in the pre-dawn cold. Willie was businesslike, knowing they needed all their time while the weather held and the *Sula* left the pier with a great pink glow firing up above the hills. *Red sky in the morning …*

'If we get ahead noo wu'll be in afore three.' It was calm still, but the tightness of the isobars meant the wind would definitely whip in fast. 'Wu'll head fur the Craig, then go right along the beach.'

They did the usual things, got the kettle on the stove, cleared the deck ready to take aboard all the creels. The plan was to pick them all up and take them in on the boat until the storm moved away. To leave them out in the gale would mean destruction on the rocks. In the shallow, jagged places where the lobsters crept they would soon be battered, twisted and useless. *The sea is no bath water, it is lumps of weight like concrete … like hooses crashin' doon on yi.*

The swell under the Craig was bad because you never got a true wave.

The Atlantic came in, hitting the cliffs with all the power of the entire ocean, then rebounded. It was all over the place like drunken dancing bears. The boat juggled and lurched but they got the first rope in and stowed. Ten creels aboard, they never even opened them up. Willie calculated it all and he knew they'd be well laden by the time they got the lot on board. The boat would be heavy. She would be at her limits. If they stayed too long under the cliff they would lose the high tide and then risk going aground picking up the inshore creels. *Time and tide …*

White water started to break on the sandbar and Willie felt the frenetic frills of the wind flapping its menacing petticoat, on its way with a big blow. They steamed away to the next rope of creels and the next. Michael deftly hooked the marker buoy each time and set the rope in the hauler. Geordie heaved the creels into a stack at the stern, knowing the urgency. Willie yelled instructions from the wheelhouse, lurching out of the door to work the hauler which screeched with the weight of the heavy tang-laden gear. Now the wind slapped with rain and spray and the deck was covered in thick brown seaweed dragged up on the creels. Michael heaved the tangles over the side, slipping and falling as he did so.

Willie's eyes flicked from sea to creels to sky. The boat began to heave, and the top-most creels fell from the stack. Geordie cursed and went to sling them back up on the pile. At last they got the final rope in, and Willie, wasting no time, swung the boat round to head out of the shallow water and home. But there was way too much loaded onto the boat. She was low in the water and the wash swilled through the gunnels. Willie tried to steer out of the swell but he couldn't put on any speed. The motion picked the boat up and carried her and he just had to try and keep her steady. He said nothing.

Then quietly, like a soft conspiracy, the deck was full with sea. In seconds they knew they were in big trouble. This was new. How to sort this, how to salvage things. What to do. There was no practise for this one. Everything was a jumble of creels and rope and baskets. They were a hundred yards from the shore and Willie, shouting, tried to cut loose the life raft.

'She'll go!'

Their words lost in the wind and the noise.

Hope tae fuck that thing releases.

Buoys were floating. Geordie was swearing and panicking; Michael caught his fear in a glance. An avalanche of water and wood slammed down on their heads. The boat tipped grotesquely. The men tumbled and slid on the incline. In seconds the stern was under. Willie scrambled towards the life raft set on the wheelhouse as it tipped. The familiar perspective of the boat went crazy.

Has he tied the fucking thing? And Michael felt for his knife.

They were all in the water, gasping and grabbing for the bottom boards that were floating around them. Baskets half submerged, bobbing and sinking. Ropes that could pull you under or save you. There was no knowing what anything was attached to. Suddenly the life raft sprang up, the release mechanism worked. *Thankchrist.* It was there, inflating, drifting from the boat, momentarily stopped by a clutter of rope in the sea. When the wind caught it, no one would be able to catch it. Willie swam heavily towards it. But as he flailed through the ice-cold water, a fish box released from its wedged position in the hull of the sinking boat, catapulted upwards through the sea. The pressure sent it up like a cork from a bottle and with a brutal force it hit Willie under the jaw and knocked him right out.

Michael, heading towards the raft, caught sight of Willie's head lurching sideways and then lolling like a rag doll. His face slid under the water and in that split second Michael thought about Willie's wife and that he would have to tell her. He never gave Geordie a thought. It was every man for himself. An onshore wind took the raft. He just needed to get to it. A life jacket tossed on the sea welled towards him, then was snatched away again by the motion into the blackness. Michael's mind and all his strength and being were fixed on one thing.

the shore

At seven o'clock that same evening, the double doors of the town hall opened and the crowd, moving as one, pressed forward, clutching their yellow concert tickets. It was a sell-out. Seadhna and Iseabail took their seats, settling into the comfortably sagging ex-NAAFI canvas chairs. The hall soon overheated, the wall-mounted electric bars glowing, as restless children gravitated away from their parents to the trestle benches at the front. They had only gone twenty minutes into the show, as Fred Weatherspoon was delivering his solo humorous song to ukulele accompaniment, when the performance was interrupted by the boom of the rockets. Everyone in the hall knew what it was at once and shifted, looking at their neighbours in the dark. *The maroons. The lifeboat.* The audience creaked in their tubular seats, moving uneasily as Fred Weatherspoon manfully proceeded with the tale of 'Walter's wanderin' coo'. It was a bad night. Equinoxes. Unpredictable wind. *Who could it be*? There was no knowing until the interval and the crowd spilled from the concert venue into the fractious night to be infected by the horror. A blind dark search was going on somewhere out on the white-topped water so far away from the warm couthy concert in the hall.

'It's the *Sula*. Willie Bremner and the McLeay boys,' announced an earnest voice with the news everyone waited for. The identity of the boat. The men. The knitting of information on the rest of the crew. The level of worry or closeness, mere spectator, relieved disinterest, or a stabbing to the gut.

The musicians and crowd mingled outside the hall, sharing a common look that spoke the inevitability of some kind of tragedy. Nights like this rarely brought happy endings.

'He was in your class, wasn't he?' said Iseabail. Seadhna nodded. Iseabail was already using the past tense.

we are

In his dream Michael was paralysed. He could see his hands but they would not move. He looked at his fingers and willed them to open and then, as if operating a remote mechanical body, manoeuvred his arm towards the rope. He saw his hand connect with the rope and willed his fingers to close around it. He could feel nothing. It was beyond cold. In the dream it seemed real, and then it seemed as if he watched himself from another place.

There was one single thread intact within him that impelled him to get the heavy part of his body up and over the huge obstacle ahead. He must do that one thing and then his work would be over. There could be only one attempt, for after that he knew his strength would be spent. Then it would be like *kirning over an engine until the battery went dead*. It was his instinct that guided him to use the motion of the sea, catch it and let it hurl his body weight up and then over into the raft. He felt the rhythm of the waves and went with a big one surging over the inflated tube, pushing down with his fists on the rope and locking his arms to dive over the slippery rubber. His head and shoulders were over and his legs trailed in the sea. With his hands still knotted in the rope, he lurched awkwardly forward and a bone in his wrist snapped when he slumped head-first into the raft and lost consciousness. It was black dark. The life raft lurched, tipping up the sides of the growing waves.

At seven o'clock Willie's wife reported the boat overdue as the concert audience settled into their seats. The lifeboat men all knew they'd be looking for wreckage and nobody could survive that cold for long. The coastguards with torches on the beach saw the life raft grounding in the tide. The same wind that blew the *Sula* too near the rocks, and the same sea that swamped them, cast Michael towards the land. With lines attached round their waists, the coastguards waded out into the water among the debris from the boat. There was plenty stuff scattered on the beach, the ridiculous kettle making it ashore complete with its lid jammed in place.

we were

Next day the town was in mourning. It was on the Scottish News. The community were good at sea tragedies. Everyone had a part and everyone could be united. It went unsaid, but everyone silently acknowledged that George McLeay was no great loss, a drunken idiot, more a liability on a boat than anything else, but Willie had a wife and two bairns. Within days there was a collection for the bereaved, boxes placed in the shops and post office. The police tried to find the whereabouts of Harry to tell him about Geordie, but he was untraceable. There were no bodies to bury.

He was dead for five minutes. Actually died. Bella wis there when he came roond.

*The whole out-of-body experience! He saw lights and angels …*whispered the shop gossips.

But it was untrue. Michael couldn't remember anything. He woke up in the hospital, as if in another world.

'A big wave, I think. That was it. Hid swamped us.'

Annie and Tom took Agnes to visit at his bedside. The sombre faces surrounded Michael, bare-chested with a plaster on his arm, and them all sitting around the bed in strange roles. His mother ashen with sunken eyes. Annie with the accoutrements of hospital visits, a paper bag of pandrops and grapes. After delivery of the hospital gifts, Annie waited a moment in the unfamiliar silence and took from her handbag a polythene bag.

'I kept this. I meant to gie yi hid sooner, hid'll be the thing that saved yi.'

Agnes looked across toward her sister, disdain mixed with sorrow as Annie placed the plastic bag next to Michael on the bed. Inside was the shrivelled fragment of foetal skin from Michael's birth, the caul.

'Hid's a good luck thing, Michael. Hid'll protect yi again.'

'Uh huh,' replied Michael blankly viewing the bizarre token which now became the centre of everything. No one knew what to say. They were unused to sitting talking in any situation, let alone this.

'Weel,' added Annie, 'the sea'll no tak yi while yi hiv that, Michael,' and after a pause, 'hid's the hood yi wur born wi.'

All were relieved when the visiting hour was over, and once they had left him Michael called the nurse over and pointed to Annie's lucky token.

'Yi kin tak that awaye,' he said.

'What is it?'

'Nonsense,' he replied, 'owld wives' nonsense.' *I dinna work wi' luck.*

In the town everyone wanted to be glad for Michael that he had survived. Once he was out of the hospital they whispered as he passed and the men nodded at him in the street. 'Michael.' And greeted him, 'Aye.'

The other deaths shifted a barrier. As the script was wrenched from their hands, Michael earned his place. In time it was obvious that no viable remains from the other fishermen were going to appear, so the town council instigated a memorial service for the two drowned men. The dismal Protestant church that always smelled of funerals was unusually packed. Michael attended out of duty but didn't sing the hymns and kept his stare firmly ahead during the prayers. Throughout the service Geordie's frightened look invaded his brain, and the sight of Willie as his head slipped under the sea and away to the bottom was something he still had been unable to describe to his wife.

While the minister assured the congregation that Geordie and Willie were at peace in a better place, safe in the arms of angels, Michael felt his stomach tighten.

Willie's wife took to combing the shore, searching for memories. For weeks, bits of the boat still washed ashore, broken painted wood and fish boxes with the fishing numbers on them. It bound her and Agnes together in the first months. *She's losing it … ye hiv tae move on …* They both went looking, going right down into the ebb, hoping to find the bodies and expecting them to look as they had done when they last saw them. Agnes forgot all the bad things about George.

'You shouldna go doon ti the shore, ma. There'll be precious little left o' him noo.'

Michael didn't say what the townsfolk were saying, that the crabs would have had a good feed.

Have you ever seen a droond body? Well it comes back up black and bloated. If they ever find anything hid'll be totally unrecognisable. The partans eat off the face first …

Willie's wife thought she found a yellow rubber boot belonging to him and took it home and cried over it. Baillie Harvey put the collected money into a post office account.

'We should divide it equally,' said John Rufus, 'Mrs McLeay's loss is as great,' and no one dared argue. The shore became a different place. It was sinister, haunted by the prospect of stumbling over the carcasses of the dead men.

What would you do if you found one of them? Yi see hoo fast the crabs strip the flesh off a fish …

It was too horrific. All of that time, Seadhna avoided the beach and it became a sinister no-go area.

Michael, however, had his new status as the survivor of a tragedy and the community needed him to reinforce the parts they all had in the loss.

Iss? Wur the close-knit community … That thing they speak about on the news, whenever there's a boat lost.

A tight-knit community … that's iss.

Aye. Tight and sweaty all right, like tense wool on four sock pins, strangling itself, came another voice.

Willie Bremner's wife had nothing to mourn over, going down to the black creel shed to sit among the tar and the tools. Before he was lost she never went there. It was his domain, a man's place. Back home at night she took one of his jumpers into the bed with her, trying to smell him. The two wee ones creeping in beside her and her keeping them there because she missed his body warmth so much. Then one morning she came over to find Michael and give him the key to the shed.

'I think somebody should use it. The stuff in it and everything. It's all fishing stuff. You have it.'

It was like handing over a spirit, if you believed in all that.

Michael took the key but it was a while before he went down to the tar shed and opened up the door. The first time he did, a cat shot out the door at his feet. It must have been in there a full fortnight without food. For a while he felt the guilt of surviving, felt that he did not have the right to pick up Willie's tools and use them, but then he tipped up a broken creel that Willie had set by to fix, and took out a roll of twine to mend the gash.

Jock Tamsin's

The McLeays were merely bit players in the official story of the town. A moment illuminated by a sea tragedy that earned a report on the Scottish News. *George McLeay, 23,* named as a missing fisherman along with *skipper William Bremner, a married father of two.* The town felt the surge of their collective drama in the tragedy, then passed on to other things. *The close-knit community has been rocked by the tragedy …* said the radio voice.

Agnes's eyes focussed on the deep sink. Her days were spent hand-washing and scrubbing on a scrubbing board. She peeled the skins off potatoes, the mucky residue mounting on the ball of her thumb, and the small cuts from knives scored her forefinger. She was always up before seven in the morning, sweeping the lino of the kitchen as if she would wear it through, beating out mats with a cane carpet beater. She never owned a Hoover. At eight she took a shopping basket along to the dairy and then to Harrald Jeffrey's, her hair brushed in a side parting, white streaks among black.

She's a witch, whispered the children on their road to school. Then she had her cleaning jobs at the doctor's and the banker's where she wiped round the toilet rims of their big houses, the stubborn shit of the banker sticking to the pan. Drawing open the bedroom curtains, she picked the clothes of the doctor's children off their carpeted bedroom floors among the must from alien dreams and sweaty nights. Then she rubbed fingerprints from the glass doors and sprayed Pledge on the polished living-room furniture. Finally she sat in the quiet kitchen, of the banker's's foreign existence, the breakfast dishes dried and stowed. Then from the top of the mantelpiece she lifted her pay in coins and secreted them into her zipped purse. A cycle of cleaning and tidying, leaving behind the gleaming brass plate and doorknob of the bank house, 'Mr and Mrs L. Paterson', the heavy wooden door closed after her.

After the wreck, Michael went back to the whitefish for a spell, but the shares were getting less. The catches were smaller, there were bigger overheads for fuel and bank loans and less and less for the crew. He did five months on a purse seiner, going for the mackerel way up in the Norwegian waters, loading them onto the filthy Klondyke ships rusting in Peterhead harbour. On those trips he avoided the nightly gambling in the mess room, getting called a tight bastard and ignoring it. Then, with his pay secure, he reckoned he had enough to set up with his own boat, something fibreglass.,

'Fir yi don't need tae paint that. I'll hiv tae stay on here fir a while, ma. Ah'll pay yi keep an' everythin'.'

'That's fine, son,' said Agnes distantly.

He bought her a new colour TV with his pay. Michael was the owner of property too, Willie's bequeathed creel shed and fifty creels, but there were still things he didn't touch. In the shed he came across a fishing bag with a bottle of rum wrapped in brown paper and two cans of Sweetheart Stout, provisions for a trout fishing trip on the loch. Such clues to Willie's life that he felt he had no right to.

Michael started off buying up a load of second-hand creels from Albert Poke, who was selling his boat with all the gear.

'Hid's costan' me a fortune in diesel and still got all me loans tae pay tae the bank. Nivver thought I'd end up a bank employee but there you are. Ah'm as good as workin' fir the bank. The big crabbers fae the continent are clearing oot the whole lot.' Albert took Michael's wad of cash from the purse trip, pausing to peel through the layers and count. The metal on Albert's creels was rusty, but Michael knew he could wind old rope round the frames to preserve what was there.

'Hid's no worth it at me age tae haul a thoosan' creels, go oot an' find some bastard's shot over yurs and the whole thing's in a bloody raffle. Twenty year ago everybody got a living with a couple o' hundred.' He paused and put Michael's cash away in his pocket. 'Aye, min, yu'll mebbe dae alright wi' singles right in where the big boats cannae git.'

fading

It was difficult to pinpoint when it started. Agnes started to repeat the same things. She used his brother's name or his father's, but at the start you could just say it was a mistake, a little confusion. She had so many names in her head, dipping in and just picking the wrong one out of the bag, it could be just a slip and nothing major. But then she left the gas on and that was hard to ignore.

Michael came back from sea and the whole house was heavy with the sweet, sickly fug of Calor. Agnes was asleep open-mouthed in the sitting room, the door to the gas-filled kitchen closed, and a pot containing three eggs, sitting on the unlit cooker awaiting water from the tap.

'Fuck's sake, mither. The place is full of gas.' Michael went to the cooker and turned it off, opening wide the back door and the metal-framed window.

'Oh Harry, yur back. Is that yur shift by wi' already?'

Michael ignored the double miss – person and time zone. 'Mither, yi coulda blown up the hoose.'

'My, there's an aful smell o' somethin'. Whit's that, Harry?'

'Wur yi cookan', mither?'

'No, I wisna, I had me tea afore.'

Michael opened the front door and let the draught flow through the building, diluting the cloying sweetness until it was gone. There were unfinished clues of half-begun activities in different areas all over the house. A cup with water in it and no teabag. The iron on, clicking and crackling with nothing to iron. Disjointed pointers to the random threads of Agnes's day.

Others noticed too and someone contacted the nurse, who bypassed Michael and instead contacted Shirley. She got the nurse's call switched through to the hotel dining room as she surveyed the white starched tablecloths. There was nothing for it; Shirley headed north to sort it all out. The house sale was barely through.

'Mam's wandering. We've got to do something about her.'

Michael was silent.

'She'll have to go into the Home.'

He had seen it happening.

'She might have to go to a place on the other side of the island. I mean, you can't just expect to get in. There's a huge shortage of spaces.'

Michael responded to Shirley's directives with Ayes and Uh-huhs while Agnes sat in the living room with *Coronation Street* on the TV.

'She's a danger,' declared Shirley, 'there's no two ways about it. She'll burn the house down and herself.'

It was all arranged. Agnes would have a two-week 'trial' period at the Old People's Home.

It was not a real trial, of course, just a softening-up process to get her out of the house. Shirley reluctantly took another weekend off to sort out the stuff.

'God, what a pile of old rubbish.'

The paltry array of clothes that Shirley arranged on the bed amounted to barely a suitcase-full. There were no books, just one school photograph of George's class and an old postcard from Strathpeffer. Clattering the wardrobe door open, Shirley heaved out the clothes that had been her father's.

'Well, she'll no be wantin' them. Whit did she keep all this for? This can all go to the dump. It's no even fit for the Red Cross.'

When they took Agnes's stuff up to the Home, the senior care-worker met them.

'Your mother's doing fine. She's a bit, ehm … confused, but it's the change of place and getting used to the staff.'

Agnes had spent the day asking everyone she met if they had seen her apron. 'I canna find it anywhaar …' Her voice trailed, her eyes drifted. Approaching visitors to the Home, she asked them all if they had seen it. 'I'll need to go home for it. Will yi tak me home ti git me apron?'

Each party of visitors that Agnes approached moved off in turn, disconcerted at the over-familiar encounter, sometimes humouring her. *Poor thing. So confused. Wur fither's in a wheelchair but at least he's still got all his wits*, and they nodded, thankful for small mercies.

'What apron are you talking about, mither?' was the start of a disconnected conversation.

'I'll need to get the washing in.'

Shirley rolled her eyes. 'Right, I'll have to go.' Shirley developed the technique of talking loudly to her mother. 'I'm getting the boat back tonight. And I have a big conference to set up for at the hotel. You'll be well looked after here, mam, and I'll be back up to see you …' – she paused, thinking that Christmas would not be practical because of the office party season – 'soon.'

Agnes was left marooned in a red high-backed chair as Shirley swept out of the communal sitting room where the television was showing a teatime cartoon. No sooner was Shirley away than Agnes was up and moving towards the door as if pre-programmed.

'Whit am I doin' here? Will somebody …?'

Back inside the kitchen of Harbour Terrace, the apron she was searching for hung on the back of the door from a hook. Michael looked at it for a second, then moved through to the sitting room where the glass budgies had survived Shirley's purge but not yet made it to the old folks' home with Agnes. That would come after the 'trial', when familiar objects could be added to the bare room. He switched the TV on in time to get the weather forecast and pulled a grease-covered engine manual from the arm of the sofa onto his lap.

Shirley had booked a van to take the furniture to the auction mart. 'It's hardly worth it, but some folk like that old stuff,' she had remarked. Shirley knew how the locals would snigger over her mother's things and indirectly over her too. With the council house purchased and her mother now out of it, she decided to give it a proper clean out, ready to let to tourists in the summer. Then, she told Michael, she would be away.

'You'll need to put your name on the list,' she instructed him. So Michael made his way to the council offices to put his name down. Single men were not much of a priority, so he was well down the queue.

'Okay,' she conceded, 'You can stay on till it's all sorted.'

from other lives

Seadhna went to the house contents sale. It was a grand social event. A public perusal of people's effects where indeed silent scorn, maybe pathos and sometimes wonder could be exuded over the lots and the boxes. Inside the agricultural shed that doubled as an auction mart, Seadhna sat on the trestle wooden benches, in for the duration. The buying public rustled in anticipation. It was an entertainment and Seadhna mused that she might find something for the cottage she hoped one day to live in.

The auction was addictive. There was an inlaid tiled table that she wanted, but it went right up to thirty-five pounds and she had to stop bidding. She also fancied a Super 8 camera but decided it would be unrealistic. It was bound to be a hassle to get film … Frustrated with the failure to get the table she felt reckless and saw what looked like a beautiful ornate wardrobe with a curved mirror. When nobody bid for it she couldn't understand why. The auctioneer looked round.

'Who will start me? Come on! 50p to start me …'. He swept another glance around the seated bidders, realising he'd have to work a bit harder a bit to shift this one. '10p then. Come on now. Plenty firewood in that wardrobe,' and with that he smiled as if it was the best bargain ever.

Seadhna was hooked. From where she sat the wardrobe looked majestic, although she hadn't inspected it at the viewing. She wasn't considering it for firewood, but as a thing of antique beauty. But where she would store it never entered her head. Up went her hand.

There was no need for cards at this auction. The auctioneer knew everybody by name. 'Seadhna Rufus.' He looked around to see if another bid might come in and then fixed his eyes on her. Others were looking at her too, assuming she must need firewood. Nobody else put on a bid and after another couple of tries to raise the figure to fifty pence the auctioneer paused. 'Sold.' The clerk scribbled '10p' onto a white piece of card which already had the lot number printed on the back, and wound his way through the crowd.

The sale was about to break for lunch before the auction of the rest of the 'big stuff' and the interval gave everyone the opportunity to inspect their buys. When Seadhna got a close look at her purchase it was, of course, completely peppered with worm. There was no way it could even be treated. It was basically powder. *That's why nobody else wanted it.* For a second Seadhna felt cheated, then she laughed. She thought her 10p was a complete loss until, swinging open the doors, she saw something inside. Rolled up, stiff and hard like a rug, were what seemed to be animal skins. Seadhna took them out into the light. *Right enough*, they were skins all right. The unmistakable mottle of seal. The two auctioneer's assistants heaved the wardrobe out the back doors of the shed and smashed it up outside, beaming as they set about their task. 'We'll be the only wans getting a heat oota this pile of old junk.' The dust rose like a fine red peat-ash mist. They couldn't even save the mirror. None of it looked as good as it had done from the distance, but Seadhna took the skins under her arm and left the pieces of worm-eaten wardrobe in the skip.

At home in her parents' house she unrolled them, stroking the rough, hard hair from head to foot. They were beautiful. The perfect construction of something once living that swam in the sea, sleek and deft. A rarity to touch, the evolutionary engineering of every perfectly placed hair. She knew that seal hunting was banned, illegal and a thing from another time, but her finger found a stiff bullet hole and played through it, hooking her into some bygone place.

Seadhna never got a reply from her job application at the Arts Centre. At first she thought someone might have forgotten to let her know, perhaps she might miss an interview, the letter had perhaps got lost. She eyed the phone, wondering if she should pick it up and call. But a passing comment overheard in the shop gave her the news that stung her. Apparently the management committee were overwhelmed with applications, attracting a lot of high-calibre talent from the south. After advertising in the national papers, there were simply so many applicants they couldn't reply to everyone. The job went to someone from London who had never been up to the isles before the interview. They had fallen in love with the place, apparently.

There were other job possibilities. The net shed that stood down by the pier was all but redundant with only one whitefish trawler taking crew from the town, and it landed and took on stores in Wick most of the time. The same Justin who came to stop the seal cull had moved into property and tourism. He approached the fishermen's co-op and made them an offer. John Rufus tried to persuade them not to sell, but all they could see was the short-term gain, the cash in their pockets. 'You'll be selling off an asset that you might never be able to get back,' John warned, but they ignored it and took Justin's cash. With that, the net shed that John Rufus had negotiated from the laird all these years back passed to Justin, who had seen great potential for an upmarket eatery. With his new Bistro now complete and the nets and creels artistically draped around the interior to provide a 'themed' feel, Justin was recruiting waitresses. Seadhna applied for a job.

'Well, if nothing else, I know I can do that,' she told her mother. In Justin's office she sat down to await his questions, deciding what she should say and what she should leave out. She told him nothing about herself other than that she had worked in an Edinburgh bar. And barely lifting his eyes to make eye contact, he said he would let her know.

other places

'There was a phone call, but not from the Bistro,' said her mother. 'Somebody called Cammy … I think it was maybe that young lad I met with you at the shows. He said he would call back … he was in a phone box.'

Cammy telephoned from a parallel universe. His whole weekend had been a whirl. Damon and Lizzie's band had finally been signed to a label and they'd got a British tour lined up supporting Sham 69. Everyone round about them felt like pop stars instead of dole scroungers. Things kicked off with a pre-tour gig at the Astoria in Edinburgh, everyone euphoric, wanting to touch success, the big world of *Melody Maker* and *Top of the Pops*. Then there was the real support gig in London at the Hammersmith Apollo. All the fan base from Edinburgh climbed aboard the Stagecoach bus to go and support them. Cammy was well in there because he had made the costumes and the record company paid an advance up front. It was like being pools winners and noticed all at same time. Respite from all being unemployed nobodies and part of the 'price of controlling inflation'.

Crash pads from Balham to Chelsea were found and the Scottish bondage army of Mohicans and stilettos descended into the big smoke looking for a pub that opened after midnight. They packed into the gig whispering that they'd seen scouts from Island Records, a producer from Chrysalis, then all spilled out among the other punk tribes that congregated.

'Jyro Day', switching to her stage name, primped herself in the dressing room with a clutch of hair pins coralling her peroxide hair into a beehive. 'Fifties meets rubber' was the image statement of the band. Jyro wore a pink tight-cut shirt dress and bolero and long black gloves studded with diamanté. She and 'Syne On' were the front people, Syne with a rockabilly quiff, tight drainpipe trousers and a selection of shirts from loud Country and Western cowboy to *Star Trek*.

'We need an image a bit moved on from punk. You know, not so trashy and a bit more glam.'

Cammy was in the dressing room too, checking the costumes, oversewing a split seam in Syne's trousers. He'd had to make ten different outfits. The stage show mattered, and Syne and Jyro had all of a sudden taken on the personas of showbiz people with an entourage. But Cammy knew that plenty people would see his costumes and come looking for more.

They all had vodkas and Pils lager and then lines of speed. Everyone felt great. They were on top of the world and nothing was impossible. The crowd whistled and surged, and even though they were just the support, they carried the show.

The Edinburgh posse were banging and shouting. The night never ended, they buzzed and danced into the London dawn. They topped up with more speed and kept going all day. Then, when it came time to get on the night bus home, everything in London was jumping out at Cammy, announcing itself in all its colour and smell and sound. He walked up the King's Road just like a king, filling up his chest with big London air.

'Fuck. This is it!'

On the bus home to Scotland, his eyes danced over the seemingly exquisite details of the bus interior as the disappearing images of lights and sleeping towns flicked past. Everything had a speed-induced dimension and interest, even the velveteen seat backs had a new allure that was all-consuming.

In his pocket he had four hundred pounds, all cash in hand, that the dole would never learn about, and because he had all that money he felt superhuman, as if nothing could touch him, and a sudden idea came that he should do something liberating, go somewhere far off. He checked the inside pocket of his Flip baseball jacket and there it was. Seadhna's home phone number at her folk's place, scrawled on the back of a table napkin from Khushi's restaurant.

'The Shetlands ... naw, the Orkneys. Ah kent it wis up north sumwhere. Right, that's whit w'ull dae. Wu'll go an' visit Seadhna in her island habitat.' His mind made up, he jumped onto a service bus on Princes Street that took him nearly all the way to the Forth Road Bridge. From there he just decided he would hitch.

When he walked out onto the tolls, he was still speeding. It was no problem getting lifts. By the A9 he was slumped in the overheated cab of a lorry delivering janitorial supplies to Highland hotels.

'Well you wurna much company, son. Take it yir pretty exhausted. Yi snored the hale way fae Aviemore,' the driver remarked after nudging him awake at Thurso. 'Did yi say yi wis getting the boat?'

'Aye,' and Cammy tumbled out of the cab as if he'd been beamed into another dimension. In an effort to get some kind of bearings he looked around, trying to make sense of the campsite with its rusty playground furniture, the drystone dykes, the fields of long summer grass and then the great swathe of blue sea ahead.

'Boat leaves fae doon there.' And the lorry driver pointed. 'Tak yi fifteen minutes tae walk it.'

'Great, ta, cheers mate.'

pictures

The summer tourist season was well underway. Each week brought a new bus tour to the hotel in the town. The same routine for each four-day tour, bags heaved from the boot of the bus and disorientated travellers looking around. They were Germans this time. The blonde hair and leather bags announced silently the tourists' visual difference. Their talk crackled with a mixture of wide, simple vowels edged with abrupt consonants. The tour from Wuppertal had been on the road for twenty-four hours with only essential stops but they were still keen to get up at six o'clock in time to get all the way round the island on the first outing of the morning.

The Germans' enthusiasm meant early breakfasts for the waitresses, who far preferred the lazier Americans even though they made a great fuss over their eggs. Michael never looked round as he passed the strangers, neither of their lives crossed in any way. He headed to the pier, intent on the work he had set out for the day, checking his creels and landing the catch to the shipping agent.

Collectively waiting outside their hotel, the townsfolk saw the Germans as one body, merely defined by nationality. There was no real avenue intersecting the differing sets of lives. Sometimes there were glimpses of common things: a small overweight woman fussing with her purse; a pacifying gentleman, smiling from tired eyes. Unspoken, the shopkeepers wondered about Nazis, keeping their guard. The relationship was commercial. There was no time, nor inclination in the busy tour schedule for it to be anything else. They would never have to know anything about Klaus and Anna and the trip that was a retirement gift from their children. Had anyone been able to converse, they may have discovered that Klaus, indeed, had been a submariner, all over the North Atlantic during the war, and they were truly embarrassed and subdued about Hitler and that old Germany ...

Later in the day the Germans disembarked after a policed circuit of the Standing Stones, and took some time to walk in the quaint street. Their wondering gaze marked them out as they peered at this holiday destination presented as a backdrop of scenic houses, quaint and angled – what they called 'Georgian vernacular'. The tour group shambled to a stop looking for a place that sold proper coffee.

'Ja, ein gute Kaffee.' And one of the party pointed them back in the direction they had just come.

The sun tempted Agnes out of the yawing double doors, the bees buzzing on the flowers planted by the community service gang. In minutes she had left the Home and reached the street. Among the shadowed gables no one knew her from the tourists. Somewhere behind the gaunt mouth and reaching eyes, she felt a familiar security, that this was a place where people would know her. If others lingered their gaze upon her they may have registered some strangeness. Looking for a second more, they could have categorised her as a local character. *Local colour.* They might have photographed her as she sat unaware on a bench. But for Agnes nothing was sure anymore.

She lived in the current second or five minutes, her memory hardly even stretching to the half-hour, let alone a day. Communication was a loop of rhetoric going through her head, manifesting itself as speech. Her legs were lumpen from the knee down. Fluid was collecting. The pleated skirt was incongruous and her clothes chosen by carers. No one else in that July street snapshot wore a tweed skirt.

Seadhna noticed the legs. The woman seemed to be walking against the tide of tourists. They were somehow too white. A heavy fleshy white, greyed by buried veins and flushed pink blotches. Thick ankles. Water retention, *You should put your feet up on a stool, Mrs McLeay.*

Seadhna walked behind and gained on her. She was in a hurry too, on a mission to meet Cammy and thrilled at the prospect of seeing someone from her other life. Seadhna assumed that Agnes was a tourist from a cruise ship … a Saga tour. In the summer, with all the visitors, you no longer expected to see people you knew on the street. Your eyes could rove around the crowds, anticipating anonymity.

The boat bringing Cammy was due in half an hour.

A foreign place.

Agnes searched among the faces for features she knew. She was expecting smiles of recognition and waiting for someone to pass the time of day with her. She misinterpreted the looks of the Germans as greetings and half responded as they walked on past her to point the way to the museum. Klaus, always polite, moved aside as she strode towards him and then the flash of contact disappeared forever.

Seadhna started to realise that the woman didn't fit the context. She was turning her head back and looking around and still moving forward steadily but her walk was different. Even her gait had different expectations from the Germans. In one of those backward glances, Seadhna recognised her.

Agnes McLeay. Michael's mother. Michael the fisherman. Dementia. Agnes pressed and massaged something into her palms like a lump of dough and drifted on in the sea of faces. She continued past her old council house without any recognition of the place. She was never aware that her things had been trucked off to the Auction Mart. The dusty trunks with the smell of soot still there from the days she lived in a tinker's tent and the stench of damp moving with her and never quite leaving Annie's folded good linen.

That's what they do, thought Seadhna. *The ones that can walk, they go off looking for their homes.* The old folk making bids to escape back to their old lives. She had seen a man once before, similarly incongruous in a checked shirt, braces and boots, striding briskly past and greeting her assuredly in the old accent, 'Hid's a bonny day fir a waak.' The surety of his step almost made her weep. His desperate purpose.

Seadhna quickened her pace to overtake Agnes and swept around in front of her, beginning a conversation that could have seemed normal in any era of her life, but even so still sounded contrived. 'Hello, Mrs. McLeay, are you enjoying this bonnie weather the day?'

'Ah hello, hello,' replied Agnes, still looking around, kneading the ball. Seadhna knew Agnes would recognise the face and the accent. She may not know who she was, but it would be enough.

'Come wi' me and let's walk along this way,' she continued, turning Agnes around to face the other direction.

'Do you ken whaar they are?'

Who 'they' were and when and where the time might be that Agnes was thinking about didn't matter. It was the thread of worry in her voice. 'Lesley and Michael. They wur gaan on the boat this morning. And I don't ken whaar thuv geen. An' I don't ken whar George is geen ....'. The face was puffed and questioning. Hurt with the slight. Wondering.

'I'm sure hid'll be all right,' said Seadhna, making her accent thick to enter Agnes's world, 'Come this waye and wu'll get it aall sorted oot.'

'I thought they wid ha' come ti say goodbye. Thur jis' been merrit.'

'I'm sure they meant tae, maybe they hid tae rush.'

Seadhna attempted to change the subject to shift the woman's thought patterns. If they slipped so easily into the wrong time maybe they would slip out again as deftly.

'Come on, I'll give you a lift in the car. Here it is, look, the red one, and we'll go a run roon' the south end. Then I'll tak you back to your place. It'll be time for a cup of tea when we get there.'

Suddenly there was Michael. 'Whit the fuck ur yi doin oot here, ma?' He was sprung into a situation he had no skills for. There could be no show of tenderness. Any feeling went unspoken. Seadhna Rufus transcending this line, muddling the unwritten codes of the place, threatened everything. She was above him. She shouldn't be in Michael's world.

Seadhna continued guiding Agnes into the car. 'It's okay, I'll put her back.' Seadhna was careful not to say 'home' because it wasn't home, of course. It was the Eventide Home. Agnes was ready to slip into a half-forgotten conversation with her son.

'Oh Michael, yi'll need tae get some coal in fir yi fither's no fit.'

'Shussh, ma,' he hissed, 'Whit yi doin oot the Home? ... Fuck, mither.'

With three conversations and three time zones materialising, Seadhna pushed on;

'It's okay, Michael, I'll tak her up. Don't worry aboot it.'

He had never heard her say his name. Names were a weakness. Names divulged too much. Bynames and nicknames defined your weakness and kept you in your place. *Tinky Mickey.*

'She's gettan' worse ... it's a pain, a right fuckan' pain when she starts cavortan' aboot.' Michael's harsh tones exposing his thread of desperation. 'Tides must be makkan',' and he rooted his mother's emotional turmoil in the cycles of the moon and the sea. He fired his cigarette into the side of the street, leaving the butt to burn itself out. Seadhna continued with Agnes.

'I'll put her up.'

Michael was walking away, his voice mellowing only as he moved off. 'Aye. Okay.'

There were no more names, thank goodness.

Seadhna arrived at the door of the Home with Agnes in the passenger seat of her father's car. It was sunny and the front doors were still open. *Not a secure establishment*, they emphasised, gently insisting that they *did* like the residents to be accompanied when they went out. The doors normally shut automatically, and were way too heavy for frail arms to push open. But on this sunny day they were jammed open, against fire regulations, for air. *Open establishment*, a small administrative white lie.

Quite naturally Agnes would have walked out of an open door into the sun. By the time she reached the top of the hill her mind would have shifted back into the old days, when Harry was there working shifts at the bakery and Geordie was still alive. Emerging out of the car seemed a natural thing too. The context hailed no alarms.

'Here we are.'

'Oh yes, oh yes.' A reflex response, brain strands slowly converging.

The auxiliary joined seamlessly in the improvisation. 'Tea's up Agnes. Been for a walk have you? You like to do that, don't you,' casting Seadhna a conspiratorial glance. Agnes was led without protest up to the door, Seadhna and the auxiliary colluding in the gentle pretence, and only then did Seadhna feel some discomfort at the deception in progress.

'Oh, we often do that,' said the auxiliary, using the royal 'we', the indication that someone else is lesser. 'Come on, Agnes, there's a cup of tea and a biscuit waiting.'

The old woman passed through the double fire doors demurely, still clutching the ball in her hand which Seadhna could now see. It was her rolled-up stockings. Before she sat down on the high-backed, vinyl-covered chair to unfurl her stockings onto her legs, a shard of desperate memory struck. Glinting through her softened brain it urged her out the door and into the long corridor for something, some vital thing.

'I've got to run. I've got to get to the boat.'

stranger

Seadhna resumed her journey to meet Cammy. She caught sight of him from the pier and felt a burst of warmth. All that time with Henry she had abandoned him. Cammy went off on a wild punk dream, where people spat at artifice and said it like it was without some sort of contrived mystery to keep the proles feeling stupid.

'Come on, we're gonna do the whole lot.' Seadhna linked his arm.

'Whaddya mean?'

'There's a whole week of it. Its pure tack but you'll have a ball.'

'Ah s'pose when in Rome an' aw that.'

Seadhna waved the programme of events in front of him. 'Your week in the islands, the upmarket tourist-snob trail to the downmarket tourist-tat trail and some Standing Stones. There's a fancy dress too. We'll have to think of something.'

Cammy recoiled in mock horror. 'Naw, fuck, Ah' hate fancy dress! D'yi no see? Ah dae fancy dress aw' the time, no jist on wan Saturday in the year. Fishnet tights fir aw' the men, Ah s'pose? Closet cross-dressers? Ah'll dress *you* up if yir *that* keen.'

'We'll have to think of something edgy … and funny and maybe even … political.' Seadhna was smiling. Connecting and drinking in Cammy's liberating infectious optimism, his confident barrage of energy.

'Tak it wur no enterin' the baby show ur the dog show … ?'

'Come on, it'll be a hoot. I've swapped shifts in the café.'

'What happened wi' the gallery job then?'

'Och nothing. Thank you but no thank you. You know. Us Red Indians don't get the good jobs. We're doing dances for the tourists … selling beads an' that kinda stuff.'

'Cynical, eh? Don't let it eat ya up, hen. A pile of pish likely onyway. Galleries ur jist rich fowks' wallpaper shops.'

They were deep in conversation, oblivious to the watching town and its folk.

Cammy slung his rucksack over his shoulder. 'You mind Lizzie? Her that geed about on they pink stilettos aw the time?'

Seadhna remembered, the girl with the painted eyes and the Corleone father.

'Her and this architect guy got a band thigither. Stage names an' aw. She wis "Jyro Day", modelled on Doris Day, and he wis "Syne On". The drummer wis "Broo Chek"!' Cammy laughed at it all. 'Ah ken. Mad stupid. A big laugh. But they actually got ontae *Top o' the Pops* an Ah hid tae day aw the costumes. It wis a ball. Wanted it tae have a bit o' style, ken. *Style punk*, if you like. Ken that's nae pure bit its jis' the designer in me,' and he winked. 'Got aw this rubber gear, an' made a dress like, wi' an off-the-shoulder kinna thing. Ah jis' got spray cans an' sprayed aw this dayglo stuff on, slogans an' that, "Kill the Rich, Fuck Thatcher", aw that. See, it wis brilliant. On fuckin' telly an' aw … They nivver thought tae censor the claes! Got paid a good fuckin' wad in cash.'

'What you hitch for, then? You could have travelled in style. Got the plane.'

'Och, just fir the hell o' it. And tae keep things real. Remind masel whar Ah come fae. Ken it's stupit. Bit yi hiv tae sometimes, eh?' He eyed her narrowly. 'D'yir folks ken y'iv got a poof comin' tae sty wi' thame?'

Cammy with a shaved head, leading his long body from the aquiline jut of his nose. He really was handsome. Big gay Cammy. Mr Flamboyant. Seadhna smiled, relaxed and felt the warmth of his honesty. He looked round the pier with confidence.

'Ah kin easy stay in the youth hostel.'

'Its fine, it's really fine. They're no bothered. Really, it's okay.' She was embarrassed that he asked, embarrassed that he knew he had to ask. Every time she spoke she felt that she drew attention to the strangeness of his open homosexuality. Strange in this place anyway. You could only be gay in cities. He was going 'Ah promis' no tae hump onythin'. It's sheep aw the frustrated guys up here shag, eh no?' Cammy just made her laugh with his bluntness. 'Whit aboot the gay scene, then?' He was flashing teasing looks at her. 'Ony hansome fermers?' He was frenetic, edgy. Taut. Then he rescued her before she took his question seriously. 'Naw, it's okay, Ah ken deepest Orkney's nay ready fir rampant homos yit … .or even stately homos fir that. Ha! But it'll no stop me lookin'.'

He saved her from her own clumsy innocence because he knew the world better than she did. This time stopping her from explaining just how redneck it was and how she felt the eyes watching them. The townsfolk would all assume he was a weirdo boyfriend. *Maybe even a druggy*. Being gay would hardly register on the radar and simply wouldn't figure. When he phoned from a call box in Perth, she could tell he was still speeding, hitching the whole way on a mad whim, all the way from the Forth Bridge tolls. A spur-of-the-moment thing. Babbling. *Yiv got tae act the man. Lorry drivers dinna like the thocht o' a poof in the cab*. Cammy was a skilled chameleon but she knew he was genuine.

Cammy winked. He loved to flirt. 'Whars the ancestral pile, then?'

Seadhna was slipping into her Edinburgh twang. Voices that marked her. She found it was so much easier when you were just immersed in one place because there was no conflict. But here with Cammy and his city-ness, so brassy and Other, it was more complex. The island voice could not be subsumed and she had to let it come through a little because Cammy could not be fooled.

'People will think you're my boyfriend. They'll a' be speekan' an' watchin' us.'

'Ah'm nae bothered whit people think … Ah like tae tease them wi' a bit o' disinformation.'

The unspoken tensions were relaxed. What you could say and who you could be. With Cammy you could be anything or nothing. Nothing in her islands would faze him.

'What made you decide to come here? I'm flattered that you should come from the ends of the Earth to see me.' Seadhna enjoying the safe flirting, the feeling of walking in male company, pretending just a little she might like him to be perceived as 'her' man even if it was only for show..

'Jis' had tae get awa' fae the poncy art world fir a blink. Fashion prima donnas. Fuckin' pop stars.' He hunched like a petulant child for a second. Then the smart was past. 'Och, its money.'

'Well, it's Shopping Week here,' announced Seadhna.

'Whit the fuck's that when it's it hame?'

'Well, it's as far away fae the poncy fashion world as you can possibly get, unless you take cross-dressing into the equation.'

'Suits me, hen. Roll me out that Scottish Island Experience.'

in our midst

'So you're a designer?' John Rufus asked and stated at the same time. Seadhna was slightly apprehensive, wondering if she would have to shoehorn Cammy into her father's approval as she had tried to do with Henry. But Cammy could talk the talk with anybody. He knew all the places they came from.

'Don't interrogate the lad,' shooshed Sadie.

'It's fine, Mrs Rufus, Ah'm happy tae talk. Yi'll hiv a joab shuttan me up.'

John's approval was subtly upheld by the offer of the car.

'Yi can take him round and show him all there is to see. Have you been this far north before?'

Cammy shook his head. They had an island virgin in their midst.

In the annual gala week called Shopping Week it was hard to steer against the flow, you either had to stay right out of it, or give yourself totally up to it. It was too bacchanalian, really, for the tourism group, way too much unbuttoned peasant ribaldry. The promotion subgroup were working hard at portraying a more quality image of the islands and the problem with Shopping Week was that no one could control what might happen. The event could not be reined in or staged for tourist benefit.

It usually all started in a suitably restrained and decorous manner with the official opening on the Monday. The 'opening' saw the small town square filled with all the people of the place and beyond. It was a time when those who had left the islands returned, engaged couples showed off their new fiancés, and aunts and uncles returned. Unseen grandchildren from Corby to Wick ran through the streets revelling in the new cousins and the penny slot machines at the shows. The crowds awaited the grand arrival of 'the Queen' as the guard of honour provided by two uneven lines of Girl Guides fidgeted. Then all those gathered as one stilled as the queen, on the arm of the lifeboat coxswain, minced in white satin stilettos, over the crooked cobbles to the flower bedecked stage.

'Best ride in the toon, is it?' Cammy twitched.

'Shhhh.' And Seadhna sent him a look.

Through his teeth Cammy was humming;

Seadhna nudged him. 'Wheesht.' All around her she could see the unmistakable family DNA of the local people reflected in the flick of an eye, the corner of a mouth or a stiff walk. In the children you could just capture small flashes of other times, distant constellations of humans, an uncle, a dead grandfather, a pale consumptive girl hollow-eyed in a Victorian school photograph. Somewhere just out of grasp was a shimmering line that could never quite be held but was there, through all the settled generations.

The band stood to attention as the procession headed towards the raised stage. An inaudible PA system crackled and the good words of the earnest dignitary performing his stiff civic duty were lost to all but the front row, who had ensured they got there early to get a good view.

Seadhna steered Cammy to the back of the crowd so that they could observe rather than be observed, and they stopped by the edge of the swingboats, so reminiscent in their primary red and yellow of the potential for running away with the circus.

'Now that I've been spotted with a man I'll be reasonably safe from unwanted attentions,' Seadhna confided a little primly.

'Aw aye! Sex-starved bachelors on the loose, is it?' he asked.

'Drunk farmers, labourers and lecherous fishermen. It's the week when you can watch the bruise count soar. The women don't wear dark glasses for the sun.'

'So Ah'm a human shield, um Ah?'

Up high on the majestic stage stood the aged Baillie Harvey. She was plumped up to even greater importance than normal with the gleaming achievement of her OBE received in the Queen's Birthday Honours list – the real

Queen, that was, although on this day it was easy to become confused. Baillie Harvey's award was for services to local democracy and she wore her medal on her jacket lapel, glinting in counterpoint with her enamel Conservative and Unionist badge. Stood next to her was the Lord Lieutenant, about to perform the crowning of the temporary and more nubile, if fake, queen. The red velvet and carved chairs from the councillors' meeting room were doubling as thrones. A crown that someone had made from papier mâché and which from afar looked just like the real thing was placed on the queen's head. The queen then royally handed her sceptre to her attendant and made her way to the microphone. There her white gloved hand stretched upwards to where the microphone rested on its stand, unadjusted from the height of the towering Lord Lieutenant, who had now sat down, a single medal and white sash on his chest.

'He looks pure ootae an Orange walk in Larkhall,' observed Cammy.

'Nobody here knows what an Orange walk is.'

'Weel that's nothin' tae moan aboot. Or dae ya mean yi'v no even entered the dark ages yet?'

'No, it's something that is good about the place. No religion or at least sectarian stuff.'

'No meanin' tae be disrespectful tae yur cultur an' aw ... bit this isna really ma cup o' tea ... Can Ah tick this offa ma "seenit" list?'

'You bored already?' Seadhna teased him with feigned disbelief. 'It's a community ritual. You see all the folk that come back for holidays. You can't hear the speeches, of course, because there is always something wrong with the PA, that's an annual ritual as well ... of technical failure. It's good if you can lip-read, or gesture-read. They're always the same speeches, anyway ... self congratulatory, "Wha's like us" and all that.'

'Tak me roon' the picturesque fishing harbour and show me the lecherous fishermen then.'

'You'll have no chance up here, Cammy. There's no such thing as "Gay".' But Cammy strode off without waiting and Seadhna trotted after him.

'Like over there. Is that one of your traditionally lecherous fisher fowk?'

Michael was throwing single creels onto the slip. They were landing in a disordered heap, the end ropes and buoys clattering behind them.

'That's Michael McLeay.'

'Lecherous?'

'Not really.' Seadhna had to think for a minute. 'Solitary.'

'Drunken?'

She found herself protecting Michael from Cammy's playful gaze. 'Doesn't drink ... or at least hardly any more. Only spirits count as drink up here, not beer ... Works on his own. He nearly drowned last year,' but she saved the story.

'Dy'a think he wid sell us some crab?'

'Dunno. Doesn't look like he's landing much.'

To Seadhna it was obvious there was nothing in the baskets, but Cammy was already striding over towards the slip. He crossed into places that Seadhna didn't go and in a second he was leaning over the railing, talking to Michael. There were no barriers for Cammy. Seadhna hung back. It was men's stuff, talking on the piers at boats, so when Michael's face began to turn Seadhna anticipated it and moved her head towards the stage and the festivities. There Baillie Harvey was assisting in the release of a wicker basket full of doves. She went on to clap herself at the success of her avian liberation. Seadhna watched the birds as they disappeared in the direction of the Auction Mart and onwards to a good feed in their coop, and her eyes lazily roved the crowd to settle unsuspecting on one figure in particular. *God, is that Edna?* All of a sudden, Seadhna had to rewind to a memory of Edna as she was when she was Norrie's girlfriend, the archetypal most popular boy in the school. They had been the dream couple, Edna with her Abba looks, whose very own teenage glory arrived when she herself became a Shopping Week Queen and was elevated above all in a satin dress and carefully twirled blond ringlets just like Agnetha Fältskog. She leant on a pushchair, smoking, her cheeks hollow. *My God, look at her.*

Edna flashed hunted looks around, sucking her cigarette earnestly as if to root herself at the filter-tipped end. As Seadhna made sense of the transformation, her eyes were drawn to the boob-tube and mini skirt and then on to the unabashed display Edna was offering the crowd. Every part of her visible flesh was mottled in great bruises, grey, brown, blue and green. *Old bruises.*

'Edna?'

Like a seal woman. Wearing her bruises like a statement, she was like a living body protest. Edna made no effort to hide them, turning her head to show the assured arc of false teeth propping out her flaccid lips. There were people in the crowd who nudged and whispered. *Shuz pat him oot fur good this time. Pressan charges an' all. Assault … yes, assault wi' grievous …*

It was tacitly known as a bad week for batterings and black eyes. Unbridled drink and the world tipped on edge, but Edna's display was something out of the norm of green tinges showing through the generous flesh-coloured panstick, the high-necked collars and dark glasses.

Cammy appeared behind her, and caught the whisper of Seadhna's shock as she reeled from Edna's brashness, or courage, or need for attention. Nobody was saying anything to her face. But someone would have to notice, to think something, to say something, and Seadhna felt like a coward along with everybody else who colluded in cover-ups. *In New York it might be performance art …*

'Whit's rang? Yi look like yi'v seen a ghost.'

'It's nothing, just somebody I used to know.'

'The boy said he'd lost all his bait ti the *sels*.' Cammy's face squinted in puzzlement. 'Didnae want tae ask whit a *sel* wis. Soonds stupid, askin' fowk tae translate thur ain language. Whit is it?'

'Seals,' Seadhna replied hurridly, 'it means seals. Its how the old folk here say it. They call them sels. Come on, let's get out of here.'

'So d'yi ken him, then? The fisher boy?'

'Kind of. Well yeah, he was in my class at school … But that's just a connection. It doesn't mean I "ken" him in other senses.'

'Like the biblical sense?'

Seadhna fired up unexpectedly. 'Very definitely *not* the biblical sense.'

'Why no? A handsome fella?' Cammy winked.

'I just would never think of him like that.'

The film reel of Michael's past rattled through Seadhna's head, justifying exactly why she should always just think of Michael as had been proscribed. Thick, stupid, destined for manual work, catatonic, strange, a peasant. The negative schema simultaneously made her feel guilty.

'He's the only one left. Big family. They all moved away but him. His brother was drowned last year, but he was a drunk.' She switched on to Geordie to deflect Cammy away from her own discomfort. In her head a voice was saying *tinker family*. Throwing in the hint of the drowning would usually divert people. It was outwith the normal experience of most and they would hook the bait and want the whole story. But already, as she was speaking, she knew Cammy was smarter than that. 'His sister cleared the house out a fortnight ago. She's gonna rent it out to tourists. She bought it, of course, in the big council house sell-off.'

'That'll be Maggie bringing power and greed tae the masses.' They both paused in a delicately flinty silence. 'Well, as it happens, Ah thought he wis really interesting. Tell't me a whole lot o' stuff aboot the mechanics o' the creels. Yi wur right, he didnae hae ony crabs.'

Cammy allowed her to make her escape. Without saying anything, he had said everything. Books and covers, judging. Prejudice. You just didn't do that crap with Cammy and Seadhna felt annoyed with herself.

'I went to the auction,' Seadhna plodded on, 'It's another local ritual. Trawling through your neighbour's stuff at the auction mart and buying up all their shite. A bit sad really, all that's left is a pile of rubbish that nobody wants.'

'Did yi get onythin guid?'

'An old wardrobe that was full of woodworm and a pile of – well, *politically incorrect* sealskins.' She was unsure how Cammy would respond.

'Wow, real sealskin. How did they come to be there?'

'The old wife's man used to shoot. They went up every year to the cull. Then it got stopped by the anti-fur people. Did you never see it on the telly?'

'Naw, too busy takin' speed an' smokin' dope ...'

They sat on the ferry pier watching the crowd from the 'opening' disperse. That was the excitement over until the afternoon. Michael's boat curved in towards Willie's boat shed, drawing an arc of deeper blue in the water with the nonchalance of a finger trailing through paint.

'Maybe Ah kid mak yi an ootfit ootae they skins o' yurs. Shame tae let them go tae waste ...'

Seadhna hesitated. 'Like what?'

'Something cool and trendy an' maybe a wee bit shocking?'

'Out of the skins?'

'Aye, why no? Like fashion kin change the world kinda thing, a statement?' Cammy was starting to imp around, the moment lightening again. 'If the peasants have no clothes, throw them furs. Yi prepared fir reed paint an' abuse?'

'Yeah, I don't care any more ... go for it, but,' and she winked, smiling, 'next on your island itinerary, city boy, is the pie-eating contest followed by spiritual communion where the Atlantic meets the North Sea. We call this package "The oceanic clash of cultures",' and she laughed.

culture clash

Seadhna herded Cammy round the sites. They did the Standing Stones, the burial cairns, the Stone Age village. 'I mean, it's the most famous Neolithic site in the world! You can't come here and not see it. It'd be like going to Paris and missing the Eiffel Tower!'

'Yeah, bit it's a' mowed 'nd tweaked ... like it's been it the hairdresser's. How kin yi tell sumbidy didna jis' pit aw' thon stones thegither tae luk like beds n' dressers? It's like us superimposan' Habitat on the Stone Age fowk.'

She hiked Cammy round the cliffs on the west of the island, pointing out the stretching blue ocean that led to America.

'Yip, this is braw. But Ah coodna hack it fir more 'n a visit. Ah ken Ah'm a city boy.' Cammy twitched with open space. He needed a tenement to pin him down. Below them the fulmars wheeled and curved silently. The two of them lay back on the clifftop grass with its padded stringy roots of sea pinks and coarse wiry leaves as the sky unravelled away to the horizon.

'If you look out there on the horizon you can see North Rona, after that it's America,' and then 'Do you know something? In the old days the ploughmen backed their old horses over the cliffs? Cart and all, the weight of it pulled everything over. The Atlantic trashed it all and it was gone ... like dumping an old car. There must be tons of old cars down there.'

''Cept a horse has a face and that's a pretty gross thing ti dae.'

'Maybe they couldn't afford to feed a horse over the winter or something.'

'Or maybe it was ritual sacrifice ... why wid ya destroy a guid kert?'

They lay on the grass and the thoughts evaporated.

'Ur ye gonna stay here?' Cammy asked her, looking at the sky, 'Ah mean here in the islands.'

'I don't know. It's a kind of a shifting place. It's not going to stay the same. But maybe I want to catch something of it before it all disappears ...'

'You could get a dinky wee croft hoos and dae water colours fir the tourists.'

'Oh please, I can't do dinky. Besides, you have to wait for folk to die before you get a house here. Or use your guile to out wit the big money from south. I've no hope.'

'Well Ah'm fed up o' squats. Ah'm wantin' hot water, carpets an' a door Ah kin shut.' Cammy fired a pebble over the cliff edge into oblivion. Too far away to hear a splash. 'See thon fresh air ... think it's killin' me. Let's get a pint in a proper pub. Ah kin see America on the telly in aw they cop shows. And crazy horses tae, fir that matter.' Cammy leaped up, agitated. Seadhna crawled to her feet, nipping a small white flower in her fingers and Cammy rounded on her. 'Hey, you allowed to dae that?' he scolded, 'Robban' wee flooers fae the ootdoors? Outdoor code, hen, Ah learned that in school.'

'Course I'm allowed, 'coz I'm not a tourist.' *I have the right*, and she cocooned the flower in her palm as they made their way back over the flaking sandstone and blue-grey clay to where her father's car was parked.

'Whit's it called then, *nature* vandal?'

'Grass of Parnassus.'

'Right, a proper pub then.'

your round

In the spartan front bar of the Central Hotel, they sat down, plastic ashtrays on round red Formica tables. Chequered lino, worn by feet round the bar. The smell of urine pervading from the gents. It was a place where women still had to go round to the lounge bar to use a toilet.

'Ah'm glad tae see the evil hand o' Welcome Inns has no reached youse up here yet.' Cammy slipped subtly into his west-coast hard-man persona and whispered. 'Dinnae worry, hen, Ah'm no comin' in here bein' all camp. Strictly for consenting circles a' that.'

Seadhna found a corner table. 'But me too, Cammy, I've got to put on an act here. I mean, I really don't feel like I'm part of the place. I don't think I ever was. Once you've left, in your head I mean, it's very hard to return.'

Cammy was always moving. 'Fuck, Ah'm gasping fir a fag.' He went to the bar to change notes. The barmaid handed over fifty pences. 'See, that's it. Exactly like you said. It's in yur heed.'

The coins clunked into the cigarette machine; Seadhna followed him over and then to the bar and he spoke as he went. 'Yi tak control, hen. Yi define yursel, then ithers will respond and reaffirm it. It's simple really. Fowk kin only react tae the clues yi gie thum.'

There was hardly anyone in the bar and they sat down while Cammy ripped the cellophane off the cigarettes. 'Act like a victim an' yi get treated like one. Act like yi'r excluded an' yi will be. Kidology, my dear Watson. Whit yi' wantin?' and Cammy headed over to the jukebox without waiting for her reply.

Seadhna sat down and her gaze drifted to the counter where a single man was leaning drinking. His cement-covered rig-boots scuffed against the tatty foot rail. He ordered his drink, then turned around to Seadhna. It was only a brief second, then recognition. It set a pulse through Seadhna that came from somewhere far back. There was no preamble.

'Whit yi drinkin', Seadhna?' the man asked, as if he'd known her all his life.

'Oh, I'm fine.' She didn't want to encourage anything other than nodding recognition.

She knew the face, of course. It was Sandy Baker.

'No no, come on. Whit yi hivan? An' whit aboot yir man?'

Not my man, Sandy.

Cammy returned, with Bruce Springsteen beginning to echo in the deserted bar, nodding towards Sandy and acknowledging his offer of a drink.

Born in the USA.

'Aye, very kind of you, don't mind if Ah dae. Pint 'o eighty, sir.' Cammy was netting the situation. Making sense of it like a detective at a crime scene. Sandy nodded again at Seadhna, awaiting her drink order. She was trapped now, as Cammy had accepted the offer.

'Half pint o' lager please,' she found herself saying, trying to minimise eye contact and readjusting herself to find a way to make chit-chat with Sandy.

'Did you put that on?' she winced.

Cammy nodded. 'Aye, whit's wrang wi' that?'

'Just didn't think it was your kind of music,' and then she found herself having to make introductions as Sandy came across with the drinks and drew up a stool, uninvited, at their table.

'This is Sandy … Sandy and I were at school together.'

It sounded as if this meant some kind of connection, as if they had all gone to Dollar Academy or something. 'We were in the same class. Sandy, this is Cammy … a friend.'

Oh aye, a friend … Sandy also was putting two and two together.

'Pleased tae meet yi,' Cammy replied with his wide open welcoming face, 'Aye, come an' join us. Always gled tae meet pals o' Seadhna's.'

Cammy held out a hand and Sandy, responding like a dog giving a paw, shook it. His leering pink face, that of the bigoted chants and grunting reading. He sat down, heaving off his heavy working jacket. The schoolboy features had submerged beneath new layers of jowl and brow. The barmaid knitted on under the optics, oblivious to Seadhna's clanging discomfort, amplified even further when Michael McLeay walked in.

'Christ, there's tinky Mickey,' yelled Sandy in shock and delight.

A class reunion, your worst nightmare.

'Aye, buey,' Sandy shouted towards Michael before he had a second to take in the bar-room, 'Come on over. Yur a stranger in this place.'

Michael nodded towards the group, not moving as Sandy settled into his position as compère for the duration. He had the whole echoing pub as his platform but turned to his immediate audience of Seadhna and Cammy. 'Aye, Michael's been a bit funny efter his brush wi' death. Died fir five minutes, they said it in the hospital. Eh Mickey? Saw white lights an' tunnels an' angels, eh?' Sandy was flicking his eyes back and fore, watching his audience's reactions and simultaneously gauging Michael's annoyance.

Michael pointed to Sandy's glass. 'Whit yi hivan', Sandy?'

'Vodka 'nd coke, min.' The jagged threesome was about to become an even

more fraught foursome. Seadhna felt her body tensing. Sandy had settled in for
a spell of diversion. Michael then nodded to Seadhna and Cammy in non-verbal
code for *What do you want to drink?*

'No, we're fine,' said Seadhna for both of them. Cammy directed a look at
her as if to say 'speak for yourself'. He was finding it all amusing.

Michael walked over, setting Sandy's drink down on the table, and made to
return to the bar.

'Come on Mickey, tell them all aboot yir visions.'

Michael didn't reply but gave Sandy a tired smirk. 'Aye Sandy, I hid a vision
o' you speakan' sense, then I kent there wis summin' wrong.'

The lines were drawn. Sandy switched focus as Michael sat down.

Seadhna watched Cammy converse with Sandy and Michael with an ease
she had never enjoyed. *Was it a male thing?* He could read a person in seconds
and he gave Sandy his full attention, flattered him, made him feel what he said
was interesting. As she sat and listened, trying to prolong the half pint of lager so
that she could stave off further rounds, the technical conversation passed over
her. She was too uncomfortable to concentrate. Sandy talked in depth about
the giant diggers they had on the building site, boasting about how much earth
they could shift in an hour as if the mechanical prowess of the diggers was all
somehow down to him. Then he *fucked* and *bastarded* over the problem with the
seam of granite. Cammy nodded, asking if they used gelignite to blast it.

Seadhna realised how diverse Cammy's knowledge was and it surprised
her that there was so much about him she didn't know.

'Ah wis in charge o' a whole scaffolding gang afore Ah came tae the college.
Big money. Ma brithurs is aw in the buildin' trade ...'. His ease with people wasn't
about coming down to anybody's level. It was about knowing enough levels to
find one that everyone could slot into. Michael stayed silent, listening to Sandy
exclaim over the size of the wage packets at the oil site. Then Sandy moved the
topic onto his pet subject, genealogy.

'So where are you from?' he asked Cammy directly. To Sandy you were
defined by place. Where it was you *really* came from. You couldn't hide from his
interrogation.

Seadhna was thinking to herself, *I always felt outside everything ... too clever, too Gaelic, too socialist, too ...* But she got in first. 'My family came from the west, and – well that made us kinda different.'

'What d'ya mean?' Sandy demanded, inferring that she had answered his question incorrectly. 'I nivvir thowt o' you as different.' Sandy wanted Seadhna to belong to his world, and Cammy to be different. To Sandy it was simple: birth dictated belonging. 'You wis jis' islanders the same as me. We aal grew up together.' His tone was almost hurt as he proposed the *Jock Tamsin's Bairns* view of life, for the moment at least, then swigged his vodka down in one as if it was an egg-cupful of Ribena.

'I know I was born here,' Seadhna protested, trying to regain her ground, 'but I still didn't feel we were locals.' She persisted, 'We didn't come in with the first longship, I mean. That's what matters to most folk here, ten generations of farming on the same land, back to the Vikings ...'

She knew she was on dangerous ground. There were things you could think but just didn't say. You could only have this conversation on an island like this, where lives could be turned so far inward on each other that the minutiae of parentage took on vast proportions of ethnic purity. Every one made up the rules to suit.

'Me mother's fae Renfrew,' elaborated Sandy, elasticating the rigid rules, 'Wis stationed here in the war wi' the Atts, merrit tae an Orcadian an' I wis born here. So is far as Ah'm concerned Ah'm definitely local.'

No one would dare challenge Sandy's status. Michael's tinker background was buried in the temporary and fleeting connections Sandy allowed. He found he had been bequeathed tenuous citizenship by Sandy. 'And Michael, you were born here too so, yur definitely local.'

If it came to ethnic cleansing you would want to keep on the right side of Sandy. Identifying what the side was could be a whole other matter.

The definitions were becoming obtuse; there was no logic to the discussion, it was all still just a means of appeasing Sandy, who would shift an argument to suit his mood. They were forging towards a kind of common view, a sense, but Seadhna was running a third commentary in her head, re-threading the uglier lumps of the discussion to something more palatable as Sandy waded on.

'Some of them incomers noo ... Weel, thur diffrint. They come here lukkan' fir the good life and they hiv no clue what life here is aal aboot … Tak the selkie lovers … Eh, Michael? The "good lifers". Them hippy seal-lovin' bastards?' Sandy waited a second for a reaction. 'The selkies can get their noses right in through the eye of a creel, tak the bait an' disappear. Thur's far too many of them, eh Michael? You tell them.'

Sandy had succeeded in snaring Michael into the lurching discussion. Michael nodded.

'Aye Sandy, yu'r right there … It started that they could get their heads in through the soft eyes. Yi ken, the hole where the crabs crawl in … and then we pat hard roond eyes on so they couldna get their heads through. But then they learnt hoo tae snap the bands that held the doors on the end of the creels, so they could get right in, an' eat everything.'

'If that hippies hid thur waye yi wouldna get tae shoot the bastards.'

Cammy offered Sandy and Michael a cigarette, detecting Seadhna's discomfort.

'But the tourists, aye them … they love 'em, eh Michael?'

'Aye, they do.' Michael talked in slow sentences that meant everyone else listened and didn't butt in. 'But we can shoot them.'

'You shoot them?' Cammy let a smidgeon of alarm show through.

'Aye, yi can shoot them if they're worrying yur gear, like. Hid's aal legal.' Michael took a ready-made roll-up from his tin. 'Mibbe if they paid me the same money to protect the seals, I wad pit me rifle away. But yi'll no get a politician anywhar tae speak up for a cull, thur aal too frightened o' thur city voters. It's the animal lovers. They environmentalists. They have no idea what it's like tae survive in this place.'

'Aye, buey, you tell them. They bloody incomers all getting up and telling us that's born and bred here what we can an' canna do. They should fuck off back where they came from. Eh Michael?' Sandy was getting to where he really wanted to be. His face was gleeful. Michael still sat with an untouched drink in front of him.

Seadhna knew where Sandy was heading and joined in to try to sanitise the discussion. 'There is a kind of a difference between the folk that grew up in this place when it was a working place and the new folk.' Seadhna felt she was translating for everyone's benefit, explaining things to a class of children. 'The folk that are part of the "viewing" culture. You know, like, "Let's look at poverty. Let's look at this quaint old town. Let's buy a piece of this couthy community life … it's all so quaint …".' She tried to find a logic to edge off Sandy's blank bigotry. Because inside she resented it too, the *incomers*. The bright-eyed eager ones, who hadn't had to suffer, who took the good jobs and came with their Costwold gentrification. 'There is a kind of economic migration … the good lifers.'

'White settlers, yi mean?'

'Aye, but the difference is money. It's class, not race.'

'Disnae metter whaur yi go in Scotland.'

'The incomers have a choice. They buy into this life here.'

'Wealthy imperialists demanding their right to buy Parma ham,' Cammy whispered under the conversation. 'A lifestyle choice.'

'Silent clearances.'

'Fuckan' English.'

'And it was poverty pushed us here. It wasn't a choice. It was an enforced move,' she went on.

'Where are the folk that used to live in the hooses it the herbur? Tell yi whaur they ur. Thur packed intae that cooncil scheme like thur Red Indians in a reserve. An thur's more dope up in that scheme than's in Wongo Bongo land.'

'There'll come a time when there's nothing left and it'll aal be fir the tourists.'

Michael drained his pint,

'Yi want anither?'

'Naw, Ah'll git this wan. Ah'm flush.' Cammy stood up. 'Got a cash payment for a big commission last week.'

Before they could ask, he volunteered. 'Costume design for a band tour. Mare money than sense, if yi ask me. But Ah'm nae complainin'.'

'Aw … yi intae the designan'?' Sandy picked up every smidgeon of information. Knowledge was power. 'Be wan o' that Art College lot o' Seadhna's, ur yi?' Men and design did not sit together in Sandy's experience of things. Michael took a rum.

'Back on the drink then, Michael?' Sandy was still needling. He would keep it up and Michael would constantly have to ignore him, quelling down the race in his veins that Sandy gave him. Always seeking out a chink. Not drinking was soft, then drinking was soft. Sandy demanded a right to your entire soul.

Seadhna stuck with a coke. She could feel control ebbing from her, and didn't want to become abandoned, helpless on the planet of alcohol. Sandy and his curiosity made her want to raise her guard, not drop it. In other company, and with another audience, Sandy would as easily refer to her as a "fuckan' weirdo wi' some foreign poof".

Eh, Michael? A fuckin' weirdo?

Michael stood up. 'No, forget that, Sandy. Ah'm awaye.'

'Whit's wrong wi' you, Mickey. Come on, have a drink. Can you no handle it any more? You gettan' soft? Yu'r no turning queer are you? Teetotal weirdo?'

'Nuther time, buey. Ah'm off.' And Michael was out the door and away, a quick incline of his head signifying his good bye to the table.

Sandy, marooned without a victory, turned to Seadhna. 'Ah'll hiv tae go efter this een. See you weemin, eh Cammy, yu'll ken whit Ah'm talking aboot? See Edna, she gets sore pissed off if I don't turn up fir me tea. Under the thumb, I doot.'

Edna? Then Sandy grinned and made the gesture of the thumb on his temple. Telling them all he had a woman, that he was a real man. Pretending for the outward show that she called the shots, not him with his fists. Sandy's show of temporary drink-addled domestic harmony with Edna. He got up and swung his large form through the stained-glass door.

my round

In the chasm of silence after Sandy departed, the jukebox began its automatic click as a random selection came on.

'Why won't they hiv a cull, then. If it's that bad? They cull deer.'

'Seals are different, it seems. They've got better PR fir a start.' Seadhna found herself grounding softly on Michael's territory.

'Is it the Landrover brigade that wid be up in erms?' Cammy poked at the cigarette butts in the plastic ash tray.

'Aye, you could call them that. There is a difference. A cultural difference …You see seals, they kept folk in these islands alive in meat, oil, food … clothes. You name it. Thurs no point killing them if you don't use the animal. The sooth folk, the environmentalists, think they're cuddly animals … Michael was right, I can see it, there'll soon be nothing for folk like him here. He's the last of something, you know.'

'It's a' Walt Disney's fault eh? Poor Bambi an' a' that. Everythin' that his a face can be turned intae a cuddly toy, hand-stitched in India by underage weans,' concluded Cammy.

'Aye. And he hated poofs an commies and union men.'

washed up

Walking through the street it was still daylight. Jeffrey's shop had shut down. The impotent sign above the two blanked-out shop windows still proclaiming *H&J Jeffrey Grocer General Merchant estd 1881*. The emporium of out-of-date cereal packets and the exotica of Arctic Rolls where lean Mr Jeffrey once presided over Green Shield stamps, the wonders of the gifts catalogue and free plastic daffodils with Surf. There were new people in the former chippy, opening a gallery, who knew nothing about the historical connections to the dirty mag *Fiesta* and the mythical previous owner who bared all. Instead, the display windows of the newly named Driftwood Gallery were over-enthusiastically crammed with hackneyed local views in watercolour, pasty oils and tired repetitions of clichéd landmarks that once were real.

'God, see whit yi' mean. Tourist tat or whit?' Cammy lingered at the display. 'Thurs nuthin' in there Ah wid paye guid money fir.'

Further along the street the new Arts Centre gleamed cathedral-like, with a large Arts Council poster in the window. Minimal precision hailed silently from the toughened glass.

'Christ, the arty set ur pursuin' us. Youse ur losin' yur ethnic innocence. Be crawlin' wi' missionaries soon.'

Seadhna allowed her eyes to glaze past the gallery, thinking *I'm not an artist. It's all a mirage.*

'Fine big fancy gallery there. No ma kinda thing though,' said Cammy.

'I can't do it,' said Seadhna, 'I mean cheat people. It's all sleight of hand ... Trickery. Once I thought it was all about something and I had something *to say* but I can't find any way to say it.'

'Weel a' they posh galleries tell yi is that the mare money yi hiv the mare expensive the shite yi cin buy, right up tae Saatchi and Saatchi, window dressers tae the Tories.'

'I've kinda lost the faith. All that time with Henry, trying to be one of them.'

'Och, nae point in regrets. Wi' his lot it's money an' connections an' you rub ma back, Ah'll rub yours. Thur art world is no wur art world, bit it disnae mean yi stop dayin' it. Thur's a kinda art that's fur us. Yi'll find a way, hen. Aw' that's in galleries is the ideal supply an' demand o' commodities created by dealers by artists also created by dealers an' sold tae rich fowks tae gie them cultural status. Fits the market economy perfect. Same as buying a Porsche. It disnae say anthin' aboot anythin' ither than rich fowk spend their money on a lot o' shite that some-one's tell't them's "art".'

'But you can't talk like that. You spend your time making money from wannabes, creating stage personas for pop stars! Fake stuff. Och, artifice then ...'

'Artyfish or artypish?' he jibed, his eyes twinkling, 'Naw naw, that's capitalism an' aw'. It's a simple transaction. They've got nae fuckan' imagination so they buy mine. Ah'm guid at it. Makin' ponces oota wannabes. An it's stupit money. Beggars choosin' and aw' that.'

They paused at the door of Seadhna's parents' house.

'Onywaye, back tae the real stuff. Ah've an idea fir yur fancy dress. Wanna hear it?'

'Och, go on then.'

'Fashion meets Performance meets The Burlesque,' and he waited for her reaction. 'Ah need a decent sewin' machine tho, his yir maw got wan? ... And Cinderella shall attend the ball.'

mean it

Michael stacked the broken creels up against the tar shed. On the seaward side of the town it was easy to pretend there was no revelry going on at all. He could hear the tannoy from the pier head sporadically announcing the progress of the pie-eating contest. There was a great cheer, followed by the compère's voice labouring through a race with little true edge to it. The real spectacle, only to be witnessed after the scheduled event was over, was when Bobbo from Brig End, the undisputed three-times-in-a-row champion, failed to contain his bellyful of cheap grey minced meat and pastry and vomited the entire contents of his stomach onto the pavement in front of the hotel. The projectile just missed the newly purchased sling-back heel of one of the Patersons' cousins from Glasgow.

Michael took out some twine and the net needle. 'Ach shit.' The gash in the creel was bigger that he thought. He'd have to knit it right back onto the base. All the time he was puzzling to think of a way to make the bait seal-proof. 'Thur clever bloody devils, grant you that …' and he cut a length of twine from the ball with his knife. 'But hid'll hiv tae be them ur me.' He spoke aloud, knowing he was unheard.

It was the match against nature, the cat-and-mouse game that kept him at the fishing. Opening the creels was always like opening a parcel. You never knew what you might get in there. Sometimes there might be a big ling. God knows how they got themselves inside, curled around, head meeting tail, that must have gone in chasing a small fish or after the bait too. Emptying the creel into the bottom of his boat, everything moving, was good. Picking out the saleable stuff and chucking out the rest. *Bloody starfish everywhere. Sucking the guts out of everything.*

Michael was determined. On the Sunday, he'd baited his creels and pushed the softened flesh of dead fish into the string and pulled down the knot real tight. He threw them one at a time over the stern of the boat as low in as he could get under the Craig. He left them out all day and overnight, then went out early on Monday morning to haul them. When the first one came up slashed and empty he put it down as bad luck. The disaster only began to follow its sickening pattern when the third creel came up. As with the first, the same thing had happened as if a malicious diver had gone through each one and released the catch from the door. The anticipation of heavy creels coming up teeming with green crabs, velvets, big partans or even a lobster was dashed into anger.

'Shit. Bloody vermin.' As dextrous as his hands, the seals had pushed their noses through the sprung-wire trap and in to take out the bait. All were empty. Picking up empty creels one after the other was sickening and Michael was resigned to it. The whole lot were stripped. *The selkie's geen through the rope wan efter anither …* There was nothing for it but to take them all in and rethink how to make them seal-proof. He took them all back into the harbour and tossed them onto the slipway, irritated even more by the nonsense going on at the pier head with the pipe band and the crowning of the queen. To add insult to injury – he pretended not to see as tourists took snapshots of him, *like you were some kind of side show.* Michael replayed the scenario in his head to ease it.

The tannoy from the pier had subsided and the country and western band were sound-checking and one-twoing into the mike. Someone was off to get a bucket of water to swill Bobbo's regurgitated record down a drain.

Below Michael's shed, that had been Willie's before, on the shingle beach there were kids playing. The tide was out and they were throwing stones into the sea. Michael became gradually aware of them as their voices pricked through the country medley. Visitors, city kids, at once loud, then conspiratorial, they were firing a shotgun at a tin, bringing it nearer so that they could hit it.

Ping! The lead hit the tin.

'Yay!' the yell went up with the infrequent hits.

'Hey, I've got an idea,' and one of them disappeared for a few minutes, then returned with some slices of pan loaf. The boy threw the bread out onto the water and a flock of seagulls descended. 'Right, Ben, I'll throw the bread and you shoot them.'

'Yeah.'

Michael knitting with the net needle repaired the worst creel and set it on end. In his head he was thinking that the seal-proof device would have to be something like a bag that would be needed to keep the bait safe and the catch would have to be modified too so that they could not just flick it open … He was trying to figure out how the whole thing would work and thinking, *Gonna slow everything doon, though, fiddling aboot wi' bags an' draw-strings …*

A yell went up from the shore.

'Yess, Yess! You got it.'

The boys were jumping. They'd hit a gull with the shotgun. The fiss of the gun concluded in a 'vip' onto the underwing of the gull and the bird collapsed maimed onto the water about twenty feet from the shore. The boys were thrilled.

'Right, try it again.'

More bread was thrown and the gulls reappeared. Another bird was shot, flapping squintly onto the water. The first shot bird was unable to collect its wing back into its sides. Michael looked up and watched, slowly transferring his concentration from the intensity of his mending to make sense of the action on the beach.

'Gimme a go.' And the gun was passed. The gulls were enticed down to within shot again, and among the flock that descended it was nigh impossible to miss. *Shootin' rats in a barrel*, and Michael rose up, automatically sticking the net needle into his back pocket. He walked over towards the stone slip above the beach and stopped at the top of the steps.

'Aye ... lads, what you doin' there?'

The absorbed boys looked up, unaware they had been watched. There was no reply.

'Are yi shootin' there?'

'Yeah ... and what of it? It's legal, we can if we want to,' and more defiant in tone, 'You can't stop us.'

'No, Ah'm no gaan tae stop yi. But yi won't be leaving the birds like that,' he shouted back.

The boys went silent. The only gulls left on the water were the maimed ones. The bread had been consumed by the squawking flock that had flown off to sit elsewhere.

'What do you mean?'

Michael felt his resolve tighten. 'Yu'll no be leavan' them on the watter like that ... in that state ... injured like that.'

'Well we'll have to. That's where they landed.'

Michael jumped down and headed to where a flattie was tied up at the high-water mark, and pushed it down the beach. His manner and tone quietly demanded co-operation and no nonsense. 'You tak this boat noo an' row oot there and you finish the job,' he directed. 'Yi need to kill those injured birds 'kis thu'll no survive.'

The boys moved towards the boat with the gun.

'No, you leave that gun here. Yi'v done enough wi' that.'

'What do you mean? How else can we kill them?'

Michael held up his hands in front of them. 'If yur gaan tae shoot birds fir fun then yi'v got tae at least mak sure the things are deed. Yi cannae leave a struggling creature tae die like that.'

'What do you mean?'

Michael was getting angry. It was the broken creels, the robbed bait. The chirpy southern voices.

'Killing wi' a gun's the easy part and if yu'r gaan tae dae that yi need tae be ready tae pit the things oot o' their misery … wi' yur bare hands. Then yu'll ken whit it really means tae kill something. A living thing. Come on, get in.'

The boys silently climbed into the boat, still defiant and sullen.

'You can't make us kill them.'

'I can mak yi sit an' watch them till a black-back comes and droons them.'

As they approached the nearest gull, it struck with its beak to avoid the boy's hand reaching down from the boat. 'The fucking thing bit me,' he yelped.

'Right, get it into the boat and pull its neck.' Michael waited.

'I don't know how,' ventured the boy.

'Well yu'll learn how,' said Michael.

The boy was struggling to reach the good wing of the bird and bring it towards him. The maimed gull twisted its neck and beak round to attack at his grip. The ungainly flapping seemed interminable as the other boys watched silently.

'Hold him over your knee and pull the head, and do it quick,' said Michael. The boy held back and held back. 'Just pull it. Sharp. Quick.'

'I can't hold it. It's flapping about too much.'

'Come on, dae it. Dae it noo. Yu'r gaan ti dae it right in front of me.'

The shrillness in Michael's voice struck a sinew of terror in the boy. At that moment he felt more frightened of Michael than of his horror of killing the bird. The bird's body felt bigger and heavier than he thought it would. The beak stabbed at him, cutting the underside of his wrist as its feet paddled about on his knee. His jeans were wet with sea water. In the panic he grabbed the head of the bird and pulled frantically.

The bird flapped on.

'It's not dead. It's not, I tried and it's not.'

But the neck and head were limp, only the twitching from the circuit of cut nerves that remained producing sporadic convulsions.

'Is that it? Is that it done?' The boy looked up at Michael, waiting to be absolved.

'Yes that's it … and that wisna so much o' a laugh, wis it?'

Still holding the dead bird, the boy recoiled back from the carcass.

'Oh no.'

In his panic his forefinger had pushed through the eye socket of the gull. The eye now attached to his finger as he withdrew in horror. He made to wipe the mess of eye and fresh blood on the smooth grey feathers of its back.

Each of the birds was dispatched in a similarly ungainly execution.

'You see killing's a serious business. Nivver tak it lightly.' Michael was speaking to himself.

By the time the job was finished, the boys were ashen-faced. One had the tension of tears about to break on his face. Michael picked up the limp birds by their legs and dumped the carcasses over the side, letting them slip away silently under the water.

He rowed the boys the few feet to the shore and the bow of the flattie ground onto the shingle. None spoke.

'Weel then. Jis' remember that if yi point a gun at something … yi truly have to mean to kill that thing, even if it means killing it with yur own hands.'

'Uh huh.'

They knew they had to say what was expected even if they didn't think it.

'Yu'll mind that noo, will yi?' He raised his eyes to search for theirs. The boys nodded weakly, waiting to be allowed to break from this strange encounter. They skulked up the beach as Michael fastened the painter of the boat to a metal ring.

'He had no right to make us do that. We could report him,' the boys whispered when they were safely back on the street.

'Yeah.'

'He's a fucking weirdo.'

fake it

In the Bistro, the lunchtime rush was subsiding. The waitresses could never keep up with clearing the tables and wiping them, as Justin never actually employed enough staff, always hoping to get away with one less wage if he could. Customers sat down to dirty dishes. The kitchen ran out of soup early on, and the new girl, who couldn't work the state-of-the-art electronic till, had screwed up the automatic stock-control system. Everyone rushed when Justin sauntered in, worried they'd be caught out for talking, not polishing the cutlery, standing around not looking busy enough. Justin moved to his favourite table as if he owned the place, because he did own the place, and snapped his fingers. He used the girls' Christian names, as if they were all friends. 'Seadhna, could we have two cappuccinos over here, please. Thanks, love.'

Justin lolled over the back of a chair, pontificating loudly to the tourists.

'So you're a local,' and the tourists prepared to drool over Justin's ethnicity.

What was it about being a local? Did it mark you as something exotic, something required in the tourist brochure?

'Yes,' replied Justin, 'been here five years now, think that qualifies me as a local.'

He had no reservations whatsoever. The tourists drew towards him. 'Then you must know a lot about the place.'

'Oh yes, fascinating history, place is full of crusty old characters, fishermen with tales as long as your arm, that sort of thing.' Justin liked the idea of being thought of as a kind of 'old salt'.

The tourists warmed to the prospect that they might have discovered their own Maasai warrior, and teased for a little more. 'How fascinating.'

'There're quite a few characters around. One old guy in particular. A right old stalwart from the old days. Intriguing name the locals have given him. "Kremlin", on account of his political views, you understand,' and Justin chuckled, inviting their class affinity.

'He's one of … how could you put it, the old guard, the local postmaster, bit of old red Clydeside, but full of history, full of history … Take this building, the Bistro here. It was in fact once a net shed. Apparently old Kremlin had to do a deal with the laird of the place to get it. The story goes he got the laird drunk and persuaded him to sign away the land that way.' Justin's avid tourist audience provided the appropriate response and 'Oohed', their curiosity switching to Justin himself;

'Indeed, but do tell us, how did you find yourself in this neck of the woods?'

'Oh, a long story. Came to stop the seal slaughter. Absolutely fell in love with the place … wanted out the rat race, bought a little property … cheap, moved on … and here I am.'

Seadhna caught the conversation as she passed. The difference she felt was solidifying, *You see? Them*, she thought to herself, *they 'fall in love' with the place. Us? Well we never had a choice. Love wasn't an option.* She loaded up the tray with knives that slid sideways onto the floor, and sodden coffee-soaked napkins, and carried on. She was not going to disavow any of them of their erroneous story. Justin didn't know the real story or that she was in fact the daughter of his 'old Kremlin'. False histories were fast in the making, and those who knew the truth kept it to themselves like the last fragile jewel they could claim as their own.

We're almost invisible here, she thought. *We're getting rubbed out, the way every tourist is rubbing out the soul of the place with every snapshot they take. Peeling away our souls. Each one thinking they are the very first to discover the place, when really they are all just following a disintegrating path.*

'Are you here on holiday? A summer job?' the tourists asked her cheerily.

'No, actually I am from here. I was born here.' *One of the last home births in the town*, she thought but omitted to say, and she loaded the unfinished cake onto a tower of dirty saucers. The tourists felt reassured by people like themselves, who were on holiday too, not people like her with a complicated history too long to explain.

'Oh, you don't have the accent. I would never have guessed.'

'No, I lived south for a while,' she replied, as if that was the reason and not that it was so much more complicated than simply an accent. In that moment a well of mixed emotions rose inside Seadhna that were made over centuries and that she knew would take more than a few lines in a tourist brochure to explain. Irrational, intuitive, instinctive and uncomfortable. Probably wrong and definitely politically incorrect. *Would a private language in which you could articulate all your incorrect thoughts help? Surely not, it would be outlawed …*

With her shift ending, Seadhna was desperate to get out of the place, with its sweaty feel and the residue of other people's half-masticated food and fish bones tidied to the side. As she slid the remains of uneaten portions of Black Forest gateaux off the plates, claggy cream coated her shirt cuffs and the leftovers slopped among the tea and soup in the swill bucket. She untied her waitress apron and tossed it in the dirty washing basket. It was Saturday, the night of the parade and she was ready to forget it all for a few hours.

myths

All the years of her childhood, Shopping Week was the magical high point of the summer. The treasure hunt, the horse and carriage, the talent show and the resident band *like a real pop group*. The Saturday night parade was the thrill and the mystery to top it all. Seadhna begged her parents to take her to the parade, and like all the others from all parts of the island they were all drawn into the old street to view the unfolding cabaret. She had sat on her father's shoulders at the foot of the road when decorated floats rolled by, and been part of the mesmerised audience, wondering at all the work, the wit, the preparation, the oneness of it, watchers and watched. She herself had always been a spectator, never a participant, and now she wanted to be part of the magic-makers too.

After her lunchtime shift in the Bistro she could devote the final two hours before the parade in preparation. Cammy was primed and ready. In the morning he hauled out her mother's sewing machine and said he would make a 'creation', the likes of which had never been seen at the fancy dress.

'As long as Ah dinnae huv tae gang in it. Ah'll assist you tae fulfil yur obvious denied childhood ambition, but that's *it*.' He pouted mischievously. 'Then Ah'll watch fae the sidelines way a half bottle.'

Seadhna clattered into her parents' dining room to a scene of clippings and threads.

'The Bistro is such crap.' She folded into a heavy chair to feel her feet ache. It was the first time that day she had finally sat down. 'Being servile, well it just doesn't come naturally. Some people must be born to it.'

Cammy sat heaped over the treadle sewing machine, his foot pumping. He'd already mended a whole pile of John's work trousers that were out at the crotch. Sadie had sheepishly appeared with a pile of them. 'Sure you don't mind, lad? Ah'm no wantin' tae take advantage of yi,' said Sadie smiling.

'You pile them there, Mrs Rufus, Ah'll be delighted. Least Ah kin dae, wi' you pittan' me up an' a'. This is a brilliant machine, by the way, thur's nothin' like a proper treadle.'

'Ay, yi'r right there. John gave it me when we got married.'

'I've got to get a shower,' and Seadhna went to wash the dirt of the Bistro from herself, as if she might cleanse herself of her entire low-paid, sidelined existence. She looked dismally at Cammy's industry at the machine, feeling too weary to bother with the fancy dress. It all seemed a stupid idea now.

'Come on, yi'll hiv tae go in noo that Ah've done aw this work. Ah wis gonnae tak a posey photee o' yi tae fir ma collection.'

'What, like a real fashion photo?'

'Aye, come on … Whit di yi think o' ma idea? "Last o' the Mohicans"?'

'Explain.'

'Weel, what's the traditional fancy-dress outfit?' Cammy danced around, excited by his idea. 'Yeah, yur Reed Indians 'n' cowboys.'

'Okay?' Seadhna hadn't still caught his thought-thread.

'So its gonna be "Last o' the Mohicans", last o' the hunters, last of the natives.'

'Oh right … God, but then nobody here'll get it.'

Cammy prattled on, undaunted by her flatness. 'See, Ah've made yi a ball gown oota they skins.'

Seadhna perused Cammy's handiwork. It was a beautiful piece of pattern-cutting, design and sewing. He had the grain of the pelts running counter to each panel of the dress so that the skins flashed like velvet.

'Cammy it's brilliant. It's a work of art.'

'Steady noo. It's jist a bloody frock.'

'Okay! Hope it's no itchy, though.'

'It's a ballgown … an' made oota sealskins, no silk, hen. Itch comes wi' the label.'

'You're on dodgy ground wi' this, you know. You really wanting word getting oot that you use *real* animal skin? Milan will boycott you, darling!'

'Pish. Go on, pit it *oan*.'

Seadhna put on the sealskin gown.

'God, it's a bit stiff. It's gonna scratch me under the arms.'

'Yi dinnae get style wi' oot some pain, hen … Hey, it looks brilliant. Bit o' lipstick on yir face, Iriquois style. Couple of war marks on yir cheek …' and he pointed and poked at her, grabbing her hair in a great twist. 'Hey, stick yur hair up in a punk Mohican. Got any green dye?'

'Okay, don't get carried away, this is not London. No one except us will understand what this is all about. It just doesn't do to stray beyond traditional fancy dress mores …'

'Yi said yi wanted somethin' political, arty an' edgy.'

'Well,' she smiled, 'I guess it's safe enough if it's so obscure nobody will understand what you are on about. It'll just reinforce the fact that everybody here thinks I'm a headcase. But … it's great, Cam. Ta.'

Cammy sat back among all the clippings and threads.

'Weel, Ah'm ready fir a drink noo.'

At that moment he could have been an Indian tailor in Delhi, with his shaved tanned head and thin aquiline nose. Every bit a cross-legged young Gandhi, except for the accent.

Seadhna left Cammy and her mother discussing the merits of Singer versus Bernina … *I could never afford a Bernina* … and headed out to buy Kirby grips and lager.

meaning

The town was quiet and the roads seemed unnaturally empty. Suddenly, round the corner she saw Michael heading towards the entrance to the Home. Her gut jumped.

'Aye.'

They could not pass without speaking. It would seem too rude.

'Aye.'

Michael didn't let the conversation linger. He made to nod at Seadhna and slowed only to say, 'It was good you found her the other day,' and carried on toward the Home. Seadhna saw the tails of what looked like ribbon trailing from his fist as she passed on to the newsagents which sold all the emergency necessities of life like tan tights, Kirby grips and beer.

Clutching the apron, Michael stepped up the stairs to his mother's room. He slipped in and closed the door. In his head the same thoughts pulsed round the inescapable dog track inside his brain. *They didn't mean it, did they, when they said they wanted out? The owld fowk. Shiz jis' sayin' it, shi disna mean it.*

The Home was quiet and there were few visitors, on account of the Saturday revellers. No staff were around. Earlier in the week, the Shopping Week queen had appeared with sweets and flowers, dispensing them to the serried ranks of chairs and home-knitted blankets.

'Mithur?'

Agnes reached out a swollen papery hand, the skin stretched to bursting over her flesh. She let her hand rest on Michael's back as he sat on the chair next to the bed.

'I thought yi'd want yur apron.' There was a pause as Agnes squinted at the floral print that Michael unfurled from his fist.

'Whit'll I need that fir?' She was almost angry. 'Ah'm no use tae anybody. What I want is a blue pill, that's whit I want. Wan that'll knock me oot fir good.' *The Eskimau weemin can waak oot ontae the ice an' lie doon.*

Michael looked at his mother. 'Mither, whit ur yi sayin', whit is it yir asking fir?'

She closed her eyes without replying. He watched her until she fell asleep, her mouth gradually slackening to the side as her pom-pommed slippers kept a blind vigil beneath the chair.

It had been hot all day and the fire escape door was wide open to let in the cool evening breeze. When the night staff came on they would shut the doors, doing the supper round and the bedtime drugs. Michael left through the open fire door and took a narrow lane straight down the hill.

The town was quiet in anticipation, with the final touches going onto fancy-dress costumes. Tractors, trailers and floats from the country farms were grinding out of secret byres. The carry-outs stowed, the kitties bulging with fivers and the farm boys, with a swig of vodka, beginning to feel a little less silly in their fake tits and suspenders. The pipers screwed up the chanters that went rapidly flat in the heat.

Mithur, yi ken I cannae ...

Michael took down the rifle and shoved a handful of bullets into his pocket. Nobody was working, nobody was fishing. Everyone was consumed with the cavalcade. He got in the boat and pulled the outboard into life. The burst of energy that he expelled wrenching the cord simultaneously snapped something inside him and he revved the engine up to top speed and set his gaze on the horizon. Once dislocated from the town, Michael began to feel a blanket of peace. *That's it. All the things of the land are small. You get right out on that blue water and everything from the land disappears*

'This is where I belong.'

He pushed down the tiller of the outboard to head for the Skerry.

disguise

Seadhna organised a back-pack of lager for Cammy to carry. 'Once I've had a few, I'll no be caring what anybody thinks.' Seadhna could feel herself brimming up dangerously. When she appeared down the stairs her mother laughed, and John Rufus, sternly engrossed in the editorial, raised his eyes above *The Scotsman*.

'Well well, Seadhna,' he remarked, which was as far as the residue of Free Presbyterianism would allow him to go in the direction of frippery. Like playing cards, fancy dress was just a bit too frivolous. John Rufus was already tacitly embarrassed by the prospect of the retirement 'do' planned by the post office girls.

Cammy walked with Seadhna across the Back Road to where the fancy dress entrants collected.

The Jackson children from the new craft shop wore black eyeliner, describing suitably squinty eyes for their Chinese outfits. One had a coolie hat made out of a lampshade and the other had her hair scraped up into a bun with knitting needles in it. Someone with a clipboard came round taking down entry details. 'And your entry? Chinky ladies, is it?'

'Chinese ladies,' interjected Mrs Jackson with nervous politeness. It was not really her place to correct the fancy-dress official.

'Well it doesn't matter which,' and the badge-wearing official wrote down the entry with an incorrect spelling that Mrs Jackson was unable to amend despite her burning inclination.

'Why can we not be Chinky ladies?' asked the children.

'Chinky's rude,' whispered Mrs Jackson, repositioning the coolie hat.

Cammy and Seadhna melted into the churning anarchy of the parade.

'God, Ah cannae believe Ah'm daein' this. Fuckin' fancy dress.'

The crowd of watchers on the road were collecting, prior to the parade moving off, and faces strained up at the floats as they arrived to assemble in the long procession. The seasoned participants delayed their entry in true professional style so that they could position themselves later in the parade for more effect. Slogans and posters declared comic lines and local wit. The mechanics from the garage had spent all week building a contraption that fired out a human cannon ball and spewed smoke into the crowd. Seadhna walked up and down the long parade as it waited for the signal to march off.

'This is brilliant.' A rusty pickup with several rows of cabbages on the back carried the title of 'Council Meeting in Session.'

'See that, Cammy. If that's not conceptual art, tell me what is?' Seadhna laughed out loud and gulped from her lager.

'All content but nae style!' But Cammy was perusing the talent. 'See him, tho? He's a bit o' all right!' and he nodded in the direction of a skinny dark-haired boy in a Tarzan outfit.

'God, no! Looks can deceive. He works in the insurance office. Totally boring. Not your type at all Cam!'

Everyone in their disguises for the night shook off the straitjacket of roles the town locked them into. The parade allowed one night of liberation when everyone was freed, when there was no editorial control, no political correctness and no comeback.

'Bloody hell, there's Lilly Barnes.' Lilly was parodying the police sergeant who led the parade, complete with beer belly and truncheon. Ahead was the horse-drawn coach of the queen and then right at the very front were the pipe band. Behind came the adult walkers, adorned in nappies, enormous bosoms and various versions of cross-dressing. Taking up the rear were the floats. Tractors and trailers, decorated, painted and festooned. The Golf Club, the Women's Guild, the Bakers, the Young Farmers, Dale, the Students, the Shopkeepers, Bolt's Engineering. Homely sets of Grannie's Heilan' Hame, Snow White *again*, and one tableau poking fun at the big issue of the day, the new ferry to the isles, which entailed an entire ship-like structure built round a tractor and trailer and towing a mini-sized lifeboat.

The 'Chinese ladies' were duly uplifted onto the back of the coal lorry, which was hosed down for the event, where they joined the throng of other under-twelve walking entries disguised as postboxes, cats, princesses and whatever was the current diet of Disney films and cartoons. Those who had aerials for the new Channel 4 had access to a whole new wonderland of dressing-up possibilities that nobody else understood. The coal lorry with its fancy dress cargo of cardboard fantasies rattled its way round the south end of the town, turning into the cavernous eighteenth-century fishing heart of the place.

Everyone was transformed by the magic. People stood at their doors awaiting the parade. Smiles stretched onto faces as the witty jokes were read. There was nudging, belly laughing, shouting and bantering, back and fore from the street to the floats.

Seadhna had enough eye make-up on to feel almost completely disguised. *This is it. This is good. I really am part of this.* The girls from the Bistro pointed. 'Seadhna, what are you like?' It was okay to be as ridiculous as you wanted.

A charity collecting tin was thrust into her hands, so she rattled it up into the faces in the crowd. Her faces. The faces of the place. They delved into the plastic bags of brown coins they had saved and fed money into the cans. Coins hailed onto the floats, a stinging copper shower. Seadhna got more and more into her part and when the parade stalled she did a war dance, whooping and clapping. She swilled lager from a can and shouted, 'Don't take my picture or you'll steal my soul!' She pointed as a camera was raised, then laughed, 'I'll put a spell on you.' Just as Michael caught sight of her and sniggered, she whooped round and round on the spot.

Cammy shadowed her slow progress with the lumbering parade as it made its way through the old streets, past the harbour and on to its final destination where the winners were announced. By then the crowd was tens deep, as if the entire population had drained to the edge of the island.

By the time the judging was over, all the adult participants were well drunk and few bothered to change out of their Saturday costumes. They all gravitated to the open-air dance with outfits ripped and askew converging in a great melee. The farm boys forgot or no longer cared that they wore mini-skirts and bras. Spirited dancers tried to find some spring on the hard pavement to rock to the cover band's Elvis medley.

Somewhere in the town, the Chinese ladies were being put to bed because eleven o'clock was still too late to be up *and you know there is a limit how much you can bend the bed-time routine and anyway, it's way too rough down there at the pier head for children. All those drunks.*

Seadhna forgot she had already spoken to Michael that day and when she spotted him her inhibitions had disappeared. 'Michael,' she greeted him like a great buddy, 'd'you want a can?' and she snapped one from the plastic four-pack.

Everything was easier when the divisions were blurred.

'No thank you, I've my own.'

'Come on Michael, come and dance.'

'No … I don't dance.' Michael stood stiffly back from her.

Seadhna, drunk, ignored him and tried to drag him over the cobbles, which he resisted. She glimpsed Cammy leaning into Sandy's ear, but only Cammy was aware of his upper lip brushing the softness of Sandy's lobe as he talked intently to him. The deafening crowd provided an excuse for their proximity. Sandy threw an arm round Cammy in a gesture that could have been all innocence. They staggered together and then Seadhna's gaze drifted away from the incongruous teaming. When he saw that she had been distracted, Michael too moved away from Seadhna but she continued to pursue him, quickly losing sight of Cammy.

'Did you see Cammy, my friend Cammy, he was over there with Sandy?'

'Is that no your boyfriend?' Michael knew she was too drunk and tried to offload her, spare her the next day's' embarrassment, the next month's returning visions.

'No, he's no me boyfriend.' Seadhna wobbled, flailing her arms.

'Well he seems like your boyfriend to me and I'm no getting intae trouble fae him.'

'Honest he's no', Michael. He's no into girls, you ken. He's gay.' Seadhna teetered. The drunkenness allowed her to fix her eyes right into Michael's.

'Well I have to go,' said Michael, matter of fact.

'Don't go. I'm all on my own. I don't know where he is. He was kind of looking after me and I've never really spoken to you, you know.' Seadhna lurched.

'Aye, you're drunk though. You'll regret all of this tomorrow.'

'No I won't.' Seadhna hiccuped. 'Talk to me Michael, I want to know about what you do.'

'Aye, you *are* drunk. You're no really wantin' tae ken.'

'How no'?'

'You ken fine. I'm smart enough to ken when I'm getting' the piss te'en oota me.'

'I'm not Michael, really.' A shimmer of despair was trickling through Seadhna as she realised the depth of suspicion that Michael bore towards her.

'Aye, we'll see. I have tae go,' and he walked away.

Cammy sprung at Seadhna from behind and caught her round the waist. 'You are *pished*, hen.'

The public toilets overflowed. Drunk men were pissing in every dark recess. A woman squatted behind a bollard. 'I wish it was always like this,' swooned Seadhna.

'See you were getting friendly with the fisher lad.'

'I was just trying to speak to him. He was real uptight, though.'

'Probably kens danger when he sees it, hen.'

'Whaddya mean? Anyway, what were *you* up to with Sandy? I saw you. You looked like you wis lickin' his ear!'

'A little kindness, that was all.' Cammy smiled. 'He's a pure confused boy. Terrified he might be a *poof*. Like so many "big men".'

'Eh?' Seadhna exclaimed.

'Well it's near enough midsummer. We all get to shag a monster or even a closet fairy till the magic wears off!'

'You didn't!'

'Naw, don't be daft. What d'ya think I am, some kinda homo predator? No that the chance wisnae there.' And Cammy flashed a conspiratorial look.

'You're kidding. You are winding me up. Is he gay?'

'Ha, whae kens? Jis so terrified o' no bein' *normal* he has tae prove he's a big man. It's a hard act to keep up, yi ken.'

Seadhna's brain tried to digest the craziness of the night, but failed. She felt she had lost something, and that still something irked her that she needed to sort. The two of them wobbled home. Seadhna had a split under the arm of her gown.

'An' Ah niver got the photae o' yi when it wis still intact. Shit.'

'It wid'a frightened the magic away, Cammy.'

an island

On Sunday morning, the street sweeper preceded everyone onto the debris of Saturday night, diligently brushing up the broken glass and the mountain of empty cans. The harbour was thick in chucked bottles and litter. Michael was up at six in the stunned morning, quiet after the raucous night, ready to set out his mended creels. He didn't let a night of lager drinking divert him from a good day on the sea and was eager to try his new invention of redesigned door catches on the creels with the impenetrable drawstring bait-bags. The sooner he gave them a go, the sooner he'd know what modifications were needed.

Cammy was up before Seadhna. He'd already been down the street to find everything closed and was sitting gauntly at the kitchen table across from John Rufus trying to trick the hangover from settling on him.

'No son, we don't get Sunday papers till a Tuesday. They have tae come in on the boat,' John explained. Cammy nodded, drumming his fingers briefly then getting up to wander around, already restless.

In the quiet morning house, Sadie peeled tatties. John listened to Alistair

Cook on the radio. Seadhna eventually appeared with a corker of a hangover and Sadie swirled the tea in the pot on the stove, ready to pour out a treacle-coloured cup for Seadhna.

'Poor old Agnes died last night, I just spoke to Heather coming off night duty.'

'Agnes McLeay?' croaked Seadhna, hammers knocking her head from side to side.

Cammy sipped a black coffee. 'Ah think Ah'm gonnae fly hame. The thocht o' goin' on that boat is makin' me boak right noo.'

'How did she go? Agnes.'

'Och, just one big heart attack, they think. It was sudden. A blessing really. She was losing her wits, poor auld wife. It'll be wan God's own job tracking doon the family. Best thing really wi' that Alzheimer's, they can live on fir years.' Seadhna made a quiet note to seek out Michael. A funeral was a legitimate excuse. But first the day had to pass, until she pieced together the night and what it all meant.

Next day Cammy went down to the ironmongers that doubled as a travel agent's for BEA to cancel his boat ticket and book onto the plane., 'Christ, that nearly cost me two hunner quid, and it's only wan way … Could get a whole box at the opera fir that.'

'Opera?'

'Aye, opera. Yi nivver been? Its fab. We got tae draw backstage when Jessye Norman wis rehersin'. It's magic, hen.'

'Cammy, I would never have had you as an opera goer.'

'Why no'?'

'Oh God, I don't know. All the things I thought I knew seem to be shifting.'

'Weel Ah ken wan thing that disnae change. Bad taste stays the same. Ah huv tae buy an ornament fur ma maw. She … wait for it,' and he shook his head in mock disbelief, 'collects frogs! So we can go tae a tacky gift shop and choose the maist stupit frog in the place. The worse it is the mare ma maw'll pure love it. Think that's why Ah hid tae leave hame. Jis' couldna share ma livin' environment way that mony china frogs.'

'It's not a bed o' roses living here either, yi ken. It's like being in a permanent *soap* opera ... where you can't get written out. The story. It's a place made of stories. You have no choice other than to be part of it ... It used to drive me mad.'

'Maybe livin' in a world o' china frogs is no that bad then. But there's nothin' says you cannae write the dialogue.'

'Not literally, of course.'

'Naw, metaphorically.' Cammy grinned. 'Aw fuck, Ah jis' said a word wi' a pile o' syllables. Gimme a tack fix quick afore Ah git above masel.'

a magician

At the airport Cammy kept the china frog in his hand luggage. Wrapped in tissue paper in a small brown box, it had 'Cotswold pottery' stamped on the bottom.

'Right. Noo Ah kin say Ah've been! Ah'm a tourist. Ah've seen hoo the ither half lives. Ah've pit masel oota ma comfort zone, an noo ma horizons is broadened. Thur's photographic proof o' me being it the most famous Stone Age village in the world.'

The flight was called. *All passengers for BEA 8330 direct to Glasgow please proceed to Departures now.*

'Come on, geez a hug.' Cammy beamed.

Embracing at airports ... people will assume ... they'll get the wrong end of the stick ... they'll think there's some relationship ... It all went through her head in a second, then she realised she didn't know when she might see Cammy again. She hugged him, letting her body collapse into him. Letting the relief flow.

'Kindness, hen, dinnae underestimate it. Many's that dinnae even get that much.'

He waved from the single Departures gate. Seadhna watched the plane trundle out to the runway.

Kindness? There is never really any knowing what the connection is between two people. Sending words out into space ... the point where any meaning is shared. It seemed either so huge it could be everything or so tiny it was almost nothing.

Cammy was like a whirlwind that came down. The Wizard of Oz twister when everything was scattered and at the same time rearranged. Sometimes all that could be hoped for was to move one tiny increment nearer to someone else, and Seadhna felt strange tears. The sadness and relief at the end of a doomed struggle, an impossible exhausting relationship, a long anticipated death, and all the new horizons that those things brought.

a ghost

Agnes's funeral took place from the small sitting room of the Old People's Home. The other residents were moved to the big dining room for the duration, although faces still craned round chairs to see who was attending. The square funeral notice announced in the shop windows that there were to be family flowers only. The coffin selection was daunting, the cushioned interiors, cotton or silk, the types of handles, shrouds or ordinary clothes. Too much choice, even with a funeral you had to make a judgement about the type of box someone merited. The family settled for the medium one. *No point pittan' quality hardwood in the grund tae rot ...*

Then the undertaker entwined Agnes's fingers over the white cloth, the tips just turning a bruised purple. The smell of powder, some strange funereal spray that was completely alien, like a foreign soap. *They hid tae brak the Cott wife's knees tae git her in the coffin, bones jist locked bent ... tendons constricted.*

Shirley asked John Rufus to speak at the funeral, adding, 'Mam was never kirky.' Even Shirley with her new correctness wouldn't have gone to the minister. The undertaker preserved his low tone of voice throughout the consultation, as they worked out the words for the notice.

'We'll share the cost.'

'Sort it all out after the funeral.'

'And what about the stone?'

'We should really put Geordie on it too ...'

'It's about 50p a letter, depending on gold, silver or whatever ... But you can think about that later. I'll drop round a catalogue.'

Shirley brought a wreath up from Nairn which said 'MOTHER' in chrysanthemums.

The hearse waited outside the front door of the Home, the boot raised open.

John Rufus, Shirley and Douglas, Malky, Jake and Michael sat solemnly in the straight- backed chairs almost too close to the polished coffin, the men strange in black suits, the second outing for Michael's wedding outfit. White shirts and black ties. Flushed with diabetes, Annie in an over-tight grey suit and Tom thin with the pain of arthritis. Shirley's skirt, cut on the cross, shimmered over her knees. Patent black court shoes on her feet.

The funeral party was completed by two of the carers from the Home. The undertaker and his assistant stood to the side, some more black suits to swell the numbers. There were just enough pallbearers.

This passing was barely a footnote in the conscience of the town, so there would be no packed church, no big silver collection for the comfort fund, nor procession of cars to churchyard. Despite the public invitation for friends to accept this *intimation as invitation*, the deadline of two o'clock went and there were no more. The undertaker, with his hands clasped behind his back, rocked towards John, whispering that he may as well start.

'Agnes Jean Bixter McLeay was born in nineteen twenty …'

John Rufus never spoke from notes. He had all the words he needed in his head. In his short eulogy he managed to find a way to elevate Agnes's life in to something dignified.

'We will remember her for the small things she did …'

He eschewed the booming distant tone that only church ministers could effect.

'… red-leading the step at the bank …'

And he looked around at the bowed heads, measuring the sentiment and the dignity of his words.

'… running to get in her washing before the rain came …'

In their minds, the mourners collected round each statement verifying them.

Yes that was her. That was what she did.

'… getting along the street early in the morning for her messages …'

In the small room, for the few minutes while John spoke, Agnes's life glowed, spoken about to an audience, made important, given a space in time. Then John Rufus stepped back, looking sideways towards the undertaker.

Excepting the fact he was an atheist, he would have made a great Kirk minister.

The undertaker directed the sons and Douglas to the coffin handles. In silence they slid the coffin out of the small sitting room, the applause from the TV snooker just audible from the sitting room. Down the wheelchair ramp shuffled the pallbearers, sliding the coffin on runners into the hearse. There was some low talk as the transport was sorted. John Rufus went in the hearse. Douglas took Jake, Michael and Malky. The company car again.

There was no speaking at the burial. Seadhna made her way to the cemetery, the small service in the Home being too intimate. The undertaker silently choreographed the progress of the coffin from the hearse into the grave with hand gestures. At the graveside they all stood alongside the strange precision-cut hole, with its smooth sides, and clean corners, and no mess of stray soil. The undertaker issued the cords to the pallbearers, unfurling them as he went round each. The coffin was lowered and settled on the bottom. Then a board of plywood with the family flowers was set on top. *Mother.*

Seadhna watched as her father went forward to shake the hands of the family, and she then followed.

'I'm sorry, Michael.'

'It was good of you to come.'

And she made her way back with her father.

Shirley had to get away back south as soon as the funeral was past and told Michael to sort out the stone.

high tide

Justin gave Seadhna the extra breakfast shifts at the Bistro. It meant getting up at six to be at work for half past in order to start serving the tourists heading back south on the boat. The early mornings were good, the unsullied day unfurling slowly, crisp unbreathed air, the roads quiet with only the early morning people around, the milk van and the street sweeper. She swung her head back, her eyes wheeling in the blue between the lurching chimney pots each side of the narrow street. This was the best time and she knew she had to appreciate it before the day got tatty and worn and she was shut away between the sweaty kitchen and the clattering dining room.

At the harbour the men were already down on their boats. They abandoned their vans and pickups on the pier and the figures could be seen making ready for the day's fishing. The axis of summer had shifted, and across the water the uncut fields were starting to turn russet with untreated dockans.

Every day she passed the place where Michael's boat lay, and most days he was there. He kept his back to her and the watchers from the pier as he baited and stowed his creels. She became familiar with his presence, each day glancing down to see if he was about, identifying his pickup and making the mental step in her mind that he would be there. She felt a quiet gladness when he was present as if it secured the start of her day.

In her head she was making up a jigsaw of his movements, a study. First she saw how he had closed himself off, how he did not turn or acknowledge the land activity. He kept himself focussed on the sea and the boat. She stored these visual clips of him in her mind as he bent, as he deftly balanced from the steps to his boat, as he stooped over the outboard. She saw how he coiled his body into the engine and wrenched the starter, his tensed muscle power that sprang the engine into life. One pull only and then he crouched as he adjusted the choke, settling the engine rhythm. He unhitched the rope and took the fenders in and moved the boat round.

She found herself daily looking for new things about him. The washed-out sweatshirts he wore, the way his jeans like a soft skin moulded the muscles in his legs. The tobacco tin that sat in his back pocket and the wet days when he wore a jersey and oilskins. She wondered about who it might be that cared about him, who made the jersey. Did he pick the pattern? Would he bother about stuff like that? She never saw him with a life jacket.

It became a habit that every day she looked for him, and felt disappointment when she walked along and saw his boat gone, away before she had woken up.

Something was creating a pull, and in her head she examined it and tested it in case it was a delusion, something to help get her through the drudgery of the bistro, the pretend joviality, the relentless stage act of forced happy servitude. She posed herself questions about her fixation and asked herself to rationalise the attraction. Once she had decided it was legitimate, she cocooned the new bubble of revelation like a fragile secret, a hidden box of good things to be opened sparingly and enjoyed.

Away from her work and the harbour she could take one of the memory clips from her store and replay it – his back under a looser T-shirt, the raggedness of his hair, the days he hadn't shaved and the black shadow showing where his beard would grow. She couldn't imagine him going to a barber's and yet she saw him with his hair clipped and tidied. She dared herself longer looks, searching him out from further away, fixing her eyes on him and keeping them there, feeding the new building current she could feel within.

The fishermen never came into Justin's Bistro – it was too posh. So when there was a day of wind that kept them ashore, they met in the old café with its mugs of Nescafé, jukebox and polystyrene tiles. The waitress persona that Seadhna had adopted was never required to respond beyond the tourists and the middle-class second-homers. But when the toilets got choked in the old café and flooded the kitchen there was a big hygiene to-do and they had to shut down until the plumbing got sorted. All the traditional clientele from the old café that was simply called 'the café' had to decant elsewhere.

When Seadhna walked out into the Bistro's dining room and saw the fishermen had taken up position at the coveted corner table, a sudden zing of unprepared shock hit her. The whole context was not in the script of her well-practised character role. She fumbled with her waitress pad, all nerves, dropping her pencil, it rolling out of her reach and in among the legs of the men. She was going to have to bend down to pick it up off the floor. She would have to grope around among their feet under the table. The cascading embarrassment had already run ahead of itself with the cumulative nerves engulfing her and producing stuttering and involuntary gestures and twitches. And Michael was there, his back to her, moving his chair away in this mini-cringe vignette to reach under the table and retrieve the missing pencil.

The others had barely noticed, pulling out their cigarettes and sweeping the menu card aside.

'Coffees,' said one.

'Aye, five coffees.'

'Huv yi any Twixes?'

'Three suggars.'

'Oh, thur's suggar on the table.' Michael half turned with the pencil in his hand, offering it out to her.

The waitress act was in tatters and a smile of relief broke out on Seadhna's face – it was out and gone before she could rein it in, realising as it spread up from her gut and claimed her face that there was nothing she could do to stop it. Her secret surveillance had guiltily come right up against an embarrassed reality. It was the kind of smile that could not be made up, impossible to pretend or act, that sent a whole pile of layered messages outwards, directed to its single receiver. The smile opened her up like a gutted fish and went straight to Michael, and for only a millisecond, cementing the involuntary eye contact, the relief.

It was done, and she knew it then as she repeated the order like a robot.

'Five coffees, then.' She took the pencil, noting his fingers, the nails worn right down to the quick, the chunkiness of his hands, the calluses, part of a tattoo showing on his forearm. Turning to the kitchen and knowing that there had been a defining moment she couldn't hide from, her head was banging. A line had been crossed somewhere. But what could be told from a look? These things could all be read wrong, could be delusional. It was the agony of not knowing. The uncertainty about whether it was matched in any way inside Michael. That was the puzzle now, the unbearable puzzle of trying to read the signs and all the things that were impossible to just come out and say.

The smile was imprinted still in her face muscles – she could feel where it had been and the surge it had provoked. Surely the kitchen staff had read it too. She wanted to keep its memory intact, and as she helped dry the lunchtime plates and stack them she relived the morning's scenario to fasten the details.

By the time her shift finished the rain had stopped but it was still windy. The men were no longer on the pier. Michael's boat lay like a tethered pony by the steps and he was gone, as was his blue pickup. She gazed down at his boat, lingering in the knowledge that he was not around to witness her greed for more proximity, more signs, more clues about him. She stared hard at the boat, trying to hammer the mystery of him into boxes in her head. Staring at the boat was the nearest she could get to him, as if it hid the key to him.

She could see now how ordered and neatly everything was stowed there, the ropes, the baskets, the confident knots, and it made her feel good – this new knowledge about him. About how there was a different way to think about Michael McLeay that in all the years she had never bothered to question. She had allowed his role to remain set in her head as prescribed by the place without ever challenging it. And as the thought dawned on her, she felt another fear – that he too might confine her to what she had been – and the shame thumped her inside.

The secret joy of a new journey that might begin was tempered by the knowledge of the invisible constraints their shared history trapped them into. Seadhna still wanted there to be a maybe, a new thing she needed to learn about, a possibility. Maybe she couldn't fix all the wrongs, but she was inquisitive now and that wasn't going to stop without her learning more.

It was a path she would need to think about. There would come a time when things would be noticed, people would pick up the signs, and she would have to know for sure where the path might go, because once the town got hold of her fragile secret, it would no longer be within her hands. The town could make it or wreck it, like a clumsy parent.

fishing

Seadhna was searching him out, constantly on watch to recognise his gait, his pickup, whether he had been on his boat. The tourists were dwindling. The English school holidays ended. It was September and the lobsters were on. *Of course, it's the fishermen's harvest too, it doesn't just happen on the land.* The land was pale orange with barley and the combines were working all night, lit up like great monsters in the fields. The big harvest moon, yellow and plump, sat lazily above the horizon like a great yolk ready to split.

She walked at night when the dark was cloaking in over the land and sea, wondering, guessing, trying to read him and draw him out. Passing the lane where she knew he lived, she felt her thoughts must be thumping out in blasting amplification all over the unperturbed town. It felt as if every kitchen window and passer-by must know her secret, as it demanded itself so loudly from within her.

She walked on the shore out by the graveyard, watching the ferry plunge into the Sound. The westerly wind cast shadows on the sea, flecking it a tone of darker blue. She walked and wondered, thinking she was beginning to obsess. The sea was the colour of autumn, whipped a more serious and darker blue. She sat on a rock, the wind slapping her hair. The tide was out and the grey sand lay wet like a lead mirror.

The crunch of tyres over the shingle announced a vehicle and an engine idled. A diesel. As she got up to walk back she saw it was the blue Hilux, Michael's. All the times she had desperately tried to engineer herself to bump into him, driven by this lurching and one-sided fixation, she had been the one in control of the story in her head. She had planned and managed the fantasy anticipation of meeting him in such a place. But the storybook fantasies she had been concocting in the safety of her private jigsaw without his knowledge or consent stood poised to crumble to nothing if extracted and tested out in the real world.

Seeing him there on the beach without the cover of other people to dilute the intensity or any easy escape excuses left them both exposed. It was too late, she would look stupid or rude if she turned away from him now and walked the other way, she would just have to brazen it out and in the seconds before their paths crossed think of something to say to him that didn't give away the crazy turmoil she felt inside.

Each step was a slow-motion panic of self examination of how she might look to him, what he might think of her, what detail or look she could impart to give the correctly honed signal to him. He stopped before her as she approached and she saw he wasn't simply going to pass by with a brief exchange of greeting. She was expected to keep walking toward him. There was going to be some sort of conversation, the prospect of which both alarmed and thrilled her. She could feel her gut shifting. He was standing square in front of her and she was flicking her eyes on and off him, scared of what an overlong glance might produce. He was taller than her, with the body fullness of someone that worked hard.

'Aye aye,' he said. Was there a hint of humour? Did he remember the night of the parade? *Oh shit.*

She felt the previous soft smile that had burst away from her uncontrollably in the bistro begin a slower, gentler journey over her face, her eyes making a similarly measured journey across the arm of his jacket, the sides of his face to his, letting them connect for a thread of telling time.

'Aye.'

'Ur ya oota waak?'

'Yeah … What about you?'

'Ach, I lost a couple o' creels and wis jist lookan' tae see if they's geen up it high water.'

'Oh I see.' She thought maybe he might think she should have noticed such a thing, but she only thought of creels on the shore as part of the accidental beach ornamentation that might feature in a tasteful photo, not as something that might matter in any other sense. Her walks on the shore were for brooding, musing and scattering fragmented thought. The shore for him was an extension of his workplace.

'I don't think I saw any.'

'Ach, Gary said he'd pat them up above high water fir me.'

Yes, that resonated, stuff put up above high water was usually claimed by beachcombers, it was an unwritten rule of the shore.

He was scanning the high-water edge. 'I see thum noo thur ower there.'

She tried to follow his gaze but couldn't see the creels.

'By that lump o' yella stuff', he helped her.

'Oh yes, so they are.' This was all sounding very limp.

'I ken whit Ah'm lukkan fir, y'see,' he smiled.

Seadhna wanted to keep him there and prolong the talking. The gaps needed to be filled or the slim connection would be severed and he would march away to get the lost gear. She tried to tease out more words.

'How do you know thur yours?'

'By the way thur pat tigithur – I bind them along the buddam.'

Seadhna had no clue what he meant. 'Oh I see – with rope, like.'

'Aye, or rubber sometimes. Anyway, we aal ken wur own creels. Like I s'pose you ken yur own writan.'

There was silence and she knew it was going to come to an end there.

'Oh well, I better go and get them.'

'Oh yes,' she said and he moved away.

After a step he turned his head back. 'Ah'm gan back tae the toon then if yi want a lift.'

She didn't really want a lift because a walk was about having a walk. But it was like a big chunk of opportunity, maybe even an offer to prolong the connection.

'Well yes, yes that would be good – I think, yes I think the rain might be coming on.'

Michael headed off along the shore and Seadhna hovered, unsure whether to stay at the pickup or what. Then she followed after him at what she thought might seem a nonchalant kind of pace. He was bending down to pick up one creel and slinging it onto his back, then the other swung from his hand. He was striding over the stones onto the sand road.

The creel was the reason for conversation.

'So ur they damaged then?'

'Nup, the buoys's jis' come off, thur fine.'

Seadhna positioned herself to walk in step with him back to the pickup. To speak, she had to look sideways at him, but he kept his face fixed ahead.

As they reached the pickup he threw the creels into the back with two metal clunks in quick succession and went round to the driver's door. The invitation had not been restated but Seadhna moved to the passenger door and pressed the handle, stretching to get her foot on the footplate. He was already starting up the engine, as if he was in a hurry to get going.

She climbed in and pulled the door shut while he swivelled his head around to reverse the truck. It mounted a bump and she swayed from side to side as it righted itself and he made to turn it round to settle on the tar part of the single track road.

'Okay,' he said, which could have been a question or a statement, and she took the communication as an opportunity to maximise the chance to look over to him and reply with a nod and a 'yes' in the direction of his eyes. As his look flicked back and fore between side mirrors he skimmed hers in the process. He made to put the gears into first, then sat with the truck idling, his foot on the clutch.

He didn't look at her but spoke through the windscreen.

'I never said right aboot the day you got me mither.'

She tried to jump through the jumble of thoughts to find the day he might mean.

'The day she wis oota the Home, wanderin aboot lukkan' fir the boat.'

Seadhna stayed rigid. 'Oh yes, that day, that was okay – I just was helping.'

'I nivver thought she shoulda been in that Home. It wis me sister, like.'

'Oh I see.'

'Like hid's no good fir them when thur oota thur own piece. Hid feenishes them tae put them in a strange place. Hid wis me sister. Hur idea, shiz whit yi might call … .hard, ken,' and he turned his face towards her, 'cold … shiz a cold woman. I hid no say innit.'

Seadhna wasn't sure how to react to this unburdening. 'Well, I'm sure you did what you could.'

'No really,' he drawled slowly, 'I coulda stopped her.'

There was a long silence, the engine still idling, and he looked full at her. 'Whit wid I ken, Ah'm jist a stupeet fisherman.'

Seadhna could not reply. She knew at once the weight incorporated in the layers of this statement. It was a challenge and a declaration of their two separate worlds. It defined the prejudice he had endured and she had been complicit with, the facile streaming that cast him irreconcilably among the stupid and the peasants as if she was predestined for something better, and yet she knew he had skills and knowledge and perception that came from a whole other set of values.

Michael stopped to let her off at the top of the hill by the harbour. The journey had been taken in silence, all the while the distance between the echoing statement cementing the impossibility of going back to mend it or soften it. That's perhaps where it simply had to stay, hanging there like an uncomfortable truth that formed the baseline to everything else.

'Here you are, will this do ya? Ah'm gonna pit these by the pier.'

'Yes that's grand. Thanks, Michael,' and she let herself claim his name just for a moment before she opened the door and slid to the ground.

From below she caught the side of the door to shut it and looked up at him. 'Michael … ?' She couldn't bring herself to give credence to the word stupid. He was protected in the cab and could look down at her and she summoned all the expression of sincerity she could to say, 'I don't think of you like that.' She closed the door before he had the chance to respond, hoping he would know exactly what it meant.

a lure

It was a whole week before Michael came into the Bistro. It was not the haunt of the ordinary townsfolk. Too many different kinds of coffee and too expensive, but he sat down and waited. Seadhna went up to take his order.

Why are there so many meanings to every tiny thing?

'What can I get you?' She avoided his eyes and he avoided hers.

'Coffee.'

She was going to rattle out the list of choices – Americano, cappuccino, espresso, small, regular – but stopped, realising it was an insult.

'An ordinary one? None of the fancy shite?' she suggested.

'Aye, none of the fancy crap. Anyway, it was you I was hoping to see.'

Michael delved into the pocket of his anorak. He was flushing. Seadhna felt alarm.

'I thought you might like this.' He handed her an unidentifiable object. 'You'll maybe think this is, ehm … stupid but I made it a long time back. When me an' me fither wis at the selkies. Could nivver think o' anyone that might want it. There was nobody I saw about … eh … daft enough to wear the damn skins.'

Michael set the sealskin purse down on the oak-veneered tabletop and Seadhna hesitated, then gabbled out an automatic 'Thank you', still unsure what the object was. Then, as she examined the purse, she changed her tone. 'It's beautiful. It's really kind of you … Thank you.'

'I know what yu'r on aboot,' he said slowly, 'I think I dae anyway. You see past the skins. Don't ken if I'm pittan' it right …'

Seadhna felt herself flushing and turned around to get his coffee. Then he shouted after her, 'Yi'v all the kit tae go ti the ball noo, Seadhna.' His manner seemed well out of character. He said her name.

She brought the coffee and clattered it nervously from the tray to the table.

'Thur's something I need ti ask yi. Can you sit?' and Michael was in charge.

Seadhna looked about. Sitting with Michael would set up a chain of whispering.

'Okay, just for a minute, it's not busy.'

'Yi'r a trained artist, ur yi no? I mean that's whit yi trained fir, awaye it the college?'

'Yes … '. She was off her guard. 'Though I haven't really done anything for ages,' she protested, hoping to cover all eventualities.

'Just that I wis needan' an artist. Fir a drawing.'

'Oh yes?' she asked, still worried, and remembering the Scottie dog.

'Me mither's stone.'

Seadhna, with all senses alert, desperately tried to avoid a faux pas that might destroy this strange delicacy.

'I mean I wid pay yi, Ah'm no wantan' it fir notheen. I got a catalogue fae the stonemasons. They had pictures in the catalogue that yi could pit on the stone, bit none o' them wis really right.'

'Yes?' Seadhna was still unsure.

'I mean it wis jis' thur designs. They didna mean anything. I jis' wondered if yi could mak a drawing … see yi can post it off, and their cutters … the stonemason's will pit it ontae the stone.'

'What kind of drawing? I mean what sort of thing were you thinking of? I … well, I'm sure I could do something …'

'Ah'm no sure o' the kinda thing. Mibbe sumtheen that has mair tae dae wi' me mither an' her, an' this place …'

'Like a wild flower or … a bird? A curlew or a gull or something like that?'

'You'll be able tae think o' sumeen' that fits …'

Seadhna stared at him.

'Okay.' She had already decided. Whatever Michael wanted, she would try and draw. 'I'll try. I could do some sketches and show them to you, and you could choose the one you liked best.'

'Okay then.'

And then there was a space when the deal had been discussed and a new place had to be entered.

'I'll go.'

'Okay.' But he didn't move.

'And the fishing, are you gonna stay with it?'

'Och aye. Ah'm up fir anither throw at the dice … Ah'm no ready tae sell tickets fir the zoo yit.' And not quite winking, looking from the corner of his eye, 'Bit if it comes tae it Ah'll train up a selkie tae tak fish fae me hand and tak the tourists oot tae watch. It's iss that's still smarter than them efter all. They kin *both* work fir me …'

He left the money on the table for Seadhna to pick up, the coffee undrunk.

'Aye aye, then.'

And Noo

Tom became sinew and bone, his flesh tightening over his arthritis. Every jolt from the metal seat on the tractor triggered pain through his body. His whole self tensed against the expectation of agony. He could not plough. Annie swelled with diabetes. In all their years in the farm they had never once locked the door. Now the big rusted key the size of Tom's palm sat inside Annie's bag. The two of them compacted into a sheltered house with a window opening onto grey harling.

Michael sat on a kitchen chair transported from beside the farmhouse stove, the favoured place of five consecutive farm cats.

'I mind the very day you were born, Michael.'

Tom clasped his hands and sat stiffly.

'Uh huh.'

'We had none of wur own … Weel yi ken that … it jist nivver happened.'

Tom glanced away. He was unsure if this was a shared conversation.

'But I mind that day. It wis a snowstorm … maybe yir mither tell't yi.'

Michael tried to a give a look of acknowledgement which did not quite become a smile.

'Well anyway, because o' that I've always thought o' you in a different waye.'

Michael felt a kind of exposure, that he had never reciprocated any bond to his aunt. It was merely blood. It never seemed anything other than technical. For a moment he felt Annie's expectation.

'It's all right, Ah'm no needan' yi tae understand it,' and Annie's face relaxed into simple kindness.'

'Ur ye wi' that lassie noo?'

There was a pause. He had to think.

'Likely.'

Michael was non-committal. The place at which a bond firmed from stray connections was still an uncharted thing.

'They say she's a good lass, Michael.'

'Ah weel.'

Annie took the key from her bag.

'Me and Tom want ye tae tak the ferm …'

Tom looked over and Annie offered the key.

'Yi'll be nedan' a hoos … a place tae set up in …'

Michael felt the embarrassment of the moment, the logic of the act, and how it was the natural progression to everything.

'Thank you, Annie …' He nodded towards Tom. 'Tom.'

And Tom nodded and made a pained smile.

'Cott has the grazing rights this 'ear, but hid's up tae you whit ye dae come the spring.'

'We ken hid's no easy fir the young fowk these days.' Annie lingered her gaze on Michael.

When the summer season was over, the local paper proclaimed it the best ever. Visitor numbers soaring, now the biggest industry in the islands, overtaking both fishing and farming. It felt like they had all been unwittingly entered into some bizarre contest in which glitzy brochures won hands down. The frantic rush of the short summer left everyone drained and relieved that it was autumn. The Bed and Breakfast hosts were exhausted, wanting to wrap the winter around them. In September familiar faces returned to the street. The metamorphoses was all but complete, from a place unconscious of its evolution through communal work and need with a meaning built round what it could do, to a place whose being became part of a fiction of what it used to be. An artifice of its past that it could market and sell.

Seadhna brought her drawings to Michael and offered him the collage of sea and sky, birds and low land. A wistful suggestion is what she thought it should be like. Not needing to explain it.

'I think its just fine,' he'd said and then asked her about the payment.

'I'm really not wanting money,' she'd said. But he took two hundred pounds from his pocket and put it into her hands. He had insisted.

'You must be paid for your work. Yur an artist.' And he had stood for a while and then she had made towards him to thank him and there in the small kitchen felt charged with an intoxicating strangeness.

'Thurs mibbe some bonnie things I cid shaa yi, oot aboot in the pieces I ken.'

'Yes,' she said. 'Yes, I would like that.'

'Next time thurs a good moon Ah'll tak yi oot tae sea an' show yi sumeen' no many folks's seen.'

And he took her out one night in his boat, in the still blackness when it felt as if everything could disappear into the secret glove of the sea.

'Di yi see it?'

'What?'

And he showed her the strange pinpricks of light whirling around the propeller.

'The lights. Hids called phosphorescence.'

And she gazed at it in wonder. All the tiny animals that glowed like magic in the black water. Not needing or looking for an explanation. Just absorbing the strange beauty. Then allowing his arm as it curved round over her shivering back. Her relief welled up within at the feel of his weight and the security it offered. She rested her face against the warmth of him smelling the sea through his clothes.

Michael drove the pickup into the yard at Tom and Annie's. The grass had already grown up through the flagstones. Behind the house the sycamores encroached on the roof; their branches leant over to scratch the asbestos tiles. Crows flew up from the heavy foliage in a flapping of green and black. All around the house, nettles thrived, waist high.

Seadhna followed Michael to the door, her awareness intense, all senses heightened, knowing they were participating in an unspoken choreography.

She waited behind him as he turned the heavy key in the lock. He did not look round, and once inside the sealed house, the empty smell of Tom and Annie's interrupted existence ballooned up into her nostrils. Seadhna was consumed by an excitement she fought to subdue, fearful lest she frighten something away. Such strangeness. So magical in its lurching newness. The heady addiction of it. In this enclosed and significant space with the complete stranger she had known all her life.

Looking through the rooms together, Michael and she, the silence resounded in volumes about what there might be. Their individual solitariness and aching togetherness in that place threatened to burst each of them out of their skins. They dared not look at each other, in case everything collapsed around them and became dust.

'Do what you like wi' it. Ah'm no interested in hooses,' Michael said.

Their eyes flicked parallel with each other like thin fish daring to meet or linger.

She reached for his hand as he made for the door and his look softened into hers.

'Ah'm ganna git rid o'them nettles'

'Wait' and she let her eyes fast on his till he clutched her shoulders and she stepped back against the heavy door.

'Hid'l be fine'

Michael lifted a set of keys from above the sink and went out to try them in the padlock to the byre. He lifted the engine leaking oil from the back of the pick-up and set it on the dank floor below the rusting hames of the long-dead carthorse. The prospect of work steadied him, planning to strip it down. Then dovetailing into the unfinished jobs Tom left behind.

The scythe hung from the rafters, made by the local blacksmith to fit Tom's frame. A frond of ivy trickled from a skylight, the waxy leaves pure in the still air. Michael took the scythe down and tried a swing. It would work for him too. From the house Seadhna heard the sound of the sharpening stone as he swished it methodically over the rusting blade.

Under the sink she took a cloth – a torn cotton semmit of Tom's and wiped off the cobwebs from the single glazed window. Long-undisturbed spiders panicked along the sill. She gathered one up in her hand and took it to the door to release it outside.

Like a voyeur she was transfixed by Michael. The special pleasure of watching someone who was unaware they were watched. The muscles of his shoulders working the scythe, the strength in his back and the steady rhythm as he moved through the nettles, felling them into a carpet of stalks. The quietness. The superfluousness of speech. In that moment she knew it would be fine.

The sweat soaked his shirt and, still oblivious to her presence, he stopped to wipe his brow with his sleeve and ease out his back. From the safety of the task he had set himself and without cover or any protective barrier in place, he turned just to catch her face. In that fraction of a second, the unguarded current of connection escaped and charged between them. Each was in the addictive place of risk with no script and no chart.

Between them everything was wiped afresh. There was no longer any past, only the present and the new story they might create.